DEATH'S BABY SISTER

BILL MCCURRY

D1260977

BOOKS BY BILL MCCURRY

DEATH-CURSED WIZARD SERIES

Novels

Death's Collector

Death's Baby Sister

Death's Collector: Sorcerers Dark and Light

Death's Collector: Void Walker

Death's Collector: Sword Hand

Death's Collector: Dark Lands (forthcoming)

Novellas

Wee Piggies of Radiant Might

© 2019 Bill McCurry

Death's Baby Sister

Second Edition, November 2021

Infinite Monkeys Publishing

Carrollton, Texas

Bill-McCurry.com

Editing by Shayla Raquel, ShaylaRaquel.com

Cover Design by Books Covered

Interior Formatting by Vellum

Death's Baby Sister is under copyright protection. No part of this book may be used or reproduced in any manner whatsoever without written permission except in the case of brief quotations embodied in critical articles and reviews. Printed in the United States of America. All rights reserved.

This is a work of fiction. Names, characters, businesses, places, events, locales, and incidents are either the products of the author's imagination or used in a fictitious manner. Any resemblance to actual persons, living or dead, or actual events is purely coincidental.

ISBN-13 (Ebook): 979-8-9853000-3-1

ISBN-13 (Paperback): 978-1-7356487-9-8

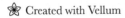 Created with Vellum

For my father—the continent on which I was raised, now slid under the sea.

ONE

I needed to kill two men and a woman before dark, and love was distracting me. Years of murdering people had taught me that when it's time to kill someone, never do some other thing first. Now I feared I might think about love in a moment better suited to slaughter, and then I would be killed myself.

To be honest, even beyond these fears and aggravations, I had found that love didn't make me as happy as it had when I was young.

I traced the lazy scar down Ella's back with my good hand, and she stopped shivering. A bit of light and even less heat twisted through the warped bedchamber window. For us, nakedness had become a kind of bravery. I felt ungrateful not to be happier, since a smart and handsome woman had just spent a frolicsome morning with me. I slid out of bed, examined both edges of my sword, and then picked up my trousers.

Shouts from some place down the hallway thumped against the carved and polished door. Shouting was such a familiar sound that I didn't even glance up from my boots. Every noise in the house flew down the hall like it was a stone trumpet, and Dina, the house-keeper, had never hesitated to stand in the kitchen and call the gardener a bastard from all the way across the courtyard. Before I could reach for my shirt, Dina screamed from the hallway, "Stop right there! I'll beat you till your ass bleeds!" Somebody heaved the door so hard it whipped open with a crack that left it quivering.

I snatched my sword from beside the bed before the door quit trembling. Ella rolled to her feet away from the door. Naked and collected, she pointed a long knife at somebody in the hallway.

A girl of maybe ten stumbled inside and fell hard on one knee without a squeak. She jumped up so fast she almost tripped on her scratchy skirt. Her hair was red like mine used to be, and it straggled down so that I could hardly see the fine new bruise around her eye. Somebody had wrapped a rope around her neck and dangled a lidded reed basket in front of her. A gooey stink oozed from the thing. She frowned at me and raised her eyebrows at Ella. Then she spotted the glass window and stared at it, her mouth hanging.

Neither rude entrances nor repugnant odors are mortal offenses, so even when I was a less discriminate killer, I would have let her live. Murdering children is distasteful in any light. She appeared harmless, though, and that concerned me. One of the best ways to kill a truly dangerous person is to appear harmless.

I pointed my sword at her face. "Child, sit down on the floor, right there, and don't dawdle." She squatted and sat without looking at me, and her hands shook as she grasped the basket.

By that time, a spare, scowling woman had followed the girl in and pointed at her. "This girl's been hexed."

I smiled with my mouth but not my eyes. "Why, thank you for that knowledge, Sal. Has anything else interesting happened while I was away? A goat born with five legs? Save anybody on their deathbed?"

Sal, the local headwoman, figured herself to be a healer. She knew enough about healing not to kill her patients outright. She knew enough about brutality and blackmail to keep everybody in the village terrified. I saw her craggy brothers behind her in the hall.

Another woman, tall and young, shoved her way between the boys and even jostled Sal aside on the way in. Her brown hair marked her a mainlander. Something had twisted her left arm to an improbable angle, and her right cheekbone had been whacked until it was sunken. "Are you deaf? Hexed! You see it, witch!" Her voice could have been used to sound the charge for a regiment.

Sal added, "Since you're the only witch around, Bib, you must have done it."

"First of all, I have never been a witch. I can't stand to cut open lizards and bunnies and pull out their guts. It's a failing, and it's held me back."

"Bib, if you can't improve things . . ." Ella kept her eyes on our visitors. She pushed some sleep-ratted blonde hair out of her face.

"I know, I should stop talking. I'll do better."

The loud young woman smirked at Ella. "Girl, don't they have clothes where you come from?"

Ella, at least ten years older than this stranger, smirked back.

"I have no prejudice against witches, but as a sorcerer, I do tend to get sarcastic when mistaken for one." I stepped to the right to get a better angle in case I'd need to stab Sal in the heart and cut her brothers' throats. "Now, I'll just point out that this is our own bedchamber, and we can be naked here if we goddamn well please. If you dislike it, you can go squat in the mud. I don't recall ever meeting you or inviting you into any intimate part of my home. So, who the hell are you, young woman?"

Sal nodded at the shorter woman. "This is Ona, a nun from the mainland."

Ona surged one step toward me and stopped when I raised my sword. She squinted at the blade for a second and then back at me. "Don't lie to me, witch! You go around telling everybody all about your death magic and dragons and wars with the gods. Just you try to deny it."

I confess that it tickled my vanity for the village folks to think I was the worldliest man ever to walk the islands, and I may have exaggerated a tale or two. I may have flat-out lied—it's one of my failings. Now my vanity had come around to vex me. "Let's set that question aside for now, Sister Ona. Tell me about this hex." I pointed with my sword at Sal's brothers. "Does it cause grown-up, rat-suck bastards to hit her in the face?"

Ella said, "The most expeditious cure might be killing them."

Sal nudged the girl with her foot. "Show him."

The girl didn't move.

Ella lowered her knife and gave the little girl a crisp smile. "Young lady, what's your name?"

The girl glared at Ella and sat straight. "Manon."

It was a common name. On the islands, almost every mother who delivered a fatherless baby named it Manon, boy or girl. It saved time later on when kids were looking for somebody to torment, and when adults decided who would get favors and who would eat fish heads.

"You don't have to be afraid, Manon," I said, smiling over at Ona. "If anybody in here hurts you, I'll gouge out her liver and give it to you for a present."

Ella grabbed a long shirt from the bedpost and shrugged into it, and then she knelt beside Manon. "It's all right, sweetheart. Why do they think you're hexed?"

Manon flipped open the basket, and my stomach clenched at the stink. Ella shielded her face and backed away two steps. The basket held ten or twelve yellow spink, a fish twice as long as my hand. Some were busy rotting.

Sal crossed her arms and lifted her chin. I had seen her stand like that when she sentenced a thieving boy to carry a bucket of rocks every place he went for a year. "We make the girl do some fishing, since she's hopeless for anything else. Three days back, she caught three fish in that one day, exactly three. Three."

"I understand. Three fish," I said.

"The next day again, three fish, and the next day, exactly three more. Today, she caught two, and Ona said bring her to you."

"Eleven fish, then. Remarkable! Let's burn her and have a party."

"Look closer." Sal nodded at the basket.

"You look and tell me about it."

Sal sighed and reached into the basket, pulling out a human finger. "First fish had swallowed this. Second fish swallowed this." She pulled out another finger. She kept pulling out fingers. "Ten fish, and they swallowed eight fingers and two thumbs. Looks that maybe they all belong to the same unlucky turd. Anything funny to say now, witch? Any jokes?"

Ona said, "You hexed the girl, so you take her."

"You don't want her un-hexed?"

Sal hissed. "She drops everything she touches, spills what she don't drop. Maybe you hexed her at birth, who knows? She's not worth the food it would take to choke her."

Manon didn't flinch. Maybe she heard that a lot. Hell, maybe her family said it to her every night for a bedtime story.

I said, "Sal, you said eleven fish, but I count ten. Your brothers doing math for you?"

Ona reached into the basket, pulled out a big toe, and held it three feet from my face. "Eleven. You clean up your own mess."

The sad thing was that all this felt sick and familiar. "Manon, come here." She scrambled up and faced me, glaring as if her eyes could obliterate me from the memory of man. I walked toward her, and she leaned away but didn't run. "Before I say anything else, I want you to remember this. I apologize for maybe ruining the rest of your life."

Her eyes widened, but she didn't step back. That was perfect. I stared into her pupils. Something was moving deep in there. I turned her face toward the window and cocked my head. Then I spotted tiny shadows with different shapes and different numbers of legs and arms swimming in the inmost sounding of her eyes.

They all stopped at the same time and stared back out at me. That was fair. The same kinds of shadows lived in my eyes and were gazing at Manon.

"Ladies, I accept custody of this child, and I don't promise a goddamn thing. As you have no more reason for loitering in my home, I give you leave to rush the hell off. And take along your dimwit chorus out there in the hall. Ella and I might wish to frolic again in a minute."

Sal frowned, grumbled, and whipped out of the room to join her brothers. Ona smiled at me, awfully sweet and cheery except for the pull against her lips by her bad cheek. She nodded at Ella and strolled out behind Sal.

"Dina!" I called out, even though she was standing right outside the door. "Take care of your niece."

Ella added, "Feed her, wash her, and find her clean clothes, in that order. And tell the gardener to bear this appalling basket away and bury it, or else fertilize something with it."

I fell onto the bed and stared at the ceiling. Back when we'd moved into this house, I had planned to spend every afternoon sitting under the crabapple tree drinking wine. I realized that could get boring, and I planned to address that by occasionally drinking whiskey. Ella was ambitious, and I had no urge to distract her from establishing her fame by solving problems for wealthy men with a vengeful streak.

Manon was about to smash my relaxation like it was a yearning boy's heart, and I deserved it. I anticipated the girl would engage in unintentional whimsy such as fires dying out when she walked past or finding a diamond buried in her breakfast every day for a week or causing every third child in the village to accidentally put an eye out with a spoon. Such things couldn't go on forever, of course. Eventually, people would figure it out and kill her.

"Ella, you may not realize this, but I dislike admitting fault."

"Once I have finished dressing, I shall faint from shock." She pulled on her trousers.

I sat up. "I confess that I may have played just a tiny part in these events. I grieve to tell you that we are facing a fearsome creature. She's slightly less dangerous than a volcano, and I'm only kidding you a tad. She's a new sorcerer who doesn't yet know it, and she might tear a hole in reality whenever she burps or slams her thumb in a drawer. She's only suffering this due to the spread of sorcery, and . . ." I shrugged.

"You brought sorcery here? You promised me you wouldn't."

"We can't know with sterling certainty that I did it."

Ella threw my shirt at me. "You lied to me!"

"No, I just said something that wasn't true. I thought it was true, though."

"Sophistry. I'm sorry, your vocabulary may not be that extensive. Bullshit." Ella hefted a boot, considered me for a moment, and then dropped it back onto the floor.

I twisted and stretched my left arm to thread my hook through the sleeve. "Sorcery should not be possible on this island. I was promised that."

"By whom?"

"Well . . . the God of Death."

Ella stared at the yellow rug, her arms crossed. A lot of women have told me I'm too hard to live with, sometimes yelling it at me, and sometimes throwing crockery or shoes. In the ten months I'd been with Ella, she had from time to time crossed her arms and stood rooted no matter what I did. She had said that such behavior was just her deciding whether I'm too hard to live with, or maybe whether I should be allowed to live at all, so I should go off and leave her the hell alone while she did it.

Ella had a right to her aggravation, but it did sting. Although Harik, God of Death, was not the most trustworthy of beings, he and I had shared a colorful relationship. He had cursed me to commit an unspecified number of murders for him, a number only he knew. I called him fancy names, like rabbit-dicked mockery of a god. We tried to cheat each other like we were sweaty men haggling over a lame, one-eyed donkey. But when I bargained for his promise that Ir would be proof against sorcery, I had judged the bargain fair. I'd clearly been too stupid to swallow spit.

I felt nearly certain that the gods didn't create us and all the world. They spent too much time complaining that creation didn't contain enough sorcery for their liking. Most of the world had been free of sorcery for years, and the gods didn't care for that, since they preyed on sorcerers like sparrows on grasshoppers.

About the time Ella and I fell in love, I struck a bargain with the gods. They could restore sorcery wherever my idle ass wandered, and it would remain when my ass had moved on. For me, it was a morally questionable task, sometimes sad and often violent. Without doubt, it was the best deal I'd ever made, considering what the gods gave me in return. But they had set me no schedule, so I rode wherever Ella wanted to go. I always found people there doing something nasty and waiting for me to kill them for it.

Shattering the veil between man and god had been more tiring than I had expected. Half a year of it exhausted us. Ella wanted to settle and take on some chancy tasks for rich men. I wanted to drink wine and ride horses, since my temperament was not suited to hard labor. Settling in Ir seemed perfect.

"Well, Harik cheated me," I said. "I'm sorry."

"We have to move now. I'm unprepared for more sorcery."

"That's an abrupt decision."

Ella turned away from me and started shoving clothes into a leather backpack. "Don't argue. Your judgment is no better than a chipmunk's. Go off and kill your malefactors and take the girl with you. You created her. I shall pack up our chattels. Dina! Assemble the staff outside!" She marched down the hallway and left me sitting on the bed.

My malefactors were three wicked thugs I had promised to kill on behalf of a slightly less horrible thug. I had regretted my promise right away. I should have paid the man what I owed him in fish or plum preserves or even silver. But I had made the bargain, and there it was—breaking bargains was not one of my failings.

I finished dressing and followed Ella into the courtyard.

Dina was cajoling the household staff into a twitchy, ragged line. I didn't know just when we had acquired a staff. I'd never expected to have one, and I didn't really know what to do with it. Ella found housekeeping and such unappealing. In fact, she'd rather drink scorpion blood than mend shirts, or sit on a couch and order servants around, so she had handed our entire domestic operation over to Dina. After that, Ella only talked about it once more, when Dina asked permission to hire her sister as a helper.

Dina must have considered that such approval extended to bringing on whatever help she felt was required. Now and then, a maid, a gardener, or maybe a fellow whose job was just to carry things around would appear. I wasn't sure how imposing our staff had become. I had counted at least twelve distinct individuals, including a couple of children, all with Dina's prominent, dimpled chin.

I wasn't worried about the money. We could pay the whole village for a hundred years if we wanted. It just itched my devotion to proper planning. When I brought it up to Ella, she laughed, kissed me, and kept on sharpening her knife.

Seventeen servants lined up outside, and none of them stood within twenty feet of Manon. She was exiled almost to the flower bed, where she fidgeted, shook, and stared damnation at her family.

As I walked toward the girl, something crashed behind me. I jumped, and everybody else did too, including Manon. One of the big wooden shingles had slid off the high roof and by chance landed on one of the chickens from our flock, which pecked the courtyard cobblestones all day. The shingle killed it on the spot.

The event told me two things. Somebody who was not me would be fixing the roof tomorrow, and I knew what Ella would be having for dinner.

Dina's daughter, Drendl, skipped over to collect the chicken. Just as she arrived, another shingle fell five feet away from her and broke another unlucky chicken's neck. Drendl yelped and ran back to her mother without a chicken.

Ella walked up beside me. "I wonder what the odds may be of that occurring twice?"

I sighed. "Do you want to wager against it happening again in about ten seconds?"

"What do you mean?"

I held up my hand. Soon, another shingle shot off the roof, executing another chicken. The staff had been murmuring. Now they chattered, exclaimed, and even swore a little, despite Ella's disapproval of harsh language.

"Would you like to bet again? I'll wager a kiss," I said.

"If you can make it stop, I'll wager more than a kiss."

I glanced to check on the servants, a normally fearful group. Most were edging toward the courtyard gate and the trail that led home. I pointed at Manon with my hook. "Ella, go hang on to

Manon if you would, please. I don't want her to escape when everybody else goes crazy and gallops out of here."

I had begun counting the time between shingles. One fell every twenty-three seconds. After the seventh execution, even chickens were smart enough to run away. A wind rose and blew the next few shingles far out into the courtyard to slay more chickens. By the nineteenth shingle, the wind had become a gale. Shingles hurtled across the courtyard at twenty-three-second intervals, and two of the last chicken-murders were accomplished by shingles on the bounce.

When the slaughter ended, twenty-three shingles had flown off the roof, destroying a total of twenty-three chickens.

The gale collapsed into a nice breeze within a minute. Ella appeared at my shoulder, holding Manon's hand. She raised her eyebrows at me and then glanced toward the girl.

"All I can say is you shouldn't stand under this roof at this hour tomorrow. Or for the next twenty-two days."

"Bib, I think it best that Manon and I both accompany you to your murders rather than stay here."

I nodded and smiled at Manon. "Do you want to come on a little trip with us?"

Manon squinted at me and rubbed her nose, her hand shaking like a tree branch in a thunderstorm. "I dreamed about killing you, old man. Or, maybe you . . . no, I'm pretty sure it was me killing you."

TWO

When I was a boy, my first day of sorcery training disappointed the hell out of me. In the weeks before it started, I had realized that, unlike other ill-behaved ten-year-old boys, I could cause lightning to burn down things. I couldn't do it whenever I wanted. In truth, it always happened at inconvenient times and places, but I was making it happen with my own unfathomable sorcerous power. I looked forward to throwing down lightning strikes whenever it pleased me. Instead, I found that my teachers expected me to crush every sorcerous impulse within me, no matter how meager. In fact, they said if I didn't make myself as ordinary as a dirt pie, they would probably kill me by the end of the week.

Once I had grown old and could recall those things from a distance, I understood that those eccentric young fellows couldn't teach me much while I was randomly burning down things around us. Also, I was learning the most fundamental lesson of sorcery— don't use magic just because it's fun or because it makes things simple. Don't use it at all if you can do something else instead. Over centuries, the teachers of sorcery had decided that if a child couldn't learn that lesson fast, it was kindest to just kill him and move on to another child. I don't mean that it would save the child from some immediate pain or hardship. But a child that lagged could rarely learn control before accidentally killing a few people, terrifying himself, and possibly obliterating large pieces of architecture in an awful or even fanciful manner. In earlier times, if the child did survive, then the friends and kin of the slain often snatched the him and put him to death, after a few bloody, spiteful tortures.

Still, at times I have wondered whether the teachers put the slow children to death out of laziness rather than wisdom. However, they were the ones with the fancy robes, not me.

Manon rode behind me on my bay mare, a beast smarter than half the people in the village ahead of us. The trail curved along knobby, black, stone hills rising up near the ocean that churned a mile off to my right. Fields of puny grass pocked the hills, too small and isolated to be worth planting a crop. The clouds scudded along low, threatening to let loose any time.

Manon's people, the villagers of Pog, possessed an admirable determination to suffer. Years ago, some awfully optimistic individuals discovered a flat, loamy spot a mile upstream from the ocean by way of a fast, brackish river. The sandy dirt would grow only feeble crops. The river was too salty for most freshwater fish and not salty enough for adventurous ocean fish. Slippery walls of rock and smashing rapids deterred any man from reaching the ocean on foot or by boat.

The villagers just about starved their entire lives, and sane people would have burned the place down and moved somewhere else. Instead, these people had endured for six generations. They bragged about it to all the passing travelers, most of whom were lost and looking for some other place.

The girl had been a quiet traveling companion on the trail to her village. I would have appreciated that quality more had we not been likely to engage in a mortal conflict some time in the future. Considering that, and the fact that she had to learn fast or die, I figured it wise to make her trust me, or at least like me.

"How old are you, Manon?"

"Twelve, I think."

I had figured ten. Manon was scrawny for her age, which was a damn shame. Now I had to deal with the moods and sarcasm of a twelve-year old. "You are a sorcerer, Manon. Or you will be."

"Why? Because you say so?"

"No, I don't have a snip of anything to do with it."

"Are you a sorcerer?" Manon asked the way she'd ask whether I was a desert reptile.

"Yes."

"Then I don't want to be one."

"There are advantages. When we ride through Pog, you can sit tall and put all those rascals and their gut-munch opinions behind you. Someday, you'll come back here and buy the whole town, rotten barrels and all. Then you can make them dance for you and feed you apricots every night."

Manon grunted. "If I had lots of money, I'd buy something better than Pog. They don't dance. And I don't want any apricots, whatever they are."

"Well, if you come back here as a powerful sorcerer, at the least, they'll flop down in awe. Some might even eat dirt to show how much they wish you wouldn't destroy them."

Manon let out a bark of a laugh. "No one in the village ever flopped down for *you*. After you ride through, we call you names. There's even a song."

"I don't need to hear it."

"I wasn't going to sing it."

The most lenient person alive couldn't have listened to that conversation and said that Manon liked me.

A few people stood by the trail as we trotted through Pog, although most stayed far back and stared. Since Manon had been produced by this place, I could expect her to be stubborn to the point of stupidity. It wasn't the most promising quality, but an unlikely number of sorcerers possessed a wealth of it.

When we had just about traversed the village, I shouted, "Pay no mind to us! We're just passing through to go do some horrible witch-craft!" I kicked my mare into a canter, and Manon giggled as we left the village behind.

I noticed that ever since leaving my house, Manon had been trembling. "Your hands are shaking. Don't be afraid. I don't hurt little girls, and I won't let anybody hurt you." I tried not to think about what a lie that would be if she was slow at controlling her power and I had to kill her.

Manon yanked her hands from around my waist, and she almost fell. I reined in, and she caught her balance. "I'm not scared! My hands always do that." She shoved them around in front of me, and they were shaking as if palsied. I had been particularly dull not to see that for what it was. She said, "Do you want to make some smart comments? I can go right back home! It's just over there."

"No, I don't have anything smart to say." I tried to sound comforting. Ella said it had shocked her senseless to find that I was good at it. "I want you to come along with me, Manon. I might need you to protect me from bears."

"Don't talk to me like I'm a baby." I thought for a moment she was crying, but then I realized she was growling like a cornered dog.

"I'm sorry. I won't do it anymore."

Manon's affliction of the hands worried me. Magic doesn't make many physical demands of a sorcerer. I had worked with lame sorcerers, one who couldn't draw a deep breath for coughing, and even a blind one. Sorcerers don't have to be clever, either. Some weren't bright enough to pour piss out of a boot, but they prospered at sorcery. They didn't die any younger than most, which was by any standard young. But manual dexterity was the one essential competence. A sorcerer grabs power with his hands from the air around him, shapes it into sometimes intricate forms, and then delivers it to sometimes preposterous places. Without quick, subtle hands, a sorcerer might still be grabbing at the air when an enemy dropped a stone church on him. Hell, a nasty child could stab him to death with a sharp stick, and then saunter off to eat cake.

None of that would matter if Manon couldn't discipline herself. Those young sorcerers who trained me had suffered more than I ever appreciated, since they often had to decide whether it was time to kill a child.

We rode along without speaking until late afternoon. Then I

called out, "Ella, please find a safe spot somewhere around and keep Manon there."

"Why?" Manon's voice caught. "Are you coming back?"

"I'll be back for sure, or almost for sure."

Ella dismounted. "I shall open a bottle of wine at twilight. You may be certain Bib will return before the sun sets."

"Don't leave me here, you dog's butt!" As Manon cursed me, she also locked her arms tight around my waist.

I tried to give her a harsh look over my shoulder and then under my arm, but she evaded me both times. "Young woman, I swear that a fighting man, or woman, could kill you with a celery stalk. I'd have to protect you when I should be killing people."

"Why do you want to kill people? I bet they're nicer than you."

Ella chuckled.

I tried not to smile. "I'll allow that's probably true, but this is all too scary and complicated for little girls."

"Don't tell me then. I don't even care." Still sitting behind me, Manon grabbed me even tighter around the waist.

The tale wasn't scary, or even complicated. I owed a pissant ship's captain named Albert Scrip, because he had made a special trip to bring Ella's bed to the island. But the flabby weasel hadn't wanted money; he'd wanted a favor. Some thugs had been taking and looting his cargo boats, and he had wanted me to stop them. Since getting killed will stop just about anybody, I had agreed. I could set the killings against the deaths I owed Harik.

Albert had bribed some fisherman to reveal the pirates' hiding spot, and a cargo boat would be dispatched to pass by this evening as bait. I knew just where the criminals would be hiding before dark, and I could murder them in a tidy fashion.

"Ella will find a little cave for you up in those rocks ahead," I said. "It might even be dry. We're still a couple of miles away from my task."

My mare jerked and fell over to the right. As I jumped free, I saw an arrow sticking out of her head. I relaxed and tumbled down the rocky slope, trying not to lose my weapon or smash out my brains. When I had slowed to a near halt, I rolled up to my feet and drew my sword.

I had thumped and bruised my way thirty paces downhill from the trail. Two men with bows and two others with swords were scrambling onto the road from uphill. A woman stood behind my mare's carcass, holding Manon with a knife against her throat. Even from that distance, I saw blood dripping below the knife blade. Ella was edging up the road toward these sneaky grease-sacks, until a man aimed his bow at her. She stopped and held her sword up at an inoffensive height.

The taller man shouted at me, "Throw the pig-poker on down the hill, or you'll be riding this fine horse in hell with matching arrows!"

They had probably outbid Albert's fisherman informant, who then told them all about my ambush. I was standing in just about the least advantageous position possible, with limited tactical options. Killing these folks would prove arduous.

Of course, I could just let them kill Manon while I escaped down the hill. If I distracted them, Ella could disappear like a sparrow. It would simplify my life considerably—I wouldn't have to watch out for Manon or face the question of letting her live. Harik might even let me count her death against my debt.

I didn't consider it with real intent. No decent person would, and I wouldn't either. I had to admit that I pondered it for a few seconds, which might have said something about my decency, but I still held a little hope for myself.

"Don't be waiting around with your thumb up your butt!" shouted the shorter man. "I killed your horse. Which of your eyeballs do you want me to sink the next arrow into?"

I shouted up the hill, "Since you haven't poked a dozen holes in me yet, I imagine you back-warts want me alive. So, I'm not going to be throwing my sword anyplace. You just come down here and take it away from me."

"We'll slit open this girl!" the woman yelled.

I laughed. "What makes you think I give a good goddamn about her?" I hadn't decided to abandon her, but those idiots didn't need to know it.

Manon gaped at me like a codfish and went pale.

My enemies hesitated. They were following a plan. I admit it was a good one, by the only standard that mattered. They were making threats from high ground and could kill me four or five times before I scrambled close enough to spit on them. Despite a few bobbles, such as my not throwing my sword away, they loved their plan, and they didn't want to abandon it. I imagined they hated to reassess things at that point.

Albert had given me the main thugs' names: Jon, Bear-Hat, and Jass. If I used their names, one of them might get shaken. In the lull, I shouted, "Jon, how much did Albert, that flabby tumor of a man, promise to pay you for delivering me?"

"None of your rutting business. Toss that sword, or I'll put an arrow through your knee." Jon, the short one, shook back his stringy hair and shifted his aim to my leg.

"Why the hell does Scrip want me?"

"Don't give a mule's fart." Bear-Hat spoke in a hollow grunt no lovelier than a mule's fart.

Jass let out a sweet laugh. "He told us we can cut off your right hand and keep it if you fight us, so be good." She was said to be the clever one.

I lowered my sword, as symbolic a gesture as ever was made. "I'll pay you five times whatever he's paying you to just go away. And you can take the girl to sell."

Manon squirmed as Jass said, "We have the girl now."

Ella was shuffling closer to the pirates now that I had their attention.

"Seven times what Albert claimed he'll give you, and you come help me kill him. You can loot everything he has. How much did the old turtle promise you?"

"Three wheels." Bear-Hat lowered his bow and scratched his monumental beard.

"Each!" Jon said.

That was a ridiculous amount, an obvious lie, but it didn't matter. "So, seven times that is fifty-nine wheels total."

Jass squinted out at the ocean. "Right." Her talents didn't include the fine points of mathematics. "But have you got them?"

I unlaced a heavy pouch from my belt and shook about three dozen small gold coins into my hand. A man could live for half a year in modest comfort on one gold wheel, if he didn't buy silk dresses for every trollop in town. I shook the heavy pouch to show it still clinked.

Jon beckoned. "All right. Toss it here."

"I'll count them out."

Jon guffawed. "Put 'em all back in."

I dropped in all the coins and pulled the pouch closed. Then I hauled off and flung it over the grimy thugs, fifty feet past them up the hill. As they watched their fortune bounce around among the rocky crevasses, I ran up toward the trail and drew my sword.

Two steps later, my sword's hilt popped out of my hand for no reason at all. I paused to snatch it up, and the hilt squirted out again, slippery as a block of soap.

Up on the trail, John, Bear-Hat, and their men were scrambling around trying to pick up their weapons, as luckless as me. Jass still had Manon clamped, but she was scanning the ground for the knife she must have dropped. Manon's eyes were as huge as pot lids, and her nails pressed into Jass's arm. I glanced down the trail and saw Ella trying to grip her sword with both hands. It shot free, banged against the ground, and clattered fifteen feet back toward home.

I abandoned my sword and half-ran, half-climbed up the slope, figuring to hell with a weapon I couldn't keep in my hand. I'd rather close with my foes while I could. No doubt Manon was creating this ridiculous phenomenon, all ignorant and terrified.

Being a sorcerer has put me at a disadvantage more times than one might think, but that day on the rocky slopes of Ir, it proved useful. I understood that the magical effect would happen a certain number of times, maybe seven, maybe seventy-one, maybe 271, or more, and then it would subside. I understood what was happening, but these shabby pirates were mystified.

Jon and Bear-Hat gave up on their bows and yanked out their swords, which flew off the trail in different directions. They rushed off and began bumbling around for their blades. I knelt on the trail and eased out my long knife, which slipped free and fell straight down. I lifted it a finger's length off the ground, and it slipped again. I heard the miserable skags behind me, cursing and stumbling.

On my sixth try, the knife stayed in my hand. I ran up behind Bear-Hat and stabbed him in the heart as he stood up with his sword. Jon was already up, but he was staring at his sword as if it might fly or recite poetry next. I cut his throat before he could find out. I glanced over and saw Ella on the ground, her arm around a man's neck. The last man charged me and swung his sword, a decent cut. I ducked, broke his knee, and stabbed him in the chest before he could start howling.

I heard a girl scream.

When I turned, I expected to find Manon dying, but instead I saw Jass on her knees, knife in her belly. She was hauling on Manon's arm like it was a rope, pulling the girl closer to her. Jass began howling, "Mama . . . Mama . . . Mama, help me!" as her mouth sprayed blood on Manon's twitching face.

I pried Manon loose, pushed Jass to the ground, and thrust my knife through her eye. The woman shuddered and sagged flat against the dirt.

Manon started shaking all over, her mouth gaping and her eyes hollow. I stood in front of her, holding my bloody knife and splattered in gore. "Manon, I know that was pretty awful, but a sorcerer must accustom herself to horrors."

She stared at the ground and sucked in a deep breath. She reached out a bloody, shaking hand and touched my arm with just her fingertips.

My own little girl had never killed anybody, but she had broken bones, and boys had been cruel to her, and she had suffered my disappointment once or twice. Manon had found out young that the world could be this brutal, and I hurt a little for her. Hell, there was plenty of time tomorrow for Manon to be a sorcerer. I knelt and hugged her, and I told her it was all right, even though it certainly was not. She hung on and gulped dry breaths while I told her I knew it was bad but would get better, and that she was the best and smartest girl in the world. That was another lie, of course, but it's what you say in these circumstances, and after all, I am a liar.

THREE

Ella plucked my pouch of gold coins from a clump of grayish weeds and tossed it to me. Actually, she threw the pouch at me, hard enough to numb my fingers. "Bib, when you departed on this errand, why did you choose to bring with you an absolute fortune in gold?" Ella had thrown quite a number of things at me these past weeks. It was behavior common among women whose patience I had ground down as fine as flour.

"I didn't have much in the line of plans." I stowed the pouch and then rolled Bear-Hat's body down the hill. "Once I killed these mongrels, I thought I'd ride on to Garhool. Maybe gamble a little and buy some wine. Look over the horses for sale."

"That quantity of gold would purchase the ten finest horses ever bred on this island, as well as a coach carved from ivory."

I hadn't thought Ella would ever know about the gold. I had loaded up that pouch yesterday, before she and Manon joined the expedition, and I'd forgotten about it amid all the finger-eating fish and chicken murders. Now I had no choice but to confess.

"I thought I might buy a boat," I said.

"Pray, is it inlaid with diamonds and sapphires?"

"Not a boat, really. A ship. A small ship!" I gave her my to-hell-

21

with-everything-but-us smile. I was convinced it had made her fall in love with me. "Small enough that with a couple of able men, we can sail anywhere in Ir, as long as we can see a speck of land. You can name her."

Ella turned and gazed at the ground. "Bib, I have no time for pleasure sailing. You know that."

I laid my hand on her shoulder from behind. "You are a driven woman, and I admire that. But even Fingit can't make magic chariots and such for the other gods without sticking his head up for a little air."

Ella spun and faced me square. "I'm not Fingit! I wasn't born a god and nothing has been given to me, so I must work for everything. I cannot play with boats or wander off for fresh air! I'm not you." She paused and blinked hard. "And I'm not Fingit, either!"

In an instant, all Ella's harsh behavior made more sense. Whenever she had brought back some crusty bandit or killed some traitor, afterward she would come home, speak sharply, and throw things. I had felt bad that she somehow couldn't enjoy her success. I hadn't suspected that her victories felt tarnished because I could have done the same and made it look easy.

"You're doing fine," I said. "Maybe I'm handy at some things, but not everything. Don't feel bad. I'm older than you, with a lot more experience. And I'm a sorcerer."

Ella didn't throw crockery or shoes or even gold at me. I count it fortunate that she didn't throw anything sharp, because there were plenty of weapons at hand. She hurled Jon's empty quiver, and although I could have dodged it, I just let it hit me on the shoulder. She climbed away uphill and disappeared over the top within a minute.

I started to follow and tell her I was sorry for whatever I'd said, but I realized that for her climbing that hill might be the same as standing with her arms crossed, except worse. Leaving her the hell alone seemed wise.

I nodded at Manon. "Sit over by that rock. I'll be finished in a minute." I dragged Jass across the trail and heaved her down the hill.

Manon sat with her back against the black stubby rock. "Why don't you rob the bodies?"

"I don't want to set a bad example. If you weren't here, I'd have them stripped to their smallclothes by now."

"You're lying."

The sun dropped behind the hills, and twilight edged in.

I sat on the black grainy road in front of her. "Manon, believe me that I'm not lying to you now. You'll be a sorcerer someday, if you live."

"I don't want to be like you."

I almost made a joke, but instead I said, "There are all different kinds of sorcerers. Do you want me to teach you?"

"Will it fix my hands?"

"I won't lie to you on that either, darling. It will not."

"Shit." She bent her head forward. "Do I have a choice? What if I say no?"

"Then I'll kill you. Untrained, you're too dangerous to let live. I wish I could just make that not be true."

Manon stood up, and I thought she might kick me. After a silent stretch, she said, "What if I say yes? What'll happen to me then?"

I stood up too. "You'll do a lot of unpleasant things and probably hate me. Hate me more. There's a chance the training will kill you. But if everything works out, you'll be a full sorcerer and able to ruin your life all by yourself."

"I guess I'd be stupid not to say yes." She glared at me. "Is it worth it? Don't lie. Will I go through all that and then wish I was dead?"

"That's an awfully complicated question for a little girl."

"I'm not a girl. I'm a sorcerer. You said so." Manon glared at me for a moment, and then turned away. She might have been sad that I hadn't crumbled into ash. "Besides, anybody can know what it's like to wish they were dead."

"You're right. I'm sorry. Is it worth it?" That was a hard question for me to answer. As a murderer, I wasn't the best person to make value judgments. "Since you told me not to lie, I won't say yes. Really, you can only decide for yourself, and then it's too late."

She examined the dimming ocean, nearly the same color now as the squall clouds whipping over it. Rain started spitting on us. "No, I won't let you teach me. You should just let me go instead."

"That's a foolish statement."

Manon turned back to me with steady eyes. "I bet you won't really kill me. You said you don't hurt little girls."

"No, but you're not a little girl. You're a sorcerer, and I've killed enough sorcerers to stack a wagon full."

Manon sighed and shook her head.

"Well, it's near dark, and you may decide otherwise tomorrow. Let's bed down back there off the path." I led Ella's gelding to the little clearing, unsaddled him, and rubbed him down. I pulled some cold chicken from the saddlebag and handed half to Manon.

"Will Ella come back?" Manon mumbled as she chewed.

I shrugged, ate a few more bites, and lay down. I listened for Ella deep into the night, and at last I slept.

For years I have expected to perish in some ridiculous manner. I've lived through some devastating experiences that no person should survive. Therefore, the gods will probably arrange for me to choke to death on a biscuit, or slip off a privy-seat and break my neck. Strangling on my own spit isn't out of the question. I base this on my numerous conversations with the gods in which they made it plain how much they don't love me.

Maybe the chicken was bad, because I dreamed I was wandering around a tavern trying to find someone who would sell me beer, until a woman sold me a mug full of scorpions. Then one of them stung me precisely between my nipples. That biting pain in the middle of my chest woke me. The clouds had lifted, and in the moonlight, I saw Manon kneeling over me. She had hauled back with Jass's knife in both hands, about to take a second run at pinning me to the dirt. Getting stabbed through the lung by a girl who struggled to wield even a fork, let alone a knife, seemed so outrageous that I thought my life was in real peril.

I grabbed Manon by the shoulders, rolled, and flung her off. She squeaked and tumbled against a tall lump of rock, and then she flopped onto the ground. For an instant, I thought I'd broken her neck, but she popped up and pointed the knife toward me. The blade shook, pointing at just about every part of my body.

I probed the sharp but shallow cut Manon had made over my breastbone, pleased that no one had ever taught her anatomy. "Manon, I respect your choice to murder me and end all doubt about my killing you. I also respect your decision not to gloat or spit curses at me before you did it. When it's time to be killing people, don't do some other thing. Kill them straightaway. Now, shed that blade and save yourself a bruised wrist."

Manon bent and set down the knife. "You don't have to kill me. I won't ever do magic, I promise. I don't even believe in spells and hexes. And don't complain about the knife. I didn't even poke you hard enough to hurt. Bib, you'd just be a coward if you killed me, so let me go. You'll never see me again."

I picked up the knife and backed away two steps, in case she should leap for it. I started to regret I hadn't resisted more when they forced her on me. "Sorry, I can't let you just wander out of here."

She spun around and kicked at the coarse black dirt. "Fine!" Then she breathed, "What do you want me to do?"

"Let me teach you for three days. If you say yes, you have a fine chance of living at least that long. I can't promise anything after that. I'm not the God of Death, and I celebrate that fact at every opportunity, with lutes and dancing."

Her shoulders fell, and she seemed to collapse a bit. In a tiny voice she said, "No. What do you want me to do right now? Since I belong to you."

I scowled at her. "You aren't my property!"

She gazed up at me, blank faced. "Oh. Will you kill me if I don't do what you say?"

"I . . . suppose that's an accurate description of things."

Manon dropped her arms at her sides and hung her head. "Then I belong to you."

It was a side of being a new sorcerer that I had never appreciated. "Only in a technical sense. Put it out of your mind and let me teach you. If you're a sharp pupil, I won't have to keep talking about killing you."

The girl stared at the ground and said nothing.

"All right, lie down and go to sleep. That's a start. Tomorrow, we'll work up to *not* crushing mountains into sand by accident."

Manon glanced up. "Where do you want me to lie down?"

I waved my hand around. "Wherever you like. I don't own this dirt."

She sat down at the edge of the trail, far away from me, her knees pulled up. "Is this all right? Master?"

"Hell, don't call me that!" I figured she was just trying to aggravate me, since she had failed to murder me.

"Fine then! Just be sure you stay over there!" Manon snarled at me, as fierce now as she had been meek a few seconds ago.

I froze and then backed away two steps. "Is that what you're worried about? That I'll molest you?"

Manon hugged her knees. "Every girl has to worry about it. Don't you know anything?"

I knelt on the road, twenty feet away from her. "Manon, learning sorcery will be painful, but I will never hurt you like that."

"You're probably lying." Manon closed her eyes and turned her back partly away from me. "Anyway, is it worse than killing me?"

I wasn't exactly sure what to say. "Well . . . it's pretty bad."

She lay down, stiff as a bridge.

"Here." I tossed Jass's knife to land beside Manon. "You keep that. That's my promise that I won't put my hands on you."

Manon picked up the knife and threw it off into the darkness. "That's a trick. You'll use it as a reason to hurt me later."

I hung my head for a couple of seconds. "I'm running out of things to say. If you feel like this, why didn't you speak up before now?"

She sat up fast, hair flying around her face, and shouted, "I did! I kept telling you to let me leave!"

"You're right, you sure did, but I can't. Manon, it may not mean pig flop to you now, but I promise not to lie to you anymore. Unless

I have a good reason. I've never promised that to Ella or my wife or to Krak, Father of the Gods."

"You're right. That doesn't mean anything at all. You can teach me whatever you want now, since you own me. It doesn't matter." Manon lay down on her side, putting her back to me.

I rubbed my punctured chest and marveled at how different Manon was from my own little girl, Bett, now dead nine years. Bett had laughed far more than she sulked and had been quick to get over a hurt. She had loved being alive, and she made other people love it too just by loving it so goddamn much. It had been a crime to take life away from her, if random events could be said to have criminal intentions.

I couldn't imagine two girls more different than Bett and Manon, who had fallen asleep, or at least gave a good imitation of it. I sat and watched her breathe, just in case during the night she tried to tear off my head with her teeth.

FOUR

I've been told that I am a magnificent companion and conversationalist for about a week. After that, every word I say is either an aggravation or an invitation to initiate hostilities. I've experienced this phenomenon many times with many different women, but only I have been present every damn time. I have therefore accepted the blame for these failures, and I wished I knew what to change to prevent so many fine women from being angry with me.

That's why I felt a moment of relief when Ella didn't expect me to talk. She walked into the clearing at dawn and faced me when I stood up. She grabbed my good hand and squeezed hard, and then looked like she might say something. Instead, she rested her forehead against my shoulder.

I considered apologizing, but I didn't know for what. I had learned that apologizing for the wrong thing is worse than keeping quiet. I could say something nice to her, maybe about her hair, which was pretty. I could say something informative or practical, like telling her about Manon's fear of servitude, or offering her some chicken. None of those seemed to the point for this situation. I sure as hell wasn't going to ask if she had decided to leave me. I didn't know how to say that, and I didn't know how to listen to her answer, either. So, I stayed still. She had my good hand trapped, and I wasn't going to stroke her hair with my steel hook. I stood like a fence post and waited for whatever would happen next.

Ella let go of my hand, walked away, and began saddling her horse. I started breathing again. At least everything wasn't over.

All morning we traveled down the trail toward the port town of Garhool. Sunshine made us sweat, and the ocean breeze dried us. Grand colonies of puffins slathered the black, pocked hills. Ella let Manon ride up behind her, hanging on. The girl was quiet and didn't resist anything we told her to do. I walked ahead, mourning my horse and contemplating how I might interrogate Albert Scrip before stabbing him in two or three different organs.

I heard a rider at midday, trotting up the trail toward us from Garhool. Ella heard it too, and we hurried over against the hillside to wait so the rider couldn't charge and run us down, should he be the surly type.

A breathtaking white mare clopped into view from around a black stone outcrop, not fifty paces away, an image as pretty as any woman I'd ever seen. A tall, solid man in green riding clothes trotted his mount on toward us, raising his hand as he came. As he closed, I saw that his boyish face was beardless and ice-pale, topped by black hair tousled so artfully he might have arranged it that way. His light skin marked him a Denzman, a man of the far south. It was a striking complexion, although I believed my own—brown as lightly baked bread—was more handsome.

When he drew rein, he nodded at me but didn't utter a word.

I said, "I am known as a polite fellow, but this road leads to my home, and you might be an insane scoundrel or traitor. Just who the hell are you?"

He smiled so hugely that I might have seen every tooth in his mouth. "I'm sorry, that was rude of me. I am Cael, from—"

"I know where you're from."

"You may, but probably not." He nodded. It was so polite it might have been an insult. "To go on, I've done a few things, mainly soldiering, but I dabble in philosophy and architecture. I even trained elephants once. My enemies call me the Drinker of Souls, but I think that's probably a joke. I would never presume to call myself something like that. I guess you are the sorcerer. You do fit the description. I'm so happy to make your acquaintance, since I've been searching for you."

Now that he and his lovely mare loomed right over me, I saw he was older than I had first credited. He must have been at least thirty-five. I said, "You have the wrong man, sir. I'm a humble goat farmer. Sorry. It's a long way back to the Denz Lands, so you'd better set off right away."

Cael took five seconds to scan the area. "Where are your goats?"

"Killed by the pox. I'll probably starve come winter."

He nodded at the sword on my belt. "You appear to be bearing a marvelous weapon. Raising goats must be more hazardous than I've heard."

"It is a chancy business."

"I'll offer you an alternative then. No less perilous maybe, but nobler and more rewarding. Come with me and set the world right."

I laughed long enough that he stopped smiling and began untangling his horse's mane, glancing at me now and then. I finally said, "Go away. Find somebody with no sex life and a lot to prove." I glanced back and winked at Ella. She had been helping Manon slide down from the horse, and now she nudged her sword loose in its scabbard.

"I've been charged to bring you with me, and if you make me tie you and haul you along in a wagon, I will." He smiled again. "Consider, Master Bib, I have never failed a charge."

So, he knew my name, but that didn't mean a damn thing. Unless he was a sorcerer too and thought he could hex me with it. He'd be surprised when he found out that Bib wasn't my real name, right before I stabbed him in the heart. "Tell me who gave you this charge."

The man shrugged. "I'd rather not say just now."

"I'd rather not cut your throat and bury you on the beach." I pointed at the beach a mile off to my right.

"All right then. I can't bring you back with me if you force me to kill you."

I smiled and imagined three ways I could pull him off the horse and kill him before he caught his breath.

He said, "The queen sends for you."

I shrugged. "Means nothing. I know several queens. Narrow it down."

"Her Eminence, Queen Mina of Bellhalt, Duchess of Gaunt, Countess Redland, She from Whom All Grace and Mercy Flow."

I winced in disgust. "That twat?"

Cael laughed deep and loud. "Yes, that twat. She commands me to bid you hello and that she hopes you enjoyed your little visit to her kingdom last spring. Even if you did scurry through the country like a rodent and never visit her once. Oh, and to give you this." He tossed a small object toward me.

Not even an idiot would merrily catch an unknown item thrown by a strange man riding along a coast that looked like it had been damned by three gods. I stepped aside and let the thing plop to the dirt beside me. It landed like a blob of grease, without a bounce or a skip. It was a small, black leather book, about the size of my hand. I didn't care about any of that. A curved, convoluted mark was set in white on the cover, the mark of Harik, God of Death.

I stepped back from the horrible object. "Cael, take this damned thing away from here. Take it right now, or I will kill you and your horse. Then I'll ride to Bellhalt and kill your goddamned queen too."

Cael backed his horse away three steps. "Just wait! Breathe for a second. Consider that Her Majesty, who's not known to be a frivolous woman, sent you this book. She entrusted it to me, the most valued of all her retainers. Three sorcerers have tried to steal it from her this past summer. Why did they do that? Nobody knows. It's an enigma." He leaned toward me, smile gone. "Bellhalt is still preferable to hell, but only by a sliver. Buildings just fall down or burn up. Lightning storms strike from the clear sky. The Rike Bridge simply disappeared. A hundred people saw it happen. More than a thousand people slain." His eyes were filling up, and he sniffed hard. "Who knows how many by now?"

"Krak's nuts, that sounds awful. I'm glad we didn't linger."

"Bib, will you ignore all that suffering?" Cael asked it the way he might ask me to help him save drowning babies. "It's not just Bellhalt. I've seen the same insanity in every land I have passed through to find you."

I shrugged at him, but I wanted to throw up. He was describing the route I had taken from the South Lands to get here. Sure, I knew I'd be opening the way for the gods wherever I went, but I hadn't expected this. Gods rarely went in for vast, arbitrary destruction. They liked their torments personal.

"Since you're not accepting my invitation, I'll just have to take you. I offer you a challenge." Cael dismounted and stretched his back.

"What, a fight?"

He nodded. "You have to promise that when I defeat you, you'll come along with me to Bellhalt."

"You are extremely amusing."

Cael drew his sword. "Promise, or I'll take you there tied onto a horse."

I nodded and drew my sword. "Well, sure. I'd never break a promise."

Manon said something I couldn't quite hear.

"Don't worry. I won't hurt you," Cael said.

"I intend to kill you deader than last night's chicken."

The bastard laughed as he lunged at me. He almost pinked my shoulder, but I riposted low. He was a tall fellow, so I figured he was ripe for an attack on the low line. I figured wrong, and I retreated two steps to take my groin out of his range. He pressed hard, and for a few seconds, I parried one thrust after another. I saw a weak spot in his guard and jumped for it, scratching his arm. Right away, I slipped aside and cut at his head, nicking an ear.

This was the point in my fights where most really fine swordsmen experience a tiny doubt about beating me. I'd seen dozens of them hesitate, and I had rewarded them with a thrust through their chest, throat, or belly. I went after Cael's weak spot again. He didn't hesitate. Instead, he almost disarmed me. I retreated two more steps to recover.

Cael smiled. "I salute you, but you've got to admit—"

While his mouth was open, I feinted toward his weak spot and slid past his guard, close enough to disembowel him. Before I could make the slice, I found that my ass was sliding across the gritty trail. Cael knocked my blade aside and pressed his sword's point against my throat.

His face split apart in that impossible smile. "Well?"

A puff of dust on the hillside caught my eye. I squinted toward it.

Cael raised his eyebrows, and this time he belted out, "Well?"

Another puff of dust appeared, right where a puffin had been standing. I glanced back toward Ella. She gaped at me, her sword dangling in her hand. Manon was peeking out from behind the horse, clutching the little book. Her chin started quivering.

I screamed, "Run!" I heaved myself upright. Cael cocked his head but didn't try to stop me. I sprinted toward Ella. "Grab the girl and run now!" By the time I reached her, she had snatched Manon's arm. I hauled them both down the trail fifty paces before I stopped and turned back toward the puffin-slaughter. back. I saw another puffin disappear, leaving dust.

Cael evidently possessed some fine survival instincts, because he reached us a few seconds later. He stood balanced, ready to cut something to bits if it would just show itself.

Ella's horse sagged, wrinkled, and went gray. It was a pile of dust in a few seconds. Manon screaked, and Ella kicked the ground. "Rutting bastard son of Krak . . ."

I almost made a joke about Ella swearing, but I was terrified that one of us who wasn't named Cael would collapse into dust next.

Cael's splendid horse shrank, bent, and collapsed in on itself until it, too, was merely dust.

"Rinonda . . ." He lowered his sword.

We watched for a while longer, but nothing else turned to dust while we waited. At last, I walked over to examine what used to be Cael's horse.

Cael scowled at me. "She was disintegrated, right there in front of us. Sorcery for sure. Did you do this, Bib?"

"I wasn't the sorcerer who did this, Tippler of Souls. And your mount wasn't disintegrated." I pointed at the long pile of dust. "When you disintegrate something, there's nothing left behind. Not a scrap or a speck. I've never seen this particular feat, but I'd guess these poor creatures were aged to death."

"Did you say aged?" Ella pushed past me.

I nodded.

Ella stared hard at me. "Where are the bodies?"

"Right here." I kicked at the dust. "Aged some unknown thousands of years in a couple of seconds. Manon, drop that book! It's cursed and venomous. Your hand might fall right off, or even your nose."

She laid the book on the dirt. "Did I kill those horses?"

"Yes, you did, darling. I know you didn't intend it, but you did."

Manon looked at the dust pile that had been Cael's horse and started crying.

"Your grief is creditable, but it won't help a damn thing, so blow your nose. Let's apply ourselves to your learning sorcery now before you kill us all. And I don't care to listen to you complain and object with a stuffed-up nose."

FIVE

Until I met Cael, I had known only three fighters who were genuine artists—technically sublime and creative, filled with a hunger to make their enemies die. They all fought dirty as hell too. One I hadn't seen in years, and most likely she was dead. The other two had each, at different times, tried to kill me. They had taught me that I might be dangerous with a sword, but I was no artist. I received that education with real gratitude, and then I killed them using magic.

Now a fourth artist walked next to me, wiping at his streaming nose with a linen handkerchief so fine it must have cost more than every garment I was wearing, including my boots. I thought Cael might be allergic to the ancient dust of his horse.

Cael said something unintelligible through all that snot, and I shook my head as I shrugged. He blew his nose and honked. "You're a decent fellow to honor your word and come to Garhool with me. When we get there, we'll find a ship and sail to the continent."

"You're full of shit."

He laughed at me.

Cael put on modest airs, but he was arrogant as hell to let me walk around free. I pondered how I should murder him. As abductions go, he was staging an odd one, but he didn't talk as if kidnapping me was a prank. He had threatened me and held his sword at my throat. That was reason enough to end his life. Also, I didn't know him or why he did anything. If something unfortunate happened, it might convince him to cut off my head. I had to slay the man, but I would probably need magic to do it.

When Ella and I had retreated to Ir, I hadn't much need for magical power, or so that stumbling goat molester Harik had led me to understand. Of course, I held on to a little for emergencies. Oftentimes a sorcerer without power is just a fellow waving his hands around and looking confused. But even without magic, I was still devious and ruthless, so I didn't concern myself about it too much. I'd have plenty of time to worry about more power when I left the islands. Cael was forcing the need for magic on me now, so I'd have to trade with Harik for power soon.

Cael wasn't my most dire problem, though. Manon might destroy us all by raining down whales, or shrinking our hats to one-tenth their normal size, all without knowing she was doing it. I needed to start her lessons on how to be as simple as any other little girl.

I guided Manon off to one edge of the path with me, but we kept walking. "You're going to learn some sorcery now. Is that all right?"

She stared at the black grit under her. "What if I say no?"

"It doesn't matter. I just asked to sound polite."

Manon sighed. "Fine."

I picked up my pace so Manon would have to walk faster. "We'll start with the most important lesson of all—how to *not* do magic."

Manon smiled. "Good! When I learn that, you won't care if I leave."

"You won't be leaving any time soon. Right now, you're as dangerous as an avalanche. With an ounce of training, you'll be no more dangerous than seven or eight trees falling at once. Can you read and write? Do any figures?"

She shrugged. "I don't let anybody cheat me on trading fish."

"Answer me this then. How much is twenty-seven minus eight?"

Manon squinted up for a few seconds. She kept squinting for a few more seconds.

I said, "Don't concern yourself about it. There's no reason you should know that."

She kicked a rock, and it bounced down the hillside. "Then why did you ask me?"

I walked a little faster. "Never mind. Close your eyes. Keep walking."

"I'll trip!"

"You'll get back up. Stop breathing. Don't hold your breath— just stop breathing. Only breathe in when you think you'll die if you don't. Now, there's a hot spot some place inside your body—could be anywhere, even your elbow. Find it. Don't give me side-eye. Do it."

After a minute, Manon sucked in a breath. "Why should I do this dumb stuff? And don't say that if I don't, you'll kill me."

"So that you won't kill any more innocent horses," I said matter-of-factly.

She tripped but didn't fall.

"Keep at it."

Manon kept at it for five more minutes and then glared at me. "I don't feel anything. I think you're lying to me."

"Am not. Find it. It's just the first lesson. Hell, a baby could do it."

Manon whipped her head away from me and whispered, "Skinny old turd . . ." She closed her eyes and kept walking.

Three hours and two skinned knees later, she said, "All right, what now?"

She had found it faster than I'd hoped. I had prepared myself for hearing her childish profanity until dark. "You found it? Where is it?"

"It's in my chest, which feels strange." She pressed her palm against her chest.

"That's good. What do you think that cloud up there looks like, and how much is seventy-one minus twenty-four?"

"A baby goat and forty-seven," Manon said right away. She stopped, her eyes wide. Ella almost ran into her.

"Come on, keep up." I waved her on. "How much is twenty-eight plus ninety-four less thirty-three?"

"Eighty-nine." Manon gaped at me, as amazed as if I'd shown her that a golden egg had been hiding in her nose. "How come I know that?"

"Magic." I bumped her shoulder with my fist.

Cael sneezed and then sneezed again, twice as loud. "That's remarkable. Manon, where were you when I built the third granary in Regensmeet? I'd have hired you as my mathematician and paid you two silver knocks a day."

I laughed. "That's a paltry wage for a sorcerer. Manon, how do you feel?"

She stopped and stared at me with huge eyes. "Bib, I'm scared. What's going to happen to me next?"

I gave her a knowing nod, full of the ancient wisdom I didn't have. "Scared is how it feels to be a sorcerer. Well, at first."

"Bib! Why can I figure all those numbers?"

I said, "Sorcerers are good with numbers. It's almost like somebody's in your head doing that figuring for you, isn't it? What's sixty-six times thirteen minus three hundred and seventeen?"

"Five hundred and forty-one." She nodded and grinned a little.

I pointed down the road ahead of us. "Now, keep walking. Faster. Make that hot place go away. Ease it out. It's not like holding your breath. It's like not breathing."

Manon started walking and pulled ahead.

I called after her, "Keep your eyes closed. And count out loud to ten thousand by thirteens while you do it."

She frowned at me like I had spit in her milk, but she closed her eyes and started counting. After three steps, she tripped and skinned her chin on the gritty road. She jumped up and kept going. When she reached 169, she stopped.

I said, "I know it's hard to understand, but you have to try."

"All right, what next?" Manon sounded disgusted.

I held my breath for a second, and then said, "The hot spot is gone?"

Manon nodded. "What next? Do you want me to hop down the road on my butt while I count to a million by sevenths?"

In just a few hours, Manon had jumped a wall that confounded most new sorcerers for two days. Hell, it took me three days, but I was a poor student. Now I wouldn't need to kill her.

I started to tell her that, but my throat closed. I almost started crying, which shocked me. She wasn't anything special. Hell, I cared about my old horse ten times more than I gave a shit about that little girl. And she was nothing like my daughter. Manon was more like a wild baboon than she was like my Bett. It didn't make a twitch of sense.

I coughed. "No, not that. Rest your brain a little. If you know any songs, sing them. But do it down the road a piece so I can't hear you."

Manon sighed and trotted ahead.

Not a speck of anything about Manon suggested she was a prodigy of sorcerous magnificence. I could hear her from thirty paces ahead of me, singing an old island tune, swinging her palsied hands in time, and almost dancing as she walked. I gazed down toward the shore so nobody would see my face if I did start crying.

I felt myself lifted and swallowed by nauseating blackness. This was how it felt when some god seized my ghost and hauled it up into the lightless arena gods used when they wanted to dupe and mock sorcerers. Men were insubstantial in the Home of the Gods. The sickly feeling would lose its grip fast since I'd have no physical stomach when I arrived. While still a young sorcerer, I had decided that the sick sensation was pure psychic loathing.

Harik must have been calling for me, and I didn't mind, either. I had been planning to go there and chew on his ass, figuratively, for lying to me about sorcery in Ir. I needed power to murder Cael too, of course.

"Hello, Mighty Harik! Have you seduced Chira yet, or is she still poking fun at your dangler?"

The God of Death answered me in a virile, potent tone, but he clipped his words as usual. "You can't annoy me with such a trivial insult, Murderer. I bring you here to bargain for a robust prize."

I have found that the best strategy with gods is to first spit in their eye. However, Harik sounded cheery about all this, which concerned me.

I drew my sword, which had been forged and named by the gods. That meant it sounded like it had been named by a teenager who discovered that only he, of all the people alive, could think profound thoughts. It was called the Blade of Obdurate Mercy, and in my world, it was about as magical as a bent nail. In this place of trading, it let me see as the gods see. On this occasion, I saw the arena of dirt in which I was standing, the gentle, care-melting yellow sunlight, the forest of trees with curled leaves edging from green to silver, and Harik with his left sandal off, picking at his big toe.

I pointed my sword at the God of Death. "Krak's nose and elbows, Mighty Harik! Why did you cheat me about sorcery in Ir? And for a god, you have some revolting habits, you drool-lapping, impotent shrew."

Harik sighed. "I do wish Krak hadn't given you that sword. Your mortal eyes aren't worthy to appreciate my immortal form."

"Given? Tell him to give it to somebody else. That thumping twerp Cael would be perfect for it. He'll haul it all over the world to show how he's helping everybody by opening the way."

Sitting high above me in a white marble pavilion, Harik jammed his sandal back on. He brushed back his cascade of black hair and straightened the neck of his robe, which was said to be the fourth blackest thing in existence. He lowered his titanic chin and turned his head a bit to the left. He always posed that way. Fingit said it was because Harik thought he appeared more handsome from that angle. It didn't seem to matter that his face was perfect, and he looked the same from every angle. "We are gods. Our ways are beyond your understanding. I forbid you to question them."

"Horseshit." I winked at the god. "Something happened, didn't it? Somebody demanded that you betray me, and like a puppy, you rolled and peed yourself. Was it Lutigan?"

Harik glowered at me. He had probably shattered a few sorcerers in his time with that glower. "Beware, Murderer. I know everything about you. Your woman risks death so often. I cannot imagine how she has survived this long."

"Was it Krak?"

Harik hesitated just a smidge. "No."

"It *was* Krak!" I said. "What's the hairy old stump planning? You owe me for breaking our deal."

"It was not Krak. I mean, it was no one. I mean, nothing at all happened." Harik stood and spoke in round, godly tones. "I am here to trade, but it seems you merely wish to whimper about a promise. What have you to offer?"

That was a fine question. Trading with a god was just like buying beer, except each beer was magical power, enough to burn a house to ash quicker than I could pull on my trousers and boots. A big house, with rooms for servants and maybe a shed or two. To buy power, I'd have to give up something I loved, or do something I hated. For example, I could promise to murder people. I'd done that once. Actually, twice. But the more the deal hurt, the more power it bought.

One time, I agreed that a god would make Ella leave me for no good reason. It struck me now that maybe a bit of that particular deal was hanging on, making her unhappy, which was making me unhappy. If I could track down that deal and wipe it out, everything would be fine again. And while that was happening, ducklings would waddle in and solve all my problems for me. I shook my nonexistent head. Sorcerers get tempted to blame magic for their own failings, and I was not immune.

Sorcerers have long speculated about why the gods want them to suffer, but they have not settled on an answer. If every sorcerer but two were wiped out, those two survivors wouldn't be able to agree on an answer. Myself, I believe that eternity must be pretty damn long. Bored gods needed something to do, and they enjoyed both pain and irony.

"Murderer, have you at last been rendered mute in awe of my magnificence? Or have you been distracted by a stray leaf, or become nostalgic for the rumbling of your own mortal digestion, which is repugnant?"

"My apologies, Mighty Harik." I swiped my forehead in a crappy little salute. "I was contemplating ways in which I could devote myself to your glory, if you were different in just about every way. Allowing all the respect you deserve, God of Death, I offer to listen while you make the first offer."

Harik rolled his eyes, saw that I was staring straight at him, and posed again. "As you will. I bring two squares to this bargain. In exchange, you must kill the little sorcerer girl."

A first offer is usually something outrageous, just to stake out a strong bargaining position. "You still have a bouncy sense of humor, Mighty Harik. I offer to . . ." I almost offered to mislead Manon about sorcery for the next week. I could keep her counting and walking with her eyes closed all the way to Garhool and back home, but I had promised not to lie to her. Well, maybe I lied when I made that promise, but her training was at a ticklish stage, and a little rage on her part could cause obscure, bad things to happen. They might happen to me. "I offer two bad head colds at times of your choosing in exchange for eight squares of power."

"I offer three squares if you kill the girl." Harik didn't shift or change expression.

"I'll get two charley horses every night for a month, and you give me four squares.

"Four squares to kill the girl."

I cocked my head at the god. "Why are you so randy about my murdering the girl?"

"She reminds me of Gorlana as a child. The bitch used to throw rocks at my unicorns."

"And peed on your golden roses too, I bet." I shook my head and smiled. "Manon has just now learned enough that I don't have to kill her, so no."

Harik lifted a palm and shrugged. "No one else knows that. You can tell them she was about to go insane and kill you all."

"Two squares of power, and for a week, any wine bottle will shatter when I touch it. I'll have to drink beer."

"Kill the girl. That is the only payment I will accept." Harik leaned forward. "Unless you secure some power, that washed-out smile that walks like a man may slay you."

"Cael? Hah!" I laughed to cover up the knowledge that Cael could probably kill me whenever he wanted.

I suspected that I was the oldest sorcerer alive, and I hadn't become that by jumping in front of arrows or failing to run while everybody else was getting killed. But I had never outright killed a child.

"If those are your only terms, then I'm wasting my time, you crusty armpit." I began lowering myself back to the world of men.

Harik sat and crossed his legs. "Unfortunate, but I am somewhat tired of you, Murderer. You will almost certainly be killed by something. Perhaps an ill-tempered rodent. To demonstrate my incomparable magnanimity, I shall grant you a parting gift of knowledge."

"I don't want it, you slug." I couldn't get away fast enough to avoid hearing it.

"I did not betray you regarding magic on your pathetic, malodorous island. I kept the bargain." Harik smiled the way people do when they're right and want you to damn well know it.

"You're just making up stories. Don't embarrass yourself."

"Oh, wise and crafty sorcerer, do you remember how you worded our bargain with care to guard against any possible lie? How you retained the power over our deal, and how only you could lift the ban on magic in Ir? Well, you yourself chose to lift it. You desired it in your heart and your thoughts."

I knew right away he was telling the truth. "You lying son of a bitch! For argument's sake, just when did I experience this desire?"

"When you had been on the island four days."

I couldn't think of anything to say.

Harik's smile stretched even bigger. "Murderer, if against all probability you survive the week, reconsider my offer."

I drifted myself back to the world of man, still walking on the trail. No time had passed there.

Ella touched my arm. "What's amiss? You look tired."

I rubbed my eyes. I could blame any redness on fatigue. "Abstruse mysteries of the everyday sorcerer. You'd be bored."

"Perhaps not."

I smiled at her. "Let me order my mind and separate the facts, manifest from subtle. Then we can get drunk and make shit up."

Ella chuckled, and I glanced at Cael. I considered that Ella could help me kill him, but she might be killed in the struggle. I should have scavenged Bear-Hat's bow. I wondered whether I could rush Cael in his sleep, or start an avalanche above the trail. There were possibilities.

SIX

Supper was sparse in our camp that night. Manon had aged Ella's and Cael's saddlebags into oblivion, so we supped on the food I had salvaged off my mare. Ella sat guard half the night and I did the other half, in case Cael decided to whack us on the head, tie me up, and carry me over his shoulder all the way to Bellmeet. Nothing so exciting occurred, however.

The next day, I expected we'd pass the inland trails that joined this little road. Those trails would dribble out travelers that would swell our road up to become the great Coast Road, which brought trade to Garhool. From Garhool, a person could travel the Coast Road most of the way around the island, or trudge inland up the Little Spine Road. In theory, they could board a ship and sail anywhere in the world, but in practice, nobody sailed anywhere except across the sea to the mainland. Half of the ships that sailed away into deep waters never came back, so exploration remained unpopular.

We started off before sunrise, and by midmorning, we hadn't yet reached those tributaries of commerce from the inland. As we rounded a bulging hillside, we spotted somebody up ahead walking and leading a lame mule. The beast must have been suffering because it crept along, and we reached hailing distance within a couple of minutes.

Ella called out, "Hello! Do you require aid?"

The traveler turned, and I saw she was Ona, the spiteful nun who had demanded I take possession of Manon. For a moment it seemed as if Ona might run, but then she waved with her crippled arm. "I could use some water, for my mule."

I yelled, "Aren't you going to accuse me of hexing your mule?"

Ella murmured, "Bib . . ."

I pretended I hadn't heard her. "Don't stop acting like a bitch at this point, nun! The gods hate weakness. Don't they teach that to little nuns?"

"Don't all sorcerers die young?" Ona shouted. "Can't you even get that right?"

Ella jumped in before I could say something nastier. "Wait there, Ona! I'm bringing water."

I scowled at Ella. "We don't have water to waste on mules!"

This time, Ella ignored me and marched toward Ona. Manon followed her, but I didn't intend to go visiting as if the nun were serving steaks and beer. Cael stayed beside me and wiped at his nose, bright red in the middle of his paper-white face. He hadn't let me get more than ten feet away from him since Manon killed the horses.

Cael pointed up the hillside next to us as he snuffed his nose. "There's a spring up there. See the wet rocks?"

"I grew up on Ir, I know its ways, and you have a hell of a lot of sand telling me about anything to do with it. Hell, the damned ocean is right there! Every rock along this coast for a hundred miles is wet!"

He shrugged and pointed again. "Wetter rocks."

I examined the hillside and saw that he was right. "God-damn eyeball-flying slayer of your sister's virtue! You're full of crap!"

Cael smiled. "Do you want water now, or do you want to drink it when it comes out of the mule?"

"If it's there, you can you can go find it yourself."

Cael shook his head. "I am not crawling up there by myself and letting you run away. You know better. You go first."

"Shit!"

I shouted our plans to Ella, and Manon ran back to me with their empty water vessels. Cael gave me a polite, little bow and gestured toward the hill. I climbed up ahead of him, pouring a waterfall of profanity and epithets back down on him. He laughed three times and complimented me once for originality.

We filled our few water bags and brought the fresh water up the road to the others. Manon ran to me and grabbed my hand.

"Finally," Ella said to Manon. "Will you speak now?"

Manon squeezed my hand tight and glared at Ona. "I'm not hexed. Why did you say I was? You ass."

Ona sniffed. "You're full of piss and vinegar, aren't you, little girl? Since you asked so politely, I guess you deserve an answer. I wanted to see Bib close-up."

"What?" Manon and I said at the same time.

"I suspect that Bib is opening the way for the gods. You are, aren't you, Bib?"

Cael stared at me. "Way? What way?"

"Quiet, the grown-ups are talking," I told him. It felt good. "Nun, I'm not telling you a damned thing about anything."

"No, no, no, hell no!" Ona walked right up to me. "Stop being stubborn and listen! Opening the way is making for a lot of suffering, and the suffering people are raising all kinds of hell. Some fellow named Agni has stirred them all up, has them killing priests and sorcerers and witches—anybody who has anything to do with gods or magic. They do have a grievance, I guess. We think the only means to solve the problem for certain is to close the way. So, if you're the one opening the way, and I think you are, we need you to help us."

"Who is 'we'?" Ella asked.

"The ones getting killed, you fool."

Nobody said anything for a few seconds. I finally spoke up. "Well, hell, I'll say it. Why don't you just kill me, tell Agni the problem's solved, and let everybody go home? Not that I encourage that, but it's the direct solution. Is that your real plan?"

"No, killing you wouldn't do any good. The gods would just pick somebody else. We want your help, but you're not important enough to kill."

Ella nodded. "Someone who does not want to take your life. Novel."

"Wait! Stop!" Cael held up his hands for us to stop, one toward Ona and one toward me. "I don't know what exactly is going on, and I've decided I don't care, except for this—can Bib do whatever you want him to do in Bellmeet? Because that's where he's going."

Ona pursed her lips. "I don't see why he couldn't work with us in Bellmeet. As long as we stop Agni, I don't care if Bib goes to the beach and eats pies all day."

Everybody looked at me.

"No." I dropped Manon's hand and let my arms hang loose in case I needed to kill somebody. "I won't do it. I won't help you or stand aside or pretend I don't see what you're doing. I won't hang myself so the gods give you somebody with less backbone, either. If you try to close the way, I'll stop you. That means I'll kill you, in case you're unclear on my methods."

"Clean out your ears!" Ona took two steps toward me. "People are dying. Women and kids. Whole families. You have got to stop being a horse's rear end and help us."

I crossed my arms. "No, I don't. I made a bargain. If you don't like it, ride your gimpy mule off into the ocean and drown."

Ona put her hands on her hips. "What kind of bargain? Just what's so good about it?"

I could have said a lot of things that were misleading, sarcastic, or just mean. This wasn't any of Ona's business, anyway, and a lie was in order. So, just to keep things lively, I decided to tell the truth. "It helps me sleep at night."

"Oh, hell, if that isn't the most ridiculous thing ever said by a man!" She shouted so loud she hurt my ears a little.

Ella gripped my arm. "He knows it's not his fault that his child died."

Ona stared at me for a moment. "Well. Well, that would be important, I guess." She shook her head and scowled. "I understand what you mean, sorcerer, but it doesn't matter. You don't know it yet, but you will help us. I don't give up."

"That's a good reason for me to be leaving you now." I walked around Ona toward Garhool.

Ella called after me, "Bib, would you first please examine the mule? I have formed an opinion, but I should like to hear yours."

I only needed ten seconds to see that the grisly cut on the mule's foreleg couldn't be helped. "This animal is doomed. You'd best kill it."

"No!" Manon screamed.

I patted the mule on the shoulder. "Manon, I imagine this is the first mule you've touched in your life, so you should question your opinion here. Believe me, it's a kindness to kill it."

"No! Save him. What good is it to be a sorcerer if you can't even help a poor old mule?"

In truth, I was holding back a little magical power for emergencies. It was enough to save this mule, even if it wasn't enough to kill Cael with any certainty. But in my universe of possible emergencies, "lame mule" was not even a speck. "I'm sorry, Manon."

"You're just worthless!" Manon ran down the road, where she stood with her back to me.

I nodded at Ona, who nodded back. I regret to say I've performed the final act for a few dozen horses and mules in my life. I drew my knife, and in thirty seconds, it was over. The mule screamed, hit the ground like a hundred sacks of potatoes, wheezed for a brief while, and went limp.

As I wiped my knife, I nodded at Ona. "Shouldn't take you too long to bury him. Pardon us if we don't stay to help out."

"You're not very funny," Ona grumped.

"Bib isn't joking about us leaving, but that does not mean you should pay him any attention." Ella shook her head and knelt to start untying the mule's pack. "We shan't abandon you to walk this road by yourself."

We left the mule beside the road and kept on walking. Ona had strapped a bag onto her crippled arm as if it were of no more use than a pole.

Manon glared at me and went to walk beside Ella. A minute later, she peered around Ella at the nun. "What was his name?"

Ona stared at Manon. "Well, my word. Who names a mule?"

Ella hugged Manon around the shoulders and kissed the top of her head without stopping.

A few minutes later, we reached the first side trail coming down from inland, weaving through a dip in the hills. By noon, we'd passed three more, each emptying onto what was becoming the Coast Road. It grew busier throughout the afternoon as we neared Garhool. We joined in with carts, wagons, and people toting sacks and bundles, either headed to town or departing. Almost everybody hauled goods of some kind. Our lack of burdens made us conspicuous.

Over a thousand souls scrambled their lives away in Garhool. A hundred or so fishermen struggled to feed the city and fell short by half. Quite a few other folks provided the services necessary to claim that a place is civilized, such as bars, gambling houses, bakeries, smithies, and brothels. A few hundred were either children or involved in domestic pursuits. All the rest labored at moving people and things from one place to another, including food to eat. Trade and transport were Garhool's reasons to exist. If it weren't for the charming natural harbor, nobody would have laid two sticks together in that spot, never mind build a city.

The Coast Road split the town into halves. On the ocean side stood warehouses, a little shipyard, the nasty docks, and a huge, splayed superstructure of offices and workshops that loomed between the road and the harbor. A huge rock outcropping separated the docks into the North Wharf and the South Wharf. The natural stone barrier stood as high as three men. On the inland side, shops and homes clung to the steep hillside, connected by a nest of walkways and ladders. Every structure in sight was made of wood, hauled from inland. The gritty soil of Garhool was never meant to grow trees. Hell, it wouldn't grow a carrot.

We walked into the city among people rushing up and down the

Coast Road, the wharves, and the hillside. As I turned toward the docks, a tall woman in the stream of people called out, "Ona! Here!"

This new woman was brown-haired, younger than Ona, and sported a nose and chin so prominent that I imagined her face was an ax-blade. She wore faded trousers and a shirt she should have pulled off and cut up for rags. Ona's broken cheek pulled her lips crooked as she smiled at the woman and waved with her good arm.

"I have to go with Kella, but I'll find you soon." Ona turned to me. "Seeing you wasn't the only reason I brought that girl to you. She would have been unhappy living her life in that nasty-ass village."

I cocked my head at the mouthy nun. "Maybe the girl will be unhappy with me. What makes you believe she won't?"

Ona grinned crookedly. "I have a good feeling about you."

Ella cleared her throat. "You must be singularly perceptive. His river of fine qualities flows too deep for most people to detect."

I put as much threat on my face as I could, and I've been told it's quite a lot. "Nun, stay away from me. If I see you again, I'll kill you in the name of Harik and Krak." I pushed past her and headed toward Albert Scrip's office.

Cael trotted up from behind me. "Bib, we'll take ship to the mainland right away. You have ten minutes to resolve whatever business you have in the city."

"You turd with teeth, I'm not crossing the sea with you. I wouldn't cross a goddamn ditch with you even if it was dry."

Cael laughed. "Where are you going just now?"

I didn't slow down. "To Albert Scrip's office."

"Wonderful! I think he owns ships. Some of them probably cross the sea."

"I'm only going there to kill the bastard! You moron!" I pushed ahead of him, hitting him with my shoulder on the way past.

Cael laughed and actually clapped his hands. "I predict that you will not kill Scrip. In fact, we'll board one of his ships and cross to the mainland on it."

If Cael wanted to throw me onto a ship, I might not be able to stop him. "We'll see." I halted and made shooing motions at him. "You walk in front. I'll tell you which turns to make."

The smug bastard didn't hesitate or even make a wry face before walking in front of me. I didn't try to stab him in the back, either, although I was tempted. He might take away my sword and beat me with it.

Ten minutes later, we were not on a ship. We had walked down three corridors, climbed two ladders, and crossed the peeling, half-rotted remains of a suspended walkway. At last, we stood at a door practically glowing with white paint. Precise blue letters spelled, CAPTAIN ALBERT SCRIP, OE, ATR."

"What do those letters mean?" Manon pointed.

Ella said, "They mean that Captain Scrip lacks a certain sort of confidence, dear. And that he's probably a bore at social events."

I pushed the latch and kicked the door open. Albert was sitting, hands flat on his desk, looking like he'd swallowed something spiny.

"Hello there, Bib. Before you run me through, I can explain."

"Cael, you go on in." I followed the Denzman into the smallish room. Besides Scrip and the desk, it contained two chests, a book-case tightly stacked with papers, and a couple dozen maps tacked to the walls in precise grids. Two un-shuttered windows lit the place. The wooden floor and walls appeared tidy enough to have been scrubbed and flogged dry that morning.

I drew my sword, and Cael stood out of my way. "Explain fast, Albert, while you still have some bits to talk with."

Albert bit his lip. "I did not try to have you captured. It wasn't me. I would never do a thing like that, my friend!"

"Did some street juggler put on your clothes and hire those nasty morons"—here I started shouting—"who killed my horse?"

"No, technically, I did hire them, but that wasn't at all the clear-cut transaction it may now seem at this juncture. I was just an inter-mediary under duress."

Ella walked toward Scrip. "Someone threatened you unless you complied. They must have threatened to kill you, and even your family."

"Precisely so! My family would have been murdered! Not just me. You understand then."

"I understand." Ella walked back toward me. "Bib, torture him until he tells you everything. Then you may kill him if you wish." She winked at me where Albert couldn't see.

Albert shifted his gaze back and forth between Ella and me, and then he almost grinned. "I have been tortured quite enough already in my life. I'm happy to tell you everything. More than everything, if possible. Four men nabbed me as I left the Lion's Elbow two weeks ago and carried me into that alley—you know, the one where you paid those three whores and asked them to forgive you . . ." He glanced at Ella. "Not important. They were a bit shabby, the men, not the whores, but intelligent and well-spoken." He stared at desktop for a moment. "They issued their death threat and demanded that I have you captured and brought to them."

"You might have just said something to me about it when you set up the ambush."

"And I would've loved to do that, but at least one of those men stayed near me all the time after that, even sleeping in my home." He frowned down at his hands on the desk and sighed. "I was forced to do their work, absolutely forced. I'm so happy that you remain free, and that my plan went to ruin. Please don't kill me."

Ella leaned back against the wall. "Why do they want to capture Bib? What would they do with him?"

"Well . . ." Albert hunched over and appeared to collect his thoughts. "It was confusing, I will say that. These people, and a great lot of their friends, revile Bib. Something about the gods, and ruining people's lives. Babies falling down wells, that sort of thing. I gather they followed you here to Ir, and not to bring you kittens, either. But what precisely do they want to do with you? I can't say. I am sorry. Do you forgive me?"

"No." I leaned over the desk. "What are their names? What do they look like? What do they smell like?" I scanned the room. "You said they're always nearby. Where the hell are they then?"

Scrip stared up at me, almost pleading, and then he sighed. "They're mainlanders, all of them. Ragged and thin, but fierce.

Their leader is some fellow called Agni, but I never saw him. The one who threatened to kill me is named Pierce. Tall, handsome, and well-spoken—voice like a buttered trumpet."

I touched Albert's throat with my sword's point. "Is one of the bastards nearby now?"

Albert glanced down as he shrugged, almost sagging. "This morning, they were gone. Departed in the night without a word."

From the doorway, Manon said, "I think something's burning."

I whipped around and realized that the smell of smoke was drifting in through the window. "Albert?"

The ship owner glared at the top of his desk and said, "Fressa's tits, Bib! You're dim as a dormouse!" He threw himself back from the desk but not fast enough. A woman wearing rags surged out from under it and stabbed him in the heart. As Albert gurgled and toppled over backward in his chair, the woman spun and jumped across the desk at me.

It was a ridiculous maneuver, since I was already pointing my sword in her direction. I transfixed her heart seconds after she destroyed Albert's. Ella knelt over Albert, but I wanted to see what the smoke was all about.

I trotted back outside, and then I marveled at my foolishness. This end of the docks could be entered at five places, three corridors for foot traffic and two large passages for cargo. Now healthy fires blocked off four of them. The wind snapping toward us shot the flames higher and threw them onto whatever happened to be downwind.

Nobody was fighting the fires. In fact, a couple dozen armed men and women were fending off anybody who tried. I watched a man toss an open cask of oil onto the least ferocious of the fires.

The South Wharf would likely be destroyed, and maybe all of Garhool, unless somebody conjured a magnificent storm. I lifted myself to bargain with Harik for the power to do that very thing. Before my stomach had settled into the Home of the Gods, Harik said, "The girl?"

"Right, isn't she a pain in the ass?" I said.

"I meant, will you kill her?"

"I know what you meant."

Harik dropped me back into my body like an anvil plunging from a tower. When I arrived, it drove me to my knees.

"I didn't take you for a man of prayer," Cael said.

"I often talk with the gods. They just told me to kiss their divine asses." I stood up, scanning the South Wharf. It was fast resembling one of the many places the gods threaten us with when we don't toady to them enough.

Only one path out of the docks still stood clear, a covered passageway. Another two dozen armed people waited on the other end of the passageway. A tall man in a bright-green shirt stood with them, smiling as they slapped shoulders and laughed. He grinned right at me, waved with one hand, and grabbed his crotch with the other.

I tried to smile at Ella and Cael, but my lips didn't quite make it all the way. "Don't worry."

Cael took two seconds to turn his head and stare at me. "Really? Did you just say, 'Don't worry'?"

Manon started coughing hard.

Ella hissed and punched me on the shoulder. "You and your gods and your ridiculous debts."

I winced. Once we were done in Garhool, the bruise would look mighty handsome. If one could see it through all my blackened, peeling flesh.

SEVEN

F ire hadn't smothered our bodies yet, but the wind blew hot
out there in front of Albert Scrip's door. My eyes watered
from the oily smoke, which made it hard to predict just how
soon we were going to get burned to death.

Cael said, "Bib, with no false modesty, I'm a peerless fighter, and
you're awfully good. But if we try to cut our way through that mob,
we'll die a useless death. A tragedy. Think of all the wine you've yet
to drink."

"That's the first thing you've said since I met you that I
understand."

"However . . ." Cael pointed toward the dockside, and I saw it
was empty. Every ship and boat that might have been docked there
was currently some place else. I didn't even see a vessel anchored
within swimming distance. "Bib, these people who hate you are
thorough. I would almost rather be on their side." He coughed a
little.

Out behind the troop of ragged arsonists, the tall man called out
in a singer's voice, "Surrender, sorcerer! Come here to the passage,
lay down your sword, and give up. I'll give you a count of one

hundred before we set fire to this passageway too." This ratty pole of a man must have been Pierce, the tall leader Albert told us about. He laughed, his arms around the shoulders of the men on each side of him, and they laughed too.

I shouted, "One hundred? Don't strain yourself trying to count any higher than ten. Not for my welfare."

"We'll kill you right dead if you resist. And I'll laugh at your ass while you bleed to death. But if you surrender . . . well, then I'll treat you well."

"I've told better men than you to go to hell, Pierce! I swear I'll kill you, and I'll piss on your grave!"

Ella leaned toward me. "Bib, I know that you must provoke every person you meet. It's one of the reasons I love you, although I couldn't say why. Now, shut up!"

"If we surrender, that filth won't treat us well." Cael pointed out at the road. "Look at the citizens they've already killed." The bodies of three would-be firefighters dotted the road.

Ella nudged me from where she stood staring back at the docks. "I suppose your enemies forced Albert to order away every ship."

I nodded. "I'm impressed. I wish I could hire these bastards next time I need to plan something nasty."

By then all of us were coughing. The fires had spread even faster than I'd expected. No storm I could conjure would douse them now, even if Harik sold me all the power the gods could scrape together.

I had been waiting for Manon to cause some insane, horrible thing to happen, something that might either save us or tear us to bits, but nothing like that occurred. She must have developed some control. I wished to hell she'd waited a few hours. Even if she killed us all in an instant, it would be better than roasting.

"You have a count of fifty left!" Pierce shouted.

I didn't bother insulting the man. I had just spotted a stick or something bobbing in and out of sight at the dock's edge. I slid down the ladder onto the terrifying suspended walkway, and I ran to the next ladder, ignoring Ella and Cael as they shouted. Ten seconds later, I stared down into a hask—a sailboat the perfect size for us to escape in. It was a shame this boat was fifteen feet below me and five feet out from the dock.

The others caught up, and Ella peered over the dockside. "Can we jump into it?"

"No, we might go through the hull. It's not much tougher than a bark raft that a kid would float down a ditch." I glanced around for a rope.

From out on the road, Pierce shouted, "I guess you want to burn. Fire it!"

Manon said, "Let's jump in the water and climb in."

"Move!" Cael yelled from behind us.

I ducked and rolled to the side. When I came up I saw the wind hurl a piece of sailcloth as big as a quilt, covered with fire. It smacked Manon and wrapped halfway around her. Both girl and cloth flew off the dock and fell into the bottom of the sailboat, toward the stern. Manon sounded like a cask of nails when she landed.

I jumped after her, aiming for the cord that moored the boat to the dock. I caught it with my right hand and hung on, and then I swung over the side into the boat. The sailcloth had blown forward and with great efficiency was setting the boat's cordage, mast, and furled sail afire. If Albert had left this boat here so he could escape with us, he had failed us all.

Ignoring the fire, I scooted over next to Manon, who was moaning. The cloth had burned a good bit of her back. It likely wouldn't kill her, but she'd need to convalesce. Her left leg was broken for sure. It may have smacked the gunwale on the way down. She squirmed a little and moved her legs and arms, so I rolled her onto her side. When I saw her jaw, I felt sick. It wasn't as much broken as it was smashed.

Maybe I could get her out of the boat without killing her, but if she went into that cold water, she'd never come out alive. That was just what Harik wanted. Well, to hell with him. I didn't intend to see any little girls die. As emergencies went, this was a good sight more important than "lame mule."

I heard Ella and Cael hit the water behind me, but I ignored them. Some seconds later, I felt them tip the boat as they climbed in. Out of the corner of my eye, I noticed the dock drifting away, and heat reaching back from the boat's bow to my face as the fire spread. I spent most of my attention on Manon.

Bodies want to be healthy, and that made the work easier. It's why the little power I had left would serve to heal Manon, although it wasn't enough to kill Cael. Bodies don't want to be dead, Cael's included.

I dealt with Manon's jaw first, in case I was interrupted. I grabbed green sheets of power out of nothingness, shaped them to her jaw, and arranged the broken pieces of bone in about the right places. I relied on her body's desire and memory to do the rest of the work and bring everything together.

As I worked, an ache came up in my own jaw. It grew to flat out pain and then to a good throbbing. By the time I was done with her, my jaw felt like it was being crushed and stabbed at the same time, and moving it even a little made my eyes roll back. I went on to fix Manon's broken leg and got rewarded with the sensation that my leg bone was being sawed in half. After all that, handling Manon's burns seemed like going to a party. I felt fortunate that even though I was given pain, I didn't feel all the pain that Manon had suffered.

When I had just finished healing Manon, Ella said, "Into the water now, unless you wish to be cooked." Cael and Ella had salvaged some unburned planks from the boat, and I hung onto mine without much caring where I drifted. Damn, it was cold, though.

I wanted to ask Ella how Manon was feeling, but my jaw was a loss just then. I stared at her and made near-meaningless gestures with my hands and eyes, but at last, she patted me on the shoulder and began talking to Cael about plans for not freezing to death. From all the shouting, I gathered they didn't have many ideas.

"Swim!" somebody shouted in the distance. "Swim! Get your asses over here!"

I pulled myself up a little and blinked water out of my eyes. Somebody was rowing a small sailboat toward us, not fast at all, and at that rate, the wind would push it too far out to sea before it reached us.

"Swim, damn you!" I recognized Ona's charming bray. Her crippled arm must have made rowing a challenge.

We swam hard, with knives shooting through my leg, and we caught Ona's skit boat before the wind blew it past us forever. Just about every child on Ir learns to sail in a skit boat. They're simple to manage, roomy for one person, and cozy for two, perfect for a romantic sail. The five of us almost capsized it trying to drag ourselves aboard. I got everyone's weight distributed around the boat, and I lay back against Ella.

"The gods willed I reached you in time." Ona shrugged. "Or maybe it was luck, or maybe you're alive because I was paying attention instead of sitting around with my head up my ass. I almost got burned to death too, you know, so . . . you're welcome."

"You stole this boat then?" Cael asked. "Not that I'm criticizing, since you saved all our lives."

"No. The gods put it where I needed it, right by Scrip's house. It would be like I was spitting on the gods if I didn't take it."

I fell asleep before anybody could contest that philosophy.

I woke up some time in the night, and the pain was a lot better. Cael was at the tiller. Everyone else lay still, maybe asleep. I examined the stars for a minute. "We're sailing north."

"We are?" Cael craned his head around and then pointed into the sky. "I thought we were sailing northwest. I've been following that star."

"That star moves around all through the night." I raised my voice. "Has anyone here ever sailed before?"

Ella said, "Only with you." No one else answered.

"Lutigan's left nipple! It's a wonder we haven't been capsized by a whale."

Manon squeaked but then shut up.

"Don't worry. They don't really do that." I began furling the sail. "Until the sun rises and we know what's what, we're drifting."

With the sail furled, we all contorted into our tiny spaces, and I fell back to sleep.

When the sun came up, at least I could still see land. Wolf's Milk Point, the northernmost tip of Ir, lay due west. "Say farewell to Ir, everybody. We won't get back until late summer, at least."

"What?" Ona sat up fast and banged her elbow on the gunwale. She growled, "Chira shred it and stick it—" She bit her lip.

I ignored her. "We're too far north to make that bit of land, with the way winds blow this time of year."

"Ships cross to Ir all the time," Cael said. "What about them?"

"It's true, and those are very fine ships, like hunting hounds. This boat is like an old, farting dog in the barnyard. It won't lie within three points of the wind, two at best."

Everyone stared at me.

"Those ships can beat into the wind and get somewhere. We could sail as close as we may to the wind for a month and never reach Ir."

Ona had become almost as white as Cael. "What do we do?"

I dropped my head for a moment. "You're like infants. We sail to the mainland. Do you see any food or water?"

The tiny provision locker was as empty as a usurer's heart. I said, "We'll die of thirst in a few days, but don't worry. We should reach the mainland in two days, no more than three."

"How will you navigate?" Cael asked.

"I think I can keep us going easterly. That may be all the precision we need to strike a coastline that's a thousand miles long. Although, we are riding low with five people aboard. I won't vouch for our survival if we hit any huge swells. If a storm hits . . ." I shrugged.

"You don't sound sure about this." Ella leaned forward and grabbed my arm.

"I'm not, but my fisherman instincts say it's so. Well, my Pa said I was a hopeless fisherman, but I'm the only sailor we've got. Manon, I'll show you how to set sail. If Cael would get his gigantic ass off that locker, that is."

"You can insult me all the way to the mainland, Bib. I'm above ridicule. As I predicted, you didn't kill Albert Scrip, and you are sailing toward the mainland on one of his ships."

"This is not a ship, you slope-brow son of a festering whore! It's barely a boat. I'll be shocked if some big fish doesn't come along and bite a hole in it and drown us all. Never talk about sailing again. It hurts me to hear you try."

He smiled at me with all those teeth.

EIGHT

The little boat wallowed up each of the swells and slid down the other side until the stiff breeze jerked it back up into the next swell. Seasickness had squeezed Ella and Ona in the first hour of our eastward run and had been wringing them ever since. Manon hadn't shown a single bit of enthusiasm for sailing. The people of Pog sort of pretended that the ocean didn't exist, since it was such an ordeal to get there and back. She approached sailing like she was learning to tie her shoes. It would be a reasonable thing to know, but not too interesting. On the other hand, Cael watched and listened as if he had to win a sailboat race tomorrow, and he'd get hanged if he lost.

I manned the tiller throughout the first day of our crossing and into the night. There was hardly room for us all to sit, so we had no hope of lying down to sleep. Ella leaned against my arm, raising herself once in a while to heave over the side. Under the yellow half-moon, I saw Cael asleep, loose and sitting upright, as solid as a pile of sand and probably as hard to shift. Manon slept with her shoulders and head in his lap. Ona was leaning against a locker, occasionally groaning and squirming.

We all felt parched at sunrise, particularly since the fire's heat had sucked so much moisture out of us. Ella and Ona appeared gaunt, but they sat up and began engaging in human activities. Ella took the tiller, and I started the next phase of Manon's training.

My teachers had taught me dexterity by tossing things at my face. They started with wooden blocks and little bags of sand. They progressed to shoes and spoons, and after that, they moved on to lumps of mud and skinned peaches. I don't want to overlook the horseshoes and chisels; they spent a lot of time throwing those at me. Eventually, they threw things like cow tongues, bowls of butter, and live ducklings at me.

I didn't have any of those things in the skit boat, but I did have rope. I taught Manon to tie some knots and made her practice them. I figured I would teach her harder and harder knots, and then make her tie them faster.

That's the training I had planned for Manon. Unfortunately, her palsy made tying even the simplest knots an ordeal. She could tie them. She tied everything I showed her, but she took at least five times as long as one would expect. By midafternoon, I told her to take a rest. She sat with Cael, mopish and licking her lips, but she didn't talk about being thirsty. Cael told her stories until dark. Some of them were his own adventures, probably imaginary, in which he'd defeated evildoers, and how the hardest part of that was figuring out which people were evil. The rest of the stories were about young girls who help the weak and needy using only wit and determination.

Ona spent some time explaining to me again how much she and her allies needed my help to save the lives of pretty much every person west of the Empire. I threatened to throw her overboard. Ona started on Ella, begging her to convince me. Ella abandoned the tiller, leaned over, and punched Ona in the eye.

I grabbed the tiller, and we didn't say much for the rest of the day.

About midnight, Ella took over again and I slept until morning. I tried to wet my lips, and then I croaked, "I expect we're more than halfway there."

Everybody nodded. No one wanted to waste breath that might have a little moisture in it.

I turned to Manon. "No more ropes today. I'll teach you something else."

"No."

"You don't have any choice."

"I do. They're just all bad. So, no. You said you'd let me go if I learned well. Did you lie?"

"I said it was unlikely, so I didn't lie." I slipped off my boot and tossed it toward her face. It smacked flat into her, and she squealed as she grabbed her mouth. Cael and Ona sat up straight, but they didn't say anything. Behind me at the tiller, Ella sighed.

"What are you doing?" Manon asked, staring at the blood on her shaking hand.

"Training you."

"This is dumb. I won't do it."

My tools for convincing her had dwindled in number. "I may still have to kill you if you refuse."

Her chin jutted out. "Kill me then."

"Fornicating pig-licker with bells on!" My voice broke, but I kept going. "You are stubborn enough to wear out an iron fence post. Hell, that's half of what you need to be a sorcerer, right there! You should just go on and learn the rest!" My mouth felt as dry as flour.

Manon opened her mouth to speak, but I put my hand in front of her face. "Here's the most important lesson of all." I cleared my throat twice to wet it a little. "If you don't want to learn that, just drown yourself now."

"Fine."

"Don't use magic if you can do something else. Anything else at all. It's how sorcerers get into trouble. The gods take part of you when they trade—things and people you love, who you are, and what you have to do." I swallowed twice, which didn't help.

Manon turned her head away from me toward the horizon.

"Someday, a god will summon you to bargain for power. They'll want you to do something, or not do something, or let them do something to you. You'll think you're smart and will win, but you'll always lose. They're gods, and that's the way they like it. Are you listening?"

"Yes." She pretended to untangle her hair so she could look away from me and my profound advice. "Don't do magic unless I have to."

"Basically, yes."

Manon smiled at me. "Do you follow this rule?"

"As much as possible."

"Are you in trouble because of magic?"

I thought to myself, *No, it's no trouble at all that I've murdered on a prodigious scale, and that I have to keep killing until Harik says to stop. Not at all.* I said, "Yes, I am."

"I don't guess your lesson is worth much, is it?" Manon smirked at me.

She went away to sulk, which in the boat was about seven feet from me. I let her be, and she ignored me. The wind held true, and we sailed toward the mainland at a good clip, but as the afternoon dragged by, thirst dug hard into all of us. We stopped talking. If it couldn't be communicated with nods and pointing, it wasn't important enough to bother with.

I sat five feet away from Manon at sunset, close enough to feel the pull when something lifted her spirit out of her body. I grabbed on, not with my hand, but with my own spirit. It sounds tricky, but it just takes learning the knack, like juggling with live frogs. I let her pull me up into the place where the gods trade with sorcerers, a place that wasn't just dark—it was absent. It was empty of things to see or touch. I couldn't hear my heartbeat, and I couldn't feel myself breathe. I could only hear what gods and people wanted to say.

"Bib? Bib!" Manon sounded terrified.

"I'm here, darling. You're all right. You've just been summoned by a god."

"Which . . . which one?" Even though her voice was merely psychic, it cracked.

I tried to sound soothing. "I don't know. We'll find out when they come to trade, because this is where the trading happens."

"Help me!" She sounded as terrified as any child I'd ever heard.

"I'll help you. Remember what I said, and don't make any trades." I made my thoughts more intense and louder. "No trades at all! Tell the gods to stuff any offers up their noses."

"What? I can't say that to a god!"

"You can, and you should. Mainly because you don't need power right now. You don't know how to do anything with it, so put thoughts of power out of your head. If you just have to say something, show the gods that they don't scare you. Call them a few names. Ignore them. It helps build the proper sorcerer-god relationship."

Manon didn't say a thing for a few seconds. "I'm scared."

"I know you are. I'll help you all I can. But a god called you, not me. I can't overrule anything you say." I raised my psychic voice again. "Don't deal! Once you say you accept a thing, it becomes part of the deal. So, don't deal. Do you hear me? Now hush. I feel a god in our presence. I hope he bathed recently. The last time I was here, Harik smelled like a colon that fell into a distillery."

"That's probably true, Murderer," said a woman's voice. "Eternity tends to distract weak-minded fellows like the God of Death. I summoned this young lady, but you're welcome here. In fact, I wanted to chat with you."

The sound of the voice both comforted and frightened me. It was wise and kind and playful. The person speaking with that voice loved you with a tenderness your mother never imagined. I had heard that voice only twice before, but that was more than most sorcerers. Most sorcerers never heard the thirteenth god, Goddess of the Unknowable, She-Who-Must-Not-Be-Named.

The first time a god brought me into his presence, fear just about destroyed me. If I hadn't been merely a spirit, my heart might have exploded. My fear embarrassed me once the ordeal had ended, since I was a sixteen-year-old man who had already mastered six years of sorcery training. My teachers told me later that lots of sorcerers handled the experience with less grace than I had. Plenty of them handled it better too.

Manon was now meeting the most unnerving of all the gods.

The girl of twelve years possessed two days of patchy sorcery training. I cherished the hope that she would be too horrified to form
coherent thoughts. That way, she couldn't agree to anything.

I drew my sword and swung a wide, ridiculous cut. The Gods'
Realm popped into brilliant view as my blade passed. Manon and I
stood in the familiar dirt arena. The marble pavilion squatted just
uphill from me so that gods could enjoy beverages and mock
sorcerers without exerting themselves. On my left, something white
foraged in a still, pale forest. On my right, meadows of infernal red
flowers sloped down to the horizon, which lay just beneath the
creamy sun. The moment the sun touched the horizon, all the
flowers turned from red to silver and I began bawling, although I
didn't know why.

The goddess leaned back on her marble bench. "So, Murderer,
you can see things here, just like us. Harik said it was so, but you just
confirmed it. Sloppy, sloppy. Oh, how could you possibly have
survived so long?"

Although I had heard the goddess twice, I had only seen her
once, and that from a distance. At the time, I had been bargaining
for my life and committing myself to an extended blight on my
spirit, so I hadn't taken a hard look. After years spent challenging
the gods, I could resist their little glamours and enticements, but
seeing the goddess was like being buried by an avalanche of awe
and lust. I practically had to work up a sweat just to think. She
didn't show herself as the woman with the motherly voice.
Instead, she appeared breathtaking, slim, and pale, with dream-
black hair, wearing a crimson gown and nothing in the way of
jewels.

I jerked when I realized her face wasn't perfect. Every god I had
ever seen had appeared ideal and symmetrical, which is more
alarming than attractive. The mind knows it's seeing something
perfect and inhuman. But the goddess struck me as just a whisper
away from perfect, the way a real, singularly dazzling woman might
appear, but with the power of a god behind it. The effect devastated
me.

I pulled my eyes away from her and started breathing again. I had lost track of the conversation, so I reclaimed the momentum by saying, "I beg your pardon?"

"Close your mouth, Murderer. I want to talk to this pretty new sorcerer girl first."

I didn't look at the goddess. Instead, I stared at the bench beside her so I wouldn't be mesmerized again. "Leave her alone, you slobbering cow. At least until she's grown up."

"She's not as young as you think, Murderer—not where it counts. Certainly old enough to be my daughter. 'Slobbering cow?' How sad. All of that sitting and drinking has destroyed your wit. One of your friends should have told you."

Manon whispered, "I'm not your daughter. I know who my mother is."

Speaking up in front of a god is a brave act. Contradicting a god is just short of heroic, but nothing good could come from Manon doing it now. It did show that she might make a fine, courageous sorcerer someday, if she wasn't killed first by any of a thousand common sorcery mishaps.

The goddess smiled, and I could hear it in her voice. "Oh, 'daughter' is just a way I have of speaking. I don't bother myself with many sorcerers, just an exceptional few. Always women, and always my daughters. You're my daughter now."

"What if I don't want to be?" She stood tall, but her voice quavered.

"Young lady, I didn't invite you to become my daughter. I stated it as a fact." The goddess caressed the bench beside her. "You are mine. No other gods may trade with you."

"I don't want to trade at all. I want to go back." Manon caught her breath and jerked her head around in different directions, unable to see as I could.

"Why, dear? To listen to that smiling cretin tell stories about himself?" She said it as if she were telling Manon to wash her face instead of eating mud pies.

"Manon, ignore this rumbling pig fart," I said.

"Poor effort, Murderer." The goddess slapped the bench beside her.

I didn't mean to, but I glanced over at the goddess and then jerked when I caught her regarding me with pitying eyes. I snapped my gaze back to the bench. "Ignore her, Manon. She's just trying to scare you so you'll bargain."

Manon turned, crossed her arms, and by mere chance stdirectly away from the goddess. "I don't want to trade. And that's final."

The goddess waited.

I took a step toward the pavilion. "She asked to take her leave. I know gods value manners as much as they value a boil on the ass, but she's turned you down twice. You're starting to look foolish."

In my peripheral vision, I saw the goddess cross her legs. "Young woman—oh, you are named the Tooth, by the way. To the gods, that's your name, in the same fashion this man's name is the Murderer. Don't you want to know why?"

I stepped in between them, an act ripe with futility. "No, she doesn't. It's probably a story so boring we'll want to eat poison."

"You may speak, Murderer, but I won't allow you to speak for the Tooth. Well, daughter?"

"Well . . . " Manon bit her lip but then shook her head. "No, I don't care. Send me home."

The goddess sat up, and I saw her brush imaginary dust off her crimson gown. "You're so willful! Delightfully strong. I can tell I'm going to be so proud of you."

I said, "Manon! You need to know two things. The goddess's daughters almost always die young, not yet twenty. Also, the goddess . . . oh, hell, I'm sick of this 'goddess' shit! Her name is Sakaj. In the last two hundred years, she's killed more people than all the other gods put together. So, don't deal if you want to live!"

"I thought you were training me to be a sorcerer. Were you lying to me? And where the heck are you?" Manon glanced around and then up.

Sakaj cut in. "Daughter, don't you want to know why I'm called She-Who-Must-Not-Be-Named?"

"Yes." Manon's voice started trembling again.

"When someone says my name, I must assume they want my attention. I am the Goddess of the Unknowable, and when you come to the attention of the Unknowable, inexplicable things happen." Sakaj held out her hands as if they were scales. "Perhaps everyone's arms and legs get turned backward. Maybe every woman in the city gets pregnant, but instead of a child, she conceives a hyena pup that chews its way out of her."

Manon didn't say anything.

"You may say my name, but if you say it to anyone else, kill them at once, lest they say it and summon me. Unless you want me to visit, that is. I have two squares of power available. What will you offer me in trade?"

Manon shouted, "Nothing! I don't even know how to do magic!"

"That's the lovely part, my darling. You already know everything you need."

"That's ridiculous!" I had rarely heard more atrocious nonsense dribble out of a god's mouth. "She can't even keep from getting hit in the face with a boot."

Sakaj twirled one finger, spinning Manon around to face her. "Just focus on something unknowable, Tooth, like how many numbers there are between zero and one, or what a cat thinks when it hears poetry. Then focus on what you want to accomplish. Don't worry about your little hands—they'll do their part even while they shake. In fact, your infirmity is an advantage. Who knows why? It's unknowable."

"Manon, this isn't right." I stood close beside her for no reason, since neither of us could touch the other.

"Not right . . . but does it make sense?" Manon stared straight at me, pleading. It had to have been by chance.

"Yes, it makes sense, but it's not good."

Manon yelled at me. "My hands make me stronger now, not a freak. Why isn't that good?"

There wasn't an honest answer to that question that an emotional twelve-year-old would listen to. "Just tell her again that you won't trade, and demand to leave. Don't lock yourself into something today. If you change your mind tomorrow, you haven't lost anything."

"Well, that's not true at all." Sakaj shook her head. "Recall how thirsty you are."

All the agony of thirst knifed me in the mouth and throat and gut. Sakaj was pulling an artful trick, since we had no bodies. I glared over at the marble step she stood on.

Sakaj put her hand to her lips. "In another day or two, thirst will kill everyone in your toy boat, unless you get water. I happen to know that the wind will die away tonight. Your boat will drift in the calm for days. Your desiccated bodies will reach shore some time before winter."

The thirst evaporated.

I turned away from the her and laughed. "Pardon me, Mighty Sakaj, but becalmed? That's pretty goat-grunting unlikely this time of year."

"So many forces and accidents affect the weather. Who knows why a wind dies off, even when it shouldn't?" Sakaj shrugged. "It's unknowable. With two squares of power, though, a sorcerer could save you all."

"You'll kill us unless I trade? That's not fair!" Manon just about whined it.

Sakaj smiled with one corner of her mouth. "I am a god. What do I care for fair?"

After a long pause, Manon said, "I don't know how to do this. I don't know what to offer."

"Don't offer anything!" I shouted. "Sakaj, trade with me for the squares. I'm willing." I gazed back at her, telling myself I didn't give a crap at all about her beauty.

Sakaj grinned up at the ceiling of the pavilion. "Harik would be incensed, so it is tempting. But no. Tooth, I'm happy to make an offer, in the spirit of vigorous negotiations. In exchange for two squares, flying insects will be drawn to you. They won't hurt you, or even touch you, but they will love you oh-so much."

"For how long?" I asked.

"Only until she dies."

I threw my free hand up. "That's a terrible offer!" I had to either turn my gaze away from Sakaj or be bludgeoned by her beauty until

I became stupider than a potato. I decided to stare in some other direction. But I was a sorcerer, and I couldn't let a god make me quiver and drool just by sitting where I could see her.

Manon bit her lip. "I won't say yes, but I don't know what to offer instead."

I shouted at her, "Don't offer anything! Let's just leave!"

"I don't want to die of thirst!" Manon shouted back at me.

I wished we had bodies so I could hug her, or strangle her. "Manon, she may be lying. Even if the wind does die tonight, we'll come up with something less disastrous than this. Hell, if we don't think of anything else, you can come right back here and deal tomorrow."

Sakaj said, "Oh, no, I don't recommend waiting, Tooth, not at all. I might feel differently about this tomorrow. There may be no deal to be had. We can't know."

Manon paused again. "Not bugs, but I offer puppies. Puppies will follow me, and only two at a time. And only for a month."

Sakaj stood and stepped down to the lower row of benches. "You're young, so I'll excuse the bald insult in that offer. How about this? Stray dogs, mature ones, will follow you, no more than ten at a time, for a year. You must provide for all their needs."

Manon scratched her head. "That's not too bad."

"Manon, please don't agree. I'll buy you three fat puppies if you don't agree." If she could have seen me, I would have gotten on my knees.

"Don't worry, Bib, I'm not going to take it. Instead, I offer . . . up to five stray dogs, for three months, and I take care of them."

"You'll provide for all their needs?" Sakaj cocked her head and smiled.

"I will."

I wanted to make everything stop, but it was too late.

"Done!" Sakaj clapped her hands. "The power will be waiting when you return. Use it however you wish. We're going to have such a ridiculous amount of fun, Tooth." Sakaj grinned at me. I sneered back, holding steady. "Murderer, that puffed-up fellow in your silly boat offered you a book. You should take it."

I glanced out at the dimming meadows of the Gods' Realm. "Why? I'd rather scratch an adder's belly than take your advice."

"I won't insult you by saying it's in your best interest. Let's just say that now it will annoy Harik ever so much. I know you enjoy annoying him almost as much as I do."

I forced myself to gaze into Sakaj's eyes. I had done lots of things harder than that, I told myself. "I won't guarantee anything. I may just fling it into the sea."

Sakaj laughed and then tossed me back into my body. It was gentle compared to Harik's brutal dismissals, but it still shook my eyeballs.

Back in the boat, I leaned toward Manon and whispered, "You're a sorcerer for certain now."

She smiled at me with cracked, bleeding lips.

I gripped her shoulder. "Being a sorcerer means that anything you love, or anybody you love, might be destroyed at any moment."

"Well . . . that's true of everybody, isn't it?"

I pulled her a little closer. "Yes, but it's likely you'll be the one who destroys them."

She squinted up at me.

"And if you're lucky, you'll care." I let Manon go.

Manon stared at me with terrified eyes for a few seconds. Then she shook her head. "Bib, you're too worried about my deal. I love dogs, and it's only three months. I can live with it just fine."

"Darling, those are almost the exact words said by every sorcerer who later wished he was dead."

NINE

The sweetest, most tenderhearted person I ever knew was a sorcerer. We sorcerers tended to be fractious, so she was remarkable. She cried every time she held a baby. I never saw her say no when somebody asked for money. She was a Daughter of Sakaj, one of the few who lived long enough to see a wrinkle on her face when she looked in a mirror.

Ten years as a sorcerer changed her. She would watch a boatload of orphans sinking and not stand up from her lunch. If they hadn't drowned by the time she was done, she'd probably go fish them out. If they were dead, well, they should have fixed their boat. She was a hard woman.

The practice of sorcery reshapes the sorcerer, and it rarely creates something better. Some sorcerers whine about that. Others accept it as the price paid for burning things up by pointing at them, or sewing trousers that let them jump up onto roofs. I don't subscribe to that shit. Sorcery may reshape the sorcerer, just like living reshapes everybody. Sorcery just does it a hundred times faster. I'm not whining about it. Nobody ever tied my hands to strings and forced me to do magic.

Ella grimaced as she watched Manon save our lives. Cael

grinned as if the girl were making candy. Ona kept a solemn face, almost serene. I don't know how I looked. Ella did squeeze my hand pretty hard and kiss my shoulder. We had a rusty bucket for bailing, so Cael held it over the side and scrubbed it before he filled it with seawater. Manon touched the water with her trembling hand, and it became pure. We drank, and I was grateful despite Manon's sorcery woes.

"Fill it again." Manon handed the bucket to Cael.

I put my hand on the bucket. "Wait. We're not in danger of dying now."

"I'm still thirsty."

"Don't ever use magic unless you have no other choice. You gave a lot up for this power. Preserve it."

"I don't think I gave up all that much," she sniffed. "Why exactly do you say it was a lot?"

"I don't know exactly, but you'll find out." I hadn't taught Manon an important thing about the Father of the Gods and his twelve children. Power made them gods, but guile made them dangerous. Normally, she wouldn't have needed that lesson for another three years.

"Anyway, I'm hungry."

"Wait, we don't need food yet!"

I was too late. Manon held out her hands over the water. A few seconds later, a herring jumped into the boat, then two more, and then another one.

"We'll have to eat them raw. I hope you're not picky." Manon grabbed a flopping herring with both hands.

Three more herring sailed in altogether, and then eight in a row. Manon held her hands over the sea again. Three more herring joined us, and then the invasion stopped.

"Now we have plenty." She smirked at me. "You knew I could stop it, right? You didn't think they were going to keep jumping in until the boat was full, and I'd cry and ask for help, did you? I'm not just some little girl now."

"No, you're a sorcerer now." I reached out, and she handed me the fish. "What did I say about what it means to be a sorcerer?"

Manon got quiet and turned her face toward the horizon.

Cael leaned closer. "I'd like to know what you said, Bib. I've never traveled with sorcerers before."

I waved my hand toward him like he was a gnat. "Hush! Go tell a story some place. I think the mast wants to hear about the Battle of Crab Falls. Again."

Manon turned back and blinked at me. "Everything I love. Everybody."

"That's right."

The girl's whole body settled, like every muscle gave up at once. She scooted over, leaned against my shoulder, and started crying. "I'm sorry I'm so stupid. And I don't want to cry, but I can't stop."

"Go on and cry. When I was learning sorcery, I cried just about every day. At least I did when I was your age."

The wind kept right on blowing all night and through the next afternoon, when Cael sighted the mainland. I suppose Sakaj had only been threatening when she said the wind would go calm, or maybe she'd been lying about everything. I still didn't believe that we would have died if Manon hadn't made that bargain.

The little boat had served us a good sight better than I had expected, so it seemed ungrateful to abandon her on the beach. We picked a direction and marched north like the damned ingrates we were. When we set out across the sea, I had plotted a course for Parhold, the closest mainland port, and Parhold was nowhere in view. But without instruments and maps, any dry land satisfied me. We walked into a fishing village before sunset. They took us in as if we were their cousins who had been lost at sea for a year.

At dinner, I sat with Gatt, the master fisherman. I had steered our boat, so he treated me like somebody of equal status. He was vigorous and gray-haired, with magnificent teeth, and he explained that we were in the Kingdom of Arrick. Parhold was just ten miles north, and he hated those sons of bitches worse than salt under the eyelids. The city had suffered some sort of big-city calamity, but that didn't excuse them from sending a troop of thugs to steal every fish Gatt caught for a week. We drank to Parhold's destruction and woe five times.

The next morning, we found out that no, Gatt wouldn't accept payment from guests, and no, they didn't have horses to sell, never mind saddles. They did expect us to accept fish cakes, bread, and fruit, although I could see they were going hungry. We picked out the smallest cakes, buns, and berries we could find, and we marched on north.

I reached for Ella's hand while we walked. "Ella, when we get to the city, I'm not sure I want to go home right away."

She paused. "What destination would you prefer? And why? If you will stoop to sharing that knowledge."

"I don't know where yet. As for why, I bet those fire-setting maniacs in Garhool will be chasing me. If they catch me, they might kill you, or Manon. I should lead them off some place isolated and kill the shit out of them one or two at a time. And Manon can't be my student anymore."

"What? How in any sane world is that possible? She's a child!" Ella let go of me so she could use her hands to exclaim over how crazy that was.

"You're not wrong, but she's a sorcerer now. She has her own destiny. I'll give her all the help she wants, but I can't tell her what to do."

"You could never tell her what to do before, so nothing has changed," Ella said sarcastically.

I laughed a little. "I should take her to a temple. They can protect her, and she can learn whatever she wants."

Ella grunted, an unusual comment for her. "So, I should go home. Will you come back? Do you want to be free of me?"

"No!" A few steps later, I said, "Do you?"

"No." She sighed. "We don't have to make these decisions on the beach with sand in our boots."

Both of us had said no, but somehow I felt like it was over.

Before noon, we saw Parhold, a smudge in the distance. As we walked, the smudge swelled into a distant city beside the water, a city that threw off a mass of black smoke that rose and blew away inland.

I shaded my eyes toward the place. "I'm not sure I want to go in there."

"Bib, we need horses. Fast, hardy horses," Cael said. "We won't find any like that at some farmstead, pulling a plow."

Ella pointed at the smoke over the city. "Cael, cease your horse discussion for a moment and pay attention. Did you take ship to Ir from this city? Was it in this state then?"

"Almost this bad. Fires were starting for what seemed like no cause. Buildings enveloped in flames, gone within a minute. I saw wood burned to ash, stone crumbled, and iron twisted up. People were fleeing the city like antelope. I had to pay a man for his place on the ship to Ir. Well, I put the coins in his purse and tossed him back onto the dock. I wish we had time to stay and help them."

"How would you help them?" Manon asked.

Cael grinned. "Someone is causing all this. I'd find them and kill them."

"That simple?" Ella put a hand on her hip, the one with the sword on it.

"No, not at all. Finding your enemy is arduous, of course, and can involve a lot of peril. But killing a person is not simple. It's a shocking act. I've done it much too often."

That was the closest I ever came to liking the smug son of a bitch. I covered that up by saying, "Cael, I'd like to browse through that little book of yours. Maybe it contains some hoary sayings that only a sorcerer would understand."

"Wonderful! I'll give it to you when we reach Bellmeet."

"I want it now."

Cael laughed. "I'm not naïve. I understand that you'll sneak away at the earliest chance, leaving me to go home in disgrace. Your promise isn't worth the food between your teeth."

I waved at him with the back of my hand. "Then keep the damn book."

Cael frowned. "Damn it. Since you won't come along like you promised, and you won't come for the book, I'm forced to be persuasive."

I laughed at him.

"Her Majesty was unambiguous about how I should persuade you, if it came to that. You know her quite well, I understand." He glanced at Ella. "I'd prefer not to discuss details. Just accept that any persuasion she thought up will overcome your objections."

We had been walking during this discussion. Now I stopped. "You'd better give me details."

Cael's shoulders slumped. "Come to Bellmeet, or I will kill everyone close to you. Ella and Manon, of course. I should also include the King of Glass and possibly a sorcerer named Desh."

"You sack-dragging weasel!" I stepped between him and Ella.

"And since Ona is standing here, her too."

Ona snorted. "You may try, my boy, and you may even succeed, but you'll wish you hadn't."

Cael didn't even glance at her. "Bib, you know that you can't prevent me from doing this."

Manon jumped in front of me. "You can't kill me. I'm a sorcerer."

I took the girl's arm and guided her back behind me. "Manon, I've known hundreds of sorcerers. They're all dead now except a handful. Hell, they may all be dead now except you and me. Keep that in mind before you start beating your chest and throwing shit around. Cael, would you really kill Ella? And kill Manon, who slept against you like you were her pillow?"

Cael shook his head. "Let's not find out."

"All right, you have me whipped. I'll go." That was a lie, of course. I sure as hell was not going with him now, not after he'd threatened us. I didn't think I could kill him while he slept; he was nearly as alert sleeping as he was awake. I'd think of something.

"Bib, you are awfully entertaining." Cael said the words, but he wasn't smiling. "Like I said, I value your promise as much as I value night soil." He nodded at Ella. "Miss, I want your promise, not his. Promise that you'll bring him to Bellmeet."

"No." Ella stepped up beside me. "And please choke yourself on an undercooked pig shank."

Cael waved his hand around at the ocean and the hills, and then he did smile. "Jumping in front of each other and behind each other like that . . . it looks as if you're dancing on the village green. Ella, please bring him as far as the Temple on Barrelshins. Then we'll reassess things. In exchange, I'll let everyone live until then. But he can't have the book."

I knew Cael didn't really care whether I had the book. I had already turned it down once, and he'd acted as if I handed him back a rotten apple. If Cael got me to the temple, that was pretty far down the road to Bellmeet, and then he could still threaten to murder Ella and Manon. He'd have given up nothing.

Cael thought he had a good deal.

I turned to Ella. "My dear, may I bargain on your behalf?"

She almost smiled but twisted it into a grimace for Cael's benefit. "If you wish. You will harangue me for a month if I say no."

I directed my attention to Cael. "I'd like to clarify the terms here. You're offering *not* to kill these ladies for now, if I go with you to the temple."

"Correct."

I nodded. "All right, I propose that you also buy us all horses and tack in Parhold."

"No. I know that you have your own gold."

I stepped back and pointed at Cael. "Now, you yourself said we have to be well-mounted, and you're the one who wants to go riding off down the road, so you are the one with the interest in fine horses, not us. You also have to promise, right now, that you will never, ever kill anybody I like."

Cael snorted. "That's—"

"I'm not finished." I started ticking items off on my fingers. "You have to tell me every damn thing you know about why Mina wants you to bring me to Bellmeet."

Cael crossed his arms.

"Also, you'll buy Manon an appropriate weapon and start teaching her how to use it."

"Well, I'd be a fool to do that, wouldn't I? If I have to kill her later—"

I held up the second finger on my right hand. "You're going to promise not to kill her, remember? Keep up! In exchange for these few extremely reasonable conditions, Ella promises that when we get to Parhold, I will honestly consider going as far as the temple with you."

Cael stared at me like I was a bad boy he was calling in from playing. "You're acting like a child. It's embarrassing. You have to come to the temple, and that's final."

I shook my head hard. "No, sir, no, but I do offer to be immensely generous and buy our horses."

"Stop it! I can afford horses."

I shrugged. "Fine, you buy the horses."

Cael put his hand on his sword. "I will kill these women right now if you keep up this foolishness!"

I pointed at Manon. "Are you saying that you would kill this child when instead you could teach her a few blocks and cuts? Are you a monster?"

"You are coming to the temple!" Cael's normally white face had gone pink.

I held out my hands in a reasonable way. "First, I have to know what Mina wants with me."

Cael clenched his teeth for two seconds before he answered. "I can't tell you that. She didn't give me leave to share it."

I stared at the sky for five seconds. "All right, I will concede on Mina's plans, if you'll promise to teach Manon to fight and not kill anybody I like."

Cael went red in the face in an instant. "You cannot avoid the fact that you must go to the temple!"

If Cael had a stroke, he would save me the bother of murdering him. "You bastard! Fine, I'm tired of quibbling with you about the temple. I'll go to the temple, and I'll forget about Mina's plans. And you don't have to train Manon. For all of that, you just have to promise not to ever kill Ella and Manon. Kill Ona if you want, I don't care." I glanced at the nun.

"Do you think that shocks me or something?" Ona shooed me with her good hand. "Just keep arguing."

I nodded at Cael. "And of course, we already established that you're buying the horses. Also, be honest, you don't really want the book, do you? Mina instructed you to give it to me, not bribe me with it, right? Do you want to disobey her?"

Cael paused, and his face faded back to pink. "And Ella promises to bring you to the temple?" He raised his eyebrows at her.

"Yes, I promise," Ella said.

Cael nodded.

"That's the bargain then." I held out my hand, and he fished the book out of a fat green pouch. The volume felt a little heavier than I expected, and a little cooler too. "I cannot goddamn believe that I gave away almost everything to you, Cael. I hate you." I spun and stomped toward Parhold, ignoring everybody else.

Behind me, Cael said in a confused voice, "I don't understand how that happened."

I glanced back and saw Ella pat him on the shoulder. "It happened because you didn't really want to kill us. And because Bib has been bargaining with gods for most of his life."

An hour later, still a mile from the city proper, we walked up to a chunky wooden outpost squatting beside the road. Four tall, dark-skinned soldiers stood wearing black armor, and carrying long pole-axes. They protected each side of the outpost as if the dirt itself might try to kill them. I waved at the closest one, a thin fellow with serious eyes.

Before the soldier could speak, I smiled and called out, "We want to provision ourselves, buy some horses, and be on our way, before sunset if possible. We don't have any business here besides that."

The man walked a few steps closer, and I realized that his skin was dark and his armor black only because soot lay thick on them. "Who are you?"

"Abandoned travelers, minding our own business and bringing gold to spend." I insinuated a bow.

Another soldier walked toward us from around the corner of the outpost. He pointed his spear at me. "What are your names? Don't try to be humorous. We're lacking patience with that shit."

"Bib, Ella, Manon, Ona, and Cael." I pointed as I named.

"Bib!" a man shouted from around the building. He trotted into view, a solid, graying fellow with big hands and one eye. He didn't resemble anyone I'd ever known. Maybe I had killed a friend of his. That seemed unlikely, since he was laughing as he ran up to me.

"Bib!"

I remember in harsh detail the faces of the people I've killed, all of them. I regret that I do not remember the faces of my companions nearly so well. In fact, I am piss-poor at it. As a result, I walk around vaguely discomforted by the idea that I might meet an old ally and not remember him. Most of my old allies are dead, many of them falling in fights I walked away from, but still, this is a failing that tweaks my pride, Therefore, in these situations I generally go along with things and hope that some detail arises to jog a recollection. I smiled. "Hello! Good to see you again!"

"Except for getting old, you look the same!"

"Hope you've been well." I wondered if he was going to try to hug me.

"Well enough, except for the eye and all those years in prison." He turned to his friends. "This is Bib!"

"Are you sure, Dorf?" asked a muscled, beast of a man with a baby face.

"I told you he'd come." He grabbed my shoulders and shook them. "He's come to save us."

TEN

I have always been a bad follower. I hate taking orders, and I hate the people who give them. To be fair, I'm also a bad leader. I suspect that everybody I've ever worked with would have chased me off into the woods, except that I was slaughtering their enemies like they were mice in a milk pail, and I was mending all their wounds.

When Dorf insisted that I meet Lord Bremmel, I did not feel optimistic. Parhold was about to stop being a city and start being a wilderness of ash and charred buildings. Dorf thought I was there to help, so this Lord Bremmel would probably ask for help too. When I was younger, I sometimes agreed to help people in crises as horrible as this one. I discovered that their idea of help was to reject all my suggestions, resent me for acting superior, put me in the most dangerous spot in the battle, and blame me for everything that went wrong, even if we won. By the time I was thirty, I had done that enough times to last me until death.

As we entered Parhold, Dorf reminisced in detail about our youthful adventures, the ones I couldn't remember, likely because they didn't mean a damn thing to me. I nodded and grunted whenever he paused. He babbled on, smiling over his shoulder at me.

Not far into the city, Dorf finished a recollection with, "Of course, Hal told me to protect your back, and Sammial did too."

Memory hit me like a mallet. "Your brothers died that day. You did too, almost."

"They were proud to die, and I'd have been too! Killing all those nasty, ass-gargling bastards, and running off the rest. You saved our city and you saved us. We helped some."

I remembered bits of those events. Somebody needed to be killed for doing something awful to some of the people. The place was sunny. I hadn't cared much about the people or the place. Some fancy rich man had hired me to steal an iron box out of the treasury. I hadn't cared about that, either. I'd cared about killing people. The rich man got his box, the city got set free, and Dorf lost his brothers, who I now remembered as both being cheery fellows. I got to enjoy murdering some men and later feeling weary and morose about having killed them.

I nodded at Dorf and grunted.

Walking through Parhold, I guessed that every fourth building had been obliterated. Soot caked every surface. Every surviving resident must have been outdoors, walking some place, tending a task, or staring at nothing. I didn't blame them for not wanting to loiter inside a structure that might conflagrate without warning.

"That was the trading house. Met my wife there, poor Anna." Dorf pointed at a mighty ash pile as we skirted it.

Manon paused and picked up something. "I found a belt buckle!"

"Place it back, sweetheart," Ella said over her shoulder.

"Why? I've never had a metal belt buckle. It doesn't belong to anybody!"

"That's right," I said. "That fellow you're standing on doesn't need it anymore, since ash piles can't wear belts."

Manon stared down at the ashes piled nearly to the tops of her shoes, and she dropped the buckle. We trudged on behind Dorf. Maybe nobody else felt weary, but I was knackered. I really had spent too much time sitting under that tree, drinking. I glanced over my shoulder and saw Manon scurry back, pick up that buckle, and tuck it into her ratty cloth pouch.

Ona saw the girl too, caught my eye, and shook her head.

Dorf led us up the back stairs of a tavern, which surprised me. I had already decided to march into this Lord Bremmel's house, take charge like the top bull, and give myself an important assignment. While on that assignment, I would inexplicably disappear, along with my friends, some horses, and everything necessary for a journey.

One lamp dangling from the center beam lit the room above the tavern. The smells of dust and oil smoke hung above cabinets, a table, and other items necessary for running a business. I ignored everything except the flabby old gentleman sleeping on an expensive-looking couch, a pair of shoes under his head for a pillow.

Dorf leaned over the man and patted his shoulder. "My Lord. I've brought you some people."

The man shook his head and groaned as he pulled himself up using the back of the couch. "Thank you, son." He rubbed his eyes. "I'll tend to them. You go guard something important."

Dorf nodded and almost tiptoed back outside.

Cael gave the old fellow a little bow. "My Lord, I don't mean any disrespect, but I'm a little surprised to find the ruler of Parhold headquartered over a bar."

Bremmel waved his hand at random spots around the room. "Sit. Sit, sit, sit, sit. Chairs everywhere." He leaned back on the couch and peered at us. "Now, who am I entertaining? I'm sorry, my house servants are all run away or dead, so would you please serve us, young lady?" He nodded at Manon. "Beer in the corner."

While Manon fetched beer out of a cask and spilled a fair amount, I introduced us. "I see that you have grave and awful problems, my Lord. I have solved a problem or two."

"Hm." He shook his head at Cael instead of me. "I shouldn't say that I rule the city. Proper master is Lord Willit, but he hanged himself. Penn, his son, went mad and won't leave his chambers. Have to slice bread and slide it under the door. Captain of the Guard ran off with

Willit's wife. The lieutenants point at each other all day and wait around for orders. To be fully honest with you, two weeks ago, I owned the brewery, which has been burnt down, may Lutigan shit on the ashes. Now I'm the only one around who will tell somebody to jump if his penis is on fire, so . . ." He shrugged. "The penis part was figurative."

I stood up. I wanted to look as impressive as possible when I sold him on our irresistible power to solve problems.

Ella stood and stepped between the old man and me. "I will help you."

"Will you? Nice of you, but what about the problem-solver there?" Bremmel waggled his mug toward me, slopping a little.

"He is an extraordinary killer. If your problem must be solved by killing people, no one will serve you better."

I sat back down. Whatever Ella's scheme was, I wasn't quite sharp enough to follow it yet.

Ella went on. "If you require a more nuanced solution, perhaps one that does not leave everyone dead, let me help you."

Bremmel sat up. "What's your name?"

"Ella Fourstairs."

Lord Bremmel raised his eyebrows. "Empire?"

She nodded.

"Well . . . some people might live . . ." Bremmel said it as if he hadn't considered it before. "Well then. But you don't really know the problem yet, do you?"

Ella leaned forward. "It's a sorcerer."

"Krak damn my in-laws, at least you know that. At first, nearly everyone said it was demon possession, except for the ones who said it was a dragon. My wife insisted it was a volcano." Bremmel dropped his head and sobbed twice, rubbed his eyes, and then grimaced at Ella. "Seems the priest has been a damned sorcerer all along. I've known him twenty-three years, but I didn't know that. Just went mad, I suppose, started burning down everything." Bremmel stared at the rug and acted like he didn't have anything else to say.

"I will help you." Ella stood. "We will."

Ella was mystifying the hell out of me, but I nodded. Manon smiled. Cael stood up, frowning.

Ella glared at Cael and pointed at me. "Do you wish him to arrive at the temple? Yes? Then sit down and nod."

Cael sat, and he nodded.

Bremmel drained his mug and almost smiled. "Good. Fine. Some other folk have offered to help. They did it to pay off debts, really, but they don't know what to do. I certainly don't know what to do." He stood and gripped Ella's arm. "You know what to do, don't you?"

"I know precisely." She patted his hand. "I shall deal with things, and you'll be able to rest. People will write songs about our victory. Did you say someone has offered to assist you? I should like to meet them."

As we followed Bremmel downstairs to the street, I whispered to Ella, "You're too subtle for me. What are you planning?"

"I plan to save them," she said coldly.

"That's foolishness. We don't know anything about this sorcerer or the city or anything around here."

Ella hissed, "I know they asked the intrepid Bib for help, and you plan to cheat them."

We detoured around three barrels of water standing at the corner.

"I feel for their plight, but I have other problems," I said.

"Their plight? Did their plight simply appear, like a mushroom? You had nothing to do with their plight. Dorf is a fool to idolize you."

Ella and I had dropped back and were trailing everybody down the street, hissing at each other as we walked. I spotted a big white dog following Manon, bumping its head against her leg as they walked.

I whispered, "Why are you so mad at me? I didn't try to hurt these people. I do intend a little deception, just to ease our way along."

"No, you didn't try to hurt them. You have busied yourself bringing back the gods, correct? Who create sorcery, which does this!" She stabbed a finger toward a gutted building. "You didn't try. You just did it. The way you do everything else."

"I don't understand any little bit of what you're saying!" As soon as I said that, I understood what she was saying. I had opened the way, which was killing these people, and now I was behaving like a selfish bastard with no pity. When I was a younger man, I probably would have been more sympathetic. If I concentrated, maybe I could remember how that worked.

Ella ignored me now as we walked, and I didn't try to draw her attention. I didn't know what to say if she started chastising me again. Within a minute, Bremmel led us into a stable yard.

Cael pointed at the stable. "Our sorcerer must like horses, since he hasn't burned that down."

"He probably likes kittens and cream too. To hell with him." I spit on the street. Ella glanced but didn't say anything.

Somebody had set up a wooden table, and three people stood up from it as we walked into the yard. A short Hill Man with sparse, white hair hung back. A dark brown fellow the size of a half-grown bear walked toward us with his hands open. A copper-haired young woman of Ir grinned at us, brushing off her tough traveling clothes that were suitable for fighting and raising hell.

I examined the Hill Man first, since every Hill Man I had ever met tried to kill me. Some had just about succeeded. He nodded at us but didn't say anything.

The big, black-skinned man said, "He won't introduce himself until you introduce yourself first. It would be rude, for he is a Hill Person and therefore superior to all other human beings." The man gave a tiny shrug and smiled where the Hill Man couldn't see. "I'm Bratt, Second of Jatter. We need allies."

The young woman stood back and examined us for a few seconds. Then she smiled. "Be nice to the old Hill Man. He's a strange one, but considerate. I just met him, and he gave me this knife. See?" She held up a curved knife of remarkable quality and design. "My name's Whit. Hurry up and tell us who you are. I want to drink with you before you're all killed."

We introduced ourselves, and the Hill Man, who was only a foot taller than Manon, nodded up at us. "I am Larripet. You have very nice manners. It shames me that I do not have gifts for you, but I will find gifts if any of us lives. I do not think we will."

Bratt smiled. "Larripet is always wise, but on occasion, he's not entirely right."

I said, "I've met one of your people, Bratt, from the farthest east. Your ass must be worn out if you rode all those months to get here."

He nodded. "My ass will still smell like saddle leather when I'm dead."

Whit stepped in front of Bratt and smiled at me. She was a Far Islander with brown eyes. They were Ir's most argumentative and aggravating people. She examined me in a way that made me glance to see whether Ella was watching. "The gods must love me after all if they sent me someone from home. I thought I'd have to die with a bunch of droopy foreigners. How'd you lose that hand, anyway? Good story? Dirty, I hope."

I shook my head. "I don't count a story dirty unless a husband gets killed, or maybe we all get imprisoned for unnatural behavior."

Whit unleashed a brilliant smile, walked right up, embraced me, and kissed me on the cheek. "Brother!"

I glanced around. Bratt was grinning at me like a nasty-minded teenage boy. He and Larripet then turned away and started whispering to each other. Cael grinned, and Manon ignored us while she threw a stick for her dog. Ella and Bremmel were nodding at two ragged men who had shown up so stealthily they could have killed half of us before we jumped.

Bratt murmured to me, "Bib, I don't believe she thinks of you as her brother. Not at all."

Whit took two steps toward Bratt. "She is standing right here, you oaf, and she can goddamned think of him however the greasy hell she wants!"

Bratt stood straight and gave Whit a slow, precise bow. "I had no thought of offending you, Whit. I apologize."

Whit said, "Huh," and turned back toward me.

Ella brought over Bremmel and the two men, who dressed and smelled like beggars. "These are our scouts, Yalley and Bits."

Yalley was a young, skinny man with a withered arm and a forest of curly brown hair. "Nothing's been happening at all down there. At the temple, I mean." He nodded at us newcomers.

Bits, a tubby, stooped old man wheezed, "Not a god-grunting thing."

"Haven't seen the sorcerer since yesterday and nothing hasn't burned up, either, thank Krak," Yalley said.

"Hope the pissant's dead." Bits spat on the dirt.

"Excellent." Ella smiled at them and pointed up the road. "Go back and keep watch. We have preparations to make."

"We can help," Bits bellowed. "We're not stupid. We're brave."

Yalley grinned. "Bits, hush! He's sorry—"

"Bite my asshole!" Bits punched Yalley on the shoulder. It sounded like hitting a ham with a mallet. Yalley staggered but didn't say anything.

Bremmel raised his hands. "Gentlemen! You have helped and been brave. Without your scouting, we wouldn't be able to fight. So, please, scout for us now."

They nodded. One of them spouted a thunderous fart, probably Bits, and they disappeared down a side street toward the harbor.

Ona, who had been standing all the way out in the street, cleared her throat. "Bib, stay out of this mess. We need you for more important things than saving this one city."

Cael said, "I agree. I pity Bremmel and his people, but what if you die here?"

"Then it'll be a sad day for you, son." I turned my back on him. "Everybody will probably bring you beer and pies to make you feel better."

Ona raised her voice, which was already the loudest voice on the street. "This isn't some joke. People in a dozen kingdoms are dying."

"I'm not joking. Everybody likes pie."

Ella stared at me with no expression. "Bib needn't stay if he doesn't wish to fight alongside us."

"Oh, I'm staying. I haven't fought a Burner in ten, maybe twelve years. This may be my final opportunity."

Ona brayed louder than a mean mule. "You stupid shit! Well, I'll tell you this. You'll have to keep your own ass intact, and you'll answer to the gods right sharp if you throw your life away like it was an old turd! I'll be praying for you, though."

"Good." Ella shooed the woman like she was a hen. "Then I needn't worry about you. You can wait with the children and grand-fathers."

Ona smiled, nodded, and walked away with no sign she felt shame at being thought a coward.

I suspected that Ella's preparations might lack some nuances. She could plan and fight like a maniac, but she had known only three sorcerers, and none of them were Burners. She couldn't understand the mundane preparations a person has to make before fighting one, or the emotional preparations, either. Above all, she didn't understand that we were almost certain to die to the last man, if the damage to the city was a sign of what we were facing.

I had arrangements of my own to make. I lifted myself to bargain with the gods, calling for Harik as I went. I sure as hell wasn't going to fight a Burner without magic of my own.

"Hail, Mighty Harik. Everybody here is singing songs about your flagging manhood—"

Harik interrupted me. "Will you kill the girl?"

"No, but I'll—"

Harik flung me back into my body so hard I stumbled.

Whit put a hand on my shoulder to steady me. "Tripping over not a damn thing, are you? Let me see that." She knelt and felt my ankle for a sprain that she damn well knew wasn't there. She jerked her head toward Ella. "The mainlander? Really? Why? She doesn't seem to like you very much. Well, that's too bad."

She didn't sound like she thought it was bad at all. She was going to be surprised. We were going to fight a Burner and do it without magic. Everything that was about to happen would be bad.

ELEVEN

My sorcerous powers are the most boring in existence. I possess the mystical power to make living beings and natural phenomena do things that they would normally do. Oh, there are bits that can be exciting. But when I almost killed myself with lightning, I realized that the exciting stuff could be fatally exciting. Once I accepted that, I couldn't think of anything more mundane than my powers.

When I found out I was just a miserable Caller, I moped for a year. I didn't care that I could make slow things happen in a hurry. My teachers might make me clear away rain showers all afternoon, or fatten up sheep overnight, and I'd daydream about leaving sorcery behind for the excitement of being a fisherman like my father. My Breaker friends were learning to simply make things *not* exist, and the Benders were reshaping anything they could see. I even envied the Binders for creating enchanted socks and magical spoons.

I never once wanted to be a Burner, though. They could spark fires hot enough to burn nearly anything, which sounds dramatic, but in fact it was a bit limiting. They couldn't even put fires out. It was either, "Burn, you son of a bitch!" or, "I'll be in the pub," with nothing in between.

But when it came to fighting, Burners were the most dangerous sorcerers of the lot. Well, maybe the daughters of Sakaj possessed a more terrifying range of powers, but Sakaj drove most of them insane pretty young.

I didn't bring Manon with us to fight the Burner. I never considered it, and nobody else brought it up. I told her to stay with Bremmel, and I told him to go hide some place before the fight. If we lived, we'd come tell him about it. If we never came, he should pack up and bugger off with Manon to some other town.

Ella finally conceded that I should share my sorcerous expertise, but I should damn well understand that once the attack began, she would be in charge. Those of us who intended to destroy the Burner then engaged in preparations. Half an hour later, we were still struggling with the first preparation.

I raised my voice at the others. "Yes, once again I'll say it, naked. Not a stitch. Bare as a baby pig. Everything you've got should be hanging out."

Dorf and two other soldiers had shown up for the fun of assaulting the mad sorcerer. The idea of fighting unclothed horrified them, and they had been arguing with me about it. Bratt seemed shy about it too. Ella and Cael just nodded, ready to get on with things. The first time I mentioned it, Larripet and Whit started taking off their clothes right away, until I told them we wouldn't be attacking until nightfall.

"I don't understand why we can't at least wear our small-clothes." Flynn stood in front of the other soldiers, arms crossed and just about pouting. "Fighting with nothing on is unnatural."

I considered stabbing the man in the heart instead of explaining it all again. "A Burner can start a fire in anything that's not alive, but he can't start one in your flesh, or hair. He starts a fire in something else and lets that fire kill you. If you're wearing clothes, he can use them to start a fire all over your body."

Lord Bremmel coughed and then cleared his throat. "Men, you'll attack nude. That's final and an order."

At last, everyone agreed that we would go naked to kill the sorcerer.

"Good." I closed my eyes for a second. "Next . . . you can't carry any weapons made of wood or metal."

Nobody liked that idea, either, and I had to wait for a lot of shouting to simmer down. Pretty soon they saw the logic, though. If you were holding a sword, the sorcerer could use it to burn your hand right off.

"Then how do we kill him?" Ella asked.

"Are you sure you want to? You could capture him. Since sorcerers seem to be popping up all over the countryside, we might learn a lot by talking to one."

Everybody was sure they wanted to kill him.

"All right, the best way is to knock him down and use your knee or elbow to crush his throat. Or bash his head against the floor until he dies. Or, if you get the chance, you can stomp his hands until they're good and crushed—then he can't do magic. Or throw a sack over his head. Most sorcerers won't risk magic if they can't see. I've always thought that going so far as blinding one was excessive." I didn't mention chopping off their hands.

Everybody stared at me. At last, Bremmel pursed his lips. "Have you done these things, sir? Or are you just spouting?"

"I haven't done all of them." In fact, I hadn't done any of them. I had killed two Burners in my life, and I had whacked both of them with Caller magic, which hadn't turned out to be so useless as my boyhood self had thought. "You do have to worry about him setting the dirt on fire under you."

"Come on, dirt doesn't burn. Does it?" Dorf mouth hung partway open.

"Everything burns. You just have to get it hot enough. Setting fire to dirt is a lot harder than burning cloth or wood. Stone too. Since the temple itself is stone, it may protect us some."

Ella slapped me on the shoulder and then stepped in front of me. "Very well, thank you, Bib. We shall require a diversion. A force attacking from the front, while the true stroke arrives elsewhere. My Lord, you said there are two entrances?"

"Yes, one on the north side, one south. I have the key, but gods, maybe he's barricaded them. Who knows why he does things?"

Ella turned to me. "I will lead the diversion. Bib, you will go through the north door, surprise him, and kill him."

I had been hating the idea of this next part. "No."

Ella narrowed her eyes. "I know you to be the most unflinching killer here. You are ideal for this task."

I took a deep breath. "You're right, and you're a damn fine leader for seeing it, instead of insisting on smashing the villain's head yourself. I won't do it." I stopped myself from wincing when I said it.

She gaped at me like I'd punched her.

I held up both hands. "I'll handle the goddamned diversion, and you go kill him. You don't have to be a bloody-eyed murderer to sneak up and knock a man on the head."

"No! My plan stands." Ella sneered at me, which I found hurt quite a bit. "You may either perform the killing, or you may retire with the others. Or find a tavern in which to drink and tell nasty stories!"

"Don't be petty, Ella. You'll stay out of the diversion because, well, because I don't want you to get burned up and killed."

Ella opened her mouth and blinked at me.

"Besides, I'm used to fighting sorcerers. If he tries to kill me, I can ward him off with magic." That was the biggest lie I'd told her in weeks.

"What about us?" Flynn asked. "We're not used to fighting sorcerers!"

"He'll spend most of his time on me. Just run alongside me but keep some distance."

Ella scratched her forehead. "I suppose it makes sense."

"Don't expect me to start making sense all the time now." I smiled and patted her shoulder. "This is a special occasion, so let's say it's settled and take off our clothes."

Ella went ahead and declared it settled. She asked Cael to go with her, figuring he was the next most effective killer.

Cael said, "No."

"What?" Ella yelled. "You too?"

"Normally, I'd be honored to fight beside you. But just now I need to bring Bib to Bellmeet. Nothing else matters. Where he goes, I go. However . . ." He turned to me. "What about that little book you wanted so much, Bib? Shouldn't you at least flip through it for anything we could use to kill this sorcerer?"

I pulled the book from where I'd hidden it in my shirt and held it up. "Is that your opinion, son? Do you want to do some magic? Maybe turn my shoes into snakes or make that table float around? No? You ignorant son of a bitch! We don't want to rush through trying to figure out a possibly magical object."

Cael cocked his head.

"All right, I'll say it another way. A way that's understandable to men who solve every problem by cutting things in half. If you're going into battle in five minutes, do you throw your sword away and grab a weapon you've never used, like a club with a rabid badger tied to the end?"

Cael smiled with his thousand teeth and nodded. Yalley and Bits had appeared from somewhere, and they nodded along with him.

Just past sunset, we stood naked and empty-handed, pouring buckets of water over each other, a futile act if ever one existed. All of our gear, including the hook replacing my left hand, was piled on the table. Ella had invited Bratt and Larripet to come kill the sorcerer with her, and the three of them had disappeared into the darkened streets north of us. They would attack when they heard us raising hell, or possibly shrieking as we were killed.

Fire slammed into existence in the stable next to us, pounding like a titanic drum as it sucked the air. We were spared listening to horses scream, since they had already been taken away before the whole city collapsed. We did get to enjoy the wave of sparks and embers that blew onto us as the near wall began falling in.

"Spread out and keep up!" I shouted as I turned onto the wide street that ran down the middle of Parhold to the temple two blocks away. Half of the buildings on the left-hand side had already been destroyed. Not a building still stood on the right-hand side. I ran, and I heard the stable already caving in behind me. It had been a rickety structure to start with. "Shout so they can hear you!"

All of us started screaming and cursing so Ella would know we'd begun. Cael and Whit ran to the right of me. Dorf, Flynn, and another soldier whose name I hadn't learned ran on the left. I didn't quite sprint. There was a small chance we'd reach the temple, and we might need some of our wind.

We passed one building and then a burned-out lot. As we reached the next building, flames vomited out the open windows on the second floor. I could see fire through the gaps in its badly joined walls. I yelled louder and kept running.

Just after I ran past the front entrance, flames launched out the doorway to the middle of the street. A blazing speck dug into my shoulder, and I smelled pitch. Flynn had been lagging and was enveloped in an instant. I glanced back and stopped shouting, since I couldn't produce anything as loud as his wailing. Covered in fire, he ran away from the burning building, as if that might save him.

After Flynn was immolated, everybody except Cael and me sped up. Fire exploded from the top floor, hurling timbers all the way across the street. A huge, flaming beam smashed Whit, sort of like hitting a duckling with a hammer. I glanced at her and wished I hadn't.

At last, we passed the deadly two-story building and made it to the second block. The corner lot sat empty except for charred wreckage. "One more block!" I yelled, which was stupid since it didn't matter whether we ever reached the temple, as long as we distracted the sorcerer.

A small structure stood on the left, maybe a shop or a tavern, and nothing happened as we ran by it. The next building was sizable, maybe forty paces long and one story high. I heard crackling from that direction, and I saw a glow through the windows. It was the last building before the temple, so I ran faster.

Then I was lying on my side in the dirt, and I swear my chest, arm, neck, and face were being seared off. It wasn't the worst pain I had ever felt, but it hurt like hell. Then, for just a moment, the sick smell of my burning hair and flesh distressed me more than the actual burns.

I didn't comprehend that anything was piled on top of me until Cael started throwing off blazing slats of wood. "Are you alive?" he shouted.

"I'll live to see you in the ground."

He snorted and grinned over at somebody I couldn't see. "Watch out for him."

I don't think I passed out, which was too bad. I probably would have appreciated that. After a while, my head cleared. Pain from the burns was driving into me, but that kind of pleased me. Burns that don't hurt are a lot more likely to kill. I sat up and tried to keep from panting.

Ten feet away, part of burning wooden wall lay broken across Dorf's body. The unnamed soldier stood between Dorf and me, hanging his head and weeping. He noticed when I tried to sit straighter. "Bravest man I ever knew. He jumped right between you and them fiery timbers. He saved your life." The soldier knelt beside Dorf and laid his hand on the man's charred head.

A bit later, Cael returned. "Bib, prepare to be astounded and appalled. I would never have expected it."

I sat up straight, ignoring the pain. "Is Ella all right?"

"She is, although disappointed and concerned. The priest wasn't the sorcerer. He hanged himself at least a day ago." Cael looked up and down the street, pursing his lips.

"Damn! Krak pound it in the nuts forever!" I started to stand up and then fell back down on my ass. "Shit! Who's the Burner?"

"Unhappily, we don't know."

"Why aren't we dead?"

"We don't know that, either." Cael shrugged.

I scanned the stars and silently put my mark on this sorcerer, whoever he or she was. There wasn't anything magical about that. I was just promising myself and all the gods that I'd slaughter the son of a bitch.

Ella came from somewhere and knelt beside me, her hand on

my unburned cheek. She sniffed and cleared her throat. "So, you're accustomed to fighting sorcerers, are you?"

"Thank you for crying for me, sweetheart, but don't drip any of those tears onto my burns. I might go crazy, or my heart might burst. No sign of the sorcerer?"

She shook her head. "Can you stand up?"

"If you have a drink for me some place, then yes." She and Cael helped me stand. "Wherever that sorcerer was hiding, he could see all those fires. Who might that describe?"

"Well, you, Cael, and Alan survived."

"Alan?"

Ella glanced toward the unnamed soldier sitting on the ground beside Dorf's body. "Alan. Dorf's son."

"Let's set him aside for a minute. I saw him almost killed twice. Bremmel? The beggars?" I gazed around but couldn't find them.

Ella said, "Perhaps . . ."

"Who's that?" I pointed to a high, lit window in a building all the way down at the other end of the wide street, seven or eight blocks away. Somebody was standing at the window, a silhouette. "Hey! Does anybody know who that is?"

Alan stood up, still looking as stunned as if he'd been whacked with a sack of apples. "That? That's Master Penn's window. Stares out it all times of day and night. Locked himself up in his room. He's mad."

TWELVE

We ducked off the main thoroughfare and jogged up the side streets toward the Magestry where Penn lived. I hoped that would keep us out of the sorcerer's view, and it must have since nothing erupted into fiery splinters beside us.

I panted, "He might just may be relaxing until we're too close to miss."

Out of the darkness, Larripet said something in his language.

Bratt laughed. "He says that since you aren't dead, you could be an immortal being and are poking fun at us mortals. He was a lot more poetic about it, though."

I didn't spend my wind to answer, since I was falling behind. My side had tightened up, and I wheezed with every breath.

Alan brought us to the garden door of the Magestry building. I almost told the young man to go on home. I didn't fancy getting him killed after his father and uncles had all died protecting me. I didn't, though. He'd become as dry-eyed and grim as a stone gargoyle, ready to slaughter his enemies. Besides, if I sent him off and then Ella got killed in his place, it would have broken my heart.

Alan pounded on the garden door, announcing himself as a city guard. Within a few seconds, a short woman opened it just wide enough to spit at us if she wanted. "Time doesn't pour out of a—sweet gods, you're nude! Go away, Master Penn is abed, everybody's asleep—it's late!"

Alan threw his weight against the door and shoved it open. The woman roared at him, but even though she was broad enough to be almost square, she couldn't force it closed.

"Kill them all!" she bellowed, louder than my pa shouting orders on his boat. Two men with spears appeared from behind her.

A man thrust a spear at Alan's stomach, but he stepped back and twisted. The spear slipped past Alan and hit Ella right in the middle of the chest. She fell backward. Cael roared as he grabbed the spear shaft with his burned hands, yanked, and slammed the spear butt back into the man's forehead. My pain disappeared as I jumped inside past Alan, who had knocked the woman down. I wrestled the other man's weapon away and killed him with it. I ran back out past Alan and Larripet, who punched the screaming woman in the throat. She started gagging.

I shoved Bratt out of the way and knelt over Ella. Blood was trickling from her chest, but it wasn't gushing.

She wheezed, "Goddamn bastard . . . shit-eating son . . . of his own whore sister!"

I probed the wound, and she hissed. It hadn't pierced or cracked her breastbone. "Remind me never to stab you in the chest. It makes you surly."

She held out her hand as she sucked air. "I'm fine. Struck me as I was jumping back . . . out of Alan's way." I helped her sit up, and she coughed for ten seconds. "I'll have an interesting scar to talk about in bed." She held out both hands, and I pulled her up to stand.

Larripet had grabbed a lantern from somewhere, and we followed him inside. No servants or guards loitered between us, and the stone stairs headed upward. I supposed everybody had run away or were dead or were hiding some place hoping they didn't die before morning. We met a boy coming downstairs with a tray of dishes. He threw it at us and ran back up. On the second floor, Alan led us toward Penn's room. The guard outside Penn's door saw us coming, leaned his spear over his shoulder, and strolled off down a side hallway.

Whoever built the Magestry must have intended it to house their family for a lot of generations. Bratt and Alan needed nine attempts and a river of profanity to bash open the thick, oaken door. That concerned me, since nine is the least auspicious of all numbers, but I put that aside. I didn't intend to be distracted by trivial things like how the universe is fundamentally constructed.

Cael pushed through the doorway past Bratt and Alan, followed by Larripet, who brushed past their legs like a terrier. Penn, a wan, slight young fellow in a purple dressing gown, was standing next to the window, hands clasped in front of his crotch. He opened his mouth to say something, but Cael crashed into him first, smacking the young man's head against the wooden windowsill. Penn flowed onto the floor like a severed drape.

"Hurry, kill him!" Bits yelled from the hallway, and Yalley echoed him.

Cael said, "I knocked him senseless and helpless. And limp. We have a few moments to discuss his fate."

"We shall bring Bremmel. Rightly, he should judge what to do. Bratt, bring Lord Bremmel here." Ella pointed down the hallway, giving orders like she was a general.

"I'll come with you." Alan trotted toward the hallway. His haggard, soot-smeared face seemed twenty years older than it had two hours before. "Lord Bremmel should hear about all this horrible crap from one of his own people."

I said, "I'll pick the boy up and toss him against the windowsill once in a while until you get back."

I wouldn't have seen it if I hadn't been talking to Alan as he walked to the door. I might not have seen it anyhow, except that this sorcerer was self-taught. New sorcerers always whip their hands around when they do magic. I've never seen an exception. Somebody has to teach them how to do it with just a finger. In fact, somebody has to tell them that's even possible. Old Bits probably never had a teacher, at least not a human one. Out in the hallway, he yanked at the air to pull power and channel it.

"Jump back!" I shouted as I ran toward the old man. Bratt jumped out of my way, I felt heat on my back as I went through the door, and then I slammed Bits against the wall. I shook him, threw him down, and kicked his head with my bare foot until he stopped moving. Penn was shrieking in the room behind me, but he soon went quiet. His clothes had probably been set afire, and now the hallway filled up with the smells of the burning young lord.

Cael and Larripet had jumped back when I said to jump, so Penn's sudden pyre had no more than scorched them. That said a lot about their reflexes and instinct to stay alive. Bratt grabbed Yalley, the other beggar, who was babbling, crying, and producing an astounding quantity of mucus. In spite of my big words about throwing people around, I found myself sliding down to the floor in the hallway. I sat with my back against the wall.

Ella found a spool of heavy twine, and she tied a cloak over Bits's head to blind him. I told her how to tie the man's hands and fingers all tight together so that he couldn't move them a twitch. Larripet was taking clothing from Penn's wardrobe, and he brought me a pink chemise with a rose-colored overshirt, along with lavender trousers. I couldn't tell whether he was helping me or mocking me, but I felt sure we were the most effete lot of killers and vagabonds on the western coast. Ella cut up one of Penn's fine cotton shirts and wrapped most of my burns.

A short while after Bratt and Alan left, Bits woke up. He thrashed his bound hands, screamed for several seconds, and from under the bag on his head, he shouted, "Effla will tear off your rod!"

Effla was the Goddess of Love, as odious an immortal creature as ever one could meet. She had long been locked in an extravaganza of malice with her husband, Weldt, the God of Wealth and Parhold's patron deity.

I could imagine how it had gone for poor old Bits. A lot of probability-defying events would have started happening around him. Effla, the Howling Chasm in Which Manhood Perishes, and that really was one of her titles, noticed him. She lured him to trust her, then she taught him, cheated him, unhinged him, and turned him into a horrible murderer. She had probably done it all so she could make a cutting remark to Weldt at some concert or picnic.

Bits shouted curses at us for a minute until Larripet whacked him on the head with one of Penn's boots. Then every time Bits made a sound, the Hill Man smashed him with the boot. Hill People don't tend to express their feelings much, but I got the impression that Larripet might start smiling at any time.

Penn died an hour later. We were still waiting for Bremmel to arrive, which worried me. When Alan finally trotted up the hallway alone, he stared at Ella. "You should come."

"Is Manon all right?" I tried to stand up.

"She isn't hurt. You better come." I squinted at him in the candlelight and saw he looked pale.

Alan led us back to Bremmel's headquarters at the tavern. Ona lay at the foot of the stairs. Somebody had slashed her throat with such dedication that she was half-beheaded. Blood had pooled and sprayed around her, and some of it was still wet. A dead man sprawled five feet away from her with a knife handle sticking out of the middle of his chest. The man's corpse wore ratty clothes, almost rags, like the fire-crazy zealots who had tried to burn us in Garhool.

"She killed him, but who killed her?" Cael asked, although I'm not sure he believed any of us was smart enough to have an answer.

"Here." Larripet pointed to a smear of blood on the tavern wall.

The killer must have run away at least an hour before, so Ella said to hell with chasing him. Alan sprinted up the stairs.

"Wait!" I yelled.

The young man didn't wait. At the top of the stairs, he charged in through the door and I heard him scream.

I stepped over Ona and hauled my cooked and exhausted self up the steps, my sword drawn. At the top, I stared around Bremmel's office. The old man lay collapsed on the couch, and Alan leaned against the wall beside him, gaunt and red-faced. Somebody had smashed in the side of Bremmel's skull. I would have testified they had used a club, since a long, wooden club lay right there at his feet. That all made sense. Nothing else in the room made sense.

A disorganized pile of bloody arms, legs, cloth, pieces of wood, slabs of flesh, and guts lay in the middle of the room, along with a brown-haired man's bearded head. I didn't recognize the head, nor did I understand what might have turned the man into this grotesque hash. I walked around the nasty pile to get a better angle, and I noticed that the little beer keg was missing.

"What . . .?" Ella shook her head.

"Krak's almighty dick!" Cael took a step back. "Was he pulled apart by dogs?"

I took another two steps and finally saw it. "No. This is what happens when a beer keg unexpectedly appears inside a man."

"Huh. Sort of a drinking metaphor," Cael said.

Ella giggled and then coughed. "I apologize. Is this Manon's work?"

I saw that Alan was staring at the floor. "Where is Manon?"

Alan shook his head, wiped his blackened cheeks with his filthy hand, and led me to the tavern downstairs. Manon sat at a table with Bratt, her elbows on the tabletop, staring into a full bowl of stew. Bratt finished saying something to the girl and then leaned back in his chair, cackling at whatever he'd said. Manon didn't even glance up. Her white dog stood under the table, its head in her lap.

I lay my hand on the table next to the girl's hands but didn't touch her. "Manon, are you all right?"

"Yes," she said as she shook her head no. "He was going to kill me too, so it's fine. That's right, isn't it?"

"You did the right thing."

"I mean, I could have just hit him on the head. Or on the knee or something, couldn't I? But I had to kill him. Right?" Her eyes were full of water, but they weren't leaking.

"Right, you couldn't take the chance." I put my unburned arm around her.

"I don't know why I did that to him. It surprised me when it happened. Almost surprised. That was a horrible thing to do to somebody, wasn't it?"

"Let's say it was creative." I patted Manon's shoulder and wondered whether she knew how she'd killed that man in such a way—and how to avoid doing it by accident. "Manon, you're a sorcerer, and nobody can judge your actions here except you."

"Well . . . I guess that I had to do it then. But it was horrible. I don't ever want to do that again." Manon pushed away her stew.

Ella reached across my hand and squeezed Manon's. "Come, let's retrieve our things from the stable yard, if they have not all been purloined by urchins."

Outside in front of the tavern, Alan was trying to explain the night's events to a pair of barking soldiers. I assumed from their nice clothes and pretty swords that they were the indecisive lieutenants that Bremmel had mentioned. Both Bits and Yalley lay tied up on the ground between them.

The hairy-faced one pointed at Yalley. "I've heard all I need to hear. We hang this turd."

Yalley yelled, "I didn't do nothing!"

The short lieutenant kicked Yalley hard. "That's fine for this pig-screwer, but with the sorcerer? We can't stop at just hanging him. Let's pull out his tongue and nail it to his balls."

The hairy lieutenant snorted. "Good! Then we'll hang him, cut him down before he's dead, pull off his arm, and beat him to death with it."

The short lieutenant nodded slowly while rubbing his jaw. "That'll let everybody know that we don't have any more sorcerer problems in Parhold."

I almost wanted to kill these cruel bastards and rescue Bits, but he was too broken and dangerous to let run free. "Let's go," I muttered to Ella.

Without making a noise, Alan pulled out his knife and stabbed one of the lieutenants in the back. The man bellowed and crashed to his knees as Alan stabbed him again. The other lieutenant had drawn his sword by then. Alan rushed him, slapped the man's lousy thrust aside, and stabbed him in the chest. He stabbed this lieutenant again, which I suppose made everything symmetrical and tidy.

Alan nodded at us, breathing hard. "Go on. Thanks, and go on your way." He beckoned to a soldier who had been watching with a stunned expression. The man trotted over to get orders from Alan.

I murmured to Ella, "I guess he's Lord of Parhold now. I wonder if he'll be alive next week."

As we walked away, Ella leaned close to me and whispered, "This is not your fault." She kissed my unburned cheek.

"Darling, you spoke differently before all these people started dying."

Ella hesitated. "Well . . ." She kissed my cheek again and we kept walking.

I had already accepted that at least part of this suffering and killing was for certain my fault. I hadn't made Bits crazy, but I had opened the way for the goddess Effla to do it. My darling Ella had clarified my thinking, though. No man could be responsible for what the gods did.

That was a sweet little argument, and I enjoyed it for about half a minute. Then I leaned against Ella and admitted that it was really a horrible argument. I just wanted it to be true. In fact, it sounded a lot like me when I lied to somebody, but Ella was lying to me for me. I imagine she didn't even realize it. I had led her into bad habits.

Or, hell, maybe she was right, and I just needed some more explanations of my innocence to back up this first argument. I tried to think up some more arguments for my being blameless in all these catastrophes, but my imagination failed me. I decided to come back to it later.

We arrived at the stable yard to find that nearly everything we'd left there had been burned and melted. I recognized just two items —my sword and Harik's little book. Both lay there as neat as if I had wrapped them in velvet and a steel vault before we left. I gathered them up with my one good hand and sat down at the edge of the street. I retained just enough pride not to flop down there.

The blistered, raw burns probably wouldn't kill me, but I wasn't going to be worth much for a while. As harsh and deadly as our lives had become, I doubted that I'd survive the next couple of days all maimed and unhandy. I lifted myself to go trade with Harik. Maybe he'd gotten bored with Manon and would want something more reasonable from me, like capturing a virgin whale.

I arrived, but before I could draw my sword, Harik snapped, "Do you agree to kill the girl?"

"Hold on, wait, you ring-tailed bastard! You're more abrupt than a boy with his first bare tit. Why do you want her dead?"

"You dare question me?"

"How many hundreds of times have I questioned you over the years? Of course I dare! Calm down. You're a god. I admit your dick is bigger." I drew my sword, and the world appeared around me. Harik was sitting on the bottom row of the pavilion, hunched forward, smacking the marble bench with his fist. He whacked it again, and a crack appeared. I said, "If you help me understand a little, maybe we can find an accommodation."

Harik noticed my sword and started, then he sat up straight, all serene and immortal. "I require her death, Murderer, and that's all you need to understand."

I made a flying guess. "Having a big fight with Sakaj, huh? Wouldn't it be easier to apologize and give her a gift she wouldn't get for herself, like some big tree that's been extinct for a thousand years? Or, play a practical joke that decapitates Trutch? Sakaj would love that."

"Your paltry intellect cannot comprehend the affairs of the gods."

"I heard that Sakaj—"

"Silence!"

I kept talking. "Maybe I'm wrong about Sakaj then. While I'm here visiting, do you want your little book? We can make a bargain about what I might do with it. I'll take and bury it in some desert, or throw it in the ocean, and in trade, you'll load me up with power. How does that sound?"

I couldn't be sure because of the angle, but I think Harik rolled his eyes. "The book means nothing."

"So, the book is very important then?" I nodded at him like I was the wisest man on the tallest mountain.

"No, I mean it's not important where you are concerned. If fact, just give it away to anybody who asks for it."

"I see. You're sending someone to fetch it from me, and you want me to hand it over with no fuss. Maybe I should just read a little from it myself every morning."

Harik smiled. "You should do that, Murderer. Go right ahead."

I couldn't tell whether he was trying to trick me into reading the book or trick me into leaving it alone. "Sounds as if that could be festive, eh? Maybe we can make a deal for the book. I offer to read, oh, three pages from it, and in exchange, you give me six squares."

Harik bellowed like a thunderstorm, "Why can't you just kill the damned girl?"

"I suppose it may not be impossible . . ."

"When you decide that it is without doubt possible for you to slay her, then I will entertain your juvenile, self-important babble!"

Harik flung me back into my body, and I threw up in the ditch.

Ella bent down and kissed my head. "Well-spoken, my dear. Eloquent as ever and accurate. Your condition appears to have worsened."

"Harik sends you his greetings. Asks if you have a sister for him."

"Fah! Let's find you the best room in Parhold." She held up a fused, flowing mass of gold the size of her fist—the coins from my pouch. "Perhaps we can scrape enough off your fortune to rent a soft bed."

I nodded up at her. "Wonderful. Just let me breathe for a minute first."

"Ella! Bib!" Cael trotted out of the predawn haze with Bratt beside him while I was still catching my breath. "Word's passing around the city that a ship from Ir just made port, so I asked Bratt to reconnoiter the harbor."

"Of course. You're my hero." I grimaced.

"He probably saved your life," Ella said.

"I know, that makes it worse."

Cael waved me away. "I'm a big enough man to accept your

thanks and put up with your pettiness, but that's not the point. Bratt saw a swarm of ragged men and women disembark, led by a loud, tall bastard. It's probably Pierce and his maniacs. Bratt didn't get a solid count, but three dozen could easily be traveling on that ship. Maybe vomiting as indiscriminately as you did here at the street's edge."

"We are greatly diminished and in no position to fight." Ella gazed at the ashy ground for a moment. "We shall flee."

"If I can flee and hobble at the same time, I agree." I held my hand out for Ella to help me stand. I spared a few seconds for some particularly repugnant cursing of Bits. "We can't dawdle. Let's steal horses and whatever else we need, and we can send the city a nice thank-you note from some place down the road."

THIRTEEN

We didn't pause to search for less flowery costumes to wear while we ran from death. Ella took Manon and her hound to find water and food, Cael hunted for weapons, and I searched for mounts. We agreed to move fast to secure those things and nothing else, even if we had to walk right around a chest of gold to fetch a loaf of bread. As we trotted off in different directions to accomplish all this, Bratt and Larripet wandered away from us without throwing us a word, a glance, or a sharp rock.

I found horses past the garden in the Magestry stable, including a beast of a bay stallion. The bastard tried to bite me and then stomp me when I opened his stall. I hadn't owned such a fine creature in years, and I told myself that neither Penn nor his father could ride this stallion in the afterlife.

I couldn't justify even five minutes to make friends with the beast, so I cursed Harik and Lutigan and Harik again just to be thorough. I left the beautiful horse behind and brought four adequate mounts around front of the Magestry building to meet the others.

Ella returned with Manon and a load of bags and flasks, and she chuckled at me struggling one-handed with a saddle. Manon had acquired a second dog some place, a rangy, spotted beast. Cael showed up a minute later with an enormous bag as well as two sheathed swords, one long and one short. He handed Ella the long one, and she smiled at the amiable turd. Then he overturned the big sack, and about two dozen pairs of boots thumped onto the street.

"I brought every size I could find," Cael said. "The boot maker's going to be sad."

Within minutes, we had shod ourselves and I was trying to decide whether we looked like street performers who had been kicked all night, or an enormous, dismembered peacock. Ella and Cael took over the saddling.

Bratt rode around the corner toward us, with Larripet walking beside him. Bratt waved at us fast, almost like a little boy. "Your life seems interesting. We want to ride along with you. If you don't mind too much."

I took a step toward them. "Hell no!"

"We make good companions. I am the Second of Jatter, the second most accomplished warrior in my country."

I threw a useless boot in their direction, far short of hitting them. "I wouldn't take the first one of whatever you are along with a dozen bowmen. Scat!"

"I'm fairly sure that we are preordained to be companions at arms." Bratt shrugged.

I stared at the fool. "Hell, we're being chased and might be dead before dark. Why would you want to ride with us?"

"The ocean is disappointing." Larripet looked at Cael, but he didn't say more.

I waited a second and then turned to Bratt. "I'm eager to know what the hell that means."

"It would make more sense—probably—if we knew what else he was thinking. He's not likely to elaborate, though." Bratt smiled.

Larripet glared at Bratt but didn't speak.

"Fine. I don't have time to gossip and share secrets with him, nor to comb each other's hair." I dragged my body up onto my docile horse, glad I'd left the man-killing stallion behind.

Ella leaned toward me. "Bib, at some future point, we may wish for allies like these. Consider it."

Accepting these near strangers seemed reckless, but I didn't have the energy for a big fight with Ella. "All right. Boys, I have reconsidered and find that you're not worth the effort it would take to draw my sword to kill you. Come on if you're coming. I can kill you later if you become a pain in my ass."

Bratt laughed.

Ella watched Bratt as he mounted, and she smiled. "He is not joking about killing you."

Bratt grinned. "As you say. But he isn't the First of Jatter, or anything like. He is a profane, one-handed gentleman of advancing years."

I turned my head and laughed straight at the man.

Manon had never sat a horse by herself, so Ella boosted the girl up and led her horse as we rode east out of the city. I would rather have traveled some random direction to confuse Pierce and his gut-flopping morons, but Parhold sat between the shore and some high, sandy bluffs that ran for miles along the coast. Only one road squirmed up and over those bluffs and then inland.

Cael pushed to the front, like he was the top goose leading us south. I didn't care. We couldn't stop, go back, or find another road. The fool could pretend to be leading us to a land full of candied apples and whores if he wanted.

Not a single tree grew anywhere on the bluff face, but as we rode higher, we saw more dry, straggly weeds. Manon's dogs charged around chasing a bunch of shocked rabbits. We crested the bluff before midday, and then Parhold fell out of sight. I had never yet seen any pursuit.

Past the bluff, we rode onto a plain of high, apple-green grass stretching to the eastern horizon, perfect except for the road bisecting it. I said, "You all head off south and make them chase you. I'll circle behind and kill one or two whenever they're busy not paying attention. In a couple of days, the survivors will be so tired and dispirited that we can kill them all with dirty looks."

Ella frowned at me. "Stop talking rubbish. You'd do just as well to cut your own throat now and save time."

I laughed at her.

Ella poked my burned shoulder, hard. When I had stopped bellowing and hooting, she raised an eyebrow at me.

Cael laughed and even pointed at me. "Besides, this road will bring us to the temple on Barrelshins. If we ride south, you could get lost. It would cause you great regret, I'm sure, because you'd never reach the temple and you'd be spitting on Ella's promise."

I admit that I had put aside any thoughts of Ella's promise.

Cael said, "Prod him again, Ella. I bet we'll hear an entirely new array of profanity." When neither of us answered, he smiled, kicked his horse, and pulled ahead.

Once Cael had stopped spouting his thin insults and ridden on, I could hear Bratt and Larripet grouching at one another. Larripet said, "You are timid. This ocean is poisoned."

Bratt laughed. "Don't try to shame me. We won. I was not timid."

"How many did you slay? Oh, I remember . . . none!"

Bratt said, "Did you want me to kill that young boy on the stairs? Or stab some stranger on the street? Or kill that terrifying little girl? Or kill you? Or—"

"Stop!" I hadn't yet seen Larripet either grin or frown, but now he sneered at Bratt. "Covet your enemy. Crave him most of all."

That sounded like nonsense on the surface, but I knew just what the old man meant. I had often rushed past my allies, or even misled them, to keep them away from people I might want to kill.

Larripet spoke up. "Ir-Man. Tell this tiny person how to make a song." It sounded odd for him to call Bratt tiny, since Larripet hardly came up to the man's massive breastbone.

I regarded the pair over my shoulder. "I don't sing a lick. None of my people do. It may be the only civilized skill we don't excel at —that and prayer."

The Hill Man looked up at Bratt as if he smelled like a fish so rotten it's dissolving.

Bratt smiled and gazed off at the millions of suddenly fasci-
nating stalks of grass.

"Ir-Man, you are not tiny." Larripet nodded at me.

"That's a kind sentiment."

"Ir-Man, you could make a song, although I would not sing it
because you are an uncivilized being." The Hill Man turned to
Bratt. "You have seen both oceans, but you wasted them. You could
have just stayed with your people and been alone. If I make your
song now, it would only make children call names and girls couple
with your enemies."

Bratt shook his head. "You're being a tiny bit unfair, Larripet.
Bib has fought sorcerers before. That's why he beat this one."

That was a fair assessment, not that I wanted to say so and
throw myself into their squabble.

Larripet turned straight toward me. "Ir-Man, teach this this tiny
person. I politely ask . . ."

I didn't hear the rest of that nauseating smear of nonsense
because I kicked my horse into a gallop. Larripet ran after me
yelling, but he fell behind in a few seconds. I rode on past Cael,
shouting, "If you sit on your ass, I may get away!"

The galloping jolted my burns like a woman beating a rug with
a torch, but I kept riding. I didn't care that it hurt. Damn everybody,
anyway.

Cael ignored my smart mouth, so I drew pretty far ahead. An
hour later, I topped a gentle rise and saw five riders on the road a
hundred paces away, standing still and facing me. They all wore
black clothes, maybe the same outfits. One man was fat and sat a
beautiful black horse. The rest were people of normal girth, with
different sorts of less handsome horses. Two appeared to be women.
A small fellow rode a rickety white nag that might not have been
able to outrun Larripet.

I should have trotted back to confer with Ella and Cael, but I
was feeling ornery, so I rode straight toward the strangers. When I'd
ridden halfway to them, the fat one raised his hand and yelled,
"Come no closer!"

I drew rein. "Why? Are you afraid of me?"

"No. Just . . . stay over there until I give you permission to come over here." The man stretched up taller on his saddle.

"Who are you then?"

"Never you mind that. Are you Bib the sorcerer?"

"Hell no. I'm Leon the cobbler. Your boots look like shit. Let me sell you some new ones before those rot and fall off your feet."

The small man turned out to be an older boy. He shouted, "We have better boots than you'll ever see! These are magic boots, so just shut yourself!"

The fat man stared at the young fellow. "Cluck, we talked about this."

Cluck frowned but nodded.

The fat man faced me again. "I know you're Bib. Harik described you to me with godlike accuracy."

"If you knew who I was, then why did you ask me? Do you lack confidence? If you're going to block roads and give orders, you should grow more spine."

The man blinked a few times.

I said, "Just who are you, toad-belly?"

"We are Death's Riders. And I am Stone-Hand."

From the saddle, I bowed toward the man just deep enough that it wasn't a flat-out insult. "That's impressive as hell. I've rarely encountered names more pretentious than Death's Riders and Stone-Hand, and here you are traveling around with both."

The man jutted his brown-bearded double chin at me. "Harik warned me not to pay any attention to your insults. You can't anger me."

"That impresses me even more." I pointed at the boy, Cluck, who had auburn hair and wore four belts—two around his waist, and one each way across his chest. "Boot Boy! I bet Chubby here treats you worse than a lizard's asshole. Is he making you ride that sack of bones?" I shook my head in pity.

One of the two brown-haired women, the taller one, stared at me. Something about the easy way she sat her horse said she might be a Caller, like me. The shorter woman, not much older than

Cluck, glared as if she wished I were already in the ground and three years rotting.

I pointed at Stone Hand and called out, "Ladies! Does this nasty pile of flop threaten you into fornicating with him, when you'd rather get beaten with a club full of nails? Be honest."

Cluck had turned red. The women started whispering to each other.

I nodded at the fifth one, an older, grizzled man. "You, I bet he says you look like a billy goat . . ."

Before I finished, from behind me Bratt shouted, "Semante!" He cantered past me toward the strangers, his sword drawn and held ready in a highly professional manner.

Three things happened one right after another. The grass in front of Bratt's horse exploded in flames taller than a man. When the horse reared, Bratt's saddle fell off, hurling him to the ground. Then a nearly incomprehensible number of grasshoppers flew out of the high grass and swarmed Bratt so that I couldn't see any part of his skin or clothes.

FOURTEEN

Bratt's subjugation proved that at least three of Death's Riders were sorcerers. They probably all were. Stone-Hand had talked about Harik in familiar terms, as if he'd just come from drinking a couple of beers with the dark master of his soul and destiny.

Ella and Cael had dismounted and were trying to help Bratt. They applied themselves, but he was flailing on the grass and shouting through the grasshopper mask. A coughing fit seized him, likely from swallowing a grasshopper.

"Just leave him lie there." I flapped my hand in Bratt's direction. "Those bugs won't eat him or smother him. They'll lose interest soon, probably before he goes insane."

The sorcerers had swatted Bratt aside like he was lint, but they hadn't really hurt him, apart from his upcoming nightmares. To have accomplished so little, they had shown me a lot about themselves. They didn't bumble around. They worked well together, so they hadn't all just happened to run into each other buying pork pies. At least three of them were moderately proficient, and they didn't panic when an armed man came riding at them shouting nonsense.

But as sorcerers they were the worst kind of amateurs. They had sat over there like gods, burning, disintegrating, and swarming, wasting power like they could squeeze it out of a cow. Any one of them alone could have stopped Bratt, but they had all wanted to whack whatever piece of him they could reach.

I shouted over the sound of Bratt thrashing. "Thanks for dealing with that arrogant pissant, Dead-Hand. Damn, he's annoying. I've been meaning to knock the shit out of him myself."

"It's Stone-Hand."

"Sure. I owe you a favor for this, so here's some advice. Whatever Harik tells you to do, just do the exact opposite thing. Yes, I'm being sarcastic, but that doesn't mean I'm lying."

Stone-Hand pointed at me and started laughing, making a show of it. A couple of seconds later, his hangers-on laughed too. He straightened his black helmet, which was shaped like the head of a bull. I laughed right along with them and reined my horse in a tight, nervous circle, rolling my eyes at Ella and making an exasperated face as I went. While all my companions were either scraping bugs off Bratt or nodding at my expression, I plucked a little flask off my saddle and slipped it into my pretty, rose-colored overshirt. I turned my horse around to face the sorcerers again.

Stone-Hand wiped his eyes, cleared his throat, and shouted, "Deliver the God of Death's book to me!"

"That sounds so ominous, it's ridiculous. Do you mean this book?" I pulled the little volume from my overshirt, where I'd been carrying it. I held it up and showed both covers. "The one with Harik's mark on the front? With a portrait of him drawn on the first page?"

Stone Hand's voice softened went up. "Really?"

I didn't know. I hadn't opened the cursed thing yet. "Yes, it's an excellent likeness, although it doesn't quite capture the scope of his chin. Son, I'm sorry. It would break my heart to forsake this earthly manifestation of the eternal grace of Harik, that dubious stain on reality's backside."

I tucked away the book and dismissed the riders with my free hand, and then I walked my horse back toward Ella and the others.

Bratt was standing now, panting and shivering. Manon and Larripet had joined in to scoop grasshoppers off his legs in handfuls.

A phenomenal bang staggered my horse and whacked my eyeballs around inside my skull. A great trench had appeared to block my way, ten feet across, ten feet deep, and fifty feet long. Dust and the smell of burning metal floated out of it. Breakers often disintegrated the earth this way, an effective but unimaginative tactic.

I wheeled my horse partway around. "Death's Riders? Are you sure you're not Death's Amblers? Death's Waddlers? I've made bigger holes peeing in the snow."

Stone-Hand hissed, proving that he could be angered by something I said after all. He gestured and created a gargantuan boom as more earth disappeared. Air rushed in to fill the trench, now fifty feet deep.

Stone-Hand bellowed, "Bring the God of Death's book! If you don't, we'll destroy you and take it!"

"All right, fine! I don't want to be destroyed. I really don't want the piddling thing that much, anyway." I pulled the dark, little flask from my overshirt, and without pausing, I flung it into the trench. I leaned over and watched until the flask hit the bottom with a flat smack.

Stone-Hand snarled and raised both hands toward me.

"Save your power, Stone. You'll need it to get down there without getting killed by a trench cave-in, or without burying the book under a hundred tons of dirt."

Stone-Hand paused and then dropped his arms.

I said, "And I think it may come a storm soon, a regular deluge, so you'd better hurry. Goodbye, Stone. If you're ever in Cliffmeet, look for us. We won't be there, but it pleases me to imagine you spending a week or two scouring the city. And the rest of you, don't let Stone here fool you into making bad trades for his benefit. You'll end up insane, or maybe cursed to pick dead fish off the same beach every day until you die."

My traveling companions and I headed east away from the

sounds of Stone-Hand shouting and the other Death's Riders sniping back at him.

"That was instructive," Cael said after we'd lost sight of the sorcerers behind a gentle roll.

"Why did you give up the book?" Bratt had to lift his head to speak to me since his horse had gone wild during the grasshopper assault and bolted back toward Parhold. Now he walked beside Larripet, who raised his eyebrows at me.

Ella scratched her forehead. "It was unlike you. Of course, crude insults and recklessness are entirely like you, but those people threatened us and you simply surrendered the book. I am surprised that they still live."

"But there were five of them." Bratt shook his head like somebody was playing a joke.

"Yes. I am surprised that they still live."

Cael pointed at my open shirt. "He didn't give the book away to those pompous raisins. He has it right there in his shirt."

Ella, Larripet, and Bratt all started objecting.

"Bib threw a jug in the hole," Manon said.

I patted the flask through my shirt. "A flask, darling."

"Flask, jug, bug, whatever you want." Manon kissed at her dogs, who were loping along almost underneath her horse.

I pulled the book out, and just then, weakness hit me from everything that had happened since the last time I'd slept. I felt like I had been piling sacks of flour for a week. I sat up straighter, which ripped pain across my burns, and my hand started shaking. I covered it by waggling the book at everybody. "I showed them a book, so they saw a book."

Larripet stared hard at the book. "Magic?"

"The best kind. Deceit."

Bratt had been staring at his feet as he walked. Now he trotted up to join me. "Bib."

I waited a few seconds, but he didn't say a thing. "What is it? Speak!"

"I must apologize to you. We are companions, but in spite of that, I must kill you. I am sorry."

"Me too." I eased my sword in its scabbard.

"Bib, wait! Stop!" Ella shouted, charging ahead and forcing her horse between mine and Bratt's. "Don't assume that this must end in death. Will you have nothing but killing?"

I knew a threat from Ella when I heard one. I drew rein and raised both arms. "Young man, I'll listen to you. I expect that when you state your full sentiment, it will be harmless. It would be to your advantage if it's entertaining too."

Bratt paused for a breath. "Bib, you're the best fighter here. Perhaps as good as the First of Jatter, my own brother. You made idiots of those sorcerers while wounded and missing a hand, and you didn't even use magic."

"Nothing you've said so far has made me mad."

"I lay in the dirt, defeated by insects. I failed." Bratt's brow furrowed. "On my journey here, I have won victory upon victory, and yet I failed in my purpose. I think that only defeating the greatest warrior can save me." He stared at me, his face calm.

"Is that all?" I pointed over my shoulder. "Cael's a greater warrior than me. Kill him and leave me out of it."

"I don't mean to insult Cael, but he is unknown and we have seen your victories." Bratt glanced at Larripet.

I turned to the Hill Man. "Did you put him up to this?"

"This avalanche began with a pebble."

"What in the prancing hell does that mean?"

"No, I did not put him up to it." Larripet nodded at Bratt. "I mean no insult to your penis."

Bratt shook his head at me. "In my country, I was defeated by only one man. No man ever defeated me in true battle, when death was the penalty. Damn it, my enemies ran away from me!"

"Lutigan's ass crack!" I said. "You're a hell of a fighter, son, I can see it, and you're pretty dangerous. It's just unlucky for you that right now, in this part of the world, you're likely to meet a lot of other dangerous people." I pointed around at everybody else. "You may not understand this, but you're about the fifth most dangerous person here." I squinted at Manon. "Maybe the sixth."

Bratt gazed straight into my eyes and clenched his teeth. "I don't have a choice, Bib. Don't worry. I won't fight you until your wounds have healed."

Ella sat tall and shot me a pleading glance. She rarely asked me for anything. Just then, her face asked me to be an idiot and not stab this young man in the heart.

I smiled at Bratt. "That's right noble. Thank you. Now, let's get back to riding before Pierce and his friends set all this grass on fire around us."

An hour before sunset, I felt one of the gods lift my spirit out of my body, with the usual stretched and queasy feeling. I didn't have a damn thing to say to Harik, so I fought. That rarely worked, and it didn't work this time. When I arrived, the nausea cut off as if my stomach ceased to exist, and my pain fell away. Nothingness surrounded me, although I knew that the Home of the Gods lay just behind it.

"Harik, I was about to name a goat after you, kill it, and heave the unclean thing in the river. I'm still not going to kill the sorcerer girl, so send me home."

"My negligible interest in that child has passed. No, Murderer, you mocked my emissaries and dismissed them. I bring you here to pay for that."

"Death's Riders may be the greatest lot of pretentious imbeciles I've ever met. I hope you don't intend to rely on them for anything important."

"Concern yourself with your own fate, Murderer. I brought you here to demonstrate the folly of your arrogance. Besides, you need power. Are you interested? Or would you prefer to wander the earth, scorched like a lamb chop, until you are killed?"

I drew my sword, and the Home of the Gods appeared around me, a little sharper and more textured than any normal place. My feet scuffed the coarse brown dirt. Harik sat above me in the marble gazebo cradling a ruby-encrusted golden chalice in one hand.

"I am interested, Mighty Harik, yes, I am. I yield to you the honor of making the first offer."

Harik leaned back on his bench. "I offer you knowledge in exchange for two squares."

"Kiss my mortal ass!" He was offering knowledge that I would almost certainly not wish to know. Those types of deals always hurt in unpredictable ways. Gods adored them. They could show off their omniscience, or at least show that they knew more than sorcerers. "I do not accept."

"You do yourself ill by rejecting this knowledge," Harik said regretfully. "It might change the course of your life."

"I offer to find your Death's Riders and give them a lesson in magic, in exchange for five squares."

Harik smiled, which was an uncommon event. "Would this lesson conclude with their deaths?"

"It's a possibility."

"Then no. Let us shift to the task I had intended the Riders to perform. Regain my favor, Murderer. Keep the book for now. Later, I will tell you where to deliver it, when, and to whom, in exchange for two squares."

"I had your favor at one time? That's a disturbing thought. For five squares, I'll deliver the book to whomever I please, when I get around to it. I'll give them a note from you, if you like."

Harik scowled at me like I was a dog that had messed in his shoe. "You shall take the book wherever you go and keep it from harm, for two squares."

I snorted. "I'll carry the book with me for a year, but I won't so much as wipe spit off it. For five squares."

Harik leaned back and set down his goblet. "I dislike the direction of our negotiations. I return to the offer of knowledge in exchange for two squares."

"What a basket of bull knockers! I've already said no." I prepared to abandon the trading arena to show Harik how much I didn't give a damn about him or his power.

"Very well, if you wish to play the coward. Carry the book with you and keep it from harm. Three squares."

I decided to stay since I thought I might make an acceptable deal about the book. "I refuse to protect the damned thing. I'll carry it with me for two years, though. Four squares."

Harik stared at me. "You should have accepted the knowledge. I shall tell it to you now, and you must hear it without even being paid. Regarding your young woman, the blonde one, you have killed her. You have already done the thing that will lead irresistibly to her death."

I had seen Harik lie a thousand times. I didn't believe he was lying this time. I let my sword's point fall into the dirt, tried to dredge up a good curse, and failed. "What did I do?"

"That knowledge cannot possibly be relevant to you now. It is done."

To be in a place where I had no physical body, it felt like somebody had just kicked the wind out of me. "Harik, you have to pay me. You made me know this."

"I am in no way obligated to do anything for you. I am a god. Consider this knowledge to be your punishment for discourtesy toward my servants."

"You have to pay me something so I can change this. I'll carry the book and keep it from harm for three years."

Harik took a slow drink from his goblet. "Murderer, you are so moronic today. You have already rejected that offer. It is void. Besides, no man may change the future, regardless of his power. That is the prerogative of the gods."

This felt like a negotiation from years ago, when Harik sold me the power to save my little girl. That had worked out badly. "Then change the future for us. You can kill me instead. I'm wrinkly and used up. Let Ella be."

"I think not. I prefer you to be stalking the land, creating mayhem and suffering on my behalf. Your blonde woman is a bit sanctimonious for my purposes." Harik leaned forward and pointed at me with his goblet. "Besides, you are the one who has killed her, not me."

I wanted to curse him so hard that everything he killed that week would pop back to life. That wouldn't save Ella, of course. I couldn't think of anything that might.

Harik said, "I have an idea, Murderer, since you seem to have run out. I know that you have not yet attempted to read my book. I shall not describe the experience so that you may savor it without prejudice. I offer you three squares if you read from the book three times, but you must do so together with the blonde woman. You both must read it at the same time. Do this by the twenty-third day from today."

"How does that help Ella? It sounds dangerous as hell, and you said I can't save her even with limitless power."

"Try to concentrate, Murderer. My book contains the magic of a god. I don't guarantee that it will change your blonde woman's fate. It is perhaps not even likely. But it is possible. To that I do commit."

That is how I came to stand in the darkness beside a stunted oak, holding Harik's book and leaning over Ella as she slept. We had paused for a couple of hours to rest the horses and ourselves, mainly the horses. After Harik's bargain, I had spent the rest of the afternoon wondering how to start this conversation. She might leave me just for behaving like an idiot and letting all this happen. Then she would die for sure.

I hate to suffer indecision, so I stowed the book inside my shirt and sat down next to Ella. I put my hand on hers, and she squeezed my fingers in her sleep.

"Ella," I whispered.

She woke right away and rolled to her feet. "What?"

"Sit down. Do you trust me?" For weeks I'd feared to ask that question.

Ella hesitated, and that pretty much told me everything. But she said, "Yes, I do."

I closed my eyes for a moment. One of Manon's hounds half barked in its sleep. Three dogs had piled themselves onto her in a heap of devotion and slobber. I didn't know where the third one had come from.

I sighed. "You're in trouble. Likely to be killed, unless together we can save you."

"Just where did you learn this entirely unexpected news? Perhaps by divining a caterpillar's fur? From the ghost of your mother? Or was it, by merest chance, from the God of Death?"

"It was Harik."

Ella looked at me as if I had just picked up filth off the road to make a necklace. "You believed him, the personification of false-hood? Did you also drink his wine and eat divine fruit while you were in his realm?"

I smiled. "He never serves refreshments."

Ella did not smile.

"I told him to take me, but he said no. He really thinks he already has you and can squeeze me however he wants. If he was lying about your death, he'd have just taken my offer to give him my life and then held it over me as long as he wanted."

Ella opened her mouth, paused, and then shook her head. "You spend too much time with these gods. You think like them. Very well. What must we do?"

"You're going to hate it a whole lot."

"I'm not afraid."

I pulled out the book. "We have to read a page out of this together, three times. One of those times may save you."

"But not with certainty. Fine." She grasped my forearm. "You must do something for me. I assume you acquired power in this labyrinthine bargain. When you heal your burns, you must also restore your hand."

I felt happy that she cared about it, but it was foolishness. "Bad idea. We may need that power for something else, and I'm doing well enough without the hand."

Ella clamped down on my arm and snapped, "So well that Cael had you supine with his sword against your throat? Really? That well? Just accept this. I'm forcing you to restore your hand. It may save your life. It is my gift to you."

"Ella, no."

She pushed my arm away like it was a rat. "You never need anything from anyone! You never need anything from me. Well, you need this, even if you are too plug-ignorant to know it, and you will damn well let me give it to you!"

I spent the next hour off to myself, pulling bands and sheets of energy out of the air, green energy only I could see. I laid on sheets to melt the burns and restore my skin. I sculpted my left hand back onto the wrist using bands. The body wants to heal, and mine remembered what it had been. The new hand was uncalloused and untanned, but perfect.

When I had finished, I said to Ella, "Want to bet how long it takes for somebody to notice?"

"Cael will notice the first time he sees you."

I grunted. He wouldn't notice if I killed him first.

FIFTEEN

The gods like it when sorcerers are in love. They think sorcerers should have sweethearts, husbands, wives, and big batches of children. Love leads us down subtle paths, where we do the things we never expected, things that are exactly unlike us. The gods use love to fool us into twisting ourselves into something they like better, or at least something they think is funnier.

Sorcerers know this. With all that foreknowledge, we make ourselves ready to resist this weakness, or at least walk around it. We almost always fail.

I did not kill Cael in his sleep, mainly because he was awake when I got there. The moon was up, and he glanced at me from where he lay. "That's an excellent hand. You should find it convenient. I'm sure I will if I need to be pulled out of a river or up from a cliff."

"Get up. We're leaving."

Cael shrugged, hopped up, and walked to his horse.

Manon's dogs were wiggling and licking her awake. The white dog and the spotted one each weighed about half as much as she did. The new one was brown, fuzzy, and half their size. Manon smiled at me, probably the first real, happy smile I'd ever seen from her. "Their names are Pokey, Violet, and Pudge." The dogs ran off in three directions as if they'd been let off a leash.

"Very fine animals. You ought to be proud. Do they talk to you?"

"Don't be stupid. They're dogs!"

Clearly, she hadn't tried yet. I didn't see the need to encourage her. She'd spend the next month distracted by how dogs see the world.

Pokey, the white one, came back with a rabbit and began devouring it with powerful smacks and snuffles. Soon, the others trotted back, each with its own rabbit. Pudge had to drag her meal along through the grass.

I mounted my horse, wishing I had time for a decent breakfast too. Cael led us east: four riders, three loping dogs, and two trotting men.

An hour later, the sun rose high enough to beam straight into our eyes. Cael and I both tried to call halt at the same time. In the end, he called a fifteen-minute halt, and I called him an oozing horse-goiter. Ella laughed at us both. I dismounted, stretched, and saw all of Manon's dogs rush off into the feathery grass. Then all three returned with rabbits, which was a bounding great coincidence.

I cleared my throat. "Manon, are you calling bunnies to come get slaughtered by your dogs?"

"They're hungry. Look at Violet!"

The dog's ribs did stand right out in the ground-skimming light. "You should save your power. Those dogs appear capable. They can hustle their own meals."

Manon turned and gazed around at the part of the countryside that didn't include me. "My mother told me to take care of all their needs. Well, they need to eat."

In my head, I heard Manon say, ". . . and you can't stop me," just like the little girl she was.

"You're wise not to call your mother by name." I squatted down and whistled. Pudge charged over to me, throwing herself against my knees, her tail flapping. I petted her and scratched her ears for a moment. "Not a flea. Teeth as clean as if they've lain in the sun for a year. I swear, Manon, you may wish you had that power later on. Save it."

Manon smirked at me. "Like you saved your power when you grew a new hand? Don't tell me to do one thing and then do another yourself."

It was a damn shame that she was right. I couldn't tell her that the hand wasn't my idea. I sure couldn't tell her that it was complicated so just accept it. "I wish you'd trust me on this. I'm telling you a true thing."

She rolled her eyes.

Ella and I decided not to fiddle with the Harik's book out there in the wilds while running from five enraged sorcerers and a deranged mob willing to burn us alive. It seemed wiser to find a more secure spot for experimentation. Even if something catastrophic occurred, we'd have a small chance to survive. We rode on east with the book still in my shirt and the dogs' bellies stretched tight. The grass became shorter and greener, and we saw more small trees. Some of them even appeared to be healthy. I thought I could smell plums, but I never saw any.

Before noon, I spotted a small village ahead. The trail passed right through the middle of it. We rode closer and stopped at four poles that had been raised a short walk from the village proper. Someone had hung from each of the poles a naked body, upside down, and evidence suggested they'd been hanging a few days. Someone had chopped off their hands, put out their eyes, and cut out their private parts. One body was an old man. The other three were children.

"Traitors of some kind? But children?" Ella blinked a few times and brushed her cheek.

Manon looked up at one of the bodies and went pale. She reined her horse around and rode off a little distance, followed by her dogs.

"I don't think they're traitors," I said. "Cutting off the hands— that's something people do to sorcerers."

"Are you saying they were sorcerers? Even the children?" Cael glanced in each direction.

I glanced at Manon and shrugged. "I'm saying that somebody thought they were."

Larripet nodded at the village. "The ones who did this are waiting in there for us to torture them. And then kill them."

"Perhaps not," Ella warned.

"If we do not torture them, our hearts will shrink until we die." Larripet ran off in the direction of the village.

"Wait!" Ella shouted.

Bratt ran after Larripet.

Cael yelled, "Maybe the people here didn't do this!"

Larripet stopped and stared back at Cael as if the man had just sneezed out three or four snakes. "If these people did not do this, they would not leave the dead to hang and rot." The Hill Man ran on toward the village with Bratt beside him.

"Oh, hell." I kicked my horse into a canter. "Maybe he knows some good tortures." I didn't even like torture, but it sounded like a good excuse for doing something stupid.

Cael, Ella, and I overtook Larripet and Bratt just after they entered the village. Manon and her dogs trailed us. I cut the Hill Man off. "Hold on, stop there! You're probably right about all this, but what if you make a mistake and torture somebody who's innocent? Will your liver swell up until you die? Something worse?"

"They are not innocent." Larripet set the butt of his spear against the ground with a thump.

"Maybe they're almost innocent. What if somebody else did that butchering, and they'll come back to kill any of these people who takes down one of those bodies? That's possible, right?"

Larripet sighed and set the butt of his spear on the ground. "Maybe."

I said, "Let's ask a few of them what all has happened here." I examined the little crowd of women and children that had gathered. "If they're a bunch of horrible murderers, I'll hold them down while you pull off their toes."

Larripet glanced at Bratt, and they both nodded at me. We all dismounted, then Ella and I walked toward the crowd. The women wore simple dresses dyed green, brown, or greenish brown. The children wore undyed tunics and trousers, and they hid in the back. The women held their ground.

Ella smiled. "Hello, I'm Ella. We are traveling east and became concerned when we saw the bodies mounted outside your town. Is anything wrong here?"

A tall, handsome woman about my age said, "I'm Zia. Happy to meet you. Everything is perfectly fine. Better than it's been in a long time. Do you want a drink of water? You can water your horses too. The tavern still has breakfast hot and beer cool. It's right over there." She pointed to a daub and wattle building that resembled every other one around, with whitewashed clay walls, a wooden door, and a thatched roof.

I glanced at the little tavern. "I could eat a bite, but later. Tell me about the unfortunates tied up on those poles out there."

Zia glowered. "Sorcerers." Most of the women made folk signs to ward away evil. Three of them spat on the dirt.

"I'll be damned! How did you find them out?" I leaned toward her for the news.

More women and a few men were joining the crowd. A stocky older man with a reddish beard called out, "I guess that every single chore around here has already been done, since the whole town is standing around here like cows. And it's not yet midday. I am purely astounded."

Zia sneered. "Go climb back under your covers, you pompous, lazy ass! Nobody will miss you!"

The man laughed. "This whole town would get burned down by some idiot, and then blow away if you didn't have me to keep you from folly. Go on you—disperse!"

Some of the women started drifting away, but Zia kept talking. "Zemm, if a bear ate you up today, most of us wouldn't notice. The rest of us would have a party."

Zemm pointed toward the middle of town. "Woman! Go! Everybody, back to work! These good travelers may have needs."

The rest of the crowd chatted with one another as they walked away. Zia picked up a rock and slung it at Zemm, but he side-stepped. She shouted, "You rutting dog! You can't stay awake forever! You just see what happens!" She stalked toward Zemm, banged into his shoulder as she passed, and threatened, "Don't be late for supper, you hog."

Zemm smiled at us. "Welcome! If you require any little thing at all, the people of Hutch stand ready to provide, for a fee of course. Provisions? Do your horses need to be reshod? This trail is uncommonly packed with stones. And without meaning offense, sir, your saddle looks like shit about to slide off a fence rail. We can offer a beautiful replacement."

I watched Zia disappear around a house. "I feel compelled to ask how long you've been married."

"Twenty-seven years! The excitement keeps me young—and vigilant."

Ella stepped forward. "Returning to our query, how did you discover that those individuals were sorcerers?"

Zemm smiled even bigger. "The most fortunate thing happened to us. I should say that the most unfortunate thing happened first. One night, a house collapsed, collapsed hard like it had been crushed by an avalanche. Same thing happened again the next night, and the one after. Seven souls killed, all told, if you can imagine it. Everybody in town walking around terrified and just about to murder each other any minute. Then Agni came. That was the fortunate part."

"Who is this savior Agni?" I asked.

"I misspoke a bit. Agni himself didn't visit us, but some of his people did. Agni and his army are marching all over creation protecting honest, virtuous folks like us from the their-asses-be-damned-forever sorcerers hiding right in among us." Zemm spat in the dirt, his smile gone. "They picked out the sorcerers hiding among us right quick. I don't know how they did it. I wouldn't ever have guessed that Gooter and his grandkids were sorcerers, but they must have been. No more houses have been crushed in the night, so it stands to reason."

I said, "It appears they didn't hold back when they chastised those sorcerers."

Zemm rubbed his jaw. "It was harsh, and I won't lie to you, I couldn't watch the whole thing. But Agni's folk are the experts, and all that chopping and blinding was necessary, they said. Those corpses are a little disturbing out there on the road, but sorcerers will stay the hell away from us as long as the poles are up. If any sorcerer tried to walk into Hutch now, they'd explode."

Ella raised her eyebrows. "Explode?"

"They might. Or they might choke or shit themselves to death or just fall over. Could be any of those, or others, according to Agni. I don't much care as long as they die."

I clenched my fist and scowled to match Zemm. "Damn right. I might want to join up with Agni. When did his people leave? And in what direction?"

"Three days back, headed south. You should join him. Eleven of our folks left to fight with Agni's people. It's a worthy crusade for sure."

I gazed over my shoulder at Larripet and mouthed the word, "Tortures?"

The Hill Man sighed and rested his spear over his shoulder.

"Hell, Larripet, does that mean no, or does it mean I should pull out the pliers?"

"No."

Zemm cleared his throat. "The last thing in the world I want is to be rude, but we sell a fine selection of clothes. I notice your garb to be a little . . . lacking in utility."

After a flurry of mercantile activities, Ella and I scraped some gold off the melted chunk she carried, and she handed the scrapings to Zemm. Then we rode out of town wearing tough clothes as simple and stylish as a dirt clod, and we left Penn's whimsical costumes behind.

I said to Ella and Cael, "Do you figure that tall hooligan back in Garhool was Agni?"

Ella shook her head. "I should think that the leader of a crusade to destroy sorcerers would spend less time shouting obscenities and grabbing at his privates."

Cael nodded slowly. "That argument would usually be weak, but in these crazy days, it sounds unassailable. Who is Agni then?"

"Who has the most to gain?" Bratt asked. "What could a man gain that is precious enough to justify all this killing and pain? Wealth? Land?"

"Agni's people seem like they won't even steal mud out of a hole," I said.

Ella regarded Hutch over her shoulder. "They carried away eleven men and women to bolster their army."

I said, "But why does this Agni want an army, anyway?"

Cael said, "Maybe he has a larger plan for conquest."

Ella said, "Perhaps revenge."

"Getting even!" I said. "Getting even for something he lost to sorcery, or to sorcerers."

"No." Larripet shook his head.

I waited for more, but he kept walking and didn't say anything else. "Is that all? Hell, speak! Don't worry. You're not close to using up your two hundred words for the day yet."

Larripet stared straight ahead. "He does not have something to gain. All he had is lost. He has nothing and can gain nothing, not vengeance, and not peace. When we see him, we should kill him right away."

"Interesting." Cael peered at the Hill Man.

I leaned in the saddle toward him. "Larripet, you sound awfully damn sure about that,"

"My sister's husband went crazy in that way."

Cael coughed, and Ella turned away to roll her eyes.

"Well." I slapped my leg a couple of times with my new hand. "We'll watch out for a man like that then."

"That will be good. My sister's husband and his men killed more than two thousand Hill People before we killed him."

SIXTEEN

I never heard my father pray. I did see him fling three salted fish into the ocean every time we sailed out of the harbor. That was supposed to show Madimal, the God of Deep Waters, that we were thankful, obedient, and terrified. Hell, we were fishermen, so of course we were terrified. The ocean loves to drown fishermen.

Sorcery training and a few conversations with gods convinced me that throwing salted fish never saved a one of us. The gods didn't care whether we drowned or found a derelict ship full of rubies as big as crabapples. My mother always chewed on my father's ass for throwing away perfectly good fish, so she must have understood the gods a lot better than the rest of us.

We talked about gods in my village, or threw fish at them, but we hardly ever talked about sorcerers. I never saw one until I started training to become one. I would not have suspected that sorcerers and gods had much to do with each other. The truth would have shocked me and probably every one of my neighbors.

So, I understood why the welcoming, pious, vulgar people of Hutch had mutilated their sorcerous neighbors, and then laughed like it was the harvest dance. Sorcerers were a thing apart, unaccountable and terrifying.

We passed another village before midday. Two bodies hung in front of it, both women. Cael didn't slow down, and none of us lagged.

In the early afternoon, the wind died away and the sun shone hot for late autumn. I spotted a mere thread of smoke to the south. I ignored it and hoped everybody else would too, but a minute later, Bratt pointed at it and yelled. That caught Ella's attention and then Cael's, and soon everybody went hustling off to save people they weren't even sure existed. Larripet glanced at me, stared at the smoke as if it smelled bad, and trotted after the others. I collected Manon and followed at a distance suitable for retreating if something bad happened.

We found a burned-out village not far past a little rise. I had thought the smoke so meager because it was far off, but in fact, the village was smoldering in no more than a couple of places. Otherwise, all the blackened doors, scorched clay, and ashes lay cold. Nine mutilated bodies hung next to the village, two of them children. Nearly forty more villagers lay scattered among the wreckage. The ones I examined had been stabbed or beaten to death.

Cael turned over some plaster with his boot. "Cleansed by fire?"

"Maybe they didn't want to butcher their neighbors," I said.

Ella led us back to the road.

Later that afternoon, I spotted a clot of people on the road ahead trudging toward us. Cael saw them about the same time, and we both halted.

I watched the people. "You've traveled through this country not long ago, Cael. Are these people you know?"

"Unlikely. The people I know don't make a habit of traveling from place to place by foot. They ride horses. Carriages, if they're elderly."

"Since they're not friends of yours, I'm eager to become acquainted."

Ella trotted past us. "Come on. You're worse than toddlers."

Two dozen travelers stepped off the road when we approached. They aged from child to grandmother, dirty but not ragged. They wore well-made, undyed clothes and solid shoes, and all of them appeared exhausted and terrified.

A teenage girl yelled, "Don't go that way!"

"Why not?" Ella asked. "There lies our destination."

The strangers eyed each other for a few seconds. The girl seemed to be the leader, or at least the most reckless. "Everything back there is gone. All dead and crushed. Everything's smashed." Her chin quivered.

Cael peered up the road as if he could see where they'd come from. "That's terrible. This whole area seemed idyllic when I passed through a few weeks ago, apart from a heroic stench of pig. What happened?"

The people stared at the ground. Finally, the girl mumbled, "Monsters."

Ella nodded encouragement. "What kind of monsters?"

The girl shrugged.

"Tall monsters? Fat? Hands or claws? Fangs? Tusks? Vile odors?"

"It was a giant."

"Only one?" Ella asked.

I grinned. To my knowledge, Ella had never seen even one giant. I hadn't either, nor heard a report of one that I'd credit.

The girl nodded.

"What's your name, young lady?"

"Ellie."

"Mine is Ella. We might be relatives. Describe this giant, Ellie. In every detail, please."

Ellie slumped but nodded. "It was as tall as four men, and hairy and blue and it had big, big eyes. It knocked down houses and grabbed people and crushed them with one hand. And it pulled out their hearts to put on a necklace strung with guts. And there was something wrong with its ears. It crushed my mum."

Cael turned his horse in a circle. "That sounds dreadful. We should go kill it, but we're in a rush, so I suppose we shouldn't."

"I have never fought a monster." Bratt drew his sword.

"No." Larripet touched Bratt's shoulder. "Men are not meant to touch monsters and other crazy things."

"You have been pushing me to crave my enemy's blood! All right, I will crave it more than anybody else! I will win, you will not die, and I will not be lost!" Bratt grinned at each of us, his chin high. "Who will follow me to kill it? I'll lead."

I leaned back in the saddle. "Oh, hell, it's probably a bear."

"No, no . . ." Ellie gaped at me.

"Or some big, murdering lunatic come down from the hills." I shrugged. "Tall as four men? How tall was it, really?"

"Big! Maybe . . . two men tall. Not less!"

Ella fished our golden asteroid out of her stiff cloth bag. "Bib, help me break off a bit of this."

Substantial straining and cursing, plus a cracked fingernail, broke off the equivalent of four gold wheels. Ella handed it to the girl. A couple of people muttered thanks. I didn't blame them for not falling down and licking our horses' hooves in gratitude. Something at least as bad as a bear had happened to them. We rode on east, leaving the survivors to trudge toward the questionable safety of the villages on the road to Parhold.

We arrived at a village set back from the road. Three mutilated bodies hung in front of it. I estimated twenty or so daub and wattle houses with thatched roofs. Such houses weren't quite as impregnable as the Fortress before Regensmeet, but they're sturdy in their own way. Something had smashed every one of these into a pile of sticks, reeds, and clay. At least thirty bodies pocked the village grounds, and a few people's chests had been torn open.

Cael nodded at the corpses. "Not a bear then, eh?"

I scowled. "Go to hell"

"Considering how friendly you are with the God of Death, you're probably in greater danger of that than I am."

"I'll take you with me. I'll need something to kick."

He shook his head and surveyed at the carnage.

Larripet spoke up. "I think we may be in the Crazy Lands. This is a crazy place. Hearts are not pulled out of bodies this way in normal places. We should leave."

Bratt put a hand on Larripet's shoulder. "You're a very wise man, but we are on this path and have no choice."

Ella gazed south onto the plains. "Perhaps we should depart the road, at least until tomorrow. We may evade whatever did this."

I pulled off my hat and wiped the sweatband. "Where is this giant now, Bratt?"

Bratt pointed down the road from where the survivors had straggled.

"And how do you know that, mighty warrior?"

Bratt opened his mouth, closed it, and swallowed.

"That's right, we don't know where this giant is now, and we don't know why it decides to turn left instead of right. If we go off trying to avoid it, we're just as likely to smack into the damned thing." I kicked my horse into a trot and led us on east down the road.

Late in the day, the wind shifted and blew chilly, and dirty clouds skimmed in. It hadn't yet rained by the time we found the next wrecked village, but a storm wasn't far off. This wrecked place was larger than the first we'd run across, or at least we saw more bodies and more piles of what used to be houses.

Larripet shouted, "Hello! If anyone wants to listen to a good idea, we should go away from here!"

Cael ignored Larripet. "This monster appears to be thorough. I wonder if that's a quality one should admire in monsters?"

When Manon screamed, I whipped around. I didn't see anything, because about that time, my horse went insane and almost threw me. It took a bit of time to control him, and he was still a fingernail's width away from rolling on me and galloping away from my smashed corpse. Once he'd settled a little, I resumed scanning the area.

Not far away, Cael sat forward in the saddle, whispering to his horse as it stamped and twitched. Ella and Manon were on their feet, so their horses must have thrown them and run. Larripet and Bratt stood with them, and all four stared at a big tree beside the road, one with leaves of pasty brown and piercing orange.

It looked like a damn tree to me. Manon screamed again, and

when I peered over my shoulder, I saw Ella, Bratt, and Larripet just standing there, gaping at the tree too, their eyes as big as hen's eggs. I stared hard at the tree this time, and our giant snapped into focus. I glanced again at Manon, surrounded by her whining dogs, and she didn't appear to be engaged in any ill-advised magic. When I turned to the tree again, the giant was gone.

I stared hard at the tree. After a moment, I saw the creature. It was obviously still standing beside the tree trunk and hadn't moved

The damn thing was supernatural for sure, since such beings can often mask their presence. The rest of its appearance also argued for a mystical origin. This giant wasn't as tall as two men. It stood no more than nine feet, say a man and a half of pale-blue flesh sheathed in patchy, light-brown hair. I hesitate to say how much it weighed. Its torso was shaped like a rough oval, as if a child had molded it and then clothed it in a blood-splashed purple jerkin. The legs and arms made up for the crudeness of the torso, as his muscles stood out like cables.

The beast's head was manlike, except the nose that was as flat as a plate, the enormous amber eyes, and the long ears that flopped over. The eyes were peering at a badly crumpled sheet of paper that the monster held by two clawed fingers. It took three ambling steps toward us, glared at each of us, and sniffed with its enormous, exposed nostrils for what seemed like enough time to dig graves for all of us and our horses too.

The giant wadded the paper up in its hand and hunched its shoulders. It chirped, "Well, you're a fucking disappointment."

SEVENTEEN

The giant's soft lisp and cheeping voice gave it away. I had heard creatures speak like that a few times in the Home of the Gods, generally saying things like, "Whatever you want, Your Eminence," and, "Look, it's still soft and wriggling, Magnificent Lord." It was an imp, one of the gods' lackeys. I had never seen one, but from their high voices, I had pictured them as runty little squeakers. My imagination had sure as hell failed on that point. This imp terrified me, but it was also kind of cute if you set aside the aura of menace and the bloody entrails stuck in its fur.

The imp let an enormous, wheezing sigh and trilled, "All right, don't run. You lot have been running away from me all day, and I'm sick of it. I'll catch you anyway, and you'll just die sweaty. I'm not going to tear you open, so that's good, right? One quick crunch, and you're lounging in the laps of the gods."

None of us ran, but I don't attribute that so much to courage as to stupefaction.

My horse had bucked and twisted toward the village and the imp, so the monster proceeded toward me first. I didn't see many soft places on it, so steel would make for a chancy attack. Along the magical line, I didn't know the beast's name, so I couldn't bind it.

The weather had turned poor, which was promising, but I'd need time to work up a good storm. One might think a storm too insubstantial to stop this creature, but when an entire thunderstorm is concentrated into a spot the size of a cheap brothel, not much can stand against it. Time was the problem, though.

"Everybody, run!" I shouted, sliding off my horse. He galloped away, and I'd probably never find him. "Damn it!"

"Damn it is right." The imp sighed. "Now I've got to make an example and pull you into tedious little pieces. I don't have time for this crap."

The imp swiped at me. I flung myself aside and rolled. Bratt ran past me, well-balanced, his sword poised for any one of six attacks.

"I always get the shit jobs." The creature slapped Bratt aside. The young man sailed thirty feet and bounced across the road, tumbling until he landed in a flaccid lump.

The imp wasn't too nimble, but it would have caught me with that swat if I'd still been all burned up. Then Bratt and I could have held hands as we strolled into the afterlife, although I'd never seen evidence that such a place was more than a half-assed fable the gods spread around. I ran away from the imp at an angle. With my new left hand, I started pulling white bands out of nothingness and whipping them into the sky. I spun, cut the other way, and drew my sword as the clouds began pulling together.

The imp stopped, regarded my sword, and cocked its head like a retriever, its floppy ears dangling uneven. "Way-Opener? Come on now. Did you plan this? Is this a trap? It can't be a pig-screwing, goddamned coincidence."

"You're right!" I'd have agreed with it even if it told me my nipples burned like stars as long as it stopped trying to hit us. "This is the Blade of . . . Awful Kindness, or whatever, I can never remember, the way-opening one. I bear it. You can see that I bear it, right here. This isn't a trap, or a coincidence."

"Not a trap?" The imp whiffed with its huge nose and then grunted. "What is it then?"

"I came here seeking you." The words leaped out of my mouth without thought.

The imp stuck out its jaw and squeaked, "Why?"

"Because . . . I heard you were here, and I want to hire you." This conversation was crumbling fast. I whipped another white band into the sky with a stirring motion.

The imp leaned in and cocked its head to stare at me with its big left eye. It gave me a slow blink with an eyelid that looked as armored as a crocodile. "Just how did you know I was here, Murderer? Yeah, I know your name, so don't try to bone me."

"You came from the Home of the Gods. You must already know how I knew you were here."

The beast snarled at me like a kitten that weighed a thousand pounds. "Are you trying to bone me? I said don't do that."

"Harik told me," I lied.

The imp squinted at me as if I had just tried to convince it that shit tastes like strawberries.

"He didn't exactly mention you by name," I held up one hand and smiled. "He said go east and I'd find something important. What could be more important than this?"

"Well . . . oh, screw it," the imp cheeped. "If I rubbed out the Way-Opener, Krak might fry me into a slick spot on the floor." It gestured around with its chin at the others, who had flanked me. "Got to kill all them, though. Chira's like a mad dog about tidiness lately. Disintegrated a unicorn for pissing upwind."

"You work for Chira, eh?"

"Uh-huh." The imp began stomping toward Cael, who was backing away.

"What's your errand? Maybe we can help you."

"I really shouldn't."

"Did you get specific instructions that you can't accept a little help?"

The imp smiled, and I realized that its mouth and teeth were just like a person's. "Not specifically, no." It stopped, opened its hand, and pulled out the wadded-up paper. It tried to smooth out the page using both palms, but it just tore the corner. "Got three more to go. Woman hit by lighting and lived, man who's licked beer off the floor, and woman who murdered her husband in his sleep.

Shit, do you believe these? I've already gathered the easy ones, like little girl afraid of the dark, and man who cheated on three wives."

I said, "Those shouldn't be too hard to find. Why does Chira want these people?"

"Do I look like some damned oracle? Reading the gods' minds? I can't always tell what Chira wants when she describes it to me—she's so divinely artful in her speech. Ought to hear her talk when she's drunk. Anyway, she doesn't want these people. Just the hearts." It reached into its jerkin and pulled out a bag leaking blood.

Ella stood off to my left. "I thought Chira was Goddess of Arts and the Forest. She who is known to be the tenderest and most humane of all the gods."

"Right. She's damned to dog shit proud of it too. Tortured more than one sorry imp for implying she's not the gentlest god of all."

I raised a fist. "We're agreed then. We'll help you find these individuals, and you won't kill any of us. How should I address you?"

"Dark."

"Dark?"

"Yes, Dark!" the creature insisted. "Aren't you a little scared? You should be scared. Men are scared of the dark, right? Dark thoughts, dark soul, all that." The imp's flop ears drooped a bit. "Am I wrong?"

"No, I'm scared," I said. I made my eyes big.

"Shit!" Dark kicked the ground, gouging out half a cartful of black soil. "Those maggot-screwing bastards back home! They said if I called myself . . . just wait till I get back!"

"We're all scared. Aren't we?" I glared over my shoulder at Cael and Larripet.

Larripet said, "I have already defecated because of my terror."

"Me too." Cael nodded.

Ella nodded along. "This is the most horrifying experience of my life."

"You dare to patronize me, the favored servant of Chira? I hate mankind! I wish you'd all die of a pestilence that makes things fall off you." Dark sighed again. "All right, deal's off. Shift yourself out of the way, Murderer. I'm going to take your friends' heads home with me, and you can be sure I'll tell Chira and Harik about your shitty attitude."

Like a toad from the guts of hell, the imp leaped fifty feet toward Cael. He ought to have been pulverized, but since he was an artist of a warrior, he leaped and simply got knocked aside by a glancing blow from Dark's elbow. He rolled ten feet through the grass and ended on his back, shaking his head. His sword had flown off in a different direction.

The cold wind arrived first, and the temperature dropped thirty degrees in two seconds. Dark stretched tall and glanced around, his gargantuan, open nostrils quivering. Then a throng of lightning bolts vaulted from cloud to cloud, throwing light that wiped out every shadow in sight. Half a second later, thunder smashed everyone flat to the ground, except for Dark and me.

I had coaxed out a nasty storm, but as a result, it wasn't too big, about a half mile across. As ridiculous as it sounds, I hadn't gotten to the hard part yet. As rain spilled out of the sky, I whipped another band up and created a sluice of wind that barraged Dark with all the water that would have been falling across the whole storm. It crushed the imp into the instantly muddy grass. Dark tried to crawl away, but I shifted the torrent to follow along wherever it dragged itself.

Just as the rain began to slack off, I sprinted to Dark with my sword ready. If its head resembled a man's, maybe it had the same weak spots. The imp was writhing on its belly, and I aimed for the base of its skull. Before I could strike, it rolled over and its hand threw me aside. It must have been unintentional, because when I stopped rolling, I wasn't dead. I lay on my side with nothing worse than a numb left arm.

I had used up the thunderstorm, and Dark wasn't likely to be distracted by amusing poetry or offers to surrender. The smart move was to grab Ella and Manon and then run while Dark was busy killing everybody else. That wasn't too promising, though. Cael and Larripet were on their feet and appeared ready to follow my lead, so if I ran, they'd run too. Ella wouldn't run if anybody else stayed. She hadn't yet learned the importance of strategic cowardice. And Dark could probably chase us all down in three minutes, anyway.

Dark had pushed up to its knees and was spitting mud. "That was just nasty," it trilled. "And insolent. After that, I think Krak might forgive me for killing you, Murderer."

I didn't think before I did it, which was fortunate. If I had thought about it, I would have hesitated and probably died. I jumped up, ran to the imp's back, and stabbed it in the base of the skull with all my strength. It was like stabbing an anvil. No, it was like stabbing a divine anvil forged by the gods. I expect the only reason my sword didn't break, along with my arm, is that it was forged by some god somewhere too. My entire body shivered, and I staggered back.

Dark laughed and stood up. Larripet ran around in front of the imp, dodged its clawed swipe, and broke his spear over the monster's head. He danced backward straight away from it, making horrible faces and yelling in his language.

The imp stepped toward Larripet and leaned forward to grab him, but the Hill Man threw himself backward onto the grass. Dark's stubby tail had lifted for balance, and I saw that even imps must eat. I stabbed it directly in the asshole with as much force as I could gather. It was like stabbing a knothole in an oak tree, and it didn't enter far. Dark froze, hissing. Ella jumped in, grabbed my sword's hilt with me, and we both threw our weight into it. We deepened the wound a hand's width.

"This is just too goddamned much." Dark's outraged voice hummed like a dragonfly's wings. "The lack of respect. Indignity. In the old days, men were brave and obedient and didn't make us run or get stabbed in the ass to kill them."

Dark spun on one leg, flinging Ella and me twenty feet across the grass and leaving my sword sticking out of its bottom. I got to my hands and knees, but Dark snatched me up in its monstrous left hand. The imp used the claw on its right forefinger tamp my arms down to my sides and then tightened its grip. I could breathe, but I couldn't move.

"I don't have time to screw around with you, but I don't want to get bitched out for killing you. But I will kill you if you're too annoying, so shut up." Dark glared at Ella and the rest. "Go away! Leave me alone, or I'll squish him! Then I'll squish you too. Go off and . . . farm something, or whatever you men do."

Dark sprinted east down the road, as fast as any horse I'd ever ridden, holding me tight in its swinging left hand. "Damn, it's cold. I don't want to dick around with this job all night."

"I can still help you," I sputtered as Dark held me tight in its fist as it ran.

Dark laughed. "Right, stab me in a tender place and then offer to help me. Harik is right—you are stupid."

"That attack was a sign of respect," I choked out.

The imp squeezed me until I gurgled.

The setting sun stood not far above the horizon when Dark arrived at the next village. He had loosened his grip just a sliver, and I used the slack to pull half a dozen white bands. If the imp didn't like cold, then I'd give it some cold. Dark walked in among the houses, paper in its hand, peering at people as they ran around shrieking and crying.

"Damn you to Lutigan's horrid armpit. This is a lot easier with two hands." Dark put away the paper in his right hand, knocked down two houses, and pulled out the paper again to squint at it. The imp used its left hand to swat a man, sending the fellow flying after banging my legs into him. I almost lost my concentration.

Dark stomped a man trying to hit it with a club, jumped twenty feet to crush a woman, and bounded the other way to smash another woman flat. "Ha! Pretty good, huh? Look! Look!" Dark's voice went even higher, and it sounded like a babbling mouse. It ran halfway across the village, knocked a man down, and said, "You licked beer off the floor! Good boy!"

I yanked a ferocious shaft of freezing air down over Dark and me. I figured the imp might be sensitive to cold, since it lived in the warm, tender Home of the Gods, and it had mentioned not liking the cold. When the frigid blast hit, I could barely stand it and I hoped Dark liked it even less.

Dark went rigid and stood up straight. "Shithead." It bent again and used one claw to rip open the man's chest. Then Dark used only its right hand to go through the process of pulling out the heart, examining it, laying it on the ground, pulling out the sack, laying that on the ground, shoving the heart inside it, picking up the sack, and putting the sack away. It cursed me throughout the whole procedure.

"What a pain in the ass. I hate you so much," Dark trilled.

I couldn't feel my face or ears, and my feet weren't much better. "Just let me go then. I can't follow you to your next gut-flinging party."

Dark kicked at a running woman but missed. "Shit! I can't just let you go after I made such a noise about keeping you till I'm done. How would it look? I'd get laughed at."

"We could make a trade."

Dark held me up in front of its face and laughed at me. The miasma that flowed out of its mouth made me light-headed. "Sorcerers and your trades. I'd rather listen to your boring-as-hell life story."

"Wait! Harik loaned me one of his books, and it's just spilling over with god-magic. He's letting me read out of it three times. Just three, and I haven't even read out of it at all yet. Let me go, with my sword, and you can read one page out of Harik's tome before I do."

Dark stopped. Most of the screaming had stopped too. "It's probably a trap. I'll bet the book's supposed to kill you, or make your dick fall off."

"It won't do anything like that. I'm the Way-Opener, and Harik's got plans for me. And why would he say I can read from it three times if the first one will annihilate me?"

"Shut up," it tweeted.

I knew a sum total of nothing about the book. It might turn Dark inside out, or it might make the imp more powerful than Krak. It might rain fire and acid down on everything within a hundred miles. Or maybe the book wouldn't do much. I didn't know about any of that. I did know that I would never get a better chance to make some useless idiot test the book before I read it.

"When's the last time a god gave you a treat?" I asked. "Sorcerers get all the attention. You and your kind get to shovel shit and have new weapons tested on you. Come on."

"Well . . . where is this book?" Dark demanded.

"I can get it." I could move only my head, so I nodded like hell.

The imp grumbled in its tiny voice. "I really shouldn't."

"If the book's a big disappointment, you can just grab me up again. I can't outrun you."

Dark cocked its head and squinted. Its floppy ears made it look like a great, homicidal puppy. "All right. Where's this book?"

"Let me go." Dark opened its hand, and I plopped out. I felt up and down my body, but nothing seemed broken. "And my sword."

Dark bent forward. "No cute moves back there. Not even Krak would blame me if I tore you into a hundred bits."

I had to put my foot against Dark's backside and lever the sword up and down to get it out. I sheathed it and pulled the book out of the new, Hutch-made pouch hanging from my neck inside my shirt. "Here, thrill yourself."

"Damn, it's itty-bitty." Dark took the book between two claws and sniffed at Harik's mark. "It's real. I can feel it." The imp sat on the ground, hunched over the book, and eased it open. "What the hell? Are you trying to screw me?"

I raised both hands. "Wait! It may take a minute for the god-magic to get wound up." I started planning my next move in case the book did nothing. My next move would almost certainly start with Dark snatching me again like an apple off the kitchen table.

Just then, a girl popped into existence right in front of Dark. She was older than Manon, maybe fifteen, and she wore her black hair in a long braid. Her strong jaw and wide forehead made her striking rather than pretty. She glowed softly in the twilight.

Dark leaned forward and squinted at her. "Well, I didn't expect that. Who is she? Who are you, girl? Did you kill your husband in his sleep? That would be pretty damn convenient for me."

The girl looked Dark up and down, but she didn't say anything.

"Talk, bitch! I asked you questions." When the girl didn't answer, Dark reached out to grab her, but the imp's hand went right through her. "Nothing but pictures. I'm not thrilled so far, Murderer."

I ignored Dark and scrutinized the image of the girl, but none of this made a bit of sense to me. She didn't resemble anybody I had ever known.

Dark stopped complaining for a moment and stared at the girl. It leaned even closer to her and cocked its head. After a few seconds, the imp leaned back and scooted away. Dark dropped the book and jumped up, still staring at the image. It shuffled back a few feet.

The girl took a step toward Dark. It turned and ran like hell, and the girl chased it. Dark swept its arm aside like it was ripping away a curtain, and an imp-size hole appeared from nowhere. I saw trees on the other side of the hole. Dark sprinted through the hole, and the girl ran through right behind it. Then the hole disappeared like a popping soap bubble.

I wished that somebody else had seen that too. Then we could have commiserated over how stupid we were and how little we understood what the hell had just happened. I started walking back up the road toward Ella and the others.

The moon was setting when I met them coming up the road toward me at a trot. I got hugs from Manon and Ella, and Cael wanted me to explain the tactical details of my escape. I ignored the oaf. Larripet stood holding the reins of Cael's horse, which carried Bratt's body.

Cael and I pulled Bratt down and laid him beside the road.

"He has gone." Larripet knelt over the young man. "Ir-man, can you bring him back?"

I knelt to examine Bratt. His big chest was shattered, and his neck had been split open. I gave Larripet a slow nod. "I'm sorry. I can't help him."

The Hill Man sat on the ground beside the corpse.

"I brought a shovel from the ruins of that village." Ella held up the tool.

Larripet made a keening sound. I assumed he was singing, since he changed pitch and threw in a strange word once in a while, but

I'd have rather listened to rats being killed. The rest of us stood some distance away and watched.

After half an hour, Larripet walked back to the road. "Bratt was unlucky. I do not relish making a song in which a monster is stabbed in the anus. My people will not think that song is noble. My brother will hate it a lot." He didn't sound upset, and I wouldn't have known the man was sad except for all the tears on his face.

"Larripet, would you like to dig the grave?" Cael asked.

"No. I would not like to go back and chop down that tree or repair those houses, either."

EIGHTEEN

We reached the town of Crakmere the next afternoon and rented rooms to get a few hours of sleep in something that resembled a bed. Ella and I had skirted Crakmere on our trip west to Ir. Ella had been anxious to reach our new home and hadn't cared to stop in the town. To me, it had looked like a coma with gutters. The dingy, open township housed six or seven hundred people in the middle of farms a mile deep, and it was about as defensible as a basket of laundry. It was not a smart place to hide from Agni and his crazy people.

The smell of cheap, greasy candles and damp wood reminded me of waiting with my mother for my father to sail home at night. I smelled a load of dust too, which she would not have tolerated for a minute. The mattress scratched my skin and mashed lumps into my back, but compared to sleeping on the damp ground, it felt like a picnic in the Gossamer Forest. Or, what I imagined the forest was like. Fingit had described it to me once while I was waiting around for Gorlana to get done ignoring me. The forest got more enthralling and magical as he got drunker and weepier.

I opened my eyes and saw Ella standing beside the bed, peering down. "You look like hell."

"Stop watching me. It's not like I'm going to hatch or anything."

"Everyone has already arisen and prepared themselves for our journey. Old man."

"If we had time, I'd make you take that back," I grumbled.

"Get up. Cael has purchased more horses and additional provisions."

I swung my legs over and sat up, knocking Pudge onto the floor. Manon, Violet, and Pokey were sleeping in a pile in the corner, along with a new furry monster of a hound she must have picked up in the last few hours. The new dog raised its head, yawned at me, and settled back down on Manon's knee. I roused Manon and her kids, and she introduced me to the new dog, Ribbon, which was at least half wolf.

"Let's go find everybody. I expect Cael bought a nag with a bony back for me, and I'll need to make him trade." I shooed Manon and her dogs out ahead of me into a high corridor, in which I drew in the first wholesome-smelling air I'd breathed in hours.

With a little regret, I grabbed Ella's hand and pulled her back into the room. "Come on—it's time."

"Stop it! This isn't the time for that sort of fun."

"I sure wish it was, but you're right." I closed the door behind us and pulled out Harik's book. "It's time for this. We need to get started, and this place sort of resembles a sheltered spot. Tomorrow, we'll be in those damned hills."

"Very well. How should we do this?" Ella scanned the room as if there might be hidden guidance on magic books if she could find the proper cupboard.

"I've given this quite a lot of thought, and I don't know. I suppose we'll hold the book somehow and open it. And read."

"Aloud?" Ella sounded a little impatient.

"Sure, that makes sense."

"You are the sorcerer in this room. Surely you can provide a sliver of guidance!"

"Well . . . Harik knows me, and he'll assume that I will decide how to read the book. Makes sense?" I raised my eyebrows at her, and she nodded. "If the thing is trapped, it's probably designed to cater to my habits. So, you choose. I don't want to sway you."

"Fine." Ella lifted the book out of my hands and closed her eyes for a moment. "Here, hold the back cover, and I will hold the front. I shall open it to a random page. Then we will read that page aloud, together."

We opened the book, and I spotted the page number—twenty-four. I said, "Oh, hell," before either of us began to read. Twenty-four was a quite unpromising number.

The page was naked of words, but it held the image of a light-house in the middle. The lighthouse was built of smooth, gray stones, and it stood on a slick rock high above the ocean. The waves were running rough. I could tell because I saw them moving. My viewpoint twisted, and it seemed as if I were looking out of a window onto a real place.

"Are we supposed to say anything?" Ella whispered.

A dazzling light blinded me, and not just for a second. Ella yelped, so I figured it had blinded her too. I would have thought that Krak had hit me with the impossibly searing light of the sun, except that the top half of my body still existed.

I slapped the book closed, but my eyesight didn't come back.

"What happened?" Ella yelled.

"I think I made a really bad deal with Harik." I started rubbing my eyes with my shirt sleeve. I heard Ella patting the wall until she found the door and pulled it open. I said, "Wait, I have a lot of experience at being blind. Let's stop for a second and think."

My vision cleared between one blink and the next. Ella turned in the doorway, and I gaped at her. A thick column of brilliant white light began just above her head and rose all the way to the ceiling. She pointed at the ceiling above me. An identical column of light stretched up over me.

"Come with me." Ella beckoned and ran down the hallway. The light moved with her, staying just over her head. I stowed the book and followed her. The house's common room had nice, tall ceilings, and our lights shot all the way up to them. We ran into the street and stared up.

The columns of light stretched into the sky as far as I could see.

"Krak! What have you done to yourselves?" Cael said, staring into the sky. "I admire the artistry, but it's damned obtrusive!"

Larripet turned away from us and shook his head.

Cael sounded aggravated. "If you're inviting every villain and predator in this land to come fight you, then this is good."

"This was not a purposeful act!" Ella whined. I almost never heard her whine.

"Maybe I can fix it." Manon raised her hands.

"No!" I yelled. "Leave it alone. We can't get rid of these things anyway. They're divine magic. We'll just have to ride fast and hope they go away."

"Perhaps we ought to ride fast and pray." Cael mounted.

I loaded my voice with sarcasm. "You go ahead and do that. While you're talking to Harik, tell him he's an infected walrus tit. Which horse did you get for me?"

Cael pointed, and I jumped up into the saddle.

From down the street toward the center of town, a man yelled, "There it is! Stop them!"

Other people yelled too, inviting us to dismount and get murdered, most likely. I kicked my horse and galloped out of town, not paying much attention to whether anybody was riding along with me.

I dismissed any notions of using trickery to escape, since unending pillars of light marked Ella and me as visible to all creation. That might have been an embellishment, but a little exaggeration didn't amount to much after your enemies have tracked you down and slaughtered you. I galloped my horse straight down the road, around the Tik Lake and east toward the hills. The others rode after me, even Larripet. Although he preferred to walk, on foot he would lag and might never see us again.

The temple on Barrelshins was really a fortress on top of Barrelshins Hill. We might reach it by midday if we rode hard enough to kill all our horses, but if I lost another horse that week, the universe might never give me a horse again. I hoped to prevent that by keeping the horses we had alive. Besides, once my fear and outrage had faded, I saw no pursuit.

Ella rode next to me. I shouted, "I wish you'd bought a spare horse for each of us!"

She made a nasty face at me.

After two hours of hard riding, we slowed to a walk so the horses could rest a few minutes. Before I could yell at Ella some more about not having spare horses, a doe bounded out of the darkness into the considerable area of light around us. It ran up next to my horse and began pacing me. Several more deer jumped into the light to join our group, and then rabbits and ground squirrels started arriving too. By the time we had amassed a hundred or so rabbits and squirrels, prairie dogs and rats began scurrying out of the darkness.

"Are you doing this?" Ella called out to me.

I shook my head.

"Well, we have become amazingly popular on the plains."

I kept shaking my head. "I've never seen this before, or anything like it."

From farther back, Larripet called, "Other animals want to eat these animals. We are lucky. No one wants to eat us."

"That makes a sort of sense." Manon made kissing sounds at her dogs, which were growling and turning in circles.

"They just want to kill us," Larripet added.

"It does not make sense!" I shouted. "Even if Larripet is right, and maybe he is, the best we can say is that it's predictable. I won't allow that it makes sense. The gods always just love for us mortal men to drive ourselves crazy trying to make sense of what they do. They laugh at us and bet on which of us will think up the most ridiculous theory."

Cael snorted. "That's an entertaining idea, but you can't know that."

"Gorlana accused Fingit of cheating at that very game while I was right there listening."

"Will I get to hear Gorlana's voice too?" Manon asked in a hopeful little voice.

"I regret that it is likely. She likes to be flattered and she loves gossip. Remember that."

Our horses began snorting and stamping. A moment later, a plains lion sprinted out of the darkness and leaped on a deer walking beside Ella. The deer screamed, and almost every animal bolted. Our horses began sidestepping, eyes rolling. Manon's dogs just watched the lion break the deer's neck. Then an assault of minor predators raced in: foxes, wild dogs, ferrets, bobcats, plus two more plains lions. They knocked down their prey, broke necks, and tore out throats in a symphony of growls and shrieks. Even Manon's dogs joined in.

I stared at the gory spectacle, and I guess everybody else did too. The lucky creatures that hadn't died right away ran until they reached the edge of the light, turned around, and ran back in. The light had become a ring of butchery, which sounded like the sort of thing Harik would enjoy.

I kicked my horse and shouted at the others to follow me. We galloped away down the hillside and left the carnage behind in a few seconds. Maybe those tasty animals would be free to run off and hide once we moved on. Maybe not. Harik knew, but I didn't care to ask.

Nobody commented on those events as we rode away. I suppose once they had accepted two limitless pillars of light as part of the landscape for a couple of hours, it was easy to accept other crazy things and move on. We did slow down a bit so we could avoid exhausting the horses, but we rode fast enough to outpace bunnies and rats. Cael complained that we were losing ground, but he didn't do anything about it besides talk.

The sun arrived, and our columns of light persisted. I could still see them just fine. They seemed even brighter.

Well into the morning, Ella shouted at me, "We're riding north-east now. I believe we should arrive at the temple before nightfall."

"That sounds right," I yelled back. "The temple's beer tastes like it dripped off a cow's lips. It's a good place to hide from insane killers, though."

Ella urged her horse closer to me, and we slowed to a trot. "Bib, when we arrive, you will have honored your agreement. You need not travel any farther east."

"Cael may think differently."

"I mean you needn't travel farther because of me." She near whispered it. I could hardly hear her.

"I know what you mean. What do you want me to do?"

She glimpsed down at her saddle as if it might be slipping. Or, maybe she was using that second to decide whether she still wanted me. "Do whatever you wish."

"Oh, hell!" I shouted up at the sky. "Now I have to figure out what you want me to do and not do the wrong thing. Shit!"

"Your lovemaking is slow and boring," Larripet said from behind us. "If I were that boring, my wife would stab me and I would not have eleven children."

"We can't all be like you, Larripet," I said over my shoulder. "You're a hell of a man. I bet you'd make a fine god."

"I know that you have just insulted me. I should kill you now, but we are in danger. If there is a fight, some person who tries to kill me might kill you instead. I will accept your insult. Besides, this is a new thing. I have never before been insulted by a man who has a penis like a grape and testicles like raisins."

"I saw something!" Cael called out from the rear. I reined in and trotted back to where he had stopped, just below the crest of the hill.

"What is it?" Ella shaded her eyes and peered along with us.

"A stellar reason to ride faster—that's what it is!" Cael snapped.

We waited for ten seconds, and then twenty.

"Why are we waiting here? We should keep running!" Manon called out.

"Not until we know more about what's chasing us," I said.

"There." Cael pointed. The pursuers lagged three hilltops behind us and were almost too small to see. "I count twenty mounted men."

"Twenty-two." I glanced at Cael. "Don't kick yourself, Cael. You can't be the best at everything."

Rabbits began hopping toward us from out of the grass and

behind the brush. The lights still stretched up from above our heads. We turned east and kept riding as fast as we thought our horses could bear.

"Do you have magic to stop them?" Larripet yelled from behind me. "I think a million grasshoppers would be useful."

"I'll hold that idea as a possibility in case they overtake us."

We kept our lead until midday, but as our horses started blowing harder, our pursuers shrank the gap. They had closed to within two hills of us, and by midafternoon, they were no more than one hill behind.

I topped a little rise and almost ran into a horse with two riders, along with a man on foot. I shouted, "You should leave this road. Some furious and determined people will be here in a few minutes. They might kill you just for standing in their way."

"Help us!" The man held up both hands, and they were huge, like a blacksmith's. His hair had gone a bit gray, but his chest seemed as broad as a rowboat. He panted hard, and so did his horse, which carried a woman of middle years and a teenage boy. The man pointed south. "We've been chased all the way from Paster by these . . . Agni people."

"Why are we stopping?" Cael rode up next to me and scowled.

I ignored him. "Answer quick and clear, or you'll regret it. Why are they chasing you, how many are there, and why haven't they caught you yet?"

"There's a dozen of them afoot, sir," the man said. "Maybe more. Save us! We saw your signal!"

"What did you do to get chased?"

"Well, it's hard to explain." He stared back in the direction he'd pointed, but I didn't see anything peculiar.

Cael dismounted, grabbed the man's shirt, and shook him.

The man gasped. "They think Anna and Zeb are sorcerers. They killed two girls for the same—killed right in front of the whole town. We just ran."

We didn't have time to pause so I could stare into their eyes and find out whether Anna and Zeb really had any power.

"We cannot leave them here," Ella said.

Cael pushed the man away. "Their mount is worn down! I feel sorry for them, but we'll be overtaken if we try to bring them with us."

Ella scanned us all with narrowed eyes. "Perhaps not. This man can ride their horse while Anna shares with Manon, and Zeb rides with Larripet, who is not terribly heavy. Hurry, change mounts!"

Cael drew a knife and stabbed the newcomers' horse in the neck. It screamed and fell sideways, throwing Anna and Zeb to the ground. He ignored the yelling from Ella and Manon, and he remounted. "Our enemies are gaining ground, so let's go."

"No, you can still take Anna and Zeb!" the man shouted. "You promised to save us. We saw the signal!"

I shook my head at the fellow. "I'd remember promising such a thing, and I don't."

The man pointed at the column of light over me. "You called, and we came. You promised."

Cael rode his horse between the fleeing people and the rest of us. "Enough! I will not allow us to be caught! If you don't start riding, I'll kill all three of them. Then no one will need to worry about who promised to save whom."

The weeping woman ran around Cael and reached out to Ella. "Take Zeb at least! Him and the girl together don't weigh as much as this murderer."

Ella pointed at the boy. "Ride with the girl. Hurry!" She glared at Cael.

"Fine! Just ride." Once Zeb had mounted, Cael led us at a gallop down the road toward the Barrelshins.

"Run away from this road!" Ella yelled back at the man and the woman. "I'm sorry we couldn't save you all."

I felt a little sorry for them too. They hadn't hurt anybody that I knew of, and they deserved help as much as any other people. Which is to say they didn't deserve much help, but they deserved it a hell of a lot more than I might deserve help with anything at all. Maybe I could have stopped Cael, but didn't know he'd get all overcome with duty and act belligerent. Even if I had known, he might have brushed me aside like a boy. He might have wounded me, or even killed me since he was in such a blazing hurry.

Of course, Cael was right. We'd have been caught, and I would've have used up power that I couldn't afford to squander, and some of us might have died anyway. If I were to be honest, that's why I didn't even raise my voice to him.

But his behavior reminded me that he didn't care about anything except getting me to Bellmeet. Anybody standing in his way could get tortured, murdered, and sent to hell as far as he was concerned. He had fooled me with his "Cael the Friendly Hero" street theater, but I needed an unfailing plan to kill the heartless sack of shit the next time we were alone together.

By midafternoon, I could make out our pursuers' plain, ragged shirts and see that two of them had blond hair. Our horses poured sweat, and they blew like whales. I began preparing to throw out some magic, maybe work up a flash flood when they rode between hills, or I could make half of their horses start kicking the other half. Any of that would take a fair amount of power, but I was holding enough.

"There it is!" Cael pointed as we topped a hill and the temple came into view.

Priests, monks, nuns, and sorcerers had built the temple 330 years before. It had been a bloodthirsty and fractious time, so they had built it high on Barrelshins Hill, with tall, monstrous stone walls, a huge courtyard, and its own water supply. A narrow road wound up Barrelshins, most of it exposed to arrow-fire from the temple walls. It had never been taken by force, although it had been starved out once.

We galloped to the foot of Barrelshins, with the crazy riders not much over four bowshots behind us. The road up forced us to trot two abreast, and they nearly snatched Larripet before the first arrows zipped over our heads. They didn't hit any riders, but they did cool the pursuit admirably. Our enemies trotted back down the hill and gathered at the bottom. I imagine they were talking about what bastards we were for getting away.

The temple lacked a proper castle's massive gate and portcullis.

A monk stood at a side door into the courtyard, staring up at our pillars of light. Finally, he led us inside without commenting. Zeb followed along, as stunned as if he'd been beaten for ten minutes.

Red Sam, a graying, chubby priest in work clothes, peered down from a peach tree. "Bib! By Harik and Trutch and their vengeful marriage, what is that light over you? Well, it's magic, of course, but what does it do? Seems inconvenient in the extreme."

"A gift from the gods." I dismounted. "I guess they didn't give you one. You must not be one of the favored this week."

Sam chuckled and climbed down the ladder. "Interesting that you've come back just now. I mean, right now. Anytime, I mean, really, welcome. Relax, we'll care for your horses, what's left of your horses. Poor things. Come ahead, refresh yourselves over there, in that door to the dining room. You remember." He ushered the others toward an open door, but he touched my arm. "Bib, wait." Sam cleared his throat. "When you've tossed a beer or two, Her Grace wants to see you."

I grimaced. "That's awfully damn sweet of her. How did the old lady know I was coming?"

"Ah, well, she doesn't drink tea and whisper secrets with me. But she knew last night. It didn't seem to make her happy, either. Be . . . well, you know, she's . . ." He shrugged and pursed his lips.

"She's a cast-iron bitch."

"Yes! And the names she called you . . ."

NINETEEN

I have rarely met a priest I didn't want to slap. Some were nice people, and some were repugnant, but too many of them were idiots. Most got offended if I didn't agree to follow them around and act like an idiot too. They spent their days and nights worshiping when they could have been drinking and chasing women . . . or men. Or, if they really aspired to be wholesome and good, they could play with their kids and gossip with their neighbors.

I have never met a sorcerer who worshiped the gods. Five minutes of conversation with a god will convince anybody that the gods are not beings to worship. They are beings to keep a close watch on if you're carrying anything valuable. If some benevolent entities created us and love us, Krak and his brood are not them.

Priests talk to gods, but they never get a direct answer. Sorcerers have actual conversations with gods, and if every sorcerer has a low opinion of the gods, priests should think hard about whether any worshiping should happen.

Nothing sorcerers ever say to priests matters. They go on worshiping gods the way Manon's hounds worshiped her.

A young monk met me in the stone dining room, empty except

for my companions. Another monk was bringing bread, cheese, and pitchers of awful beer to the long, scarred tables. Two hours later, everyone and their chubby bellies dozed on benches, except for me. I eased myself off the bench and took a step toward Cael. He opened one eye and watched me until I sat back down.

Red Sam opened the door, leaned in, and whispered, "Bib, it's time." He grinned and shrugged.

I trailed Sam across the courtyard, the tiny orchard, and through another door. We walked into a stone corridor that must normally be dim and sad, but light showered down on me from Harik's aggravating gift.

Sam smiled back at me. "Thanks for the light, Bib. Helpful, really. I hate those goddamned candles! Sorry. Blow out all the time . . . no oil for us priests, though. Sad. Come on." He led me through a minor canal of moist corridor, through turns, up steps, and down ramps. At last, we wandered into a large room that was bright with windows and lamps. I detested rooms like this one, with religious tapestries, lots of hard furniture, and a well-organized desk in the corner. The twelve guards with drawn swords didn't charm me, either.

Sam bowed. "Your Grace."

Marta, the temple priestess, sat writing at the desk. A black quill held her graying hair in a bun. She waved at Sam without looking up, giving him leave to go. He went. She scratched a few more words with a different quill, and laid it in a box that was just the right size to have been made for that purpose. She stood and smoothed her gray skirt, then stretched her back while she scruti-nized at me. She squinted for a few seconds at the light rising from me to the ceiling. Then she grunted and ignored it.

I had met Marta on my trip out to Ir. We had stayed at the temple for two days, and Marta had allowed me a couple of curt conversations. She'd granted us permission to come calling at the temple again some time, though.

I smiled and even insinuated a bow. "Hello, Your Grace. Thank you for saving our lives. That was nice of you."

Marta grimaced. "Bib, you have caused a lot of trouble. I mean serious trouble. A lot of people have died, and a lot more are now ruined. You're a sorcerer, that's true. But if I give the command for you to die here, you will die." She crossed her arms. "I think I should kill you right now. Is there any reason I shouldn't?"

That was a disappointment. "I'm serving the gods right now, Your Grace, so you should wait to kill me until I get done with that." That was stretching the truth, but I did owe Harik two more book readings and some unknown quantity of murders. And there was the minor task of continuing to ride around opening the way for the gods wherever I took the sword.

"The gods all hate you. Well, some just dislike you. I read the portents—don't think that I don't. Your death wouldn't grieve them. They might even hold a party."

"It's a good thing I'm on my way to make right all the things I've done wrong."

She took a step toward me. "Which things?"

"All the ones you're talking about. And if you want to mention a few more, I'll make them right too."

"You're known to be a liar. You're lying to me now." She grimaced as if I smelled like something under the privy.

"If I'm going to get killed, you'll be the first one I take with me. And that is not a lie." I took a lazy step around a chair so I could kill her in two steps if I needed to.

"It might be worth it . . . you may be the worst criminal in my lifetime."

"I am not the worst!" That hurt my feelings a bit. Then I jerked when I realized maybe she was right.

"How many men and women have you murdered? Not killed—just murdered straight out? You could have walked away. Dozens? Hundreds?"

That hit me pretty hard. "I admit that you're right, I've done that. Harik commanded it, but I agreed to the bargain . . . and I enjoyed doing it."

"You see? And now this opening of the veil between the gods-

and-us business? You've made a mess of it. Things disintegrating, houses burning, and people walking off into wells. You deserve to die. But . . . maybe you can help us repair things. How can we close the way? Restore the veil between the gods and us? You screwed it up. You must know how to put it back."

"I don't know a damn thing about it. Krak said to take this sword and ride around with it, so that's what I'm doing. Register your complaint with him."

Marta narrowed her eyes at the sword on my belt. "It's the sword? Really?"

I realized that maybe I shouldn't have shared that information. "Sort of. It's complicated."

"I thought it might be the sword. Well, I don't need you anymore then." She nodded at the guards. All of them stepped toward me.

"Wait!" I pulled out Harik's book and held it up. "This can destroy you all. Everything on this hill! Vaporized."

Everybody stopped. Marta said, "That sounds like another lie."

It probably was a lie, but she didn't know that for sure, and neither did I. "It put this dumbass beacon of light over my head. It can do just about anything." I turned the book so she could see Harik's mark.

She stepped back and inclined her head. "All right. I'd hate for you to destroy the temple. Let's discuss it. Sit down." She pointed at one of the chairs around a huge oak table.

"That's damned kind of you, but I think I'll stand here with both hands on this tome of unfathomable destruction. And what did you mean about people walking into wells?"

Marta shrugged and glanced down at her empty hands. "That's one of Agni's rallying cries. It speaks of the thousands you have made suffer."

I stepped toward Marta and yelled, "Who the hell is Agni, anyhow? Where can I find him? Can we buy him off?"

The guards fidgeted, but none of them came at me.

Marta walked around her desk and sat down. "If I tell you what I know, will you sit down and talk?"

"Sure. After you're done."

Marta leaned back in her chair. "Agni doesn't care about Bib the man, only about the way-opener—which you happen to be. But now I see that what she really wants is the sword."

"Agni's a woman?"

Marta nodded. "Gossip says that the gods came through the veil you opened and turned one of her neighbors into a demon. It made her children and husband all walk into the well and drown. In the same afternoon. Everybody thought she killed them, and they punished her."

"That's an awful tale."

"Isn't it? She decided to stop all this, and other suffering people joined her. Hundreds of them. Maybe thousands, I don't know. She's just a farmer's wife—I don't know how she does it. Maybe when she kills you, she'll be done. Probably not, if it's the sword, though."

"If she wants to rest, why the hell is she killing people all over the countryside instead of just me?"

Marta sighed. "Maybe those hundreds of people who follow her think the problem is bigger than just you. Marta slammed her palm against the desk. Now, sit down!"

"These are terrible things," I said, "and I wish the gods weren't using me to do them. But the gods are using you and Agni and all her people too. They want all of this to happen. Killing me won't stop it."

"Let's find out. Kill him."

The guards all stepped toward me again. I jumped up on the chair and then onto the middle of the massive table, pulling a red band out of the air at the same time. I knelt and slammed my palm against the tabletop. Nothing happened for a beat, and then the table exploded out toward all the walls.

It was an appalling waste of power. Dead wood wants to rot, and just a little power is needed to urge it along to rot fast. Dead wood does not want in any way to explode. The pressure required is outrageous. But I could no more kill twelve armed men with my sword than I could hammer out a horseshoe with my face, and I preferred not to be slain that day.

When the table exploded, I dropped straight to the ground and scanned the room. The big flying splinters had smashed every window and shattered every lantern. Two tapestries had started smoldering. The concussion had hurled ten guards against the paneled walls, and most of them lay still on the stone floor with giant splinters sticking out of them. Another guard was struggling not to fall through a window, and the last one was coming fast to chop off my head. I didn't see Marta and didn't have time to search for her.

I slipped past the running guard's sword and stabbed him under the arm and into his heart. The guard who was climbing back in the window never made it. I thrust into his belly and shoved him out. I trotted around the room to the guards who were still moving and cut each throat with a neat slice.

Then I looked toward the corner for Marta. I flinched when Ona stood up from behind the desk, bloody and wincing with two deep cuts on her crippled, broken arm. Gaudy strips of shredded cloth stuck to the blood around one of the cuts, and I recognized what remained of a magical disguise torn up and ruined by a splinter.

Ona looked damn good for a woman who had been just about decapitated a few days ago. I paused to let my mind catch up. Well, she had disguised herself as Marta today, and probably killed the priestess. Ona could have killed that poor woman in Parhold and disguised the corpse to look like herself so we'd think she was dead. Why would she do that?

While my brain bumbled, Ona threw herself out the window, a ten-foot drop. I ran to the window and saw Ona sprinting toward the road down the hill, holding her broken arm with her good hand.

"Agni!" I shouted.

Without even peeking back at me, she raised her good arm in an obscene gesture. Her wounded arm dangled for a moment, and she stumbled but picked up her stride again right away.

Before I could jump through the window, I heard the far-off

clank weapons behind me. I ran back to the door to the room. Distant shouts and the sounds of fighting echoed out of the hallway. Ella yelled for me, or maybe I imagined it. I turned my back on Agni and sprinted back down the twisting corridor that would take me back to the courtyard. When I reached the courtyard door, I heard fighting just on the other side.

I decided not to charge out into the yard to get cut in half by somebody sneaky. Instead, I cracked open the door and peeked out. Nearly thirty of Agni's nasty followers were pressing Cael, Ella, Larripet, Manon, and her dogs into a cut-off corner of the courtyard. Even counting the dogs, the crazy people outnumbered my friends more than three to one.

A few zealots already lay in the dirt bleeding. I saw Cael kill one and spin to hamstring another. Larripet jumped around like a flea, stabbing with Bratt's dagger and then rushing somewhere else. Ella was being pressed hard but didn't seem hurt. Manon appeared a little dazed, but her dogs were protecting her, snarling and biting. I saw a man hit Violet with a heavy club, and she yelped as she fell over.

I helped Ella first. It wasn't because she was in the most desperate situation. It was because I would kill every other creature in the courtyard to keep her alive. I slaughtered two men in two seconds from behind, and she killed a third. A man charged in from the side and hurled Ella to the ground, and three others almost overran us, but I held until she got to her feet. We took small cuts and blows, but we began rolling up the line of enemies toward Cael and Larripet.

I glanced at Manon just as a woman thrust a spear into Ribbon, her last defender. The woman aimed at Manon, with three men running toward Manon from the other side.

"Manon, run to me!" I shouted.

Manon did not run to me. She screamed, and all four of her attackers shouted, stopped short, and began writhing. They fell down, wriggling and straining in silence, weapons dropped, grabbing at their belts. Within a few more seconds, each of them broke in half at the waist with a pop, blood splashing as the upper body fell away from the lower.

Cael killed the last of the fanatics. Everybody had taken quite a few cuts and bruises, and Ella sported what would probably be a spectacular bruise on her butt. All of Manon's dogs were alive, but none of them could survive. Pudge's back was broken, and Ribbon was oozing blood where he'd been stabbed. Manon was running from one to the next, petting them and weeping. Pudge dragged herself toward Manon using just her front legs.

"Manon, maybe you can heal them," I said. "I'll help you."

She rubbed at her face, which didn't help. "I think I just used my last power."

I did not choose that moment to lecture her on power conservation. "Maybe you can trade for some more. Let's go talk to your mother." I lifted us and called for Sakaj. Then Manon called for Sakaj. Then the two of us together called. Sakaj decided not to answer us.

"Maybe I can do something." I lifted myself and called for Harik. It was stupid to trade for power, to trade away something I might regret losing, just to heal some dogs. I called for Harik anyway, but he ignored me.

I had a little power left. Healing dogs would be ridiculous when later I might need to heal people. Hell, that power might be needed to save *my* life. Healing dogs was not how I lived to become so mature. But I couldn't stand there and do nothing. Manon was lying on the ground hugging Violet, stretching her other arm out to let Pudge lick her hand. I remembered how my little girl, Bett, suffered when her dog was killed, as if she were being killed too. That was just a sliver of what Manon was suffering.

I felt as if Manon were falling into the river and I couldn't pull her back up. I touched her shoulder. "Manon, I've got enough power to save one of them, but just one. You'll have to choose."

Manon sat up and stared at me with her mouth open. She squinted through tears at Pudge, then at Ribbon, and back at Pudge. I suspect that the sorcerer in her wanted to save the monster dog, the one who could protect her. The little girl in her wanted to save Pudge.

At last, Manon whispered, "Pudge."

I knelt down beside Pudge while Manon went around giving the others their final pettings and hugs. I tried to pull a green band out of the air, but nothing happened. I tried again, and still got nothing. I knew I had enough power.

I sat on the bloody dirt and assumed that all I knew about this situation was wrong. I walked through everything that had happened, step by step, and then I knew.

"Manon, your mother said you have to take care of them yourself. All their needs. Pudge needs to be healed, but I can't provide for her. Your bargain with your mother is stopping me."

"What can I do?" Manon wiped her wet cheeks, leaving a smudge of blood on her nose.

"They're in pain, darling, and they won't get well. We have to put them out of that pain."

"No!" She sniffed and hugged my arm.

I waited.

Manon sagged. "Would you do it?"

I pulled out my knife and knelt beside Violet, but I couldn't force the knifepoint toward the dog. Something like an invisible hand pushed me away every time.

"I'm sorry. You've got to take care of all their needs. May your mother have dry heaves for eternity."

She hugged my arm tighter. "How do I do it?"

"Here's my knife. I'll show you."

Manon was crying hard when she kissed Pokey on the head. I held her while she used both trembling hands to put the knife to the dog's skull. Her hands shook so hard she had to try three times, and the dog gazed at her with total trust every time. Then it was done. She went to Ribbon next, and then Violet. By the time she got to Pudge, she looked like she'd run twenty miles and then been beaten with iron rods. Manon killed Pudge, and I took the knife.

Ella laid her hand on Manon's shoulder. "Let's clean you up and find a place to rest."

"No." Manon sniffed as she studied the ground. "I have to bury them too."

I fetched a shovel from the garden for her. Manon dug four graves along the orchard wall. A monk huffed over to complain, and I grabbed him. Before I threw him against a tree, I saw in his eyes that he really didn't know what the hell was happening. I just pushed him back into the courtyard. When Manon finished the burials, Ella led her away.

I had failed that little girl at every turn. She knew nothing about being a sorcerer, and I hadn't prevented her from making one mistake piled on top of another, leading her to this grief. Ella would probably have considered it from three angles and said it wasn't my fault, and hell, she might have been right. But no other person had a hope of preventing all this horror but me, and I had profoundly failed.

I joined the search for survivors in the temple. A good third of the temple's residents had died. We found Marta's body hidden in the stable loft, throat cut. Ona must have murdered her.

That evening, I explained to Cael and Ella that Ona was really Agni. They seemed just as shocked as I had been.

Cael said, "I assume that Agni's disguise was magical."

"Sure, and Ona's corpse in Parhold was some other poor woman disguised to resemble Ona. I mean Agni. Shit! Anyhow, Agni may hate sorcerers, but she has a Binder chained up some-where making magic trinkets for her."

Cael pulled out a rag to start cleaning his sword. "Agni's people were bold infiltrators. It's too bad you didn't kill Agni when she was fifteen feet away from you."

I ignored that. "We should find some beds."

Cael kept on at his task. "We're not staying. Every hour we delay, more people die."

"Manon needs to rest after all that shit."

"She's a sorcerer. She can squeeze up some courage and mount her horse."

"Cael, did you take a sharp look around the priestess's office? What do you think happened to those guards? You don't have to answer, because I know you're too ignorant to have an answer that's worth a good goddamn. But if you keep flapping on about no rest, something like that's going to happen to you. You beat me in Ir, but you have no conception of how things have changed."

Those were big words for me to say with just a tiny amount of power in reserve, but we stayed at the temple that night.

TWENTY

People have called me foolish and reckless, and often they were correct. Even childish has been an accurate description sometimes. But not even those who despised me have called me stupid. I knew that I was partial to Manon because she reminded me of my own little girl, and I had exercised discipline to make sure I didn't get too emotionally attached.

My discipline got blown all to hell in that courtyard. Every time Manon stabbed one of her dogs in the head, I felt it. By the time she killed Pudge, I would have done about anything to keep her from hurting that way.

Ella and I lay in the priestess's opulent bed, with Manon asleep three rooms down. The girl had rejected comforting and had insisted on sleeping in a bed of her own. As for Ella and me, naughty behavior was nowhere in our thoughts. We had bathed our exhausted selves, and sleep would hit us like a feather avalanche almost right away. I wanted to say something and wasn't clear about what, but I had no time for strategy.

I opened my mouth and let it fall out with no preamble. "I want Manon to be our daughter." The words shocked me so that I stopped breathing, but I knew they were right.

Ella didn't speak.

She was lying down facing the wall, so maybe she had already fallen asleep. I spoke louder. "I want us to adopt Manon. She doesn't have anybody."

Ella rolled over toward me, her head on the pillow. "I had understood that she is to remain here at the temple, and that they will care for her."

"This place is beaten to hell. We can't leave her here."

"Perhaps, but we can take her elsewhere. There must be others who can tend her well and lovingly."

I sat up. "I want us to do it."

"That makes no sense. We lead dangerous lives. Some would call them insane. Bib, you know I've raised other people's children, several of them. I promise you this would be a torturous life for a child."

All I really heard her say was that she had raised several children, a fact I knew already. I started getting more excited about the idea. "She's a sorcerer. It'll be the perfect life for her. Hell, she'll thrive better than we do. I never expected to have another child, and I know you didn't either, but she's here and she needs us."

Ella lowered her voice to not much above a whisper. "I'm sorry. No."

"Why not?" I prepared myself to explain away any objection.

"Just . . . no."

"Go on and say why!"

"Bib, she is not your dead daughter!"

It felt like she'd broken off the bedpost and hit me with it.

"And I am not your dead wife! You must leave them behind."

I mumbled something. It may have been an apology. I might have called her a razor-hearted bitch.

Ella didn't answer me. We stared at each other for a minute, and I don't think either of us breathed. Then I got out of bed and walked into the hall, not caring much that I was naked. The priestess's office was two doors away. No one had moved the bodies yet because the priests and monks were still in shock. I dragged a corpse away from one corner of the room. Then I pulled the stupid religious tapestries off the walls, shoved them into a pile in that corner, and slept on them.

I woke up in dimness the next morning, and I saw that it was raining. I struggled upright, groggy, and was halfway to the door before I realized that my pillar of light had disappeared. I had expected it would dissipate eventually. It had stayed for about a day, which I felt was a pretty happy definition of eventually.

I walked back to the bedroom, but Ella had left. Harik's book was missing too, and panic knifed me in the stomach. She might try to open it if she was angry enough. I didn't know whether she, a non-sorcerer, could even open the thing by herself, but if she did, then whatever happened would be bad. She might not live through it. For all I knew, everything on the hilltop would turn to liquid and drain away.

I ran into the hallway and almost knocked Ella down. "Give me the book!"

"I don't have it." She put her hands on my chest. "Bib—"

"Who has it? We have to find it! Right the hell now!" I realized that I'd been ridiculously casual with the book.

"Wait. It's not in your possession?"

"No!" I snatched my trousers. "Go get Manon. If she has the book, take it away from her and bring it straight to me."

"And if she does not have it?"

The book in somebody else's hands could be just as dangerous. "Take her with you, get on your horses, and ride away from here. At least three hours."

Ella swallowed, and some color leached out of her face. "Perhaps she is searching for breakfast and everything is all right."

Manon wasn't off searching out breakfast or sitting where she had buried her dogs or hiding anyplace I could think of. Everyone started scouring the temple for her, but after about an hour, Cael started giving orders for our departure. Ella threw clumps of mud at him until he shut up about leaving.

A few minutes later, Larripet loped into the damp courtyard where the rest of us were standing around like geese, having searched all the places we could think of. "The girl is not in the smaller stable. Her horse is not there, either."

Ella gritted her teeth, turned away from the Hill Man, and kicked a handy stone across the courtyard. "She ran away? With the book?"

"The horse probably did not take her prisoner, but these are the Crazy Lands." Larripet shrugged.

"Why would she run?" Cael asked.

Everybody else turned to me.

"I suppose I'll go ask."

I lifted myself and called for Sakaj, but she ignored me. I called for Harik, who answered right away. I arrived at the place of absence, where bargains were made.

Harik drawled, "Be quick, Murderer. I am enjoying a warm afternoon with a young lady."

"Why, that's sounds charming, Harik. I'm sure she and your wife are good friends."

"If you want something, I require that you kill the girl in exchange."

"Are we back on murdering the girl? I thought that was part of our colorful history." I drew my sword, and the Home of the Gods appeared. The afternoon was indeed warm and soothing. Harik sat above me in the marble gazebo, his hand on the knee of a woman so beautiful I had to look at her three times to accept it. Harik whispered to her. She smiled, rose, and strolled away with a grace only a magical creature possesses.

"Harik, why don't you show the imagination worthy of a divine being? Too much fornication can dull the wits. Prove me wrong. Come up with something besides killing the girl. Make me a different offer, and we'll knock this out in a minute."

"No. I am Death, and I have spoken."

"I am a drunkard, and I have sung about women in washtubs. You aren't intimidating me. I'll go to Fingit instead. He's probably pissed off at you about something and willing to bend a rule."

Harik smirked. "Just now Fingit is scrupulous about avoiding even the least of infractions. He is not favored by our father."

"Then I'll go to Krak." That was a bluff. I wouldn't go to Krak unless I was chained, and barbarians were about to pour molten lead down my throat. "I imagine he'll be fascinated by whatever grab-ass you and Sakaj are playing."

I had only been speculating about Harik hiding this—whatever it was—from Krak, but Harik's teeth slammed together like an anvil hitting an iron floor. "Do you believe yourself mighty enough and clever enough to blackmail the God of Death?"

"I do not, but I'm blackmailing you anyway. Should I go find Krak?"

Harik glared. "Very well. We will bargain on terms other than the child's life. What is your offer?"

"Wait a minute. I might decide to kill her after all. It depends on how much trouble I'd have to go to. How far away is she?"

"How transparent. Unworthy even of you. If you want to find her, just ask. And tell me what you're offering."

"To hell with the girl then. She just aggravates me. I guess we're done. Good luck seducing your friend. Maybe she thinks plagues and starvation are erotic." I slid back toward home to the world of man.

"Black Drifting Whores of the Universe!" Harik snapped. "Come back here, Murderer! Yes, yes, I want you to find her. She is riding north to the Bole and plans to toss my book into it."

"Why? The Bole must be nothing but a hollow tree. I sure haven't been there to open the way. Whatever she tosses in will just get covered up by leaves and eaten by bugs."

"That is not— well, nonetheless, she travels there now and leads you by half a morning. If you are unwilling to kill her, you must prevent her from reaching the Bole. In exchange, I offer one square."

I didn't know what Harik's word choice meant, if it meant anything. I stowed it for later examination. "Unless you offer four squares, I'm going back to bed."

"If the girl destroys the book, you will be unable to keep your bargain with me and your woman will certainly die. It might even cause the girl's death. You could achieve two dead daughters and two dead wives."

I almost yelled at him, which would have been unproductive. Harik's good opinion didn't concern me, or his anger. But when a sorcerer bargains and loses his temper, then bad bargains and tragedy follow. "What a sweet sentiment, you cross-eyed jackal. Why is Manon going to fling your book into the Bole?"

Harik waved his forefinger at me. "You need not know that. I doubt that you could understand it."

"Ah, so Sakaj is sending her there to heave your book into the Bole and destroy it, but you don't want her to. Unless it's more complicated and subtle than that?"

The corners of Harik's mouth twitched. "No, that's exactly it. There is nothing more intricate involved."

"Huh. Well, I'll just concentrate on the wolf whose teeth are in my ass right now. I'll take four squares, but not for preventing Manon from reaching the Bole. I'll stop her from destroying the book, if you like."

"That could be acceptable, if you take the book away from her and then do not leave that spot until you speak to me. Two squares."

"Three."

"Three . . . but if you fail, you will kill the girl and every other person who is present at your failure."

"I don't think so. Instead of killing—"

"No! Those are the terms. Accept them, or return to your bed and enjoy congress with your woman quickly, for she will soon die."

The sensation of ramming my sword through Harik's chest overwhelmed me for a moment. My options were meager, however. "I agree."

Harik smiled at me like I was good to eat, and he hurled me back into my body.

Fifteen minutes later, I urged my horse around Barrelshins and away through the damp hills with Cael, Ella, and Larripet behind me. I knew these hills well, and I figured Manon would get pulled into one or two winding, dead-end ravines. We'd catch her, barring some awful misfortune.

Cael had objected to chasing Manon. In fact, he had shouted at me and drawn his sword. Ella and Larripet then pointed their weapons at him on Manon's behalf, and I promised that if he didn't shut up and follow me, I'd use magic to make his testicles come out his nose. I couldn't really do that, or anything like it, but he respected the threat and agreed to come along if we promised to meet several conditions. I said yes and then ignored him while he described his terms.

The day remained heavy and wet, but the rain held off. About halfway between noon and sunset, I spotted feathery smoke rising into the mist. The valley we were riding through curved that direction, so I followed it along. Soon, we found a saddled, roan gelding grazing. Manon's horse was black, but I'd seen this one before. One of Stone-Hand's band of sorcerers had been riding it, a woman I suspected of being the Burner. I didn't see that woman anywhere, or her corpse.

Larripet grabbed the horse's bridle, and we brought it with us down the valley. When we rounded the hillside, we spotted a small tree smoldering and spewing smoke. It leaned in the middle of a circle thirty paces across that had burned until the bare earth blackened. A tight scattering of toast-colored stones as big as barrels lay fifty paces away from the tree.

Nobody was standing around claiming this to be their work. I expected to find a crushed woman under the stones, and I was right. The Burner was there, pretty well broken up and dead beyond my ability to help her. I couldn't make out her face, but her ripped-up, gory black clothes matched those that Death's Riders had worn.

Cael had been surveying the surrounding grit and tall shank grass that passed for countryside in these hills. "This woman's mount ran back to where we found it, and four horses galloped away toward that hill." He nodded west across the valley where a stone-jumbled slope rose to a hilltop. "Stone-Hand."

I shaded my eyes and scanned the hill. My vision was as pure as it had been when I was a boy, and I didn't spot any sorcerers up there ready to drop half a hillside onto us. "What about Manon?"

Cael said, "I believe she rode away along this valley, to the north. She hurried, but not as if she were being chased."

"Look at this!" Larripet yelled from halfway up the hillside next to us.

I scrambled up to join him. From that vantage, I saw that the rocks weren't as scattered as I'd thought. They spread out just enough to make a good semblance of a hand, as if it had smashed the woman like a bug.

"Well, that's rather artistic," I said.

"That is not a normal thing." Larripet shook his head. "I will tell you again: these are the Crazy Lands. We should leave before we find the cows that shoot acid from their eyes."

TWENTY-ONE

My wife could flatter and chide anybody into doing nearly anything. She could've convinced me to give up everything in my life that displeased her, but she only talked me into giving up about half of those things. She let me keep the half I loved. That proved she was a woman of high character, because many of the things I loved were foolish and bad for me.

She never taught me the art of swaying other people's intentions, or maybe I was a hopeless pupil. Either way, it seemed I couldn't persuade Ella and the others to do a goddamn thing, or at least not the important thing, which was to stay behind while I dealt with Manon. I explained that if I failed, I would be obliged to kill every one of them. Cael laughed as if I were telling a joke, and he made it clear he wouldn't let me get more than fifty feet away from him. Ella, grim-faced, declared that she would come along regardless. Larripet muttered and growled to himself, shaking his head. Then he climbed onto his horse and stared at me.

I feared that Manon had traded with Sakaj for more power, so I didn't give up trying to convince them. I stood on top of the rocks that had smashed the Burner into a sack of shattered bones and explained to my idiot companions how ignorant we were about

Manon's current power and state of mind. I yelled a lot, and at last, they offered to trail me by a hundred paces. They had chosen a poor distance, and I told them so. It was so near that they might be caught up and obliterated if Manon decided to kill me, yet not far enough to escape if she decided to kill them. But they couldn't believe that such danger might come from the little girl they knew. They listened no more seriously than if I were describing how fairies make rose-whistles. I gave up.

When I saw how Manon had pulverized the Burner, I shifted my thinking about the pursuit. Her feats might now only be limited by her imagination and by how much power Sakaj had given her. Yet I had an advantage. I had ridden hundreds of horses before Manon was born, and hundreds more since. Manon had sat atop two horses in her life. Horsemanship would be a greater advantage than magic in this chase.

I rode fast, straight toward the Bole. In the afternoon, I spotted Manon ahead, crossing a stream in a narrow valley. She didn't appear to have seen me, so I rode up and over to the other side of the closest hilltop. I knew where she was going. If I drove my mount hard, I could keep hills between us for the whole journey and arrive at the Bole first. She would never see me.

It was a slick plan, and I felt a little proud of it until she rounded a hill in front of me and entered a defile fifty paces away, staring at me over her shoulder. I gave her a gigantic wave to show I didn't mean harm. Of course, from her side, it might appear I was showing how I intended to swing my sword when I cut off her head.

A towering mound of earth bounced out of the ground in front of me, like a block of soap popping out of water. My horse reared, but I kept him from bolting. The mound closed off the defile to a height of twenty feet. It was an impressive barrier, but Manon had a poor grasp of how horses work. I retreated a hundred paces, rode up the slanted side of the defile at an angle, and came down the same way on Manon's side. She couldn't resist stopping to admire her work, so her entire obstruction merely doubled her lead, which wasn't great to start with.

At the end of the defile, Manon hesitated, maybe considering whether I'd be prettier flattened by rocks or by dirt. Then she turned her horse and galloped away into what soon became a gentler valley. Even though she weighed just a bit of nothing, she couldn't ride as fast as me. That was a raw fact, and I closed with her at every stride.

When I had chopped the lead in half again, I found myself sliding off the side of my horse. Manon had disintegrated every bit of my saddle and tack. I cursed as I snatched my running horse's mane and pulled myself back up. I felt a little disappointed that Manon had been so unimaginative, and more disappointed that she had wasted all that power instead of just snapping the cinch.

I could ride about as well bareback as I could in the saddle, so Manon's feat gained her not a damn thing. The gap between us shriveled to thirty paces, and then I convulsed from a pain in my gut. It felt like somebody had dropped three or four frisky porcupines into my stomach. Then one of them began chasing another down through my bowels. I vomited as everything in my system exploded from both ends.

My horse didn't slow a lick. I gave Manon a floppy wave, and my body spasmed to expel whatever was left. I waved harder, intending defiance, but I halfway hoped she'd think I was surrendering.

The girl slowed a bit, twisting to peer over her shoulder at me, which let me draw a few paces closer. That was what I needed for the paltry amount of power I had left. With my right hand, I pulled a yellow band out of the air, and then another, and I began throwing bands around all four hooves of Manon's horse. I yanked the beast to a dead stop. Even a good horseman would've been thrown. Manon hurtled over her horse's head, tumbling, and smacked flat onto the ground. She lay still. Right away, my porcupines fled to make somebody else pray for death.

Manon twitched, but her eyes stayed closed. She moaned when I said her name, but I doubt she would've known a chicken from a crocodile.

I said, "If you hadn't destroyed my saddle and every damn thing on it, I could give you a drink of water." I shifted to hold her head in the crook of my arm.

Everybody else caught up, dismounted, asked whether she was dead, and made smart comments about how I smelled. Ella brought a flask, and she wet Manon's face before I dribbled water onto her lips. In a few seconds, Manon squinted up at me. Her eyes snapped open and she tried to roll away.

I gripped her hard and said, "Darling, it hurts me that you'd trust some damned god more than you trust me."

She stopped struggling.

"I won't hurt you. I don't plan to ever hurt you, and if I did, it sure wouldn't be on an exhausting hot day like today. What did your mother tell you?"

"That you'd kill me if you caught me."

"What a tale! She should have given you milk and gingerbread when she told it to you. What else?"

Manon sat up and hung her head, shaking it. "Not much, really."

"What did she say to do with the book? Exactly? Which words did she use?"

Manon closed her eyes and took a breath. When she opened them, she seemed years older. "She said to toss the book into that tree—the Bole."

I gave her a sharp nod. "Good. She used that exact word? Toss?"

Manon didn't hesitate. "Yes."

I squatted and leaned toward the girl. "I figured that to be the case. Harik used that same word. For unfathomably powerful beings, they tend to be mighty literal and consistent. It's a failing, so remember it."

"Really? Gods have failings?" It was as if I'd said apple pies have rat turds.

"More than the night has stars. Instead of chasing around and making each other shit our pants, let's work together like profes-sional sorcerers. We'll poke the gods in the eyes. Hold onto that book for now, but you promise to hand it to me later."

She stared into my face from two feet away and gave a lopsided grin. "Fine."

I sat down beside the girl.

Manon sniffed and scooted away.

"I know, I smell like something that fell out of a sick goat, but that's not my fault, is it? Why did you let your mother talk you into this ridiculous task?"

"She gave me lots of power." Manon shrugged.

I waited.

"And she made it so that dogs will stop following me." She spat that out fast.

That was about what I'd expected. I grabbed her hand and squeezed it. "It's good that you won't have to suffer like that again. But you don't seem too relieved."

Manon shook her head. "I know I should be. But I'm not. It doesn't seem very important."

"What else did you give your mother?" I tried not to sound all that curious.

"Nothing!" Manon smiled a little. "I got something from her, actually. I don't have to remember how much it hurt. I remember that it did hurt, but I don't remember feeling it."

I cast my eyes down, not too far since I was sitting on the damn ground. "Did you ask for that?"

"No, she just offered it to me." Manon kept smiling.

I gripped her shoulders and turned her to face me. "Manon, she cheated you. That was a gift for her, not you. Gods will ask to take away what you feel, or what you remember. They do it for the pleasure of making you decide to change yourself for them."

Manon cocked her head and thought for a moment. "I don't feel changed. A little . . . ." She paused, unsure of herself. "Distracted."

"How do you feel about the people of Pog?"

Manon sneered.

I chuckled. "You don't need to tell me, I can see. Maybe this trade with your mother doesn't mean much. Probably won't affect you at all."

Manon paused and then quietly said, "You're lying."

"All right." I let go her hand and nodded. "It will affect you, but maybe not too much. I can't say."

Manon nodded back at me. "What are we going to do at the tree?"

I smiled. "It will be astounding. We'll either show the gods our metaphorical backsides, or we'll instantly destroy everything between here and the ocean."

Manon frowned, and it hurt a little to see how composed she was.

I covered it up by patting her on the shoulder. "I expect our results will be somewhere between those extremes."

After a short rest, we rode north until sunset, crossing a sizable stream in which I washed myself. Then we camped in a little valley that fended off most of the night wind. Manon walked off to lie down by herself instead of curling up beside Ella. I lay down, and a minute later, Ella came to stand over me. I rolled onto my side away from her, and I heard her walk away.

The next morning, every part of me hurt, including my eyeballs and earlobes. I hadn't believed that Manon could harm my flesh that way. It turned out she hadn't. She explained that she had reached out to the uncounted tiny bits of vegetation that live inside every person. Most people are not aware of such things at all, and the truth would terrify or revolt many if they knew. Manon had known after Sakaj told her. The girl had then forced the ones in my guts to grow, twist, poke, peel, and generally raise hell, all at once. It was as clever a feat as I'd ever seen.

I wondered how I'd handle Manon if she decided to kill me outright. Maybe I could just stand there and let her kill me.

Manon and I developed our plan on horseback. We rode easy, since I wanted to reach the Bole about midday. I had traveled there when I was younger. The place wasn't evil in the way of rapists and child killers, but nobody was in there giving away cake, either. The Bole existed for ending things, or beginning them, with oaths and compulsions. Harik had sent me to the Bole to kill the first man I owed him. If Manon and I were going to creep into the Bole, I preferred to do it under the bright sun.

The Bole didn't occupy a lot of ground, maybe as much as a puny village. It stood on an island right in the middle of a small, round lake, so it resembled a bushy castle surrounded by a moat. Its dusty pine trees stood thick, and their towering caps swayed even when there was no breeze at all.

After seeing how Manon had handled me during our chase, and how haggard we both seemed now, nobody insisted on coming with us. Cael said he'd bend to trust me this one time. Manon and I left our horses behind and walked to the lake's edge, with water so clear we couldn't tell whether it was five feet or fifty feet to the bottom. When I stepped off into it, Manon grabbed my arm, but I took her hand and led her out. Despite how its appearance, the deepest water only came to her chest.

Once among the trees, our feet swept ankle-deep needles and pinecones aside. I sauntered as if I were headed to the tavern to drink and lose all my money—not that anything in the Bole would be impressed by me. The smell was like being slapped with a handful of pine branches, and by the time we'd taken ten steps, it had grown as dim as twilight.

We walked into a small clearing. A huge tree stood there, not a pine tree and clearly deader than hell. I had seen trees in nearly every part of civilization and even on the frontier, but I had never seen another tree that was kin to this one. Its dead, brown bark hung like crusty armor. Half a dozen men couldn't reach around the trunk, and it sent twisted, shattered branches a hundred feet up and just as far in every direction. A dark, man-size hole gaped in the side of the trunk facing us.

"How do we know the Bole even works?" Manon knelt down and peered at whatever might be inside the top of the hole.

I pitched a big pinecone into the hole. It blazed like a young fire and then exploded with a crack as it fell. A few sparks died on the moist ground inside the hole, but every other bit of the pinecone burned away before anything touched the dirt. "Got anything you want to get rid of forever? Besides the obvious?"

Manon shook her head and sighed. "Just like in the plan?" She pulled the book out of a large pouch she must have filched off the corpse of a priest or monk. She held the little volume in both of her shaking hands and achieved a bit more control.

I drew my sword. "Just like we planned. Wait for me to say go."

We intended for Manon to gently toss the book into the opening at its very top. I was hoping that the book, being full of divine magic, would not be destroyed in the first instant. I was hoping the same thing for my sword. If the blade disintegrated right off, I'd look foolish when I tried to whip it into the hole and knock the book back out before it could be annihilated.

Manon would toss the book into the Bole. I would prevent the tome from being destroyed. We would both honor our bargains, go skipping back to the temple, and be eating mince pie with cream by tomorrow night.

I said, "All right . . . go!"

Manon tossed. I nipped my blade in and slapped the book. Then I was lying on the ground.

Somebody was shoving knives, nails, glass shards, and an iron spike in and out of my skull. I opened my eyes onto the dimness of the Bole, and it was like pressing my eyeballs against the sun.

"He's awake!" Cael boomed in the voice Krak used to call up volcanoes.

"Bib!" Ella bellowed. "Can you hear me?"

I nodded my head a fraction. My skull felt like it was banging around inside a temple bell. I whispered, "Did it work? Does you still have the book?"

Somebody nodded. I think it was Manon, but I couldn't be sure because there were two of her.

"Ella, you got here mighty fast," I whispered, using no more breath than necessary.

Nobody spoke until Ella said, "I did attempt to hurry. However, you did not recover quickly."

"Well, what time is it? I can't tell how late in the afternoon it is among all these damn trees."

Manon patted my arm. "Bib, you've been lying here for two days."

TWENTY-TWO

Ella and Cael sat me up against a tree trunk, but not the one that had nearly killed me. They chose one of the safer ones that merely swayed around without the wind and threw deep, unnatural shade. I stayed awake throughout the procedure, although dry heaves made me wish to get knocked out again.

"Why didn't you take me away from these haunted trees?" I murmured.

"We tried," Ella said, wiping my mouth. "Every time we attempted it, you stopped breathing. When we lay you back down, your breath returned."

"That was probably Harik's doing. He told me to stay put once I saved his little book."

I felt Harik reach out to me right away, coming to the sound of his name like a boy to the smell of pies. He lifted me out of my body, and I didn't fight him. I knew that every pain would disappear when I reached that spot of dirt where the gods make sorcerers stand to trade. I guess it's divine dirt, but I felt a little insulted whenever I stood on it. It was as if the gods thought mortal men would pollute divine grass with their feet.

"Oh, nicely done, Murderer!" Harik sounded on the edge of

giggling. "Considering the limited scope of your powers, I harbored grave concerns. However, you mastered the situation with a competence that astounds me!"

"Mighty Harik, giddiness is unbecoming in an immortal being." I mentally reached for my sword so I could see, and I realized that some considerate soul had removed it as I slept. I supposed they thought an unconscious man would never recover unless he was disarmed. Maybe that was common knowledge among old wives and learned physicians alike. Perhaps wounded kings had perished because of a too-sharp spoon in their belt. I knew my sarcasm was unproductive, but damn whoever took it. Unreasoning kindness has led more people to folly than bald self-interest ever could.

"Next, Murderer, you will take the book across the sea to the Northern Kingdoms."

"The hell I will! Once Ella and I have read it twice more, I'm going to bury it under the nastiest privy in this kingdom. I would say in the world, but it's not worth going that far out of my way."

"I see." Harik shrugged. "Well, if you have no interest in the honor to be earned, as well as the power, I shall bestow both upon someone else."

"Stone-Hand? Oh, yes, he's perfect for this task. Perfect. I can't think of another man better suited."

Sakaj's voice sounded in the nothingness. "Please do entrust the book to your toy sorcerers, Harik. It would be a gift, just as if it were my birthday!"

Harik shouted, "Sakaj! You are not welcome here!"

"Really? I believe . . . yes, this is my name right here, carved into the bench. I find that terribly welcoming."

"Come back later!"

"I want to be here now, and so does the Tooth. Don't you, dear one?"

"Yes," Manon answered from some place.

"So, if you cannot say anything edifying, Harik, just be still and try to learn something."

Harik said, "Temerity is all you have left, you slut. Bark, bark, babble, babble. Hah! No one heeds a failure."

Sakaj giggled. "I'm experiencing a trivial delay, nothing more. My glory will be even greater when you . . . well, it will be greater."

"Get away! Go sit on your own bench!" Harik said it as a command, but there was a whine in there someplace.

"You mewl like a human. And ew, your robe feels sticky!"

I cut them off. "If existence has endured under the rule of gods like yourselves, it might thrive under children who pee their beds and eat their own snot."

Manon chuckled.

"Quiet, Murderer!" Harik boomed, with no hint of whining. "I may choose to destroy everyone you love. You will take the book to the Northern Kingdoms in exchange for two squares."

"Why?"

"Your limited mind is not meant to know such things."

Sakaj giggled. "Harik can know things, however. His mind is certainly not limited. If anything, it's receding."

"Silence!"

I jumped into the brief lull. "Unless I know what this celestial pissing contest is about, I refuse to play."

Sakaj proclaimed, "It is war, and the victor will sit at Krak's right hand for the next hundred thousand years."

"Oh, come on. Really." They couldn't have missed the sarcasm if they'd been chimps instead of gods.

"Oh, she's correct. It is war," Harik assured me.

Sakaj sighed. "Murderer, your intellect really is rather constrained. If we explain further, it might destroy your mind, I do promise you that."

I could be sure that whatever these two transcendent beings told me was bullshit. They were squabbling with each other over something. I imagine the loser might be embarrassed in front of the other gods, but nothing cataclysmic would happen to him, or her. There would be catastrophes elsewhere, of course, but they'd fall on the people the gods pulled into this fight.

I said, "If I'm too stupid to understand, then I guess I'm too stupid to help. Manon, are you coming?" I began drifting back toward the rhapsody of pain waiting for me at home.

Sakaj called out, "Tooth, while you fulfilled the letter of your bargain, you still failed me. I don't blame you, though. The Murderer is old and devious. Now you will make it up to me."

"Bib says you cheated me!" Manon sounded angrier at Sakaj than she'd ever been at me.

"He's a liar. He admits it. Brags about it!"

"He doesn't lie to me," Manon said with perfect calm.

"Oh, my dear, of course he does. Come, haven't you caught him in a lie just recently?"

Manon didn't speak. I had lied to her, just days ago, when I said her deal with Sakaj probably hadn't changed her. Manon had caught me on it too. She wouldn't have forgotten.

Sakaj laughed like an old maiden aunt telling a dirty joke. "I see now that Harik's little book wasn't meant for destruction in the Bole. Again, not your fault, dearie. So, I'll offer you another task. Take the book to Bellmeet. Just that. It should be easy, since that deadly, smiling man who loves his sword more than his member wants to go there. I can be happy with the book in that city."

"Pathetic. The Murderer will take the book to the Northern Kingdoms." Harik droned on. "He is cruel, devious, and incalculably deadlier than the Tooth. If she interferes, he will carve her like a squab."

"What about the sword-loving man?" Sakaj asked.

"The Murderer will slay him too."

Sakaj sniffed. "Ignore him, my lovely Tooth. Take the book to Bellmeet."

I said, "Let's leave, Manon. There's no call for us to be involved in this."

Manon stayed quiet for several seconds. "What will you offer me to do it, Mother?"

"Manon, please stop!" I snapped. "This is a horrible idea! Remember, I was right about the deal with the dogs. Trust me!"

Manon spoke to me in a businesslike way. "I trust you—mostly. You're mostly honest with me, but not totally, so I've got to protect myself, even from you. When you chased me, I couldn't escape, and that's no good. I have to do better."

"I didn't kill you."

"Thanks for that."

Of course, Manon was right. A sorcerer should never trust another sorcerer, at least not completely. I almost reminded her about how I had held her while she killed her dogs, and how I had comforted her. Also, how I hadn't goddamn yelled at her for wasting power. But she had traded away how she felt about all those events, so she had forgotten how those events had made her feel about me. For the first time in my life, I started to feel old.

I pleaded, "Manon, don't make this deal."

Sakaj laughed a gorgeous, ringing laugh. "Murderer, you are embarrassing yourself. Tooth, I offer you one square."

"Seven."

"I wouldn't pay seven if you took that book around the world twice! Two. And I won't hear of anymore, as punishment for your cheek."

"Fine. Two," Manon grumped.

"Done. The power is waiting."

Harik said, "I might almost have considered that to be entertainment, sister. I may hire the two of you for my next party. Murderer, I offer three squares to take the book to the Northern Kingdoms. You needn't even kill the Tooth if you don't wish. Just tie her up and leave her in a gutter, or however you want to handle it."

I wished I could sneer at his repulsive, perfect, godlike face. "No."

"Very well, four squares. No more!"

"No. No forever. I won't do it for any amount of power."

"Ridiculous!" Harik sounded outraged. He was probably standing up now. He did that when he was really pissed off. "You can't extort the God of Death!"

Sakaj said, "Why not? The other gods do it all the time."

"Shut up!" I could imagine his spit flying. Harik went on: "Murderer, five squares. Do not reject it."

"I reject the hell out of it. As long as Manon is taking the book some place, I'm not taking it anywhere else."

Silence.

"We're leaving now," I said. "We have to get an early start for Bellmeet. If you two are going to fight while we're gone, make it count. I look forward to hearing about dead gods next time I visit."

Manon and I drifted down and dropped back into our bodies.

I studied Manon's eyes. "Now do you trust me?"

She bent and hugged me from the side, putting her ear against my chest. "Mostly."

"Not completely? Krak's pits! Do you want me to cut off my head in your service?"

"No, but you could still go make that deal if you wanted to. In an instant. Maybe you've already done it."

I pushed myself to sit up straight. "I haven't, and I won't."

"I believe that you believe that." Manon let go and stood up, brushing her knees. "You're not always too dependable, though." She walked off and disappeared into the trees. Larripet watched her, glanced back at Ella, and then followed Manon.

I reached out. "Help me up." Ella pulled as I stood, and then I leaned over to steady my head and the pains that wanted to burst it like a rotten grape. "I don't understand why she doesn't trust me. I never had this problem with my daughter—" Ella crossed her arms and glared at me, so I changed my next statement. "Ella, you know all about kids. What am I doing wrong?"

"It is not what you're *doing*. It's what you *are*. She's right—you're undependable. It's the quality I find hardest to overlook if I want to love you."

I opened my mouth, but nothing came out. I felt as if I'd had an enormous goiter on my forehead for years and no one had told me.

"Bib, a few days ago, she was at home with her family, however detestable they may have been. She was spirited away, and now where does she belong? With you? With her mother the goddess? With Cael, or me? With Larripet, may the gods forbid it?" Before I could give her a stupid answer, she went on. "She's still a child. Who can make her feel safe?"

"What can I do to help her?"

Ella shouted, "Stop lying! And do the things you promise!"

I could have spoken up and promised to do those things, but it

199

would have sounded a bit guileful, so I just nodded. Ella grabbed my arm to steady me as we walked out of the clearing, but I stopped. "Bring Manon back here! And make sure she brings the book."

Ella cocked her head and stared at me. "Why in heavens do you want me to do that?"

I took a deep breath and stood on my own. "We're going to read the book."

"In the Bole? Isn't it a place that personifies some great magical power, one that could not be honestly called benign? I should think that any other place in the world is better suited."

"I'm counting on that book to save you from a preordained death. I hear that changing the future is a difficult thing, and I hope the Bole will shove more power into the book, like it was a heavenly sausage. If it doesn't work, we'll get killed, or maybe we'll be turned into worms and stepped on."

Ella squeezed my arm, smiled, and ran off into the trees. I leaned against a tree trunk and practiced not falling down while she was gone. Soon, she trotted back into the clearing with Manon.

"Please hand me the book," I said.

Manon fished it out of her pouch and passed it over, not hesitating.

I held it up in front of me. "Let me choose the page this time." Ella nodded as we each held onto one of the book's covers. I thumbed the page edges before I flipped open the book. It was page three, the most auspicious of all numbers, and the one I was trying to reach.

Page three contained a black rectangle. Nothing else had been marked on the page, and nothing lay inside the rectangle. The blackness seemed to have depth, like a lightless hole. Ella lifted her hand as if to reach inside, but I knocked her hand away. She shook her head and murmured something.

"As far as extra-powerful, divine, magical phenomena go, this one fails to inspire me," I murmured back.

"Is that all?" Ella asked.

"It seems to be." I closed the book.

"You must have done it wrong." Manon reached for the book. "Try another page."

I held onto the book and frowned at Manon, prepared to make a sarcastic remark, but a man standing behind Ella stopped me. He was huge, a head taller than me, broad, shaggy, armed with at least four sheathed blades, and a bit transparent but glowing. More men stood behind him, and some women too, arrayed all the way back to the trees. Maybe three dozen of them stood silent, still, and not quite solid.

"Ella, don't be fearful, but you've acquired a retinue." I nodded toward them. "They're standing behind you."

Ella didn't turn to examine her new friends. She stared past my shoulder, took a big step back, and swallowed twice. The enormous man shuffled out of her way.

I turned and found men and women standing there, just as insubstantial as Ella's. They filled my half of the clearing, and they packed the spaces between the trees, as far back as I could see. There was no way to count them, but I knew exactly how many there were.

The closest one sneered at me and drew his semi-visible sword. I drew mine right away and pointed it at him. He held out his arms to each side and walked toward me until the tip of my blade touched his chest. He sneered. "The gods damn your heart, Bib. You still live, and with both your hands. The gods are cruel that you stand before me and I'm unable to crush you, to tear your flesh and to open your veins, you ripe squirt of feculence."

I started breathing again. "Why, hello, Vintan. I missed you too."

TWENTY-THREE

Manon peered behind us for the fifth time in five minutes. Then she stared over her other shoulder, twisting in the saddle to get a good view straight back. "What do they want?"

"I guess most of them want to kill me."

"Can't they tell you?"

"Not unless I ask them, and I don't care to ask."

In a way, that was a shame. I had killed some fine conversationalists over the years.

I broke down and glanced behind me too. My great herd of near-transparent people was still following, spread out in a fan behind Vintan, the Denzman sorcerer. Far back and off to my left, Ella's modest escort trailed her. There were some important and subtle sorcerers in my group. Manon could learn a lot if she talked to them. Hell, I could too.

I half-expected Manon to demand that I let her converse with them, but she didn't say anything like that. We rode along side by side, following Cael. He had sworn he could lead us right across the countryside to Bellmeet, and to hell with all the roads that were probably bubbling over with Agni's zealots.

After a minute of silence, Manon blurted, "How many people have you killed?"

"Not many dare ask me that question. When they do, I tell them I don't know, because I let Death do the bookkeeping. That's a lie, though. I've killed two hundred and forty-three people, and that's how many ghosts are gliding along behind me. I wonder if they have to watch out for my horse's droppings? There's a metaphysical question with multiple layers for you."

"How many were women?"

"Fifty-seven." I said it flat out. It was a fact.

She hesitated. "How many children?"

"None."

"Two hundred and forty-three is a lot." I couldn't tell whether she was horrified, or impressed, or didn't care.

"I'll allow that it's an excessive figure. Ghastly, really. When you look at it over twenty years, it's about a dozen a year. But I've killed most of them in these past ten years, since I started killing for Harik."

Manon paused for several seconds. "No children?"

I shook my head.

Manon frowned and guided her horse off away from me before dropping back toward Ella.

I had accepted some hearty abuse from Vintan, a man I'd killed less than a year ago. I could understand that he was still tender about it. I felt no guilt over his death, since he had chopped off my hands, imprisoned me, and tried to stab me to death after he cut Ella's throat. He may have thought he was serving his king loyally, but when I met him, he was a horrible, baby-murdering waste of his father and mother's sweaty fun. When I got tired of hearing him curse me, I pulled my sword away so that it stopped touching him. I suspected that would cut off his ability to speak, and it did, which was the highlight of my morning.

Cael had promised we'd make Bellmeet the day after tomorrow, in the afternoon. We had ridden out of the hills, and tree-dotted, green countryside rolled off into the distance. The sight was a sweet promise that winter was still far away. That promise was a raw, heartless lie. I smelled snow in the air. If it didn't hit us by tomorrow night, then I'd assume the gods had stripped me of my weather-sense for being a mouthy aggravation amid their serene existence.

We hadn't prepared for harsh weather. We had shed Penn's whimsical garments back at Hutch, and at the temple, the monks knew how to dress for no more than rain and a nippy wind. We hadn't brought a single cloak or blanket with us. I had mounted up and chased Manon down the road as if we existed in eternal spring-time, and my foolish companions had chased along after me without a thought. We'd pay for that tomorrow.

At midafternoon, we stopped for a few minutes to rest ourselves. I sat against a tree rubbing my bare feet, since none of the boots Cael had brought to us in Parhold were a good fit. I had cursed him about it for two days, but insulting him about boots had finally become monotonous. Besides, he was a reservoir of other qualities that begged for ridicule.

Larripet walked over and sat cross-legged in front of me. He stared at me and didn't speak.

At last, I said, "I already said I don't sing, and I don't dance, either. If me scratching my nasty toes entertains you, then you're welcome to sit. I would appreciate occasional applause, however."

The Hill Man flicked his gaze to the side and back, almost as if he were nervous. "I have never seen dead people follow someone."

I waited for him to say something cryptic about diamonds, or fornicating lizards, or such, but he just watched me.

"It's a novel experience for me," I said at last.

"I have never heard of this happening anywhere." I realized he was tapping his little finger on the sheath of his knife. Although unlikely, I had to accept the possibility that he really was anxious.

I raised an eyebrow. "Doesn't this kind of thing happen all the time in the Crazy Lands?"

"I know all the songs about the Crazy Lands. Dead people that follow their killers are not in any of those stories."

"So, you want to write a song about it?"

Larripet shook his head. "No. The song must be about you."

I snorted as I pulled on my right boot. "But I'm not civilized. You said so. That's bad luck for you."

The Hill Man leaned forward. "Maybe you are a civilized person, and I cannot see it. Do you know about all the gods?"

I squinted at him. "Better than you do."

"Can you make something useful?"

Grinning, I said, "I can make people wish—"

Larripet cleared his throat and gave the tiniest shake of his head. "Can you make something useful?"

"Um, yes."

He nodded. "Do you protect the people who depend on you?"

"Sure."

"Are you honest and truthful?"

I shook my head, certain to fail this test. "No, I'm not."

"Good."

I raised both eyebrows.

The Hill Man sat up straight. "You say you are not truthful. If that is so, then I cannot believe you. So, I cannot believe you when you say you are not truthful. That means you are truthful."

"A convoluted argument. You should be a sorcerer."

"You are a civilized person then, and it is lucky for me. Put your other boot on. Your feet are distasteful." Larripet jumped up.

"Wait! Since I'm civilized now, and the song is about me, I deserve to know what's so important about it."

Larripet frowned but nodded. "I will write a song loved by all beings. That includes gods and animals."

"Well . . . I don't know whether I'm the right subject." I pulled on the other boot.

"You are all I have."

"So, this is your purpose?"

"Yes." He nodded. "Also, if I do not write an exceptional song, when I go home, I will be killed by my brother."

"I'll try to be interesting." I stood and walked the other direction, passing Cael on the way to my horse. "Larripet is writing a song about me."

"Oh, 'The Drunkard's Anthem.' That'll fill a void."

Near sunset, Cael found a nice, tree-covered hollow by a stream. We gathered up firewood and ate the last of the hard bread and bacon. Tomorrow, we'd be hungry as well as cold.

I watched Ella on the other side of the fire, flanked by her victims, and I decided I'd been unreasonable and too sensitive. She hadn't meant to hurt me by throwing my wife and daughter up at me. Or, maybe she had, but even so, she was worth a hell of a lot more than my hurt feelings.

I walked around the fire, and she looked up at me, at my retinue, and at me again. I said, "I'm sorry I acted like an ass. You may not have been totally right about my family, but you weren't wrong, either. I shouldn't have run away when you were trying to talk sense to me. Do you still love me?"

Ella said, "No."

I stared at her, expecting her to say it was a joke or an exaggeration or a coughing fit or something besides no.

She stood up. "I knew you were a killer, but . . . not like this. I couldn't truly imagine it until I saw them all. I know you had reasons, but . . . why didn't you kill yourself instead? You should have." She walked away, straight through her ghosts, who stepped aside to make a path for her.

I stood there and stared at nothing. I wasn't prepared for Ella to wish that I had cut my veins open when I was young, and that the world would be better off now if I had. However, she had asked a meaningful question, and she wasn't the first one to ask it.

I'm not special, nor am I destined for any particular thing. When I die, it will not be a notable event. But the world has a habit of making things change, and I've walked through a lot of changes. Whenever I've thought that the future looked like broken hearts and rotten teeth, I wondered whether things would change later in the day. It cost me not a damn thing to hope that they might.

That hope was how I walked back around the fire instead of through it, how I sat down instead of running away, and how I threw a stick into the flames instead of ramming it through my eye.

I turned away, right toward all the people I had murdered. Their presence had complicated my life considerably, but I suppose that was fair since I had killed them. In truth, I owed them nothing at all. They would disappear tomorrow, or so I predicted, and I could go back to remembering them as they'd been the moment I killed them.

I thought for a bit about how much I didn't owe them, and how life didn't seem to mean a damned thing, and then I stood. "Line up, ladies and gentlemen. I will hear you out one at a time."

A scarred young woman in a fancy shirt stepped forward. I drew my sword and touched the point to her chest. She said, "You piece of shit. You killed me when I wasn't looking. I never got to have Puall's baby. He probably got married again when I didn't come home."

I remembered her, an awful bandit who had worked for a more appalling bandit. She had just chopped through the back of my friend's neck when I killed her. He had been in love too. I could have told her all that, but I just nodded and waved the next one over.

The night wasn't long enough to listen to them all. They produced a slight glow, which helped me locate them and see the hatred on their faces. One hundred and eight of them unburdened themselves to me that night. That's an especially ill-omened number.

Four of my victims forgave me, and one of them joked about the whole thing. Mostly, they shouted abuse. A lot of them complained that if I had just walked away instead of fighting, then they would have too. Quite a few accused me of killing them when they weren't looking, as if deadly combat had rules. Some had thought up pretty creative tortures for me, and those ghosts wanted me to be clear on the fact that I should suffer them forever. A couple of them just stared at me and wept.

I recognized Larinz the Sorcerer when he stepped up. I touched his chest with my sword and waited.

"Bib, I won't moan about what was or wasn't fair."

"I appreciate that."

"Even though you did kill me when you could have let me live."

I didn't answer that. I didn't recall the events that clearly, and he probably remembered his death better than I did.

Larinz set his jaw before he said, "Everything I knew, all of the wisdom that my eyes and hands gathered in my life, is gone. I can't share it with anyone. You didn't just kill me. You killed everyone that my knowledge could have saved. You ruined everyone who might have been inspired. You didn't just take my life. You rendered it meaningless." He smiled at me. "Now Harik has sent me back to you, a known liar, so that I may tell you the truth. You shall never know peace, Bib. There is no victory for you, no prize, and no rest."

He must not have expected a response from me, because he walked away without waiting for one.

"Well . . . you were a piss-poor sorcerer!" He kept walking as if he didn't hear me.

At the merest first light, I turned away from the ghosts, sat against a sapling, and covered my head with my arms. I blamed Harik for making me kill all those people, and I cursed him in whispers. My brain had gone numb, and my stomach was trying to fall through my body into the ground.

Then I realized I hadn't killed these people at all, not really. They had killed themselves by fighting me. Or else some other thing would have killed them soon, so I was just jiggling with the timing of their deaths. Besides, they all had a chance. Any one of them might have gotten lucky and killed me first. Maybe they could have gotten behind me or set a trap, so it wasn't my fault.

That relieved my mind for a few minutes, until I gave up lying to myself. I had killed them all, not Harik, and not fate. And I had never understood, deep down, what I had taken out of the world. That wasn't the worst part. The worst part was that whenever I listened to one of them tell me about their death, my heart felt a little thrill. No matter what they said, a part of me imagined the satisfaction of killing them again.

Manon knelt down beside me.

I rubbed my face. "Is it important?"

"Of course it is!" She poked my arm.

"All right."

"Those people over there that you killed—were they evil? Mean and dangerous?"

"Some of them were, but some were just doing their job, and their job was to stop me. Or to be in my way."

"But you killed a lot of bad and dangerous ones?" Manon shifted and made me meet her eyes.

"Yes, that's true."

"I don't see any children." She made a show of scanning the dead people as they glowed in the twilight.

"That's true too. I didn't kill any elephants or sharks, either." I started to stand, but she dragged on my arm to keep me sitting.

"I trust you then. Really. I know you won't kill me, and I know you'll protect me." She spoke with care, and I heard every distinct word.

I patted her hand. "Sure, I'll keep you as safe as I can."

"I want you to be my father."

"What?" I whispered.

"I don't have any family, and you don't either, so we should be our own family." She grinned and bounced on her knees.

"It's a serious thing. It's not that simple."

Manon stood up and faced me. "Tell me what's not simple about it. Make me a list."

I had wanted this, but at that moment, it terrified me. I started to count off all the obstacles, but I stopped at one. "I appreciate the trust, but this isn't like picking out a ripe piece of fruit. I don't know that you really understand."

Manon lowered her voice. "Do you love me like a daughter?"

I took a breath. There wasn't any going back. "Of course."

"Do you love me more than your first daughter?" she asked in the same quiet voice.

"Hah. Don't be pushy."

"I love you too. This is going to be wonderful. You'll see!" Manon ran around to the other side of the camp, right to where Ella had begun saddling her horse. They talked for ten seconds before Ella glanced at me and then turned her back.

TWENTY-FOUR

Once the sun showed a sliver, we rode off across the grassy flatland that was about half covered in trees. Once in a while, some shady stretch would refresh us to the point of feeling brisk, and then a sunny stretch would press warmth back into us until we reached the next shade. Everybody else enjoyed as perfect a ride as one could wish for. I wished I could ride off and leave everybody behind, but now I had a daughter to think about.

At midmorning, I explained that a harsh, piercing storm would arrive before dark, and I felt a twisted bit of satisfaction when I did it. Everybody had laughed at me except Ella, who had rubbed the sleeves of her long, woolen shirt.

The dead disappeared toward midday. I didn't see it happen. They were following me, and then the next time I glanced back, they were gone.

Just before sunset, a layer of clouds slid right over us in only a few minutes. Hard wind charged in with the front, playing warbling chords on the branches. The air chilled to near freezing, and then rain started drizzling off and on. I predicted that the storm would strengthen before it petered away, and this time everybody nodded.

Cael demanded that we push on through the night to reach

Bellmeet as soon as possible. I didn't argue. I was too busy rubbing my hands together and blowing my warm breath on them. From that point, we paused only to rest the horses. We never met anybody during the night, and if Agni was working hard enough to find me in the pure dark, in that storm, way out where just about nobody lived, then I might lie down and let her kill me. She'd have earned it.

Throughout the night, we shivered, rubbed our arms and faces, and lay against our horses' necks for warmth. The sleet started around midnight and lasted until dawn when it turned to snow. At first, the wind blew the snow to hell and gone, but soon the wind dropped off and snow piled up past a man's ankle. The misery didn't quite make me wish for death. I wished for Cael's death.

Before noon, Cael turned straight east. I didn't feel like talking to the man, or anybody else, so I hung back and ignored everything around me. That was a good way to get killed, but I felt like daring the universe to kill me.

Within an hour, Cael fell back to pace me. "Bib, you haven't insulted anybody for hours. Are you sick?"

"Go away. I'm cold, and the sound of your voice gives me a queasy stomach. You're probably lost already, you strutting buffoon. Are you sure Bellmeet's not some place behind us?"

Cael shrugged. "I know where it is and how to get there. The Rike Bridge is gone, so we have to cross the river at the ford upstream."

"Well, that will be pleasant as hell for you. The river could be running high for all I know. I would promise to bring news of your drowning to your loved ones, but I can't imagine you having any. Not even a blind dog could love you." Stripping some skin off Cael lightened my mood just a whisker.

"You have loved ones. Is that making you happy?" Cael asked.

"Well . . . no, but it still might. I'm not yet dead."

Cael squinted at some far-off trees. "In my experience, happiness is rare."

"That doesn't mean I can't fight for it."

"Should you? I saw all those people you killed, Bib. What makes you think you deserve to be happy?"

The possibility that I might not deserve happiness was a novel thought, like the idea that trees might not deserve dirt. "I've got as much right to be happy as you!"

Cael laughed hard. "What makes you think that I deserve to be happy?" He kicked his horse and galloped ahead before I could answer. I decided that I hadn't wanted to answer him anyway.

That afternoon, we stared down at the unfortunately named Fatt River. It could only have been running faster if it were the Fatt Waterfall. The soldier at the ford's way station warned us that the current would push us a good distance downstream during the eighty-pace journey across the muddy water, but he promised that our horses shouldn't have to swim, or at least not much. The wind had petered away to nothing, so the snowflakes floated down around us now. It was still so cold that I dreaded peeing more than getting stabbed.

I had found a fine opportunity to murder Cael.

The plan to kill him had just appeared in my mind when Cael halted us at the crest of the shallow river valley. The dim river ran down the middle of a great, snowy course with the gentlest of curves, dwindling in both directions as if it were painted by a fine but depressing artist. The water was beautiful, in its way, and I hoped Cael would appreciate losing his life under it. Well, I didn't really care what he appreciated. I just wanted him dead before he became all dutiful again and killed one of us for some urgent but stupid reason.

Fording a calm river on a sweet day can kill a man if his luck is bad. Horses step in holes or panic, men fall and get tangled in reins, and deadly creatures may be disturbed. On a horrible day like today, a man would only need a shade of bad luck to die. I planned to create some bad luck for Cael in case he couldn't find any for himself.

I might have decided to use magic to drag Cael's horse under-water, and Cael with her, and then hold them there until he drowned. However, I couldn't abide such cruelty to a horse. Instead,

I would be forced to use the water itself, which would drain my power more than I liked. Water is willful, hard to shift when it's still, and hard to stop when it's moving. I planned to redirect the running water so that it slammed Cael harder and higher than it hit anybody else, over and over until it swept him off his horse to drown. I would assist with the dismounting process by aggravating his horse into gyrations.

Once Cael was dead, I would put on a sad face for Manon's benefit, although I felt sure Ella would know exactly what I'd done. Manon and I would ride on to Bellmeet, nip inside the city to make Sakaj happy, and ride back out again. Then we'd invite Ella to ride home with us. Maybe she wouldn't revile me quite as much by then. If nothing else, she and I needed each other to read Harik's book one last time.

Cael led us into the river, and I made sure to follow just behind him. When the water had risen to my shins, I pulled a white band out of the air and made an invisible channel upstream from Cael. It created a freakish, tall, and narrow wave that shot right up at him. The wave smashed into his entire left side but only shifted his horse a little. Cael shook his head and peered around.

I sent another white band upstream and shouted, "Damnedest thing I ever saw! This river must not like you much."

Cael shook his head again but didn't look back. A breath later, another wave, as high as Cael's head, smacked into him. It knocked him half out of the saddle, but he pulled himself right back up. This time, I hadn't paused between bands, and just as Cael settled back into the saddle, a third wave hit him. At the same time, I whipped a yellow band around his horse's right rear hoof and squeezed. The horse jerked while the water shoved Cael sideways.

The wave left Cael swimming, but he had twisted his hand into his horse's mane. He coughed water as he struggled to get his leg back over the horse. Behind me, Manon started screaming, and Ella called me a couple of salty names.

I spun two fingers to pull another white band, but my horse twitched and then sidestepped. Somebody snatched my wrist before I finished.

"Ella! Leave it alone!" I yanked my wrist free and glanced back, but Ella hadn't grabbed me. She was still riding four horse lengths behind me, past Manon, who couldn't have grabbed me either. As for Larripet, I could hardly even see him past Ella.

"That doesn't belong to you," a woman said from a distance, but I couldn't spot her or tell the direction of her voice.

"I apologize. Do you mind if I borrow it?" I tried to speak as if I had picked up her spoon by mistake, hoping not to inflame the situations.

"I know you," the woman said. "I should thank you for opening the way."

We had reached mid-river, and my horse was swimming. I glanced at Cael, and he had almost pulled himself back up.

I dipped my head in a salute. "You're welcome. Happy to do it."

"Don't boast. You polluted my river with your vulgar sorcerer magic. I should replace your hands with your feet." It sounded like she was hissing these threats into my ear, but I knew she could be anywhere in the water around the ford.

Cael was in the saddle again and whipping his horse to hurry out of the river. In another few seconds, my chance to kill him would pass.

"Oh, River Spirit, if that balances things between you and me, could you let me go kill that son of a bitch up there?"

The spirit laughed from some place I couldn't see. "I shouldn't say we're balanced, not at all. You're beloved of my cousin."

"The Blue River Spirit? Yes, we're close, close friends."

"I despise that graceless fishhook," she said in an icy voice.

That jarred me, but I tried for a smooth recovery. "In fact, I don't like her that much, either. I was just trying to be polite."

Fifty paces away, the spirit popped out of the river and right back in. A second later, she sprung up beside me, dove away, and then showed herself eighty paces upstream. The whole time, she laughed like a nasty boy with a trapped fly. "You're embarrassing yourself, Sorcerer." She collapsed back into the water.

"It's just that I'm so pathetic compared to an elegant river spirit like you." It was easy to say because it was so true. I glanced around. "Where are you, anyway?"

The spirit laughed again. "Hah! Do you think you can bind me as you did my cousin?"

"Absolutely not." The bank lay only ten paces away now, and Cael was already riding up onto the dirt. I drew rein. "Beautiful spirit, if you're planning to mutilate me at the very edge of your river, please don't. Maybe we can make some arrangement."

Manon rode up beside me. "Who are you talking to?"

I ignored her.

The spirit said, "Oh, we can make an arrangement. Yes, we certainly can. Here are my terms. Stop spewing your nasty magic into my river. Also, never step into my river again . . . unless you bring me a present, damn you! Don't you know anything? What sort of sorcerer are you?"

"A thoughtless one. I apologize, Fatt River Spi—I mean, Spirit of This River."

"Why don't you say my name?" the spirit asked evenly. "It there something wrong with Fatt River Spirit? Is that what you are implying?"

Ella and Larripet had joined Manon near me in the shallow water, all watching me talk to nothing.

I said, "Your name is gorgeous, Fatt River Spirit. I didn't mean to say otherwise. Well . . . can we go now?"

"You may go. Remember what I said."

Cael yelled from the riverbank, "Hurry! It's not safe!"

We all rode up the bank, where our horses stood blowing and we sat shivering.

"Something tried to drown me!" Cael said it so fast he stuttered, and his horse sidestepped. "Did anyone see it?" He had half-drawn his sword.

I turned toward the river and shaded my eyes. "I might have seen a school of big fish. I can't be sure."

Ella called out, "Bib tried to kill you."

Cael cocked his head at her. "What?"

"Ten years ago, he would have succeeded, but he is quite decrepit now. Age has slowed his hand."

Cael backed his horse away from me and drew his sword.

I realized that Ella wasn't inclined to forgive me soon, if ever. "Darling, that's rough treatment. Do you want to knock out a couple of my teeth and make me wash your chamber pot too?"

"Make him ride in front of you," she told Cael.

I frowned at them both and sat my horse, listening to the river splash and Manon sniff her runny nose. An odd drone picked up, and I wheeled around in case the river spirit had come back to kill us all. Larripet stared back at me, thrumming and whining a tune that sounded like hummingbirds set afire.

"Fine, I'll ride first." I pointed at Larripet. "But he's going to put unflattering things about you two in my song."

I led us south along the riverbank toward the Green Gate of Bellmeet, the biggest city within a three-week ride. Over fifteen thousand people crowded the place, and another few thousand farmed the valleys and fields around it. At least that had been true ten years ago when I had last visited, and a nasty visit it had been.

Bellmeet sat on the main road running from the inner kingdoms out to the western ports. Also, the Fatt River deepened just enough at Bellmeet to barge goods down to the southern ports. Dozens of miles of fertile land surrounded the whole mess, and Bellmeet attracted everybody who grew, made, bought, sold, or stole things. When the King of Bellhalt had built a stone bridge across the river a century ago, other monarchs were said to have complained that it was nothing but showing off.

Most working people lived their nasty, turnip-eating, watery-beer-drinking lives on the west side, behind the White Gate. Important places like trading houses and temples sat on the east side, behind the Green Gate. The important people who did things in temples and such lived behind the Green Gate too. If a few common people managed to sneak past one eternally guarded gate without permission and cross the bridge, the second gate would catch those stragglers.

When we reached the northern tip of Bellmeet itself, I rode

down the open corridor between the steep riverbank on my right and the high East River Wall on my left. The Rike Bridge had indeed disappeared as Cael had said, leaving just stone foundations. All five of us stopped when we reached the open Green Gate. The lack of a bridge pushed us to within a hard rock's throw of the tall gate doors.

A short, broad man in light mail blocked the way. Two guards with spears flanked the opening, and two more guards with crossbows leaned over a short, stone wall above the gate. All of them looked to be mainlanders—fair with brown hair.

The short guard strolled toward us, pursing his big lips. He nodded at Cael. "Sir."

"Dabs. We're here to see Her Majesty. Please, send a message ahead."

"Can't spare a man." Dabs spat on the road. "Sir."

Cael smiled. "A child could hold this gate with two men. A sick child. You can manage to do it with three for a few minutes."

Dabs crossed his arms and stared at Cael.

I ached to cut open that man's veins. His friends too—I might as well murder them all while I had my sword out. But I didn't so much as whistle or make a mean face. Maybe these fellows would kill Cael for me.

Cael sighed. "Fine, it's not important." He rode toward the gate at a walk.

"Wait!" Dabs called out. "No hill-rats on the green side." He jerked his chin at Larripet. "You go back around. You can get some dripping whore to ride you over on the white side, shit-skin."

Bellmeet had never welcomed people of a different shade, or even more than tolerated them. But unless Dabs was meaner than most, the city's hospitality had deteriorated since my last visit.

Larripet sat his horse with no expression. I couldn't predict whether or not he was about to jump on Dabs like a wildcat from hell. Larripet would probably sit there just the same way if Dabs had invited him home to meet the family. However, since I had known him, the Hill Man had been touchy about his version of proper manners. It puzzled me. Then he raised his eyebrows at me.

"Hell no!" I said. "This is the part of the song where every man fights his own fight."

Dabs scowled. "What's that crap you're saying?"

Cael raised his hand. "Wait! The Hill Man is with me. I'm bringing him to see the queen, so step aside."

"I don't serve you, ice-face. He stays outside." Dabs pointed at me and then Manon. "These two look pretty damn dark too. They can't come in, either."

Cael leaned down toward Dabs. "You'll be guarding a barge south to Gullhullet if you don't move."

Dabs raised his hand. The crossbowmen up behind him lifted their weapons shoulder-high, ready to make big holes in somebody.

I let my head drop. This promised to be the kind of fight where death comes easy, no matter how skilled a man is. I decided to take control of the situation with a decisive move. I fell off my horse and lay still on the dirt.

The only one who moved or commented right off was my horse, who whickered and took a step away from me. Then, as I'd expected, Dabs took charge. From the corner of my eye, I watched him walk over to kick me. His eyes popped wide when I grabbed his kicking leg and pulled him down to his knees. Then I smacked him in the throat, and he gagged.

Cael shouted, "Stop! Everybody, stop!"

I don't think anybody stopped. I sure didn't. I stood and hauled Dabs upright while he coughed, keeping him between the crossbows and me. Both spearmen ran toward me. I heard a short cry and saw a crossbowman fall backward with a knife handle sticking out of his chest.

"No! No killing!" Cael yelled. His horse almost reared.

One of the spearmen angled away from me toward somebody else, probably Larripet. I didn't think Ella could make that throw, and Cael didn't seem to be in a killing mood.

I shoved Dabs at the closest spearman and sprinted to get against the stone wall where the last crossbowman couldn't see me. I had drawn my sword by the time Dabs and his man had sorted themselves out. They came at me at the same time. I ducked the spear, parried Dabs, and cut the spearman deep across the thigh. He fell to one knee just as Dabs swung again. I cut his hand half off. He was still staring at it when I cut his throat. It felt like a hot meal after working in the cold rain all day—satisfying.

I kicked the spearman to the ground and grabbed his weapon. The crossbowman had leaned over the wall to aim at me, so I stabbed him in the face with the spear.

"Bib! Stop!" Cael screamed.

I killed the wounded spearman with his own weapon, thrusting through his heart as he lay on the dirt. Then I dropped the spear and snatched up my sword. "All right, I'll stop."

Cael scowled like he wanted to cut strips off me until nothing was left. Larripet stood over the body of the other spearman, thrusting experimentally with the dead man's weapon. Ella frowned at me and then gazed past as I were nothing but dust in the air. She had stayed on her horse throughout the fight.

Manon had stayed out of it too, but now she smiled at me. "I didn't come help because I knew you could kill them all. Two hundred and forty-six!"

Larripet turned to her. "What does that mean?"

"Bib has killed two hundred and forty-six people."

"Thank you. That is an important thing for me to know."

"You've made an enormous mistake," Cael said, tight and fierce.

"Mistake?" I sheathed my sword. "They might have killed us all. You could have a bolt through your damned forehead right now. You should thank me." I mounted and rode toward the gate. "I know the way!"

Four strides later, I drew rein. "Wait, the queen still lives in the High Tower, doesn't she?"

Cael frowned. "No, it was destroyed after the bridge."

"Then I don't know the way."

"Fine! Stay close, and don't kill anyone else!" Cael rode through the Green Gate ahead of me.

TWENTY-FIVE

I galloped into the city behind Cael and passed two guards standing twenty paces inside the gate. One pulled on a bell rope with gusto. The other threw a rock at us, and that would have been funnier if he hadn't whacked my left elbow. My arm tingled, and I cursed at him, but I had to admire his spirit.

"Where are we going?" I shouted.

"Residence," Cael shouted back, pointing north.

Cael turned right onto a narrow lane, about as wide as a wagon. That road headed straight away from the Residence. We were riding too fast for me to shout an objection, so I had to trust that he knew the city better than I did. It seemed likely since I had last been there years ago, and he'd only been gone a few months. I had to look twice when we passed a building buried in cow skeletons. Not bones. Fully connected skeletons.

After two blocks, Cael turned right and then right again onto the Harrow, the main road running through Bellmeet from the trading house to the Residence. I saw people in the distance, hustling like a formation of soldiers. Cael turned again.

I twisted to check behind us. Everyone was following along, although Manon had lost her reins and was hanging onto her horse's mane as if the street was ankle-deep in serpents. I glanced at the pale buildings as we passed; most of them dripped with wooden carvings of people, animals, and scrollwork. The walls appeared dingy, though, and I saw actual garbage on the street. In the Bellmeet that I remembered, the first thing a person did in the morning was clean the street in front of his house.

When he reached another small lane, Cael turned left and crashed into seven or eight soldiers headed the other way—I never made an exact count. Cael's horse sent one hurtling into a wall, and he kicked another in the head as he rode through. I couldn't draw my sword fast enough, so I drove my horse against the wall too. I pinned one man, and another threw himself down to escape getting squashed. Manon rode on past me and joined Cael. By the time Ella rode through, the other soldiers had closed in. She kicked one, but another grabbed her and hauled her out of the saddle. She slammed hard onto the stone street and didn't get up.

I slid off my horse and drew my sword as I ran toward Ella, who was surrounded by three men ignoring her. Two ran toward me, and one turned back toward Larripet.

"Don't kill anybody!" Cael yelled from down the lane.

I killed both soldiers within ten seconds, or at least I gave them mortal wounds. They had hesitated, not wanting to hit each other by mistake in the narrow street, so I left them both bleeding to death. Larripet had reined in his horse, and the soldier facing him waved his sword high as he ran at the Hill Man. When the soldier had almost reached him, Larripet thrust his spear into the man's chest and pulled it back. It looked nearly as fast as a frog's tongue.

I lifted Ella, who had blood flowing down her cheek and a gritty scrape across her forehead. She tried to stand, went limp, and tried to stand again.

"Hurry up!" Cael yelled.

"Come help me, you floppy-dicked oaf!" I shouted back.

He didn't come help. I boosted Ella up to Larripet, and he pulled her the rest of the way to lay her across the front of his saddle.

"Bib!"

I turned to tell Cael to entertain himself by counting to eleven, but instead, I saw a soldier's sword swinging down hard not two feet from my head. I ducked and shifted aside at the same time. The sword took off a sliver of my hair and scalp. I prefer to attack with thrusts or small slashes, but I got mad and took the man's leg off at the knee. He toppled over shrieking, and to apologize for being so crude, I thrust my sword through his eye.

I jumped onto my horse and shooed Cael with my free hand. "Go on! Don't sit around on your thumb!"

"Too slow." He shook his head as he turned his horse. "Too late." He galloped away down the street, which wasn't quite heading toward the Residence, but at least it wasn't heading directly away.

Two minutes and four turns later, we at last, with no doubt, were riding toward the Residence. We had passed one big building burned to the timbers and another so covered in rose vines that I couldn't see the house itself. We galloped down Salt Street, a wide avenue that crossed the Harrow where it passed by the great Salt House. A huge salt field lay just downriver from the city, and everybody in six kingdoms who wanted salt bought it from Bellmeet. That commerce must have died for the time being, because the two-story Salt House had collapsed sideways, as if a giant had mashed it.

We rounded the corner onto the Harrow. Then we hauled the reins to wheel our horses. Two dozen soldiers with spears stood two ranks deep almost a block away between us and the Residence. Before we could ride ten strides the other way, another dozen men ran out from hiding and closed off the street behind us. Ten cross-bowmen stood scattered among both groups. Somebody had laid a sweet ambush.

"I'm sure glad you took us down all those back ways, Cael," I said. "It paid off."

Cael didn't answer me, which was fine. I imagined he was just as disappointed as me.

A finely dressed, dumpy man stepped up through the double row of soldiers and called out, "Oh, it has all the stink of treason to me. Killing the queen's men has just got to be treason. It stands to reason." He chuckled. "I'm sorry, that was horrible. Treason, reason

—ouch." His voice sounded happy and friendly, but he wasn't smiling. "At least you died fighting."

"I surrender, Nubba," Cael said, sitting high.

"What's that? You say you want to throw Her Majesty in the river and sit on her? How dare you? That's just awful."

"He didn't say that!" Manon yelled.

I whispered, "Please don't do anything, Manon." Then I yelled at the dumpy man, "Nubba? Seriously? Tell me that you locked your ma and pa up in a shed and burned it. That could be the only punishment for a name like Nubba."

Nubba laughed, and it sounded like real amusement. Cael turned in the saddle and stared at me.

I muttered to him, "Does anybody in this city even like you?"

Cael shrugged. "The queen."

"Let's go see her then." I raised my voice loud enough that Manon and Larripet could hear too. "When I ride, you ride like hell after me, and don't stop to fight anybody." I started pulling blue bands from the air with the fingers on both hands.

Nubba yelled, "That's so sweet, you two declaring your love just before you die. Now, men . . . wait!" He hiked up the hem of his silver-embroidered cloak and skipped back half a dozen steps. "There, you can kill them now, Captain."

A graying fellow, about my age, yelled, "Attack!"

I didn't have enough power for this, nor even a quarter of the power I needed to do it properly. It forced me to skimp on the niceties, and on some of the necessities too. It was bad enough that I had to rot the wood from a distance. Dead wood wants to rot, and that was in my favor, but putting my hands on it would have made things far less taxing. Also, I needed to do everything as near to the same time as I could. When I was a young sorcerer, I would have fumbled it and might have died.

I would have preferred to rot every wooden item within fifty paces of me in the interest of thoroughness. However, I have probably never possessed enough power all at once to accomplish that. That forced me to be selective. I kicked my horse and began whipping out bands, starting with the crossbows. I rotted a ham-size chunk of wood right under each crosspiece. When the men tried to fire their weapons a moment later, the weakened wood gave way and the crossbows exploded, hurling stocks, quarrels, and steel crosspieces in all directions.

The crossbowmen had begun screaming and cursing by the time my horse reached the soldiers between the Residence and me. I threw blue bands and rotted the spear shafts one by one, one foot back from each spearhead. Each rotted section was as long as a kitchen spoon and not much sturdier than ashes. Four soldiers thrust at me, and the spearheads hurt like a son of a bitch, but they just tumbled away when the shafts crumbled.

I reined in when I had passed the soldiers. I waved Cael and the others on ahead with one hand while I kept on rotting spear shafts with the other. I labored at it until everyone had passed through the line of soldiers, and every man near me held a useless weapon. Then I turned to follow Cael as he charged up the Harrow toward the Residence.

Rather than destroying all the spears held by the nearby soldiers, I had saved my last little chunk of power like a good, conservative sorcerer. One of the squint-face bastards I had ignored flung his spear and hit me right above my left elbow, which was still tingling a little from the rock that had pegged me at the gate. The spear fell out right away, but I felt blood seeping from what must have been a ragged puncture in the back of my arm.

The Royal Residence squatted at the end of the Harrow like a stately toad. The low, stone building took up most of that end of the city. The damn thing was so hideous that the queen had refused to live there when her father died. Almost all of Bellmeet's structures had been built from wood and then carved with a certain amount of charm and even artistry. The stone Residence was spread out—high, severe, and hard as hell to get into. A gate fortified with spikes, iron bands, and copious murder holes guarded the only entrance. Arrow slits dotted the outside walls, and plenty of platforms sat on the roof for throwing or slinging nasty things down on unwelcome visitors.

The guards on duty at the Residence hadn't ignored the

warning bell. As we rode closer, I made out at least forty armed men and women on the ground. That many or more might have been staring through arrow slits, anxious to put a shaft into one of us nasty strangers. I remembered that they'd be using real bows, not crossbows, and could shoot at us three times in a minute, easy.

Cael raised his hand and stopped fifty paces out from the gate. "Bib, I want you to promise not to kill anybody. If you go crazy like you did at the city gate, then we'll all die."

"You may not be bright, but you're right this time," I said. "I promise not to kill anybody. I think I can cripple them if I concentrate."

"Bib!"

"All right, I won't attack anybody unless they attack me first."

Ella had sat up in front of Larripet on his horse. "Promise me too." She slurred her words just a little.

"Fine, I promise! Should I kiss their hands and sing ballads too?"

Cael dismounted. "Shut up! And follow me." He walked toward the gate. The rest of us did the same as he bellowed, "It's Cael! I'm bringing four friends! One is the man Her Majesty wants!"

One of the guards, a young woman, shouted back, "Come on then. Walk slow." When we had come within ten paces, she said, "Stop! Wait right there!"

The guards had nothing obvious in common except a yellow tabard and light skin. They carried all kinds of hand weapons and wore different clothes and armor, some whimsical. Some were still teenagers, and a few were older than me. All of them sized us up as if we were something they might have to swat and throw out the back door. I couldn't resist smiling and waving at a few of them.

The young woman doing the talking didn't wear or carry anything that especially said she was the boss. Her brown hair was cut short and her nose had been broken a few times. Her smart, wide-set eyes crinkled when they saw Cael. She strode up to Cael and grabbed him in a big hug. Then she said, "Every day she asks whether you've come back. Twice a day. Sometime more. Stay here." She let out a high whistle as she walked back toward the gate, and two men ran inside.

I heard shouts and footsteps behind me. Nubba's men were raising a respectable dust cloud as they charged up the street toward us. I eased my sword in its scabbard. "Manon, I have squeezed out all the power I care to. Please, please don't do anything! Not until I say so. Then I ask that you do something to stop them. Cael would rather they not die, but that's up to you. He can't give you orders, and I can't either."

Manon grabbed my hand, and hers was shaking especially hard.

I had become aware of whistling and hooting behind my back while I made my plea to Manon. Now the lead Residence guard ran past me toward Nubba's crew. A few seconds later, twenty or so guards followed her. They stopped an easy rock's toss away from Nubba's men, and they waited.

Nubba's soldiers closed on the guards, and I expected a profound bloodletting. Cael held his ground, and I did too. The guards didn't know me from a hole in the ground, and they might decide to kill me before they worry about the soldiers.

The soldiers halted just more than spitting distance away from the guards and started yelling profanities. The guards shouted back some fine curses of their own. A couple of soldiers scraped handfuls of dirt off the street and threw them at the guards, with about as much effect as throwing feathers. A soldier took down his trousers and showed his ass to the guards, and three more joined him. A guard exposed his private parts and waved them at the soldiers.

I muttered, "Cael, I remember going to concerts and plays here years ago. Is this what Bellmeet culture has come to?"

"I'd like to tell you no." His face pinkened.

"Everybody, stop! Stop right now!" A woman's voice, piercing but not shrill, split the sounds of insults, foot-scraping, and flatulence. A few soldiers and guards didn't quiet down right away. The boss guard on one side and Nubba on the other whacked them into silence.

The queen walked right in between the guards and soldiers, and she glared around at everybody. She was as tall and slender as I remembered, with skin less fair than most mainlanders, and brown hair almost light enough to be blonde. I had to stare hard to see the gray in it. She wore a long shirt and short trousers, fine enough to cost two months' journeyman wages. Her knee and hands were grimy, as if she'd been digging in the dirt when she was fetched.

"This is unacceptable." She showed her teeth. "I don't care who started it, and I don't care who stabbed whom. I will not have my valued fighting men and women fighting among themselves! You don't have to love each other. You needn't even like each other. But you will not engage in open hostilities!"

The queen looked around and flipped her long braid back over her shoulder. "I pray to every god that I am not killed in my home some night by a crippled drunkard because my guards and my soldiers were all off flapping their asses and dicks at each other. Your behavior demands punishment of the direst sort. Nubba? Syd? I leave that to you. You know what needs to be done."

"Yes, Your Majesty." Syd, the head guard, bowed.

"Certainly, Your Majesty," Nubba said, bowing lower.

When the queen turned away, Syd bowed even lower as she sneered at Nubba.

Mina, Queen of Bellhalt, stared around at us all. "Well? Go do your jobs. Is it your job to stand in the street and gape at me like a codfish? No? Then scamper!"

Everyone trotted away except for Mina, Nubba, Syd, four guards, and us. Cael knelt. I glanced around. Ella knelt next, and then Manon. I didn't see anything good coming from acting like an ass just yet, so I knelt too.

Larripet asked me, "This woman owns this city?"

"Yes, and all the country around it."

"She owns the soldiers who are loud and easy to kill?"

"Every one of them."

Larripet glanced at Mina and then back at me. "I wish I could give her a dog."

I blinked. "That . . . I'm sure that would be nice."

The Hill Man nodded. "A dog will not lie or betray. It cannot pretend to love. It is the right gift for a king."

I knew better than to expect elaboration from the man. "Or a queen. We'll look for a dog, then. I mean it."

Larripet knelt too.

Mina held out her hand to Cael. "I wasn't sure that anyone could do it, but you did." She jerked her head toward me. "You brought him. I have never met a person more loyal and able than you, Cael."

Cael bowed his head. "Thank you, Your Majesty." I was kneeling in just the right spot to see his face. He was smiling, but he had the eyes of a regretful old man.

I spoke up. "May I stand up? I'm old and infirm."

"Horseshit. Yes, you may." Mina waved a careless hand at me.

"Well, I'm here, old girl. What do you want with me?"

Cael hissed but didn't say anything.

Mina clenched her teeth. "You must answer for your actions. And your actions have been heinous."

"I have heard that a lot recently."

TWENTY-SIX

I could have been King of Bellhalt if I hadn't turned down the job. That's what I told my fellow drunks sometimes when it was early morning in the tavern. It impressed most of them, since they were too crocked to tell a boiled chicken from four boiled rats sewn together. One tavern owner proved that to be true.

Mina and I met not long after I first left Ir. I had survived several dozen mistakes that commonly killed new sorcerers, and I planned to cure every ill that my elders had been too timid to overcome. This happened years before I started murdering people for Harik. Mina was almost twenty years old, ancient to still be unmarried. Despite her highborn and wealthy family, she had earned a reputation for disparaging behavior, such infamy that every suitor decided that no amount of wealth and power was worth it. Gossip said that some suitors decided to give up while in midair as she tossed them into the garden pond.

We met in the market square and fell in love two days later. I can't imagine what she liked about me, but she was smart, generous, and ready to eviscerate anybody who pushed her. We enjoyed each other's company in secret, since few people would have approved of our romance. She assured me that if her father found us out, he'd send a hundred men after me and then nail me over his door like I was a wolf that poaches sheep.

Mina started life far down in the line of succession. Two assassinations and an epidemic changed that, putting her father next in line for the throne, just behind the sitting king. That king started a war and then died in it. The same war killed Mina's father three months later. Mina became queen and won that war. I watched her do it.

A lot of Mina's subjects complained about having a queen instead of a king, and some important people met in secluded rooms to discuss doing something about "that mouthy little girl." After she had them arrested and hanged, people began adjusting to the idea of a female monarch.

To me, being a king sounded like sitting around and listening to fat men who wanted things, while servants brought me whatever I told them to fetch. I felt inclined to try it out, and I told Mina so when I asked her to marry me. I did not understand at that time how much smarter she was than me. She said no. She also said I'd be a horrible king, an awful consort, and probably not much of a husband, either.

That seemed abrupt and painful too, but no argument or plea could change her mind. I left the kingdom of Bellhalt downcast and without purpose, riding east to find out what would happen to me next. A few years later, I did make a tolerable husband, or so my wife told me.

I had visited Bellmeet once since Mina denied me the throne. Twelve years had passed, and my wife had just died. I didn't arrive with a bunch of hopes, but I hadn't expected to be run out of town, either. Mina welcomed me, and I think she was sincere. But she had acquired a husband and three little boys, all with uncommon, dark bushy hair, and not a one of them appreciated my existence.

That first night, some men grabbed me out of bed, tied me up, and hustled me to a dock. They rowed me miles downriver and threw me up on the bank, still bound. Then they gathered all my possessions up into bundles and threw them into the river while I watched.

"Never come back here," Mina's husband grated. "We'll do worse."

Profanity, epithets, and curses to the gods lose their spice when said through a gag.

Her husband kicked me and laughed. "Don't come back."

Now I was back. When guards shooed me into a big audience room, I peered around for Mina's husband. I couldn't remember his name, so in my head, I called him the Jackal's Crotch. For Mina's sake, I might not kill him the moment I saw him. It might upset the kids too, although I didn't see them, either. Unless he was hiding behind one of those tall, pretty tapestries, he wasn't in the room, but if somebody didn't apologize to me pretty damn quick, I was going to start taking heads.

I had participated in this kind of throne-room nonsense more than a dozen times. Mina sat on a raised chair at the front of the room, and Cael stood down on the floor to her left and Nubba stood on the dais to her right. Four guards stood within easy reach of her. Ella, Larripet, Manon, and I stood facing her on a gigantic, burgundy rug in the middle of the room, like pigs waiting to get picked out for supper. I figured to hell with that.

"Where's your husband, Your Majesty? Off on some vital, uninterruptable errand, maybe?"

Nubba stepped forward to block the path between Mina and me. "The Prince Consort died almost three years ago." The soft little fellow put his hand on what appeared to be a well-used sword. He'd have killed me for sure, if nasty looks had been fatal.

"Well, I am sorry about that. I assure you I've changed my mind and don't want to be a king anymore, just to be clear about things."

Mina had smiled at the back of Nubba's head when he tried to intimidate me. Now she scrutinized me, and her smile drained away. "Bib, you're no longer so clever as you think. Age, I suppose. My youngest son died with his father."

I thought about my first daughter as I lowered my voice. "I am sorry about that, Mina. That's a hard thing."

When I used the queen's given name, Cael clenched his teeth and glared more profanity at me than he'd spoken since I met him.

Before he could will me to die, the big door behind me clattered open. Syd, the captain of the guard, hustled in with nineteen guards. They planted themselves so that I'd be forced to fight at least three of them to reach the queen, no matter my line of attack. Syd stepped in front of me and gave a little nod, as if she'd just walked into a crowded bar and joined me at my table.

A small crowd of people had followed the guards in. Most of them wore expensive clothes, but a few wore the clothing of working people, bakers, and carpenters. One wore rags, and I could smell him from where I stood. They gathered into clumps on each side of us.

I examined all these people for a moment. I judged that none of them was any deadlier or pompous or repulsive than they first appeared. "You know I love an audience, Your Majesty. Since Cael threatened and bargained and cheated for hundreds of miles to get me here, what do you want?"

"I brought you here to fix all this, Sorcerer."

I raised my eyebrows and lifted my hands.

She went on: "The inexplicable disappearance of great structures. Buildings destroyed by lightning storms that come from nothing and disappear in minutes. Sheep bleating in harmony for days."

"For five days? Five sheep? Five note harmony?"

The queen jumped up. "Yes! How do you know that? Do you see? I think you're causing all of this. Even if you're not, you will make it stop."

"Oh, I was just guessing." Five was a likely number to guess, or at least it was likely for a sorcerer to guess. It was a strong number for any animal that walked on four legs. Four legs plus a head was five, which was a low prime number. The only number more auspicious was three. I hadn't been able to resist the chance to aggravate Mina.

Mina barreled down off the platform toward me. Although she was slim, she staggered a guard when she shoved him out of the way. "Don't try that shit with me! I know you better than anyone." She pointed at Manon. "She's not your daughter. You're helping her out of guilt, probably." She pointed at Ella. "She's your latest punch. I know that look. She's sick of you already." She pointed at Larripet. "He's . . . I really have no idea, but that's not the point!"

"I'm sorry, dear, but I can't do what you want. It is beyond my ability to put things back the way they were," I said.

Mina spun toward Cael. "Did you give him the book?"

Cael nodded.

She took another two steps toward me. "He gave you the book!" She said it the way she might say, "You have two arms!" Four guards shifted to stand on each side of her.

"He could give me a book, a pony, and a poke in the eye." I shrugged. "None of that matters. The way is open again. The gods have been freed. We can't stop them."

Mina grabbed the front of my shirt, and I didn't resist. She shook me like a fly in a bottle. "Did you do this? Tell me the truth, you prevaricating bastard!"

"The gods are doing this. But I did help them along a little—not that I meant for all this horrible shit to happen."

Mina pushed me away. "You didn't mean it—you just did it!" She glowered at Ella. "He just did it. Right? Just like always."

Ella pressed her lips tight and gave the tiniest nod possible.

"I should have you killed." Mina walked back toward her chair. "Tortured. Kept alive to torture for ten years. All your friends too."

Nobody besides me was meeting the queen's eyes now. Some turned sideways or crouched a little, as if that might make them invisible.

Nubba shouted, "Krak! Lutigan's ass hairs!" He shook his left foot, and a small rat fell out of this trousers leg. For a moment, nobody else did or said anything while Nubba swung and twisted his other leg. Two more rats fell from that one.

Nubba pointed at me. "Stop! Stop this right now!" He drew his sword, but he dropped it when a rat crawled out of his collar and up the side of his head. He swatted but missed the rat and hit himself in the eye. I stepped to the side with four guards pacing me, and I stood on my toes to crane my head. A line of rats ran to Nubba from the wall behind him. Some launched themselves onto his body, some burrowed inside his clothes, and others swarmed any exposed skin. The line of rats was followed by a mass of rats emerging from under the back wall.

"Kill him!" Nubba screamed, flailing at rats and at his clothes. "Sweet gods, kill the sorcerer, kill him, hurry!"

Syd looked at Mina, who shook her head. "Go help him, dear."

Guards pressed in close to Nubba, swatting rats off him. The small army of rats was becoming a large army of rats. Rats must have been coming from all parts of the Residence, and maybe from the city outside.

I could have helped him, but I wasn't wasting the last of my power on Nubba. Rats that small wouldn't kill him anyway, unless he inhaled one and choked to death. He finally fell and rolled back and forth on the dais. I've disemboweled men who didn't scream as loud.

The queen sat in her chair, ignoring Nubba with her face propped in one palm. Nubba's screams hit a crescendo. He must have been ruining his voice. Mina beckoned me, and the guards snarled as they let me through.

Mina took a deep breath and nodded toward Nubba. "Bib, can't you help him somehow?"

I cocked my head at the suffering man. I didn't like the familiar looks he'd been giving Mina. "I can buy him a drink and tell him about all the people who have it worse than him."

She hit me on the chest, but not half as hard as she could have. "Help him, or the only way you will leave this city is in a dozen separate jars."

"I'll do what I can, but it may not be much. You have a new sorcerer some place in the city."

Mina closed her eyes and nodded at me. "I know."

I leaned in toward her. "He or she could be anywhere and could be anyone."

Nubba shrieked louder, and we spun to see. Guards had cut off all his clothes to get at the rats, but without his clothes in the way, a whole lot more rats could invade his private areas.

Mina shook her head at me. "No, the sorcerer can't be anywhere or anyone. He's upstairs, and he's my son."

"Which one?

"The only one I have left."

I considered the stairs. "You could be wrong about him. These things are pretty near random."

"The recent bizarre events happen disproportionately often to Nubba. Martel hates Nubba. He thinks Nubba is going to replace his father."

"Is he?"

"Maybe."

"Huh. You threw me out as a possible husband, but you may decide to cuddle with that? Either I have serious problems, or you do. I want to meet Martel. I might help him a little. Or, I could wait a week. Maybe Nubba will get murdered by a stray shingle."

TWENTY-SEVEN

"You hit my son in the face with a horseshoe! Three times!" Her Majesty stalked into my room dragging her fourteen-year-old son by one hand, and she hurled the horseshoe in question at my throat. I snatched it out of the air before it whacked my windpipe and made me gag.

"Don't concern yourself—I'm done with all that. Tomorrow, I'm throwing a baby snake and a horse turd at him." I winked at Martel, who was a lanky boy with calm eyes. He tried to turn his bruised, red face away as if this embarrassment could be ignored. I imagined his current situation felt less desirable than death.

Mina sneered. "I asked you to help him! This isn't help. You're deliberately humiliating him to spite me."

I set my cup on the table for more wine. "I am not. I'd have to care more about you to make the effort."

Manon grasped one of the bottles in front of her with both shaking hands. She poured my cup half full and spilled about the same amount on the table. Neither of us mentioned it or flinched.

I picked up my wine cup. "Thank you, darling."

"Bastard!" The queen didn't quite shout it at me, but I'm sure they heard her in the next room.

"I know you own every damn thing around here," I said, "but you're no more important to me than the last barmaid I toppled. Fond memories, but I didn't pay much attention to anything she said."

Martel gasped and clenched his fists. Defending his mother from me ought to give him back some self-respect.

Mina hissed, "I'll have you tortured to death."

Manon, who hadn't yet acknowledged that Mina was in the room, looked up at her blank-faced. "You shouldn't talk to sorcerers like that, Your Majesty. It's not nice. Bad things happen to people who aren't nice."

I smiled at the girl but said, "Manon, let me handle this, please."

Mina took two steps toward the table. "Bib, if you don't whip some respect into this smug little girl, I will!"

I winced and shook my head. "Please don't say that. I don't give Manon orders. She's a sorcerer, and don't you go thinking less of her because she's short."

"Thank you, Father."

Martel had glared back and forth between Manon and me. He might have been deciding which of us to hit first. He settled on me. "Bib, apologize to my mother!"

"Don't you respect my opinion, son?"

"Not on this. And I'm not your son!"

I nodded. "That's fair. I do admit, I'm acting like a right sideways bastard. But then I'm a sorcerer, so who can tell me to stop?"

Mina held up a hand. "Martel, no. He's charming, but he's as dangerous as a tiger. A diseased tiger that rots off your toes and hands."

Martel yanked free and charged right up to the table. "Apologize," he said in a cold voice. "Maybe I'm not a sorcerer, but if you don't apologize, I'll make you turn me into sand or burn me alive to keep me from killing you."

Manon smiled a charming smile at Martel, and he faltered when he glanced at her.

I held up both hands. "I apologize, Mina. I shouldn't have expressed all those rude opinions. Martel, I admire how you stood up to me." As a rule, I don't apologize, but I would have eaten a good deal more dirt if it helped Martel forget that his damned mother had hauled him in here like he had shit the rug.

I nodded toward Manon. "Martel, would you please show Manon around the Residence? Show her any interesting trees or ugly, old tapestries?"

Manon glanced at me and locked eyes with Martel. "Please? I'm sorry too."

Martel paused, stood tall, and nodded at Manon. "All right." He frowned at me. "But we're going to the armory!"

Manon squeezed my forearm, gave Mina a stiff curtsy that was a twitch away from mockery, and skipped out of the room ahead of Martel.

Mina I sat with a groan. "Control her, Bib, or she'll come to a bad end. I won't have any choice but to do it myself."

"Really? What would you do if your son was acting like her?"

She gritted her teeth. "I would smack him until his eyes crossed."

"Would you do that once he's a sorcerer? When he can burn a company of your soldiers to flakes of ash? When he can collapse whichever portion of this fine residence he chooses?"

Mina pursed her lips, and then she sat down across from me. "Give me a cup."

"This is the only one."

"Give." Mina poured her cup full and raised it. "I hate you too." She sipped. "What must I do? I can win wars and gut traitors and slap shitty little courtiers around, but . . ."

"You won't like it."

"I don't like anything these days."

I stared at the queen with as much gravity as I could scare up. "Not every young sorcerer lives through his first year. Their chances aren't much better than a baby turtle's."

"What?" she whispered.

"Sorcery is a perilous business. Since you asked for my advice, I'll throw you a ton of it. Let me help him get some control even if it means I make him walk like a chicken and lick every tavern door in the city. I should finish that up by tomorrow."

She grimaced and nodded.

"Then you go hire some rude, nasty old monk to tutor him for a couple of years, to prevent the boy from turning himself to silver or some other whimsical thing. Then ship him to the temple on Barrelshins for another two or three years. Or, send them a wagon loaded with gold and ask their best teacher to live here for a while."

"That is what you suggest?"

"Damn right." I took a drink. "Oh, and it doesn't hurt anything if you want to love him, but never pity him. If he starts pitying himself, he might as well jump in the ocean and spare us all this crap."

Mina sat rigid and lay down her cup. "You stay, Bib. You teach him."

I didn't laugh at her, since she looked so terrified. "No. Either you or Manon would die within the first month. And don't even talk about me sending her away."

"I could imprison her and force you to stay."

That time, I did laugh.

Mina scratched at a scar on the tabletop and glanced over at me. "I hear stories. She'd be powerless if I cut off her hands."

Just for a moment, I imagined Mina's throat slashed open and spurting blood. I tapped my fingers on the wet tabletop. "I know that's your fear talking, and that you'd never do something like that."

Mina stared at me for a couple of seconds. "Of course not, that would be horrible. But Martel will be the next king. I must protect him in any way I can. Any way that's not horrible."

"Sure. Do you want another drink?"

"No." Mina stood and smoothed her rich, quilted shirt.

"Don't hurry off to plot against me just yet. We need to resolve my payment."

Mina started. "You never mentioned payment. Don't you have a sacred duty to train young sorcerers for free, or something like that?"

I raised an eyebrow at her . "Does that sound like me?"

She frowned. "What's your price? Is it too much to hope that you simply want money?"

I drummed my fingers on the table and let her wait about ten seconds. "I want two things. First, tell me everything you know about this book you sent me." I held up Harik's little book.

"What a disappointment for you. There's not much. A man infiltrated the library a few months ago, a sorcerer. Or at least he possessed a little power and an ocean of gall. We killed him in the library beside a shelf holding sixty-year-old harvest records, some mummified amphibians, my grandfather's love poetry, and that little book—which no one had ever seen before."

"It just showed up one day while you weren't looking?"

"Yes. I had touched that shelf dozens of times. Gran'ther wrote some darling poems. That little book was never there before. No one could open it, not a finger's width, so I locked it away. A few weeks later, another sorcerer tried to steal it, and then a month after that, a third sorcerer took a run at it. By then, horrible things had begun happening around my son."

"So, then you sent Cael lumbering across the countryside to find me—bringing the book."

"Bib, you had sneaked through my country months before." She started talking faster. "How could I know what curses you had laid down? Certainly, I sent Cael to find you and to bring you here!"

"You're right. Your story disappoints the hell out of me. You could have at least embellished it with some pretty girls or a pillar of fire. Fine then. For the second part of my payment, I want your most precious piece of jewelry."

Mina stared at me.

"For every five seconds you make me wait for an answer, I'll add on your next most precious piece of jewelry, whatever it is."

"This is ridiculous. You're just being greedy."

I could barely believe that she was talking to me about being greedy. "Isn't your son's life worth a bracelet, or a tiara? Now you owe me your two most precious pieces. Shouldn't have hesitated."

Mina stood and turned away. "Very well. I'll send them with a servant." She walked out into the hallway.

I shouted after her, "I'm off to examine your son's face. I can stir up a good onion and goose-shit poultice for those lumps."

Her footsteps clopped, then echoed, and then faded. I drank another cup of wine and walked after her into the hallway, turning and almost banging into Larripet.

"Have you been standing here?" I walked off toward the barracks, and he followed me.

"You laughed at the queen, and she did not kill you." He pursed his lips before saying, "It will be in your song."

"Hell, ignore that, I wasn't brave. She has a tender spot for me because we used to get wiggly under the trees at night."

Larripet raised his eyebrows. "You fornicated with the queen? That will definitely be in your song."

"Fine, put it in."

"Did you love her?"

"I suppose I did." I walked a little faster.

"Where are the children you made together?"

"We never had children."

Larripet raised one eyebrow. "Did you love her?"

It surprised me that the question hurt a little. "Well . . . I suppose not enough."

He grunted, turned, and walked right back the way we came.

The barracks sat in one of the Residence courtyards. It was a square wooden building big enough for fifty bunks along the walls and three trestle tables in the middle. It smelled as musty as fifty hard-working people, but not as musty as fifty hard-working people who didn't wash. Six open windows lit the whole space with bright winter daylight.

I hoped to cajole a few guards into fencing with me, as we'd done the past two days. I wanted to keep myself sharp and exercise my frustration with Mina, who had forbidden us to leave the Residence. She had hired excellent guards. Every one of them could have commanded men and women elsewhere. She must have paid them well and treated them even better. I started off thrashing them one by one. Then I started humiliating them in pairs. Today, I thought I might cut three out of the herd, slop some beer on them, and see if they'd fight instead of stand there with big eyes.

All the guards must have been out guarding things that afternoon, because I couldn't hear anybody sitting around the barracks bitching. I saw only Ella and Cael standing beside a nasty, junk-strewn table. They were leaning in, heads together, as they murmured to each other.

I had feared that Ella was done with me, but I hadn't known it to be fact until then. I stepped halfway back into the hall, anticipating the waterfall of wine that would slide down my throat as I hated her and then shoot back up as I hated myself.

Without even winding up, Cael slapped Ella's face with a crack that echoed off the flat, wooden walls. She staggered back three steps, steadied herself, and spun to sprint toward the far door. Cael ran after her.

"Rat-suck bastard!" I shouted, and I chased Cael across the room, knocking a chair out of the way as I went. I ran through the door and crashed into two gaping servants. One fell and smacked onto the wooden floor. The other screamed and dropped a box of pewter mugs. While stumbling my way through the mugs, I spotted Cael disappearing through another doorway on the right.

I kicked the last stray mug and followed Cael into a modest, square room that stored the guards' bedding and such, along with three more staring servants. Cael shot through a door in the opposite wall. A braid of cloth on his wrist snagged the latch and tore, and in that instant, Cael turned into a squatty man wearing a shirt full of holes. Somebody I didn't see slammed the door shut. Just as I reached it, I heard a wooden bar drop on the other side.

A couple of things happened then. First, I reminded myself that sorcerers shouldn't lose their tempers, because angry sorcerers do stupid things and get killed. I wished I had remembered that thirty seconds earlier.

Second, I rolled to my left and came up in a crouch, facing the middle of the room. While I was rolling, some arrows struck the barred door, or near it, or not too near it. Eight Residence servants stood on the far side of the room, four aiming their bows at me and four reloading. Agni stood behind them.

I could have rushed them, but I'd have to draw a weapon, or else go after them bare-handed. They might be no more accurate than a blind man with no hands pissing in a high wind, but even so, they could hit me when I closed to within five feet.

Agni said, "Bib, when you're finally dead and have to explain yourself to your gods, tell them the way will be closed soon."

I stood. "Happy to. Any other news to pass on to the gods? Recipes to share?"

Agni sighed, and her shoulders eased down, like a tight sheet floating to the grass. "No. Tell my babies they can finally sleep because I killed you. And say to be patient, that I'll come for them soon."

"I've never killed any children, you raggedy-ass fanatic!"

"You murdered mine." She sounded certain—as if she was just saying that fire is hot.

The servants had all loaded up their bows by then, and Agni scowled at me like I was something nasty in her shoe. I had a bit of power saved, and I didn't anticipate any upcoming threats to my life more severe than this one.

I whipped a blue band over a man-high pile of cotton bedding. In a moment, I rotted it down to wisps and bits. The entire pile collapsed on itself, hit the floor, and exploded to fill the air with eyeball-sticking, throat-choking rotting cotton debris throughout a good part of the room.

I didn't dawdle. I hopped back over to the door, listening to arrows smack into the wall behind me as I went. I assessed for a moment. The servants were yelling and arguing, and Agni was screaming over them, an appalling racket. Now I could just walk over and kill half of them while they were blind and reloading. Maybe the other half would panic and shoot each other. Then Agni and I could talk about just who the hell was murdering children and who wasn't.

The door behind me whipped open, and a burning rod ripped all the way through my torso from back to front. I squinted down to see a sword point sticking six inches out of my belly. "Shit!" I yelled. I followed up with a much less energetic, "Son of a bitch."

Behind me, whoever held the other end of that sword gave it a grinding twist. I saw Agni in the middle of the room, laughing and pushing between her flunkies to reach me. My arms and legs gave up, and I dropped onto my knees as I tasted blood. Then I grabbed the sword blade. I guess I thought I'd hold on so that asshole couldn't twist it again. Or maybe I planned to push it back out, turn around, draw my sword, and cut off his head—and then die, because I had already used up my tiniest bit of remaining power.

This was a marvelous time to visit Harik. That idea vanished when the nasty goon behind me yanked his sword back out and then shoved me. I collapsed onto my face, and that was all.

TWENTY-EIGHT

The rope woke me up—the imaginary one being dragged back and forth between the two holes in my torso. Without thinking, I grabbed for my belly and tried to sit up at the same time. Something knocked my hands away, and something else pushed my shoulders back down. I tried to say, "Stop that!" but instead, I croaked like a petulant frog.

"Stop wiggling," Manon's voice said.

I opened my eyes. Manon was kneeling over me with one palm pressed against the exit wound in my belly. She moved the other hand around in the air, jerking and trembling. Two of the guards had pinned my shoulders.

I swallowed, spat out a little blood, and cleared my throat. "I wasn't aware you knew how to do that," I whispered.

Manon gave a little head shake, flinging off drops of sweat. "My mother taught me."

"How much did that cost you?"

"Shut up! I'm trying not to put you back together wrong!"

I closed my eyes and breathed for a bit as the rope stopped dragging. Then phantom pliers started pinching. Soon, Manon began breathing faster, and then she grunted.

I gave her a tiny grin. "Sorry, darling, I know it hurts."

"Say something else obvious. If I'd known it would be like this, I might have let you die." She sounded mad at me for getting stabbed.

"Why didn't Agni kill me, I wonder."

Manon didn't answer, but she narrowed her eyes as a slicing pain ran from my hip to my shoulder blade.

A minute later, Manon sat back and wiped her sallow face with her sleeve. "How's that?" she wheezed.

It might have been better. I felt a stitch in the middle of my belly, and it wasn't from running. Manon had connected something in not quite the proper place. It didn't feel fatal, though. I hated to discourage the girl, but without correction, she might kill somebody next time. "Thank you, Manon. That will save my life just fine, although something is a little twisted in there."

She hunched over her belly and grunted. "I'm not surprised. It was my first try." She didn't seem to be embarrassed or regretful at all.

"Don't worry. I won't ask you to go in again and fix me."

Manon pressed her palms to her own belly and winced. "Sit up then."

The guards hauled at my arms to get me there, and I blinked around to get my bearings. I was sitting in the same storeroom, in just the spot where I'd fallen when I was run through. Some wisps of rotted cotton still floated around. Two more guards stood at the doors, and Larripet was squatting by my feet.

Larripet said, "You looked dead, but you were not. The killers were lazy and careless."

Manon was fumbling for something on the floor that I couldn't see.

I grasped her forearm and said, "How do you feel now, bedsides impaled?"

Without shifting, she scrutinized the store room's floor. She felt the smooth stone underneath her, and then shook her head. "I feel all right, I guess. Lift your legs."

I was forced to groan, but I lifted my legs just a fraction off the ground.

Manon patted the floor under me and shook her head.

"I know that you're free to ignore me," I said, "but if you feel like telling me what you gave up to your mother, I think that could help us both."

"No." She didn't pause to blink.

"I'll assume that not telling me was part of the bargain."

Manon had been investigating things like she'd lost a pin, but now she stared at me without so much as twitching. If Sakaj had made Manon forget something, she might not know what she had given up, only that something was gone.

She looked so serious that I smiled, but she didn't smile back. I tried not to seem worried and said, "Well, I'm tired of sitting in my own blood. Help me up and hand me my sword."

Manon bit her lip.

Larripet stepped over to squat beside me. "The lazy killers took it."

I sighed, and the stitch inside me yanked. "I suppose they would have."

"They also stole your book that is cursed. You should send them a present for that."

"No, they didn't." Larripet and one of the guards helped me stand. I patted my upper thigh. "I strapped it to my leg."

"Why?" Manon asked.

"Too many people know I carry it in a pouch around my neck."

Larripet stared at me like I was a little boy who had just dropped a clay pitcher. "You carried the book of death next to your penis?"

I thought about that for a moment. "I suppose that might have been a flawed plan."

Syd met us during the walk back to my room, snapping out questions about Agni and her imposters. Manon, without slowing, ordered Syd to follow us, and Syd jumped aside rather than be run down by a twelve-year-old girl. Ella and Cael joined us a minute later, also barking questions about the attack.

I yelled, "Damn it, I'll act it out in a play for you if you shut the hell up until I sit down with a drink!" Yelling aggravated my stitch, so I resolved not to do any more of it.

At last, I sat at my table and poured some wine. "Cael, help me convalesce. Find a sword for me. Without one, I feel as naked as if my ass were hanging out."

Cael shook his head but left. Syd interrogated me while Ella stood in the corner. I hadn't noticed Manon leave, but she had gone.

During Syd's questioning, the queen stalked in. "Will your wound interrupt Martel's training?"

"No, he'll be catching baby snakes tomorrow just as planned."

She half turned toward the door, stopped, and gazed at me with some concern. "So, you're not in much pain?"

"Hell, it's a scratch compared to a broken heart." I winked at her.

Mina gave me an impatient look that I remembered from when we were in love, and she swept out of the room.

Syd asked me some more doubt-smeared questions. Then she told me not to leave my room, and she marched out.

Ella sat down across from me. "I didn't truly think you could be dead."

"I should be as blue as a peacock's testicles right now. Except for Manon, I would be. How did she find me?"

"It seems improbable. I understand that some guards discovered you and ran to find aid, but they met Larripet first. He hurried away and brought Manon back with him a few minutes later. It is a mystery as to how he knew her whereabouts."

"No mystery." I drained the cup. "He heard about Martel's plan to show her the armory."

Ella reached out, and I handed her the cup. Instead of filling it, she gathered up the four wine bottles and set them out in the hallway.

I grinned. "That's funny, but don't try too hard to make me laugh. My guts may tear apart."

"You are recuperating, and you drink too much even when healthy." She beckoned, and a servant walked in with a tray. I squinted hard at the man, but nothing about him said danger. The ones who almost killed hadn't seemed dangerous, either. He set down the tray, and Ella served me a bowl of nasty soup, a heel of gritty bread, and a mug of small beer thinner than water.

I started to bitch about it, but I was too tired. I dipped into the soup.

Ella stood over me. "So, Agni was here. We must assume she wore a magical disguise. Everyone we meet now is suspect."

"Really? I guess I ought to kill everybody. But I thought you don't like it when I kill everybody I meet. Are you changing your mind? I'm not an awful, repulsive murderer anymore?"

Ella paused. "That was cruel."

"Damn right it was. But cruel's not so bad compared to killing half the country, is it?" I knew I was being a bastard, but my bitterness was spilling over. I swallowed and remembered what I'd told Mina about sorcerers and self-pity.

Ella closed her eyes for a moment. "You cannot anger me."

I gaped at her. "For almost a year, all I've done is anger you!"

Calm, she said, "You cannot anger me today. Bib, I discovered something about Cael."

"Do you want me to kill him now? Let me warn you, I've already tried to kill the man more than once." I grinned at her.

"No! Hush now! He committed many reprehensible acts as a younger man."

I smiled at her in a way I knew she liked. "Maybe he was just bragging about it. He can see you're partial to bad men."

Ella grabbed my wrist, sloshing beer into my lap. "Be still! Cael's . . . immoral acts were as horrible as yours. Indeed, worse. Don't raise your eyebrows at me! Think of atrocities you find too appalling to commit. Likely Cael is guilty of them."

"Why tell me? I don't care about his conscience."

"Cael has sworn fealty here to perform good service and make amends."

"That's sweet of him. Has he done enough noble quests to make him a good boy now?"

Ella pushed my wrist away and cast around, probably for something to throw at me.

"Wait, don't fling that chair at me in a frenzy of not getting mad. So, Cael is making amends? When will he have made enough? Be done? Or will he be making them forever?"

"At least he has stopped creating death and pain wherever he goes!" Ella had raised her voice, and her cheeks were getting red.

"You might want to count up the murders. He's killed about as many men as I have since we met him. But that doesn't matter. Say that Cael indeed used to be a murdering son of a bitch. Then Mina convinced him he can make up for it all by taking her orders and doing her good deeds. Bullshit! Ella, she fooled him as slick as a charlatan at the village fair. Mina's deeds aren't particularly good, or at least no better than anybody else's. Even if they were good, once you do terrible things, you can't say that they never happened just because you do some good things later on. I bet Cael knows that by now."

Ella crossed her arms and stared at the floor. I figured I might have a long wait, so I gnawed off a chunk of bread. I stopped mid-chew when she leaned across the table toward me and bellowed, "At least you could have tried!" She kicked over the bottles when she ran out into the hallway.

The next day, Martel achieved a reliable level of skill in not destroying everything around him without thinking about it. I didn't know whether he'd make a good sorcerer, or a good king, but he was a good boy, not too polite, and I liked him. He failed more than most, but whenever he failed, he just worked harder.

I wanted to get on my horse and chase Agni right away before the sun set. Of course, I wanted revenge. But mainly, I could not begin to imagine the punishments that Krak would heap onto me if I didn't recover his stupid, way-opening sword.

Before I could escape from Bellmeet, Mina insisted on a celebration dinner for just her, Martel, and me. She backed up her insistence with a couple dozen blades. So, I said good evening to Manon and Ella, grunted at Larripet, and slouched through a meal that ended up making me smile even though I had intended to be rude.

Long before dawn the next day, somebody hammered on my door. I snatched my new sword and hurled open the door.

One of the guards smiled at me from the hallway. The oil in his beard glinted in the torchlight. "I thought you might be all hung over there, Bibber. Insensible, I mean. Her Majesty invites your stinking ass to eat breakfast with her on the terrace."

By the standards of the queen's guards, it was a tolerably polite invitation.

The lantern-lit terrace overlooked the city from behind a stone railing. Trees, shrubs, and elegant statues lined the space, which was big enough for an expensive wedding and cold as hell. The weather had turned again, and bits of sleet smacked my face.

I didn't pay the weather much mind, since Mina stood with Nubba at one end of the terrace, backed by Syd and thirty guards. Manon and Larripet stood off to the side. There wasn't a breakfast table in sight.

I swaggered toward her. "You sure are sweet to have your cutthroat chorus serenade us before we go, Your Majesty. We're in a hurry, though, so they'll have to sing us two songs next time we're in town."

"You're such a sassy bastard." Mina grinned a little and narrowed her eyes. "I missed you, Bib. However, I have a task for you."

"Pretend I'm laughing. It's too cold to actually laugh."

"The Residence is no longer safe. I need you to escort Martel to the Winter House."

"I'm sorry, I have other business."

Mina lifted her head and sat even straighter and taller. "I meant to say that you *will* escort Martel to the Winter House."

"I will *not*. The Winter House is five days' ride. Have Cael do it. He must have some rapes and blasphemy to atone for."

The queen flinched. "He cannot. He's not here."

"Too bad. Unless ten of your crusty oafs tie me up and carry me there, I'm not going."

"Ella will be there."

"What?"

Mina nodded. "Oh, yes. Cael left with her yesterday."

I blinked a few times.

"More properly, he abducted her and is transporting her to the Winter House. Now, don't threaten us. If you do not bring Martel there within a week, I have ordered Cael to kill her."

I had run three steps toward Mina with my sword drawn before I stopped myself. Guards surged to put themselves between her and me.

"Breathe," Mina called out from behind her guards. "Don't foam at the mouth—think it through. If you refuse, Cael will kill her. You know that he will. If you try to kill me instead, I suppose you'll kill quite a few guards before they cut you down, but you'll die for nothing. Ella will be killed anyway."

I wanted to slap myself for being outwitted like this, but I couldn't imagine how I might have predicted this particular treachery. I sheathed my sword. "I'll take him. But this isn't nice. And bad things happen to people who aren't nice."

Mina smiled and nodded at Syd. The guards split off as if they'd rehearsed this like a battle plan. Syd and a dozen of them made a circle around the queen, and the rest trotted back into the Residence, with Nubba following.

I said, "I want . . ."

"Wait."

"Do you want me to wait until Ella's head is falling toward the floor?"

"Here he is."

Martel walked through a door toward us, followed by a guard.

Mina met her son at the door, ushering him in. "Bib, I would like you to meet Martel."

I squinted at the boy and realized he was slouching, something I had never seen Martel do. This fellow had Martel's height, build, and coloring, but he also had fearful eyes, a pointy nose, and skinny lips.

It was a little too much aggravation. "A decoy? All this shit, and I'm escorting a damned decoy?"

Mina hissed, "Martel is my son! Do you think I'd send him away when he's in danger?"

I glared at Mina for a moment and then turned to the boy, who had started shivering. "I know it's cold, son. We'll find you something warmer. What's your real name?"

The boy now known as Martel threw up on my leg.

TWENTY-NINE

The Winter House perched in the southern hills of Bellhalt. It was not a place to visit in the wintertime because of its fine climate. It had been named the Winter House because it was cold every damn day of the year. Mina's grandfather had commissioned it as a manor for the royal family, an austere retreat at the top of a deep, expansive hillside covered with charming gardens and pools. By the time construction started, the predatory old reptile had invaded most of his neighbors, so a manor was no longer practical. His architect revised the plans. The finished Winter House lacked gardens or pools or any scrap of charm. It did have thick limestone walls, three turrets, and a fine defensive trench.

The queen had detailed two hundred soldiers to ride along with us. I told her she should instead send them all to damnation and follow along behind them herself.

She groaned and turned away. "Just take them! Krak! For once in your miserable existence, can you try not to make everything as difficult as possible?"

"I'm not being difficult. I am going along with your nasty-ass plan. I won't be difficult until I get back here."

"If you really don't want them, you will have to kill all two hundred of them. That is the only way they will stop following you."

I agreed to take the damned soldiers.

Manon, Larripet, and I gathered up our few trail-battered possessions, and a servant brought us new cloaks. As we saddled our mounts, three bodyguards escorted Not-Martel into the stables. He leaned against a stall door and watched one of the men saddle his horse for him.

I called out, "So, what's your real name, young man?"

He didn't look at me. "Martel."

I muttered to Manon, "This is going to be fun."

Manon reached up and hugged me, stretching tiptoe to lay her cheek on my chest.

I hugged her back and said, "I love you too."

She whispered, "Nubba plans to kill you when we come back."

I whispered back, "I don't doubt you. He smells like a damned schemer. How do you know?"

She stepped back and stared at me.

"Your mother's been a busy teacher, hasn't she?"

Manon nodded, gave me another quick hug, and walked back to recheck her horse's saddle.

Midday was a memory when we finally rode out the Green Gate. I blamed the two hundred dawdling soldiers who had stepped on each other, stopped for snacks, and run back to get the swords they'd forgotten. That might have been exaggeration, and I judged them harshly, but I sure as hell lost half a day because of them. I shouted at the captain to ride faster, even though the stitch in my guts stung almost every time my horse set down a hoof.

The sleet had dwindled during the morning, but it charged back with fury late that afternoon. The sun had disappeared behind layers of dim, racing clouds, but full dark hadn't yet arrived when we reached the ford. Not-Martel and his bodyguards rode with Manon, Larripet, and me. A hundred soldiers rode ahead of us, and a hundred rode behind.

I hadn't forgotten to bring the river spirit a nice present this time. I felt for the calfskin pouch containing the queen's most precious jewelry. Supernatural creatures tended to covet the best of any particular thing: the purest salt, the sharpest sword forged by the oldest smith, the handsomest man they ever saw, and that sort of thing. The queen's best jewelry would appeal to the spirit's vanity. I hoped to hell it would. I had called on Harik to bargain before we left, and he had ignored me like I was a dandelion. I was impotent as a sorcerer.

The river spirit had threatened only me, and in Bellmeet, I hadn't heard of any travelers at the ford being swept under or smashed to death on the rocks. So, I didn't expect the spirit to slaughter the first hundred soldiers as they crossed. There was no certainty, of course, but I figured warning them of possible death by supernatural means might diminish their enjoyment of the afternoon. If the spirit wanted to kill them, no warning would save them.

The lead soldiers rode across the ford, which I noticed was a fair bit deeper than it had been when I'd attempted Cael's murder. The soldiers reached the far bank unharmed, spread out, and waved for us to cross.

I raised my hand, and everybody on my side of the river stopped. "Wise and beautiful spirit, I have brought you presents and an apology. I'm sorry for fiddling around in your lovely river uninvited." I held up the calfskin pouch and removed an astounding emerald choker, followed by a magnificent diamond necklace. "Will you please allow us to cross?"

The head bodyguard said, "Who in Nubba's flabby ass are you talking to, Bib? Are those Her Majesty's necklaces? You just put those back and hand them over!"

"Hush, or I'll feed you to the monsters." I pitched the jewelry into the river.

Every bodyguard, soldier, and decoy-boy within a hundred feet started babbling.

The river's surface went still, flat, and smooth. It wasn't just placid. As far as I could tell, the entire river stopped flowing. The spirit's enormous voice pounded me and everybody else near the river. "Your gift is enchanting, Sorcerer." She giggled at herself. I cringed when the giggle echoed back off the hills from two miles upstream, where the river bounced down in a waterfall. "They're lovely, and just my color. Would you like to see them on me?"

"I'd be honored, just truly honored."

"Well, you won't!" I felt the power of her voice pressing my eyeballs out of shape. "You won't, because you brought me that woman's second-finest jewelry! Do you feel such contempt for me that you assumed I wouldn't know?"

I wondered for an instant whether Mina had tried to kill me. "It's an innocent mistake, merciful spirit! I will ride back directly and fetch you every speck of jewelry that the queen owns. Did I mention before that this is the jewelry of a queen?"

The river exploded like a three-day-old pig carcass lying in the sun. It knocked me off my horse straightaway. I grabbed for Manon, but the smashing water pulled her away. It threw me underwater and spun me, and I couldn't tell which way to swim for the surface.

A ragged limb rushed into me, gouging my leg, and I grabbed it. I assumed that it would float, so I swam in the direction it pulled me. I reached air and sucked it, then took a wave in the face. I think I swallowed a small stick. The surface was jumping and dragging me along. I couldn't see a single other person.

A half-sunken tree trunk appeared and crashed into my left arm. I shouted as I bounced off. Then an eddy threw me back into the log, and I swore while it smashed my arm up some more. The arm was dangling when the tree had finished with me, so I used my other arm to grab on by the slick nub of a broken branch. I tried to haul myself higher and failed.

A hand reached down from the top of the tree trunk, and I grabbed for it. We made a fine grip, and then my savior slid right over the top of the log and into the water, taking me with him. I held on to the hand. If I survived, I might want to kill him later.

I fell out of the water and straight down into a layer of shin-deep mud. Dropping the idiot's hand, I scrambled off my ass and drew my sword. I scanned fast for threats, then slowed down, and then stared around me, my sword's point drooping. The river had gone dry, except for the muddy riverbed. I couldn't see water in any direction. I peered upstream, and then farther up the river course. Even the waterfall had disappeared. I paused to scrutinize it and realized that a new hill had appeared right where the waterfall had been. It was probably busy starting on a new lake up there.

Off to my right, Manon stood about a hundred paces beyond the former riverbank. She waved at me and then nodded off toward the flatland running up to another clutch of hills.

The lake-creating hill had not simply appeared out of nothing. Manon had picked up a hill and moved it over to where she wanted it. I could see the dark expanse on the flatland where it used to sit. I started to calculate how much power it must have cost but quit when I realized that "staggering" would do for an estimate.

I whispered, "Darling, what are you trading away?"

Manon waved at me again. I saw that her hand didn't quiver or even tremble.

The idiot who had grabbed me started coughing and spitting behind me. I hadn't yet paid much attention to the mud-slathered lump, since disintegrating rivers and migratory hills had distracted me. He knelt in the mud and said, "Thank you . . ." in Not-Martel's voice. He spat again and tried to wipe his mouth, but he couldn't find any clean part of himself to wipe with.

I needed to deliver this little grunt. If I didn't, Cael would demonstrate all the spine of a bunny rabbit and kill Ella. I needed to mind him better.

Just as I made that decision, my arm started throbbing and each throb shoved barbed spears of agony all the way through it. I shivered all over for a few seconds and fell straight down onto my butt.

Larripet appeared beside me, muddy only up to his knees. He laid me back in the muck and made Not-Martel hold up my feet. I just lay there and sweated.

Larripet said, "Good songs have a few parts that are not as interesting as other parts."

I nodded.

"I mean no disrespect."

I pulled a deep breath. "Thanks."

"I would not say that it is stupid to try to be interesting all the time."

"No?"

"I would not say it."

I laughed and regretted it. I figured that the tree had broken my arm in two places, or maybe three, but the broken bone wasn't sticking through my skin anyplace. I lifted myself and called Harik, but he didn't answer. I tried other gods in the order of how much they didn't despise me: Gorlana, Fingit, Chira, Weldt, Fressa, Effla, and on down the list to Lutigan, who hated me most of all. None of them answered me. I wasn't in danger of being ripped apart or smothered in the next few seconds, so I didn't go to the desperate extreme of calling on Krak. I hesitated and then called for Sakaj, but she stayed silent too.

After some more sweating and panting, I felt solid again, so I sat up. Manon stood ten paces away, staring at me.

I smiled at her. "When we get home, I want to shift the orchard to the other side of the pond. I wouldn't mind some help with that, sweetheart. Shouldn't take you more than a minute or two."

Manon shrugged a little.

"I don't want to burden my daughter in my old age, but would you please help me with this busted arm?"

Manon inspected my arm for a few seconds. "Turn it over."

I gritted my teeth and shifted so she could see the other side.

"No."

"I'm sorry?"

"No. You can bear it."

"Manon—" I stopped then because she was staring at me as if I were no more than a fellow she had passed on the road once.

Manon walked away. "Some horses lived."

I yelled after her, "Manon, tell me what you paid. I'll figure out how to help you."

"I saved us, so don't whine."

THIRTY

F orty-six soldiers and two bodyguards survived the river calamity. The other bodyguard drowned while boosting Not-Martel onto that tree trunk. I wished to hell he had lived. Or that one of the others had died too. Forty-eight was an ill-omened number, dripping with nasty portents. Forty-nine was a bit less awful, and forty-seven was auspicious.

That didn't mean that we were fated to die or fail. In fact, it might mean nothing. But in general, numbers like those meant that the universe intended to slap and kick us, and maybe spit on us a few times while we struggled along.

We camped beside the dead river. Larripet set my arm and bound it to my body, while Not-Martel, whose real name was Heath, told me his life story. His farm boy life had been as interesting as mud, and he told the story in immense detail, even describing smells. Since I had been encouraging the young man to speak, I felt obliged to hear him out, at least through age seven.

The next morning, Manon, Larripet, Heath, and I mounted up on four of the surviving horses and took four more as spares. Some of the soldiers bitched about that, but they quieted down when

Manon frowned at them. Two of them even apologized. We departed at dawn along with sixteen soldiers and bodyguards, trotting south beside the dead river. I knew the way to the Winter House. Mina and I had run away there once for a private frolic when we'd been making big eyes at each other.

Yesterday, on the ride up from Bellmeet, my horse's gait had aggravated my gut stitch. Now, while traveling toward the Winter House, riding encouraged my arm to ache, burn, and throb, and sometimes all three. By evening, I had become a wrung-out, sweaty mess under my cloak. Sitting back against a scraggly tree, I stretched out my legs and ate one-handed.

I smiled at Manon once, raised my eyebrows, and glanced at my arm. She reached across the campfire and stabbed me in the heart. Well, she actually blinked at me and then looked away, but it felt like the same thing.

I lifted myself and called on Harik, but he didn't answer.

On the second day, we passed a village of no more than fifty people. Four poles had been raised, and naked, mutilated bodies hung from them. They appeared to have been hanging for a few days, but in the winter weather, it was hard to tell. All four had been children. Some of the soldiers wanted to take down the bodies and bury them. Others wanted to rush into the village and kill whoever had done this horrible thing.

"These torturers have traveled on," I told them. "Agni did this, or her scruffy herd did it. She figured they were sorcerers. See how she cut off their hands?"

Heath said, "Why do they cut off the . . ."

"Their privates? I don't know why these killers would do that, except for being vengeful, terrified sacks of shit."

"So, these poor little babblers was sorcerers?" a soldier asked.

I shrugged. "Probably not. Just unlucky. Or they made a neighbor mad, or they were one mouth too many to feed."

I convinced the soldiers to ride on without taking time to bury those sad folks. That was wise, since we passed two more villages that day and four the next, and every one of them displayed cut-up corpses. Usually, two or three poles stood outside a town, but Agni had lined up seven at one place.

Late on our third day of travel, a rider appeared from behind a distant dip on the plains, cantering across the winter-killed grass. I didn't alter our course to meet this rider, but he swung east and rode fast to catch us. When he neared, I drew rein because I recognized Stone-Hand, Big Boss of the Death's Riders. He galloped toward us, his belly jiggling and his magnificent horse blowing like it was fit to die.

Stone-Hand stopped twenty paces from me and bellowed, "Halt and hear the word of Harik, the God of Death!"

"We're already halted, Stone. Do you want us to ride on a for a while so we can halt again?"

The pompous lump of butter paused. "No, don't do that." He started yelling again, "Mighty Harik commands you—"

"I don't see your baby ducks behind you. Did they get lost? Suffer misfortune?"

"That is none of your affair!" He glanced at Manon and then back at me. "They wait close by, prepared—"

I beckoned the sorcerer. "Hell, invite them over, Stone. We're not standoffish."

Stone-Hand glanced at Manon again, and then he sagged. "Bib, may I speak to you alone?"

I raised an eyebrow at Manon. She gave the tiniest shake of her head. I examined Stone-Hand. His armor, helmet, and mount appeared as fabulous as ever, but his face was grimy and tired. He looked years older.

I nodded at the big sorcerer and rode with him out of everybody else's earshot.

Stone-Hand rubbed his face. "I'm asking a favor. Harik sent me with a message, so please listen while I say it. You know how he gets when you fail."

"Tell him to take his message and wipe his ass with it."

Stone-Hand jerked and stared. "I can't do that."

"You'll live longer." I shrugged. "Why can't he whisper this message into my ear himself? I've called on him dozens of times."

"I'm not positive. He behaves as if he's testing me, but once, he let slip something about rules."

"Let slip? Do you mean he's not perfect? He makes mistakes?"

Stone-Hand grinned. "I didn't say it."

"What's the message?"

"Harik commands that you join forces with Death's Riders to destroy the Dread Reshaper of Worlds." He glanced at Manon again.

I couldn't help laughing.

Stone-Hand spoke up over my laughter. "You can lead us if you want to, Bib. I don't want to lead anymore. Stop laughing! The entire world is in danger!"

"No, it's not. Harik does this kind of shit all the time. When he first told you about me, what did he call me?"

"Um . . . the Marrow-Sucking Blade of Damnation."

"Pretty good. Now that we know each other, Stone, does that describe me?"

He grinned again. "Maybe."

"You can tell Harik you've delivered his message. I'll devote profound thought to it. Stone—shit, what's your real name? Not your real, real name, but the name they call you at home?"

The man pulled off his helmet and scratched his balding head. "Dunn. Bib, how long have you been a sorcerer?"

"More than twenty years now." I knew exactly how many days, but the approximation would do.

"Krak! I've been one six months, but it feels like sixty years. Damn it, a year ago, I was sitting at a desk copying out writs and pleas."

"Dunn, sorcerers should never give each other advice, but do you mind if I give you some?"

"Go ahead."

"You should refuse to talk to Harik for at least a year. When you do talk to him again, your first words should be, 'Climb straight up my ass, you dick-flopping baboon.'"

The big man turned pale. His mouth opened, but nothing came out.

I turned my horse toward Manon and the others. "Goodbye, Dunn."

That night, a cold front shocked us with heavy sleet. I hadn't felt it coming. Maybe Harik had sent it. By midnight, the sky cleared, the wind died away, and cold air bit down on us. The full moon rose before morning, and by then, ice had sheathed the dead grass. The entire plains glittered like stars. When the sun rose orange, the whole world east of us seemed to be afire.

I wished it was real fire. Damn, it was cold. It stayed cold all day, and my broken arm clenched hard enough to take my breath away. None of us spoke. We kept our heads down and pushed our horses until they were blowing hard. Then we switched to our spares, back and forth to keep our mounts better rested. The soldiers, who lacked spare horses, fell behind early and dropped out of sight by midday.

Another single rider appeared as we left the grasslands and entered the Southern Hills. I thought it might be Dunn coming back to chat, but the rider approached for a few minutes before cutting away north. He shot off twice as fast as any horse should run.

"Magic horseshoes, maybe." I shaded my eyes.

"Just wonderful," Manon muttered. She sat tall and took a breath.

"You might need that power for something else more important later," I said.

She glared at me.

"I'm making an observation, that's all. He is pretty damn far away, though."

"Well, fine!" Manon sounded like a regular little girl who hadn't ever killed anybody. One who might cry when she killed horses by mistake. Then she turned and regarded me like I was no more than a bridle, or a piece of dirt. "Are you going to lead?"

I led. We halted late and got up early to ride on. The next after-noon, we reached the Winter House. An easy, half-mile slope rose up to the house, a slope twice as wide as it was long. The architect had pushed the house back in between hills, so the slope was the only practical approach. The slope could be an issue for defenders, since the slope itself would deter an attack about as well as a pork pie sitting on the ground.

The square Winter House stood two stories tall, and its pale limestone walls measured eighty paces on each side. Mina had told me her grandfather envisioned a beautiful structure, with real glass windows set into carved openings. In the end, no windows existed on the ground floor, and the upper windows were better suited to firing arrows than to artistic contemplation. The house was not a proper fortress and would never hold against a real assault, but if fewer than a hundred men attacked, they would get an ass-whipping.

I rode up the slope at a walk while the others waited at the bottom. Half a dozen soldiers waved me off and walked partway down the slope toward me. More soldiers stood at the door and in the trench. Before I reached any of them, I shouted, "Cael!" I put some more guts into it and bellowed, "Cael! Come out here, you no-dick bastard!"

The soldiers turned and stared at the house. Cael walked outside and waved at me. Ella strolled out with him, unbound and not looking abducted at all.

Half an hour later, we all walked into the Winter House's main room full of bright rugs, scratched leather furniture, and a huge fireplace. It was the only common room in the house that served no military purpose. I wanted to cut out Cael's heart so much I was shaking, but I had only one arm and no magic. I didn't want my vengeance limited to gushing blood on him as he transfixed me.

Ella spoke first, turning to Heath. "What's your name, young man? I'm Ella."

Heath blushed and muttered, "Martel."

"That's a fine name. Are you hungry?"

Heath smiled and fell in love with her right then. I watched it happen, and his face described the whole thing.

I didn't have time for romance. "Mina sent Heath here as a decoy, in case somebody tries to murder Martel. She ordered us to escort him."

Ella squinted at me. "Ordered? That seems unlikely. If she

ordered you to travel here, you would ride at a gallop in the other direction."

"You know me well, darling. But she also said that Cael had seized you, hauled you here, and would kill you if we didn't show up with Heath in a pretty snappy fashion."

Ella laughed. "How silly. Her Majesty asked me—asked *me*, mind you—to prepare the Winter House for Prince Martel, since I know what is required to raise a child of nobility."

"And you didn't say a goddamn word to me before you left?" I realized I had clenched my fist, and I made myself relax it.

"The queen said there was great haste. And . . . I was angry with you."

"So, nobody abducted you?" I pointed at Cael. "Why the hell is he here? Did he work as a governess in his blood-splashed past?"

Ella laughed. "No, I—" She cocked her head at Cael. "Why *are* you here?"

Cael held up both hands. "I knew that Bib would come. He loves you too much. You were never in real danger."

Ella's jaw dropped open. "You . . . were . . . planning to kill me?"

Cael shook his head with vigor. "I wasn't planning to."

"*Was* there a plan?"

"Yes."

Ella raised her voice. "Did it involve killing me?"

Cael sighed. "Yes, it did."

Cael's first mistake was going along with a plan that involved killing Ella. His second mistake was standing there while she bounded two steps toward him. His third mistake was nobly waiting to let her slap him. She did not slap him. She pounded him on the corner of the jaw with an uppercut. From that point, he was off-balance. He staggered back, but she pressed him. She kicked him in the knee, and when he bent over, she broke his nose. He covered his head with both arms and retreated two steps. Ella rushed right along with him, grabbed the front of his shirt, and pushed him staggering back two more steps. Then she shoved him into the huge fireplace. Somebody had built the fire up nice and high against the winter freeze.

As Cael howled, Ella stalked away. She had demonstrated to him that his artistic fighting skills didn't mean shit if he stood there and let himself get hit. That would be a good lesson, if he lived.

THIRTY-ONE

Not many sorcerers tend toward serious, philosophical thoughts, and I myself have been less philosophical than most. Of course, I sat around at night with other sorcerers, drinking and arguing over how to most efficiently destroy various things: ships, wheat fields, troops of horsemen, and such. We speculated about why we always heard crackling sounds when Lutigan spoke, and why numerals predicted success or disaster for no reason anybody could figure out. We did it for fun, and none of it mattered a damn.

I wouldn't say that I idled where thinking was concerned. I developed a fine sense of the value that oaths, memories, and suffering might have in a trade. I planned dozens of attacks, diversions, and escapes. But I have spent most of my life thinking about how to do things, not thinking about what things meant.

As I walked along the dim Winter House upper hallway with Ella, I wished that I had cultivated more reflective powers of thinking. The gods were snatching new sorcerers, especially children, and wringing out everything worth having. Killing and destruction followed them like starving dogs. Agni and her mob were swarming the countryside and murdering everybody they thought might have a little magic in them. Harik and Sakaj were playing some kind of crazy god game, and maybe all of this was happening because I had been riding around opening the way for the gods. I didn't know what it meant. I didn't know whether it meant anything.

Ella stopped at a plain wooden door. "She has been quartered here. Bib, let's not do this."

I reached around her to unlatch and push the door. It opened with a greased whisper. Candles tossed wobbly light in the small, windowless room. A cheap table held a large, empty bowl with a spoon, and a nice chest sat against the wall. A well-blanketed bed sat against the other wall, and a gaunt young woman squinted up at us from where she sat on the bed's edge. Bones stretched the skin of her face, and her eyes widened as she leaned toward us.

"I'm gone," she said.

"Hello," Ella said to her as if sharing a secret. "Are you cold?"

The girl stared at me.

I'd have been shocked if she were cold. She wore a blanket over two cloaks, and only the gods knew what clothes she wore under that. I figured her for sixteen or seventeen years old.

Ella touched my arm. "We should leave her alone."

"Any speck of knowledge she gives us could save our asses."

"Fah!"

I shrugged. "All right, probably not, but thoroughness is a virtue that I don't intend to abandon now." I smiled at the girl. "My name is Bib."

She sat forward and whispered, "I'm gone."

"Can you tell me—"

"I'm gone." She blinked at Ella. "I'm gone."

I murmured to Ella, "The soldiers found her?"

Ella was inspecting the bowl. It was so clean it might have been scrubbed. "A patrol discovered her a day's travel from here, wearing rags. If they had not found her, she would surely have perished in the recent turn of weather."

"Hold up one of those candles, Ella. Young lady, look here at me."

The girl stared at me without twitching, and I found shapes

269

swimming and wriggling deep in her eyes. I picked up one of her hands and examined the sheath of callouses and scars on it. "She's a sorcerer—a Binder."

The girl grabbed my sleeve. "I'm gone." She started sobbing and wailing, tears running, but her face stayed calm.

I pulled the girl's hand off me as gently as I could, and then I reached out to pull back her blanket.

The girl didn't flinch, but Ella stopped me. "You needn't further examine her physical condition. Trust me that the mutilation she received from whomever held her is as revolting as I have ever seen."

"I expect that Agni chained her up and forced her to make disguises and magic horseshoes and magic pants. Who knows? Agni kept her at it until the girl had traded everything to the gods. Everything that meant anything. It might have been kinder to let her freeze."

"Do not dare kill her!" Ella hissed.

"I wasn't contemplating it." I let the girl's hand drop. "Young woman, can you tell me about anything you've created?"

She stopped crying and sighed.

"Anything you've built. Maybe some small thing, maybe a weapon."

The girl turned away from me and stared at the wall, which I didn't consider a promising development. If I'd had any power, I could have healed her body. I'd never have been able to change what she had allowed the gods to do to her mind.

I plucked the wooden spoon off the table and put it in her hands. She didn't seem to notice. I gritted my teeth and pressed my hand against her back, which I figured held a crop of bruises and wounds. The girl moaned.

Ella shouted and punched me in the ribs, which staggered me, but I kept watching the girl. For a few seconds, she turned the spoon in her hands, then she put the handle against her leg, grabbed the spoon's handle, and pulled as if she were stretching it up over her head. She bent the spoon against her leg until it snapped in two. Then she let the pieces fall onto the floor.

While I was thinking about what the hell that had been, Ella kicked me in the shin.

I hopped. "I'm damn glad there's no fireplace in here! Do you want to cram me into that chest?"

Ella glared but held off whacking me. After she had thrashed Cael, he had rolled himself back out of that fire and survived, but the flames had burned his shoulder and leg black. The scars would likely pull on him enough to slow him as a fighter. He'd have to settle for being an amazing swordsman but not an artist. Ella had told me she feared that she might have overreacted, and she had avoided Cael since she thrashed him.

I rubbed my shin. "Ella, I don't know that I learned much from this poor girl. I need to contemplate it for a while. Young Lady, I'm sorry that I hurt you. I hope it helps me kill that horrible bitch that did this to you."

The girl ignored me, lay back on the bed, and started whispering, "I'm gone." She was still at it when we left the room.

As we walked down the torchlit stairs, Ella asked, "Did that justify her pain? What could you really learn from it?"

"If it means anything, whatever she created was long. Or part of it was long. Like a sling."

"Or a whip?"

I nodded. "Or maybe a flag."

Ella squinted over her shoulder at me.

"A flag that inspires your troops to fight harder. Or run faster, or never get tired. Or a horn. A horn could do all those same things."

"Hah! A bow is far more likely than any of that rank speculation."

"It depends on whether Agni has much in the way of imagination."

"Are you implying that I do not?"

"Look, here's the courtyard!" I pointed, ignoring her question.

We walked to the center of the small courtyard and stood shoulder to shoulder, dead grass crackling under our feet. I pulled out Harik's little book so we could read it for the third time. Together we held the book at reading height.

"Ella."

"Yes?"

"Is this the last thing we'll ever do together?"

"It will be if the book obliterates us," she said flatly.

I smiled. "For argument's sake, assume we survive."

"No. I'll ride with you back to Bellmeet. That may be the last." She sounded as if she were pretty sure it would be the last.

I nodded and tried not to let it distract me from the death magic ritual we were about to perform. "What page do you want to read?"

"I don't want to choose."

"I don't either. Let's not choose. Let's just read the last page." I grinned at her. "What kind of morons read the last page? Harik would never expect it."

I held my breath as we opened the book to the last page. It showed a big oak tree just sitting on the page with nothing inked around it. A great network of roots spread below it. Masses of bright green leaves covered the right half of the tree. The left half was dead and rotting. Fat roots anchored the right side of the tree, and shriveled roots lay under the left side.

We waited for a few breaths.

"Is that all?" Ella arched an eyebrow.

"I can almost guarantee it's not."

I closed the book and stored it in my pouch.

Ella stood in one spot, scanning the courtyard. "What should we do?"

"It's almost suppertime. Let's eat."

Ella walked toward the courtyard door.

"Wait!"

She stopped, and her eyes followed my line of sight. I nodded at the ground. The grass had come to life when she walked over it. It grew taller as I watched, and a couple of bugs jumped out. She took two more steps, and grass crawled to life as she passed.

"An interesting phenomenon," she said, "but hardly as shocking as dead people. You try."

I walked in a different direction, but nothing happened. I walked back toward her. When I stepped on part of her new grass, it died back to gray crispness underneath me. I laughed. "We could solve an age-old, imponderable mystery right here. Which is stronger? Life or death?" I stomped up to her, killing off all her new grass as I went.

Ella took three more steps, drawing grass back to life with each one. I followed, massacring grass right behind her. Ella rarely giggled, but she giggled then. She ran around on her bountiful feet, and I hauled my devastation around after her. We used Harik's curse to wipe out each other's work, aggravate one another, and laugh the whole time. I didn't even mind the pain pushing itself through my broken arm.

After a couple of minutes, I spotted Larripet standing in the courtyard door. He nodded. "This is not interesting at all."

"I wish you could try it," I said. "It's the power of life and death on an insignificant scale. But I can't just let people read out of Harik's book for fun."

Ella stood beside me, grinning.

Larripet said, "It is good that it makes you laugh. Two hundred men and women are here to kill us."

Five minutes later, Cael, Ella, and I stood with the garrison captain in one of the short turrets, examining the long slope below the house. Through the twilight, I saw at least two hundred people and as many horses. They had made camp toward the bottom of the slope.

"Your hill-rat can count," the captain said.

I said, "Captain, I am proud to fight alongside you, and if you keep talking that way, you will never leave these hills alive. That is not a joke."

The captain stole a glance at Cael, who nodded. The captain stared out at the newcomers. "Well . . . I wonder why they don't attack?"

Cael said, "They may not be well-trained. If they attacked at night, they'd kill each other as often as they'd kill us."

"Or they're waiting for friends who would be sad not to share the pleasure of gutting us all," I said.

"Maybe both." Cael touched his shirt over his left shoulder.

The captain rubbed his chin. "I can't hold them off with my thirty men."

"You're right about that," I said. "I guess we'll just have to attack them at dawn."

THIRTY-TWO

I didn't intend to attack two hundred horsemen at dawn, or at supper, or at any other time. It sounded quite dashing when I said it, and I hoped everybody would be thinking about what a brave son of a bitch I was while I considered ways to escape. I would bring Ella, Manon, and Larripet along, and I might allow Heath to come too if he was quiet and respectful. Nobody else had claim on my loyalty. Cael could crawl back into the damned fireplace if he wanted.

I strode down the south hallway, my boots slapping on the slate floor and each torch flame quivering as I whipped past. The Winter House stables pushed up against the building's back wall. Once past the stables, a slick, chancy back trail led down and away through the hills. It wasn't necessary that I scout the path ahead like this, but I preferred that my escape not be inconvenienced by any unexpected barred doors or caved-in ceilings.

When I shouldered open the stable door, Manon stepped out of the shadows to block my way. "I've been waiting. Did you sit down for a meal and a nap? Let's go."

"Pardon me and my dragging ass," I said. "Wait here while I bring the others."

"What others?"

"Larripet, Ella, and her future husband, that boy."

"Leave them."

"That's mighty harsh."

Manon stared at me.

I tried again. "They can keep up. Well, the boy can't, but I'm sure Ella will tote him in her arms." I smiled.

"They can't keep up with us—we're sorcerers. If we try to bring them, we'll all die. I'd rather let them die now so we can kill Agni later."

I couldn't work up much fury toward the girl. Any number of times over the years, I had sounded about the same as she did now, whenever people I didn't give a shit about were involved. "Manon, let's talk about it after I bring them." I turned, but she grabbed my arm. When I turned back toward her, she stepped aside. On the stable floor beyond her lay a fused pile of wooden slats, leather tack, iron horseshoes, a bridle, and most of the parts of two soldiers. Or maybe three soldiers. It was dim, but not so dim I didn't recognize the same sort of work she'd done on that zealot who killed Bremmel.

She pointed at the hideous mess. "Don't bring the others back here."

"Let me go get my cloak." I hurried back out of the stables.

I didn't intend to leave Ella behind, no matter what Manon wanted. The girl might be full of magical power, but she was young. I had spent half my life cultivating trickery and contempt for the notion of fairness. But I didn't have enough magical power to wilt a daffodil, and I feared that trickery alone would prove inadequate for overcoming her.

Soldiers had begun running or at least walking fast on errands all over the Winter House. A slaughter was coming, and all the smart people would be gone before it arrived. I began considering options. Most were nearly impossible. The rest were insane.

Magic would surely improve some escape options to no worse than improbable. Harik had been snubbing me, but it had been a couple of days since I last asked to come visit. Sometimes when my circumstances changed, his tolerance for my presence changed too.

I searched out a quiet spot in one of the storage cellars. Sitting with my back against a cask of nails, I asked myself what I wanted. I wanted Agni dead. I wanted my companions and I alive to laugh at her corpse. I resolved to keep those things in my thoughts, and then I lifted myself to call on Harik.

Harik hauled me up so fast I almost didn't have time to feel queasy. "Murderer, what a dreadful situation you have burrowed yourself into. Would you care to simply consign your existence to me, in the interest of expediency?"

"Mighty Harik! Where have you been all this time? Did Sakaj finally give you permission to come out and play?"

Harik paused, but I couldn't see him. Damn Agni for stealing my sword. He sniffed. "I have been occupied with amusements unfathomably more entertaining than you."

"You do realize that Fingit isn't really stealing your nose, don't you? So, what do you want me to do with your stupid book?"

"Oh, just throw it on the ground somewhere."

"Did we save Ella's life?" I asked, trying to sound like I didn't care.

"Is she still alive?"

"You know she is!"

"If she dies within the next few weeks, or months, you'll know that you failed." I heard the smile in his voice.

"You nasty sack of piss! I hope birds shit on your black robe."

"Don't be overwrought, Murderer. That woman doesn't love you anymore."

I wanted to tell him he didn't know that to be true, but he did know it. I knew it too, and I wasn't even a god.

Harik laughed. "Just state what you want, Murderer."

I concentrated on what it would take to achieve my purposes. "I want five squares. That's the number of fingers on one of your hands, in case you're unclear. And of course, I want you to make the first offer. And it had better not be killing Manon!"

"No? Then we're done."

Harik slammed me back into my body.

I stared at some dusty coils of rope for a minute and failed to think of a way to overcome or trick Manon without my own magic. I tried to imagine her taking pity on us all, but it seemed as likely as her flying us all to safety on a giant goose pie. If she wouldn't let the others leave, I'd just have to stay with them. When Agni attacked the house tomorrow, not many of us would survive, but maybe I could make sure Ella was one of those. Hell, maybe Agni would trip in front of me and bang her head, and I could slice it off.

I climbed the stairs to the main floor and wondered where Ella would be. Before I stepped into the hallway, Harik snatched my spirit and pulled me up.

"Murderer, if you fail to make a bargain now, you will not survive."

"Shit, you're the God of Death. That should tickle you. Or maybe you'll lose points if I die right now."

"Points?" He sounded oblivious. For Harik, that meant he knew what I was talking about.

"Points! Lose a turn! Get a penalty, take a handicap, have to carry a monkey around on your shoulder for the next round! Whatever it is you and Sakaj are playing at."

"Stop babbling—you sound like a madman. Here is my offer for five squares. All who love you now will soon come to revile you."

I laughed. "That hardly sounds appealing, but I appreciate that you made an offer. How about this: I will stop drinking for a month. A lunar month."

"Unacceptable. You will soon come to hate all those whom you love."

"No, but I offer to hate them whenever they remind me of you." I knew he could see me, so I winked.

"Is this the moment for sickly humor? Do you want me to abandon you to destruction? Never mind. I offer that you will never have another child."

"I don't plan to father more children anyway," I said.

"It should be easy then."

"Wait, do you mean only natural children?"

"Neither children of your body nor children you adopt."

I yelled, "You greasy pig-licker—this is a trap! If I agree, then you'll go kill Manon."

"Is she your daughter now? She cares no more for you than for a dirty bowl."

"That doesn't matter. She's still my daughter."

"Desist! Murderer, she is not your daughter. You have known her for less than a month."

I dug in my heels. "That doesn't matter, either."

"You are so pathetic. You care nothing for this child. You're simply nostalgic for your real daughter."

I prepared myself for rage, for the urge to ram my sword through the God of Death's head. Then I prepared myself to control that rage, so I wouldn't say stupid things and make rueful trades. I did not prepare for everything inside me to shrivel, which is what happened. "I miss both of them. And I don't trust you not to kill Manon."

"Fine. I promise not to kill her, nor cause her to be killed by some other agency."

"You can promise her a golden ball gown and a ship full of kittens too. I still don't trust you."

"My offer is that you have no more children," Harik said. "Accept it or not."

"Wait. Tell me what Manon has been trading away."

"I'm sure I have no idea." Harik sounded oblivious again. Well, sometimes he really was.

I jeered, "I suspected you were too stupid and unperceptive to know such things."

"Ha! What a blunt attempt at manipulation. I simply have no interest."

I stayed quiet.

"Murderer, what about my offer?"

I tried not to think. I tried to become an empty place.

"Murderer! I can see you right there!"

Quiet.

"Fine, you repulsive little man! I can make some guesses about what the girl traded. A lot of memories, not all, of course, or she would be flopping on the ground like a carp. I suspect that most of the foundational memories are gone, the early ones. She would have many recent ones, but the emotion would be stripped out. That's typical of Sakaj, that shrew. Oh, the girl's infirmity touched everything in her life. Removing it was clever. Satisfied? What about my offer?"

"I might accept it, but I also want to buy part of Manon back."

"Hah! That presents challenges. Of course, no challenges are too great for a god, but restoring that sort of thing is tedious."

"I want her memories back. As many as she can get," I said.

I heard him yawn. "Make an offer."

"Mighty Harik, I don't offer a damn thing more." Harik was some place out in the nothingness where I couldn't see. I smiled with a load of arrogance for his benefit.

"Amuse me with your explanation of that."

"I don't want you to waste any effort on how she feels about me. Give her the early memories. They make her who she is."

"Ah. Well, if you want to be so selfless, and you agree to have no more children, it might not be too much trouble to perform this restoration. I insist upon two conditions, however."

"Damn it! Anything else? Do you want me to braid your hair?"

"Be still, Murderer. First, I want you to understand that this trade changes nothing. Your being is not rooted in sacrifice or kindness or love or feeding woodland creatures. You are a killer. Do you understand that?"

"I hear what you say."

"Superb. Second, I want you to take ten squares instead of five."

"What?" I had calculated things to a fine balance. Five squares wouldn't let us stroll to victory against Agni, but we could make a decent showing as we retreated into the hills. On the other hand, ten squares could make me confident enough to get us all massacred. "Why? I mean, is there a condition?"

"Oh, yes! You must use them to kill your enemies."

"Is that all?" I felt like I was strolling into a trap I couldn't see.

"Yes, it is. Go on, Murderer. Go kill your enemies."

Without the power, we'd all be killed tomorrow. "Done."

Harik flung me back into my body. I only stumbled a little. I ran back down into the cellar and spent five minutes healing my arm and then another minute repairing the stitch in my belly. Then I trotted back to the stables.

Manon hadn't left. In fact, she hadn't moved more than a couple of feet, and she stood staring at the parts of the two or three soldiers she had scrambled. "I didn't need to do that."

"I have no business judging you."

"No, you don't!" Her brow furrowed. "I kind of wish somebody would, though. It's confusing."

"Try to set it aside. You'll feel better in a couple of days."

Manon gritted her teeth. "Bib, did you do something to me?"

That would have been a wonderful time to lie, but I decided not to. I took a casual half-step toward Manon. From that close, I felt I could knock her unconscious before she turned me into a pile of elbows and guts, if I distracted her first by driving a couple of horses mad. "I asked Harik to give you back a load of memories. Nothing you didn't have before."

"You didn't have any right to do that without asking me!" She yelled it with more rage than I would have expected.

"I guess not, but I figured you might be happy with them once you got them. I'm sorry. You can sell them right back to your mother, I bet."

"I gave them up to keep you from dying. I can't imagine why I did that."

"Thank you all the same."

"What a big waste."

I shrugged.

Manon shouted, "I hate this! Am I supposed to be happy about it? Well, I'm not! Why not?" She hit me on the chest three times.

I stood there and let her hit me. "Be patient. Wait a few days before you give up on being happy."

She whacked me again and then stepped back. I didn't see any deadly hand gestures or finger-waving. She was crying. Maybe she was sad. Maybe she was pissed to holy hell. "What did you pay, you turd? I don't even care that sorcerers aren't supposed to ask each other questions."

"It wasn't cheap, but I got good value."

"Fine!" She rubbed her cheeks with her sleeve. "I'll wait, but. . . this is so confusing! Let's leave, fine, let's go. Well, go on and get the others if you love them so much! Even if it kills all of us."

"Even if it does. We all escape together."

Harik seized me with such violence that the jolt of nausea hit me even before everything dissolved. "Why are you talking about leaving?"

"Because I don't want to get beaten to pieces by a couple hundred crazy people."

"I see. Are you referring to your enemies?"

"Yes, I mean my enemies! Well . . . shit."

Harik laughed. "Kill your enemies, Murderer. Do not run from them. Renege on our agreement at your peril."

Harik whipped me back into my body as if he'd fired me from a siege engine. I collapsed onto the stable floor.

Manon stepped back and watched me shake my head as I stood up. "I'm going to tell everybody that you fainted while you were talking about them."

"Have Larripet make up a little song about it too. Manon, dear, Harik has tricked me into fighting Agni's mob tomorrow. You don't have to stay. If you're smart, you'll run."

Manon stepped past me on her way back into the house. "Well . . . don't call me 'dear' anymore."

THIRTY-THREE

To hell with dawn. I climbed up to the Winter House roof at midnight to start attacking Agni and her torturing ass-hangers. I guess most of them slept right through my early assault, because I didn't hear anybody shouting or running around.

The cold had eased to just above freezing, so I slung some lazy white bands into the sky and pulled the temperature down to a hard freeze across the whole hillside. Yesterday's sleet hardened into a flat crust of ice. I took a slow, lazy time for all this, which burned less magical power than a rushed job would have.

Before dawn, I called in storm clouds to give me some options. By then, Manon stood with me on the roof. I had healed Cael's burns, since we could benefit from an artistic fighter just about then. He and most of the soldiers were guarding the gate and manning the windows.

Ella and Larripet joined us on the roof.

I jerked my chin at them. "You two will probably be more useful fighting on the ground with Cael."

Ella snorted. "He might prefer that I not stand behind him with a naked sword."

"Did you ask him?"

"I did not. He may choke on his own teeth for all I care."

I nodded at that. "Hate him all you want—it won't bother me. Larripet?"

"I think we will all die soon. But if I live, I want to watch your death."

"And you should, for artistic purposes. All right, you two will be my reserve force. Go get shields." I lifted the big, round shield I had brought up from the armory. If I squatted, I could almost hide my whole body behind it. Manon held a smaller shield.

Ella squinted at my shield. "I don't . . . oh, I see, perhaps the Binder created magical bows. Or slings."

They disappeared for a while and returned with round shields just as the sky was showing light. I squeezed the storm clouds while I pulled the temperature even colder. A healthy freezing rain began falling to thicken the ice on the slope.

At last, the sun rose high enough to show our enemy.

I said, "Lutigan's liver and asshole damn it forever!" During the night, Agni's army had about doubled in size. Over four hundred of her zealots swarmed the bottom of the slope, clumping and spreading out in no logical pattern I could detect.

"If anybody is thinking about running, now's the time," I said.

"I can't leave that boy to die," Ella said.

Manon and Larripet didn't say anything.

Agni's army shifted itself to begin the attack. I had been hoping they were just undrilled fanatics, and they fulfilled my hopes. Men and women trotted in bunches up the slope. At the thicker ice patches, they began slipping, struggling, and even falling. Within fifteen minutes, the whole mess of them straggled across the bottom half of the slope in confused lumps and bunches.

I nodded at Manon, and she gestured. Long cracks opened in the ground underneath the closest sixty or seventy zealots, but the fissures didn't gape wide. Then rocks the size of tombstones pushed up out of the cracks. The fissures started eating people. Their screams blended and echoed, even through the rain. People scrambled and ran, but the stony teeth broke legs and crushed bodies before pulling them underground.

Those closest to the slaughter turned and ran. The ones behind them, who couldn't have seen what happened, kept scrambling up the slope. It was like dropping ants into a jar and shaking it.

I ended the rain and stilled the wind. Then I lavished power to twist the water in the air. That cost more than I wanted to spend, but when fog swallowed Agni's army, I smiled. Manon reached out to open some more hideous maws in the ground. More screams drifted upslope as fog-blinded people were eaten.

I could have pulled down some lightning to kill those bunched-up maniacs by the wagonload, but it would waste power something terrible. The sun had lifted high enough to shine in my eyes, and I raised the shield to shade half my face.

"Help!" One of our soldiers ran out onto the roof and pitched forward onto his face. A ragged woman appeared out of nothing and pulled her sword out of the soldier's back. Something on her forehead evaporated in a flash of fire, leaving a black burn above her eyes. She winced and ran toward Ella. I saw more of Agni's people charge out onto the roof, and there were probably some I didn't see.

I yelled, "Put your back to the edge! Some are invisible!"

Ella blocked the woman's swing and killed her before retreating toward me. She, Larripet, and I gathered with Manon behind us. More of Agni's people ran onto the roof until we could see eight attacking us at once. A woman bobbled for no reason, so I took a chance and jumped out to slam my shield against the empty space to her right. A man with a club appeared flying backward to land on his butt. I slashed a woman across her blackened forehead.

Five raggedy attackers faced us when three more appeared from nothing, fire blazing for a moment on their foreheads.

"There!" Manon yelled. "You can see them all now."

We killed all of them over the next two minutes. Larripet took a cut across the ribs that oozed blood, but no one else got more than small lacerations.

The fog had blown away without my holding it steady, and the temperature had warmed back up to about freezing. My thunderstorm was drifting, so I worked on pulling it back together.

Agni's mass of fighters struggled on up the hill, gaining speed and screaming like Lutigan's fourteen hundred vile foot soldiers. Manon gestured, and a patch of ice behind the army disappeared. Fifty people in the front stumbled and fell, squirming and pounding the icy ground. I squinted and saw them coughing up water.

Manon grunted as if she'd been hit. I glanced and saw she was pale and sweaty. She raised her hands but dropped them instead of killing all those people rolling in the cold mud. "I have to stop. I mean, I don't have much power left."

I shouted, "That's fine. Just stand back and yell if anymore run up here to kill us."

"It's just . . . I don't know what it is, goddamn it!" Manon pounded her fist on her leg. "Just don't worry about me. I'll stop as many as I can!"

Far off to my right, away from Agni's army, I spotted Dunn and his sad sorcerers galloping up the hill.

"Please don't kill them," I said to Manon, pointing at Death's Riders.

She nodded. "All right. Well, I won't kill them first."

Dunn shouted something.

"Manon, what did he say?"

"He said to please kill him now." Manon rolled her eyes. "I don't know what he said! I'm busy fighting, unlike some people here."

Agni's fanatics were three-quarters of the way up the slope, so I didn't have time to fool around with Dunn.

Manon shouted, "Wait!" She gestured at the ground. Instead of maws opening, the earth beside the Winter House wrinkled. The wrinkle rolled and grew down the slope and became a wave of dirt. It rushed through Agni's army, throwing people left, right, and into the air.

I turned to Manon. "What about your power?"

She shrugged.

I assessed Dunn's little sorcerers' club, and one of them was staring hard at me, a woman I figured was a Caller, like me. In her place, I'd be preparing to calm our horses when that crusty old sorcerer up there spooked them. I didn't try to spook them. Instead,

I pulled and threw enough yellow bands to clamp all the horses' hooves, and then I yanked them all sideways. The horses fell on their sides, throwing Death's Riders into the mud. I squeezed the bands as the horses scrambled up. The beasts bucked, snorted, side-stepped, and ran off down the slope.

Stone and his sorcerers dragged themselves upright and pointed at me, the horses, and each other. I reached up and squeezed lightning and a grumble of thunder out of the storm. Death's Riders froze.

Three arrows smacked into me one after another, and I staggered. Two struck the edge of my shield, and the third pierced the fleshy part of my left shoulder. The bowmen had grouped their shots with fine accuracy, which likely meant magic bows.

"Shields!" Ella shouted.

I squatted behind my big shield and peeked downslope, but whoever was firing had hidden themselves damn well. "Does anybody see them?"

"There." Larripet pointed.

"Where?" I saw at least thirty bows. Three more arrows slammed into my shield.

Larripet walked toward me, his shield still up. "In the middle. Left and down."

"My left?"

"There is more than one left?"

Three more arrows smashed into my shield, which started to splinter.

"Are you acting dumb to make sure you get to watch me die?" I yelled at Larripet.

He stood taller and said with dignity, "I do not decide such things."

Three arrows slammed my shield again, one on the boss, and it fell to pieces. I dropped flat, certain that it wouldn't help me. If they were firing magic bows, they wouldn't miss just because I moved a couple of feet. Ella took a step toward me holding up her shield, and then she hesitated.

"I see them!" Manon screamed.

I heard two arrows hit wood and another hit flesh, and somebody small fell on top of me. I rolled to my knees, and Larripet slid off me, two arrows in his shield and one in him. I grabbed the shield and covered as much of us as I could. Ella knelt next to me a moment later. I heard enormous crunching sounds, as if a gargantuan monster was chewing up a stone church, but I didn't pay much attention. An arrow had driven all the way through Larripet's neck, cutting his spine. He'd been dead before I got to my knees.

"I stopped them," Manon yelled. She nodded toward a pile of boulders that hadn't been on the slope a minute ago. She knelt beside Larripet's body and frowned. "What now?"

Ella looked over the edge of the roof. "We must do something. Cael and his soldiers have attacked so that we won't be overrun."

"Call him back," I said.

"How?" Manon asked.

Ella didn't wait to ask. She knelt and grabbed the edge of the roof, lowered herself, and dropped, rolling when she landed. She ran out toward Cael while I spun more white bands into the sky. By the time Ella reached Cael, I had the wind sweeping water up above my storm into the high, bitter air.

Cael and the soldiers fell back toward the house. Once they cleared the field, I dropped hail onto a good part of Agni's army. I goaded the storm to pull in moisture from miles in every direction, and I threw more moisture at the hail as it fell. It started as the size of peas, but within a minute, hail the size of plums was smacking into the zealots, who covered their heads and ran for shelter that didn't exist. I spent more power to grow the hail to the size of apples. I couldn't see or hear Agni's army by then, but I imagined them jumping around and trying to hide in the mud.

I spent another whole square to pound Agni's people with apple-size hail for five minutes. Then I let the hail ease away to nothing. More than two hundred men and women lay on the muddy slope. Some were moving, but most weren't. Another hundred or so had fled the slope and were riding away from the Winter House. More than two hundred horses on the edge of the hailstorm had run free.

Dunn and his riders stood off on one side of the slope. I had held off smacking them with hail, despite temptation.

Manon and I ran down the stairs and out the gate.

I said, "I hope to hell we killed Agni."

"Let's hurry and search for her." Cael was already running and yelled back over his shoulder at us. "If she's not dead, we'll need to chase her!"

"Will somebody please pull this arrow out of me first?" I admit to whining those words.

Ella tended the wound, which was minor for a battlefield arrow wound. I drew my sword. She grabbed my arm. "Bib, do you intend to slay the helpless wounded?"

"Well, not when you say it like that. Why don't you walk the field with me? We can hunt for Agni, and you can point out the wounded ones you don't want me to kill."

Ella crossed her arms and stared at the ground for a few seconds. Then she said, "Very well," and led me onto the battlefield.

THIRTY-FOUR

Throughout the morning, Ella and I walked the whole battlefield, scouring it for Agni. I hungered to kill all the maimed and wounded zealots, but Ella saved several dozen from me. Even so, I had destroyed 149 people during that morning's fight.

I had also killed two children.

Never once had I thought about Agni sending children up that hill to die. I should have. She was a rank butcher with a broken heart who knew, without a scrap of doubt, that she was right. I should have predicted that she'd use kids. Both of the dead, brown-haired boys looked about twelve years old, and hail had beaten them to hell. When I found the first one, I threw up until my sides cramped. When I found the second boy, I felt numb.

We did not find Agni.

Cael and some soldiers gathered horses for our pursuit. Cael chose to come with us, frowning the whole time like he'd bitten something bad. The soldiers would stay to guard the Winter House. I didn't chide them over it, since it was their duty to defend it.

Dunn volunteered to chase Agni with us.

"Why the hell do you want to do that?" I asked. "I thought you wanted to roll over and do puppy dog tricks for Harik."

Dunn climbed up onto the horse he had begged from us. "That's funny, Bib. No, we can do Harik's bidding later. Agni is our common enemy. We're all sorcerers."

We buried Larripet in haste beside the Winter House. I suppose I didn't mourn him as much as I should, considering he saved my life twice. He had been brave and reliable, although inscrutable and overly personal at times. I remembered every person I had ever killed, but I had long ago lost track of the men and women who died fighting beside me.

As we mounted, Death's Riders started arguing about who would ride which horse. I yelled at Dunn and told him he had the heart of a snake and the dick of a toad. That got his people's attention. While I waited on him to settle his people, I leaned toward Ella. "I never learned much in the way of facts about Larripet. I feel a little bad."

"He and I spoke at length." Her eyes crinkled as she smiled.

"Do you mean that you talked, and once in a while, he said a few words about flamingoes or anuses?"

"No, not like that. He wished to talk about Bratt. The young man loved Larripet's niece, which was looked upon with disfavor, since Bratt was an uncivilized person. The girl's father, a perfectly hideous man, demanded that Bratt perform three heroic feats."

"And Larripet rode along to help out?" I watched Dunn whacking one of his riders with a coil of rope.

"Gods, no! He hated Bratt."

"Well, then he cried more over Bratt's body than I would have expected."

"They had months to become friends, as well as common cause. Larripet's brother had required him to accompany Bratt, to record his feats in song. Yet if the brother disliked the song, he had the right to kill Larripet." Ella rode up and blocked my view of Dunn and his idiots. "Pay attention. The Hill People think quite highly of songs. You should feel flattered that he chose to write one about you."

"Well, I suppose I do." I shrugged and leaned to look around her.

Ella bent forward to adjust her horse's bridle while she glanced at me. "Larripet propositioned me, you know."

"What?" I yelled.

"Twice. It was terribly sweet. When I declined, he thanked me and said he would ask again another time."

"I'll be a ring-tailed bastard," I sighed. "I didn't know a damned thing about the man, I guess."

At midday, Ella, Manon, Cael, Death's Ridiculous Riders, and I rode away from the Winter House following Agni's trail. Her people outnumbered us by an awful amount, but they were fleeing, fearful, and vulnerable to quick, clever attacks. They must have been poorly mounted, or at least not as well mounted as us. Unless one of the gods stuck his foot right in the middle of our business, we would overtake her in two or three days.

That night, we halted to rest for a few hours, and I lay awake thinking about the little boys I had killed. I am not much given to maudlin introspection, but I am given to anger so pure that I just have to share it with everybody in sight. I prodded and kicked every-body awake and demanded that we continue the pursuit that very moment. A couple of Dunn's people, Cluck and Pister, objected, but Dunn shouted them into action with a presence I hadn't suspected of him.

We rode as fast and long as our horses could bear. That meant stopping for two hours of sleep the second night, and then we pushed on deeper into the western march of Bellhalt. The weather turned sunnier and warmer. We rode out of the flat, dead grasslands and into craggy, wooded hills covered in bare trees, with occasional gullies, streams, and patches of underbrush.

In the afternoon, we topped a rise and found a wide, curved stream set in a broad gully below us. I stopped and signaled every-body else to do the same.

"Not too stealthy, are they?" Dunn whispered.

I spotted half a dozen of Agni's people across the stream,

hunkered down behind trees too small to cover them. I hissed for us to ride back over the hilltop out of sight.

"We aren't too stealthy, either." Cael pointed at a couple of the zealots as they pointed back at us. Another one crawled out of his hiding spot and sprinted away up the hill.

I slapped my leg. "Shit! No use creeping around behind bushes now." I turned my horse and rode back over the rise, putting the stream out of view. "Let's decide how to kill them."

We created a straightforward plan. It avoided optimistic complexities that sow confusion, stupidity, and the deaths of people who aren't supposed to die.

Ella, Cael, Manon, and I would creep off downstream, and then I'd pull together some storm clouds. At my signal, Dunn and his dolts would walk right back over the hill where we'd first appeared. They would hurl some splashy, distracting magic across the stream to get every last fanatic's attention.

When Dunn's craziness started, the rest of us would hustle across the stream, except for Manon, who was no more dangerous with a sword than she was with a spoon. We'd surprise Agni's people from the flank, kill twenty or so—like chicks in a snake pit—and then retreat across the gully. Manon would cover our escape, and we'd all rendezvous downstream to plan our next attack.

I allowed about three hours to ease the storm clouds together. While I worked at that, I said to Cael and Ella, "Why aren't either of you bitching about how you're the one who ought to lead this foray?"

Cael shrugged, and Ella said, "We have no purpose here other than killing. I acknowledge your expertise."

I was the expert. I tried to put those dead kids out of my thoughts for the thousandth time or so.

Once I dragged the clouds together, I squeezed them and thunder grumbled the signal for Dunn to begin. Dunn and his lackeys provided a hell of a show. Half a dozen trees fell crackling and smashing across the stream. Three flaming arrows sailed into brush piles, and a battering wind whipped the brush into snapping columns of flames. The ground on Agni's hillside stretched itself up into a fanged, demonic face ten feet tall and thirty feet wide.

People beyond the stream ran back and forth. It seemed that their only purpose was to panic. The shouts, curses, and screams made that a likely assessment.

Ella, Cael, and I sprinted into the gully and up the other side. Before I could run too far up the hill, a titanic boom sounded behind me. I spun back around. Manon teetered on the edge of a just-appeared pit, eyes huge and arms flailing. Before I could step toward her, she fell in. Her scream stretched for most of a second and then cut off.

I forgot all about stealth. Dunn and his sorcerers were sprinting in the direction of their horses. I screamed, "Damn your goddamned lying tongue, Harik!" while I hurled more white bands into the sky.

The lightning may not have killed Dunn and his shitty little murderers. They possessed the durability of sorcerers after all, especially the Caller. Even the second lightning strike could have failed to finish them. The third strike obliterated them without doubt. The fourth and fifth might have seemed unnecessary, but I threw them to remind Harik, and everyone else who might hear about it, not to challenge my willingness to kill for love.

Before the thunder had faded, I was running back to the pit that had taken Manon.

"Manon!" I shouted as I knelt at the pit's edge. She didn't answer. I could just see the bottom, about fifty feet down. She lay unmoving on the dirt, her left leg twisted under her in a way that legs aren't supposed to twist.

"Bib!" Ella shouted from behind me, and I heard swords clash. She and Cael faced five of Agni's fanatics, and more were scrambling across the gully toward us. I drew my sword, and within thirty seconds, we had killed all five. Seven more had reached us by that time, and we started fighting them too.

"We have to retreat!" Cael shouted, jumping backward out of a sword's reach.

"Bugger that! I'm not leaving Manon."

A stream of howling zealots sprinted and scrambled and sometimes fell down the hill toward us. We could kill any five or six of them, but if thirty showed up at once, they would fall on us like an anvil.

"Retreat!" Cael yelled.

"All right, back to the pit!" I shouted as I killed a tubby, bald fanatic.

We put our backs to the pit and kept fighting. I remember flashes of the next minutes. I killed four men in twenty seconds, only to get stabbed all the way through the thigh by a woman. I cut her throat with my knife. Cael and Ella were shouting like maniacs, and I realized I was too. I came face-to-face with Ellie, the girl whose village Dark had wiped out. She snarled and swung a club at me. I whacked her on the head with the flat of my sword, and she collapsed. Four people swarmed Ella and pulled her to the ground. At least two of them stabbed her before I knocked them off. She didn't get up. I tripped and fell because so many bodies lay on the ground, but I rolled and thrust my sword into a woman as I came up.

Pierce, Agni's tall thug, appeared in front of me. He swung my stupid god-named sword at my head—hard. I'm sure he had won a lot of fights because he was strong and battered his enemies. I leaned to my right, his sword whipped beside me, and I stabbed him in the groin. He staggered back, shrieking. I knocked him down and cut his throat. I didn't want him to suffer; I just wanted him dead. I pulled open his fingers and grabbed my sword.

Manon had likely been killed. Ella might have been dead too. Cael had taken a big wound in his side when he kept the other zealots off me as I fought Pierce. Now Cael was wavering. I had started limping, and I bled from half a dozen places. Everything was horrible. I thrust into a man's belly as he swung at Cael, and I felt more alive and thrilled than I had in months.

Two men charged me, but they slowed at the pile of bodies. I knocked one down, killed the other, and stabbed the first one in the throat before he could sit up. I whipped my sword in an arc, flinging a line of blood across the closest fanatics, and then I howled. Every man and woman nearby hesitated. I stabbed another one in the belly, and like a moron, I beheaded the woman next to him. I raised my sword, lifted her head by the hair with my free hand, and laughed. Agni's minions faltered, and then they ran. I limped after them, yelling for the cowards to come back and get killed.

I staggered back to Ella and knelt. The throat wound was a miracle—it wouldn't kill her or even hurt her much. I healed her ragged belly wound just enough to keep her alive. Then I limped away to pursue the fanatics.

Nobody challenged me at the gully or on the way up the hill. Near the hilltop, three men with swords came running at me. The first one almost killed me when my wounded leg wobbled. I escaped with nothing worse than losing some more scalp and half my ear. I killed that one, and I got lucky when the second one slipped on his friend's blood. As I killed him, my leg collapsed all the way. The third man smiled awfully big about that until I reached up from where I knelt and stabbed him in the throat.

I found Agni sitting against a tree as I hopped on one leg toward her. Her crippled arm appeared shattered and had been poorly splinted. Her left ankle had swollen up like a melon. Hail had bruised most of her face purple and green.

Agni said in her braying voice, "Well, I guess you've shown up to brag about what hot shit you are."

I didn't intend to converse with her. I hopped closer with my sword pointed at her heart. Agni pulled away a cloth that was draped over her bent legs, revealing a wooden box clamped between her knees. She yanked off the lid, and something like embers or crushed rock exploded into my face.

I fell and rolled onto my back, calling her a lot of bad names, the nicest of which was "spewing cavern of an elephant's ass." I didn't drop my sword, though. When I rubbed at my eyes, I felt blood and I seemed to be blinded.

I heard Agni crawling away from me across the scraggly dead grass. During an unfortunate time in my life, I had spent a considerable number of months in complete darkness, and now I could tell within a hand's breadth where Agni was. I rolled back over, got one leg under me, and launched myself at her while thrusting with my sword. She gasped, so I stabbed her again. I stabbed her two more times before she stopped groaning and lay still.

I got to one knee again, hung my head, and tried not to pass out. If I did, we might all die.

THIRTY-FIVE

Agni had blinded me in one eye and half-blinded me in the other. I could see well enough not to bash into things, so I healed my leg a bit and hobbled fast down the hill. I tumbled and fell once, but it was into a soft bush. I found Cael leaning bare-chested over Ella, pressing his ripped-up shirt against her belly wound.

If I believed that the gods gave a damn about us, I would have thanked one or two of them for Ella's clean neck wound. The belly wound was made by a crazy man who had twisted his weapon something awful. I healed her enough to be sure she wouldn't die, or at least not from this hole in her body.

I was breathing shallow around my belly pain when I turned to Cael and reached for the wound in his side. He edged away. "See about Manon first."

"How in the name of Lutigan's ass crust do you suggest I do that? Float down there like a dandelion?" I pressed my hand against his bloody cut, and he hissed. Somebody had cut him up worse than Ella. I started pulling him back together. "Cael, you're near dead. If I had stopped to pick up walnuts on the way down the hill, you wouldn't care about your wicked past anymore. I need you to chase down a few horses and bring me back some rope. Now! Run!"

I staggered over to kneel beside the pit, carrying the pain from Ella's and Cael's wounds. Manon hadn't moved. I shouted, "Manon! Hello! Say something or wiggle if you can hear me!"

She didn't speak or wiggle.

Ella started groaning behind me. I heard her roll over, and she crawled to the pit to kneel beside me. She grabbed my arm and held it. "Is Manon alive?"

I shook my head and healed my leg some more. A minute later, hoofbeats thumped from around the hillside. Cael arrived on Stone-Hand's fine horse, carrying three coils of rope. He started fumbling to knot them together, so I took them away from the oaf and did the job in a dash. "Fisherman's son," I said.

Cael tied off the rope, and I grunted my way down it to the bottom of the pit. I jumped the last feet and landed in loose, powdery earth that fluffed up nearly to my hips. Manon lay cushioned in a pocket of the stuff, drawing shallow breaths. If she had turned the dirt into dust, then she had saved herself. I straightened and healed her broken, dislocated leg, which would have hurt like a scorpion in the nose if she'd been awake. It hurt enough to make me cry.

I dragged my legs behind me to Manon's head, and I found a huge lump above her ear. It would have killed her soon, so I hurried to heal it. As she got better, more and more angry little men with hammers beat on the side of my skull. I rolled onto my back and waited for something that didn't hurt to happen.

Cael led Dunn's horse to pull us out of the pit. I lay on the ground and patted Cael's shoulder when he leaned over me. "Thank you, sir. This almost makes me regret those times I tried to kill you, you hypocritical piece of shit. Don't wake me up unless you . . ." I fell asleep.

I opened my eyes and saw a clear black sky full of stars and a gibbous moon. Most of the pain had gone.

Manon was sitting beside me, and she touched my neck. "He's awake."

Ella knelt beside Manon. "Is he lucid?"

"Enough to argue every damn one of you into tears," I croaked, sitting up. In fact, I felt better than I had expected, although my leg throbbed. I counted up my remaining power and found I had almost two squares left. "Does anybody still have a serious wound? I'll help with that, but the small stuff will have to get better on its own."

Manon and Cael walked off to gather firewood.

"We found Agni's corpse." Ella flinched as I pressed my palm against her belly. "You did a thorough job."

"Let's have a party. We can dance." I winked at her in the firelight. "Do you think Agni's army will just go home and tend goats now that she's gone?"

"Perhaps, unless some new leader just as charismatic and fierce appears."

"Fierce and sad—don't forget that. I did kill her children when I brought the gods back. I'm done with you." I let go of Ella's body and sat back.

Ella felt of her previously perforated belly. "You are not responsible for those deaths. The gods manipulated you."

I wanted to let her believe that, but she deserved a little truth. She'd suffered enough with me to pay for it. "What about all the other deaths?"

"The gods manipulated you." She didn't sound so convinced.

I didn't answer, because Manon and Cael arrived with firewood. They built the fire up higher. We dined on hard bread, dried beef, and not-too-rancid bacon from Dunn's saddlebag. Agni's army may not have dressed well, but they had carried gallons and gallons of beer.

"I don't see any reason to return to the Winter House," Cael said, wiping his mouth. "Let's go back to Bellmeet."

"Hell no," I said. "I'm going home to Ir. I don't intend to ever pass through anyplace unless I've been there before with this sword. Never. The gods won't exploit kids and make people crazy in any new places, because I'm not going there." I smiled at Ella. "Come on home with me."

She patted my hand. "No, I need somewhere new. I shall travel east, which means passing through Bellmeet. Cael, we will travel together that far. Do not mistake that for any sort of forgiveness from me."

Cael looked down. "I understand. If it's possible to earn your trust again, I'll do whatever's required."

Ella hurled a rock at Cael, who dodged. "You are a damned idiot! I've never trusted you. Now I despise you."

"Well, that was all nice and amusing," I grinned. "Manon, do you want to come home with me?"

"No, I don't, and I don't want to go to that clump of dog crap I grew up in, either. If I ever the village of Pog again, I'll toss it into the ocean. Ella, can I go with you to Bellmeet? I feel like I need to be there. Besides, I'd like to see Martel again."

I stared in the direction of Ir, hundreds of miles away. "Shit. I don't want to go home by myself."

Ella said *tsk-tsk* to me as if I were a toddler. "Don't pout. It is unbecoming in a man of your years."

I shrugged. "Hell, I've been to Bellmeet before. The way for the gods can't get any wider there than it already is. I'll come with you too, just to spend time in a city where I can raise hell in an unconstrained manner!"

We faced a four-day ride back to Bellmeet. I had already said everything I wanted to say to Cael for one lifetime. Manon rode along staring ahead, and when I talked to her, she answered me with one or two syllables, if she answered at all. I talked with Ella most of the time. We laughed more and fought less than we ever had as lovers.

On the third day, Ella turned in her saddle without warning and told me, "Bib, you needn't return home by yourself. You can stay with Pres for a while." King Prestwick of Glass was a young man we had once rescued over his objections, but in the end, he forgave us.

I snorted and pointed at her. "Funny. There's nothing to do there but visit a brothel or own a brothel. Those are both worthy undertakings, but the thrill fades pretty damn quick."

"If you had a worthy task there, would you consider it?" She held up her hand. "Do not answer yet. Am I correct in my understanding that numerous sorcerers, young and old, still live in the lands through which you have passed? And more will continue to appear as children grow into their power?"

"That's probably so. Almost certainly. No, I see where this is going. You want to gather them up and wipe their noses and teach them not to blow their damned heads off. Is that your plan, Governess?"

"Why not? Do you deny that they would lead longer and happier lives with training? With guidance on how to deal with mendacious gods? And everyone around them would be safer as well, since the lands will contain fewer reckless, uncontrolled sorcerers."

I regarded Ella with all the gravity my soul contained. It wasn't much, but I used it. "You don't have any idea about the terror you would create. None at all."

Ella laughed as if she were going to the crossroads fair. "I want to build a school. I will convince Pres to sponsor it in his kingdom."

"Well, I guess you'll probably build it then, since I've never once convinced you not to do something you wanted to do. You're sure not going to get me to run it."

Ella laughed and waved a hand as if she were discussing supper. "Krak's elbows, I never considered asking you! I shall conscript Desh for that position." Desh was a young sorcerer we had traveled with—smart, skilled, and dispassionate. He'd be perfect for this.

"What in the round hell do you need me for then? To throw horseshoes at their faces?"

Ella smiled the smile of a woman with pure certainty of purpose. "Someone must seek out these sorcerers. That"—she leaned over in her saddle and punched me on the shoulder—"is the perfect job for you. Consider it. As a favor to me."

I would have told anybody else to go bite themselves in a nasty place. "Fine, I'll consider whether I want to lose my mind and go get immolated with you and Desh."

"From you, that is nine-tenths of the way to yes."

I didn't tell her that this ridiculous, terrifying school sounded a bit like a happy situation, and that I had become mistrustful of happiness.

We crossed the dead Fatt River downstream from the city, beside a grounded barge. Then we rode up along the east riverbank to the place where men were dumping dirt into the riverbed beside the Green Gate. Now that the water had gone, it seemed Mina intended to create an earthen crossing from one gate to the other.

The gate guards didn't try to stop us, but one of them said, "I see you got rid of your little hill-rat. One less of those crusty bastards to spread plague."

I charged my horse and kicked the man in the face. As he staggered, I jumped down and drew my sword.

"Bib, you don't have to do it!" Ella shouted.

I paused. In my mind, I had already taken that man's life. Holding back felt harder than falling and stopping myself just by thinking about it. Ella was right, though. I didn't have to kill the little shit-stain. I had a choice. I stepped back, sheathed my sword, and mounted my horse. I couldn't quite tell myself that I wasn't going to kill him. I settled for saying that I wouldn't kill him right then, and that never killing him was a possibility.

We arrived at the Residence. Syd embraced Cael and said Her Majesty expected us to join her on the terrace—scouts had reported our return. Syd talked about the new dirt bridge as we climbed through the Residence. When we walked onto the terrace, Mina and four guards stood at the farthest point from the balcony. The weather had snapped cold again, and a brittle breeze made the potted trees sway just a little. Heavy tapestries fluttered against the wall.

I stopped after four steps. The tapestries didn't move enough. Syd had been too friendly, and Mina stood rigid as a stack of iron angles, although she smiled to welcome us. "Something's wrong."

"Where?" Manon glanced left and right around.

Two dozen guards stepped from behind the tapestries. I heard Syd draw her sword behind me.

Mina held up both hands. "Just be calm. We don't have to fight, and I prefer that we don't."

"We won't have to fight if you just let us leave," I said. "Will that make you happy? We'll say nice things about you in all the other kingdoms."

Mina shook her head. "Bib, you're as much the dashing smartass as ever. Relax, I don't want you." She pointed at Manon. "I want her."

THIRTY-SIX

I stepped in front of Manon, which didn't make a damn bit of sense. Ten guards were aiming arrows at her from angles I couldn't block. I waved at Mina. "Stop, just hold on. We can fix this."

"She murdered Nubba." Mina pointed at Manon.

I raised my hands to appear inoffensive and harmless. "Do you know that for absolute certain?"

The queen raised her voice. "We found a piece of him in every room of the Residence."

Manon raised her eyebrows and made an innocent face. "He was going to murder you. I'm not sure why I thought I should kill him for that, but I did."

I whispered, "Manon, you may have to surrender unless you want this terrace covered in blood two inches deep. I'll help you escape tonight."

Manon glared past me at the queen. "Your Majesty, I don't trust you a thimbleful. I won't surrender to you. Let us go this instant, or I will kill every one of you on this terrace. Maybe I'll kill your whole city." Manon glanced at me and whispered, "Not our people."

Martel sprinted out of the doorway into the Residence. "Don't fight, Manon, just for now! I'll protect you. Nubba was a traitor. Well, I think he was."

The queen screamed, "Martel! Go back inside right now! Guards, take the prince inside!"

A guard grabbed the prince by the arm. As he was pulled away, young Martel the almost-sorcerer shouted, "If I can't save you, Sakaj said she would."

The air twitched and then vibrated as if somebody had hit an enormous, soundless drum. The wind cut off, and the whole terrace went cold silent. Several dozen little birds fell dead out of the sky onto the stones. I grabbed Manon by the shoulders, but she just stared past me as she twisted her fingers.

A high, tweeting voice said, "Damn it to dog shit, I was this close to bagging a fat nymph."

I spun and saw Dark sniffing the air right among half a dozen guards. They jumped, as shocked as if the Residence had sat up and begged for cookies. A hole in the air stood behind the imp, a portal just like the one it had used to escape the glowing girl.

Behind me, Manon said, "Kurrip, I bind you. Kurrip, I bind you. Kurrip, I bind you."

"You squinty little bitch!" Dark trilled.

Manon smiled at the queen and then nodded at Dark. "Kill everybody up here that you've never met before."

"Sure, sure . . ." Dark grabbed a guard in each hand and slammed them against the wall. They squished like plum pies.

"No!" I yelled, raising my palms toward Manon like she was a naughty child, and it did just as much good. Manon stepped back and scanned the terrace.

I heard somebody roaring behind me and glanced over my shoulder. Cael was sprinting toward Mina, and Ella was running toward me. Syd stood gaping at the imp. Then she shook her head and charged Manon. I drew my sword and hamstrung Syd as she passed.

"Manon, send it back!" I shouted.

Manon shook her head, although her brow furrowed for a moment.

Dark had crushed four more guards, and then it pulled one apart in a shower of blood.

I seized Syd under one arm and beckoned Ella. "Grab on!" We dragged the dazed guard captain toward the portal that Manon had made for Dark.

The imp killed the last three guards near it. Then Dark leaped all the way across the back of the terrace, over Mina and Cael. When it landed, guards flew like ninepins. Four arrows fired by guards near the doorway smacked into Dark's hide and bounced off.

I shouted, "Cael! Help me!" He glanced at Mina, who nodded. I beckoned, and Cael sprinted toward us at the portal.

Seven of the guards near the Residence door screamed and gushed blood when potted trees appeared inside them. I glanced back at Manon, who raised her eyebrows and shrugged Four guards were hustling Mina away from Dark, but that was the wrong direction for escape.

At the portal, Ella and I stood Syd up. The guard captain stared around blinking and didn't fight us.

I snarled at Ella and Cael. "Drag those planters over here and knock them over!" Then I shouted at the imp, "Dark! You missed one! She's the leader!" I pointed at Syd.

"Huh? Leave me alone. I just want to finish this bullshit and go home."

I shrugged. "If that's what you want, but you won't finish unless you get this one."

Dark stomped on a guard and walked toward us. "Yeah, whatever you say."

I whispered to Ella and Cael, "Get ready to push him in."

"What?" Ella squeaked.

"Push him in that hole!" I dragged Syd ten feet farther past the portal, away from Dark.

Dark ran toward us, stopped, and jumped at Mina and her guards. He knocked them all flying with one arm, like they were game pieces on a table. They smashed into the wall and bounced off.

"No!" Cael screamed.

Beyond Dark, I saw more guards running out from the Residence. As the imp ran toward Syd, I knelt and grabbed the two small trees we had tipped over. I couldn't make them grow much in a couple of seconds, but I poured in power to make them twist and writhe. As the imp trotted past, the branches grabbed its ankles and squeezed.

Dark bent and swatted at the branches. "Asshole." It didn't sound impressed.

Ella and Cael slammed into the imp's side while it was bent over and leaning toward the portal. I jumped up and hit it a second later, and I broke my left hand. Dark threw out its arms to take a step, but we heaved and it toppled sideways into the portal. As Dark fell, it grabbed Cael with one of its flailing hands and dragged the man through with it.

The portal snapped shut with Cael and the imp on the other side.

Manon was leaning against the balcony, relaxed and gazing out over the city. She didn't seem to care that we'd banished Dark or even care that we existed. I ran toward her. "Manon, damn it, kick your mother's ass out and stop whatever you're doing!"

Manon waved her fingers toward a sizable wooden building on the main boulevard, and it collapsed. The ruined wood contracted and squeezed down into a ball the size of an old oak stump.

"Stop that! You don't have to do this!" I shouted, reaching for Manon's arm.

Several dozen flagstones rolled up off the terrace. They threw Ella and me backward, away from the balcony. When I sat up, Manon still stood gazing over the city. Ella lay next to me on her side, eyes closed and writhing. She must have banged her head on the stones.

Manon said, "We can talk later, Bib. My mother has chores for me. You know how that goes."

I did know, and damn it forever. "Hell, your mother must have told Martel her name, and he didn't know better than to say it out loud. Shit, she probably encouraged him." I could almost see the piece of herself that Sakaj had put inside Manon. I saw the outline, but that didn't help any of us one damn bit. "She doesn't belong here! Throw her out!"

Manon didn't answer. She shrugged and wiggled her fingers at something down in the city.

Unless Manon decided to bash herself unconscious against the stone balcony rail, I couldn't stop her. I lifted myself and called for Harik. He answered me without even a pause.

"What do you want, Murderer? I have a hunting celebration to attend almost this very moment."

"Mighty Harik, I want to shuffle some things around inside the Tooth's mind again. You did such an admirable job last time. I'm sure no other god could match you."

"No insults? You must be having an inconvenient afternoon."

I drew my sword, and the bargaining arena appeared around me. Sunset seemed near, and the leaves in the little stand of trees had turned red and silver. Harik sat on one side of the marble gazebo. Sakaj sat on the other, as far away from Harik as possible. Both twitched and readjusted themselves on their benches.

I swallowed the impulse to call Sakaj everything from a rat fart to an elephant's infected scrotum. "Why, Sakaj, the Terrifying and Mysterious. Since you're in attendance, I can deal with you and avoid inconveniencing this oozing wart of a god."

Sakaj sniffed twice. "I'm sure that you could, if I were the tiniest bit interested. I love my daughter as she is. She's so beautiful today, don't you agree?"

I stood tall and prepared myself to shout and demand things, since I had nothing to back up my position. "I want you to let her go. Actually, I want you to quit the world of man for today. Let the Tooth and her mind go free."

"Why in the Void and Vicinity would I do such a thing? She's having fun. You never let her have fun." Sakaj pouted and then laughed.

"Make an offer," I said. "You'll find me flexible on terms."

Harik held up one hand. "No deal may be made with the Murderer unless I sanction it."

"Yes, fine, keep your toys in a pile for yourself." Sakaj leaned back and even stretched her legs a little. That was a clue. I wish to hell I knew what it meant. "Murderer, you must leave Bellmeet immediately. Don't even pause to grab a spare shirt. You must ride straight to Cliffmeet and wait for me to contact you."

"Bah!" Harik waved like he smelled something bad. "I can do far better. I will drag Sakaj out of your world and also provide two squares. All you need to do is slay the rest of the guards in that pokey little city."

Sakaj purred at Harik, "You intend to drag me somewhere?"

"It wouldn't be the first time, would it?"

"I allowed you to do it. You're so pathetic."

Harik stood up and jutted his chin at Sakaj. "You adopt this aura of mystery, as if no god can perceive your ways! You are as simple as milk."

Sakaj stood too. "Which of us is wearing a robe that's not the blackest thing in existence, but merely the fourth blackest thing? It couldn't be the ever-impotent God of Death, could it?"

Harik shouted, "So, who is winning then? Someone who's not you!"

"Fish-screwing parasite!"

"Deprecating hole!"

I shouted, "Who's winning? What do you mean who's winning?"

"I didn't say that," Harik said, his eyes shifting. "Nor anything like it."

I stared at them. "I hope you get bitten on the tits by a grumpy mule. Both of you. This is never going to work, is it?" My position was hopeless, so I was forced to rely upon mindless folly. I pulled a deep breath and bellowed, "Father Krak!"

Both Harik and Sakaj stared at me with their eyes stretched wide.

"Father Krak, I'm calling and annoying your blinding magnificence because these two divine turds are engaged in some kind of shenanigans that I fear you might not like."

Krak's roar sounded from some place beyond the gazebo, and maybe beyond the next mountain for all I knew. "Whoever you are, stay right there! And you had better be a lot more amusing than you sound!"

Sakaj and Harik sat down again and faced away from Krak's voice. Sakaj examined her fingernails.

Krak bounded into the middle of the gazebo like a silverback gorilla but with infinitely greater presence and vigor. He glared at me. "You have five words."

"Harik says he's winning."

"Winning what?" Krak grew a foot taller while he said those two words.

I shook my head. "He won't say."

Krak narrowed his eyes at Harik. "What the flip-floating, void-scratching hell is this about? And don't lie. I despise liars. I plan to disintegrate ten liars before supper." Krak relaxed one finger of his closed fist, and a pinpoint of light escaped. It felt like my skull had been hit with a chisel. Harik swallowed hard, and Sakaj had a tiny coughing fit.

Harik said, "Father, we're playing a harmless little game of strategy and guile, and there's nothing injudicious about it. We just do it to keep our wits sharp for the next war, and it really is quite the challenge in its own humble way . . . do you want to play?"

"No, I do not want to play!" Krak roared with the power of a whole herd of elephants. "I have important things to do! I do not have free time to adjudicate your pissy arguments about rules, especially with this darkness-damned sorcerer right here listening!" Krak pointed at me. "If he wasn't the Way-Opener, I'd crush him with one finger right now. So . . . what is this game, anyway?"

Krak had been clenching both fists, with his neck veins standing out on a mythical scale. Now he relaxed just enough to tilt his head to one side. Since eternity is mighty long, I have often suspected that gods were keen on all kinds of contests and gambling.

Sakaj jumped up and babbled, "It's so simple that it's silly, Father. We each choose one game piece. Whoever's piece causes the most death and suffering wins! But we can't let the pieces know that we're playing."

"That sounds ridiculous." Krak frowned in disgust.

"No, no, it requires subtlety and callousness," Harik said. "And, well, I'm winning!" He didn't clap his hands and jump up and down, but I wouldn't have been shocked if he did.

Sakaj took three steps toward Harik. "You drooling fool."

"Quiet! I'm talking," Krak said.

He hadn't been talking at that exact moment, but I didn't intend to quibble.

Krak crossed his arms. "Well . . . what are the stakes?"

"A chariot!" Sakaj smiled.

"A magical chariot?" Krak raised his chin. "Something new that Fingit's built?"

"No . . ." Harik reached into his robe and withdrew a chariot small enough to fit on his palm. "Sort of a trophy."

"That does nothing? Huh," Krak grunted.

I glared at the tiny chariot. For that, hundreds of people had died.

Krak turned on me. "You called me here for this stupid shit?"

"That's not the only thing, Father Krak. I want to trade . . ." I jerked when I remembered that Krak could make—and enforce—trades on behalf of all the gods. He could make any deal. I came to save Manon, but the gods, those divine beings with the morals of hyenas, had been violating hundreds of kids the way Sakaj had been violating Manon.

"What. Do. You. Want?" Krak shouted at me.

"I'm sorry, Father Krak. This is a trade that I can make with none but the Father of the Gods."

"Fine, talk fast."

"I want the gods to leave every sorcerer alone until he turns sixteen years old. No contact at all." I said it the way I might ask for a fallen leaf.

Harik frowned. Krak stared at me as if he couldn't tell what kind of bug I was. Then all three started to laugh. I waited for them to stop, and it was a long wait.

"Unbelievable." Krak was still giggling. "Why would we ever do that?"

"In the old days, gods didn't contact children as a rule," I said.

"Well, these aren't the old days, are they?" Krak and Sakaj started laughing again.

I nodded and wondered whether I could get away with an obscene gesture behind my back. "No, these aren't, but you gods—not you personally, Father Krak—are using up these kids in a hurry. If you waited, they could give you a lot more trades in the long run."

Krak squinted at me. "Just what are you, Murderer?"

"A sorcerer."

"Goddamn right! Don't try to tell the gods their business."

"I'm just asking for this one thing, Father Krak. If you agree, I'll cultivate new sorcerers so that they'll be even more valuable over time. You'll come out ahead."

Harik raised his hand like he was waiting for permission to talk. "Oh, no! You want to cultivate sorcerers anyway, Murderer. I know about the school. That's no offer at all. No, you must promise to always keep traveling to new places without stopping so you can open the way for us faster."

"No, I won't do that . . . I'll move to a new place every six months."

Krak waved. "Forget it! We'll talk to all the children we please, when we please."

Sakaj said, "Even should we plunge into insanity and entertain your demand, you can just forget the whole idea of sixteen years old. Thirteen years old would be more appropriate, I think." Krak nodded at her. "Oh, and I'm so sad to say that it wouldn't help the Tooth at all. Everything you purchased for her from Harik? The Tooth just sold it all back to me."

I felt like I couldn't breathe. I squeaked, "Why?"

"Let me see . . . I think she mumbled something or another. Oh, that's right. She said that it hurts too much to remember."

I started to panic. Manon might be gone. But Sakaj was probably lying. I clenched my fists and swallowed. "I want her back. What will it cost?"

Sakaj smiled like the mother you wish you'd had. "She is mine, dear. Every little bit."

"But . . ."

Krak smacked the marble floor with his fist, and it shattered. "Damn, you're boring! Listen to me! We're not lying. We don't care enough to lie to you."

I didn't know what was true and what wasn't. Nothing was working. This was why you didn't call Krak. I thought about losing Manon, and I sagged. I almost tried to stab Krak in the eye, but I pushed down the urge. Then I twitched with a new thought.

I let my sword hang loose in my hand. "Fine, if you want it that way. Unless you agree to my terms, I won't find and train sorcerers. Instead, I'll kill every damned sorcerer I find. I'll starve you out."

"Don't threaten me, you nit!" Krak whispered. "I will obliterate you. I will destroy you so profoundly that no one will remember you existed. Your mother will never have been born." He bellowed, "I will go back and wipe out your forefathers for ten generations!"

I bowed to the repellent bastard in apology, but I also let my sword rest on my shoulder. "I would never do something as presumptuous as threaten you, Father Krak. I know I'm a horrible, flaming pain in the ass to the gods, but please don't destroy me. You haven't killed me yet."

Krak grinned. "I should annihilate you just for saying that."

"Father Krak, it might inconvenience the gods not to cheat and abuse children, but it'll benefit you over the long run. And if you agree to my terms, I won't ride around murdering every sorcerer I see. Come on, if gods can't take the long view, who can?"

"I don't destroy you right this very damned minute because I choose not to, and for no other reason. Do you understand?" Krak didn't shout, but I felt as though he'd slapped me anyhow.

Harik laughed. "Your offers and pleas mean nothing, Murderer. You are a killer, but you won't wander around killing sorcerers for no reason. It's not in you."

"I've slaughtered forty-one sorcerers, including your sock puppets, the Death's Riders."

All three of them laughed at me again.

Every sacrifice that Ella, Manon, and I had made seemed meaningless. If I had been less of a killer and more of a negotiator, maybe I could have tricked these gods into a deal. But I couldn't think of how to do it. I could only do one thing.

"All right," I said.

I dropped back out of the Home of the Gods and found myself still sitting on my ass on the terrace. I pushed up and winced when I banged my broken hand. I flexed it a bit, and it hurt like a flaming son of a bitch, but it moved.

At the balcony, Manon was still waving her fingers. Another building, this time farther away, collapsed. Far-off screams sounded from people on the street.

I took two steps toward her, and my sword flew out of my hand. It clattered off across the terrace. "Manon, come back. I know you can. If you come back, I'll protect you from your mother. We'll slap around every damn god that exists until we get your memories back."

Manon didn't answer me, but the guards behind me started shrieking.

"Manon, stop. You don't have to do this, no matter what your mother says." My mouth was dry, and my chest hurt. I walked toward her, and the sleeve above my unbroken right hand seized so tight it snapped my wrist.

Two more steps, and I reached Manon. I didn't talk. With my broken hand, I snatched out my knife, almost too fast to follow. I stabbed her in the base of the skull so she wouldn't have a moment in which to destroy me. My hand had time for one immense throb before I dropped the knife. She fell straight down, small and easy as a pillow.

I trudged to my sword, knelt, and wrapped my broken hand around the hilt. Then I called Krak, who lifted me back to the Home of the Gods. I stared Krak in the eyes, then Harik, and then Sakaj, calm but hard. "I will kill every sorcerer."

The three gods glanced back and forth at one another. Krak said, "I suppose you would. Let's deal then."

That next moment, I almost panicked because she was dead, and I couldn't take it back. But I pushed all the grief down to bargain. In the end, Krak agreed that the gods wouldn't contact sorcerers until they turned sixteen. I agreed that Desh and Ella would train new sorcerers without me around to screw things up. I wouldn't stay in the same place for more than two months, and I would take Harik's little book to the Northern Kingdoms. The specific location would be revealed later by Harik, that ass-chapping spit lizard. I gave up more than I should have, but I was distracted by the need to stop myself from screaming.

Krak lowered me back into my body with an uncharacteristic lack of severity. I dropped the sword, picked up the knife, and threw it over the balcony. Then I sat down and pulled Manon's body into my lap.

THIRTY-SEVEN

When Ella sat up and saw me with Manon's body, she shouted and grabbed me by the shirtfront. She yelled that I should have shaken her or gotten her attention somehow. We would have found some other way to stop the girl.

Ella screamed, "You didn't have to kill her! She was almost your daughter! You are a goddamned soulless monster!"

I tried to explain why I'd done it, that I hadn't had another choice that would help anybody a bit. I don't think I explained things well. I might have babbled and mentioned chariots. Whatever I said, Ella didn't find it persuasive because she yelled at me some more and knelt to take Manon's body away from me. I shouldered her aside without standing up. She stomped off, calling me more names as she went.

I really hadn't had any choice but to kill Manon.

Some time later, Martel touched my shoulder.

"I had to do it," I said.

"You saved a lot of my people, Bib, including me. Maybe you saved all of us."

I hadn't thought about that. It sure as rat shit wasn't the reason I had killed Manon. I nodded at the boy as if I cared.

317

Martel squatted beside me. "Manon's demon killed Mother." He just about moaned the words.

"I'm sorry for that." I really was.

"I shouldn't ask this, but . . ." He licked his lips. ". . . but I know that you were bargaining with Krak during the battle. Fingit told me you were doing it. Why did you choose to call on Krak?"

"I didn't choose anything. I didn't have a choice." The boy was foolish for asking such an obvious question, but it didn't seem important enough to mention.

"Oh . . ." Martel cleared his throat and patted my shoulder. "Bib, let's take her away from this awful place."

I followed the boy into the Residence, carrying Manon. Six of the surviving guards escorted us to a big sitting room, where a table stood covered with cushions and pillows. I lay Manon down on it.

Martel said, "Go rest. These ladies will care for her." He nodded toward two older servants in the corner.

"I . . ." I noticed the women behind me and then glanced around the rest of the room. There were rugs, some furniture, candlesticks, and a pitcher. Nothing stood out. Manon was there, so I shrugged.

"Go on."

I walked to my room, passing several servants who looked away when they saw me. A fancy-dressed fellow coming toward me stopped, turned, and near trotted back to disappear into a side hallway.

When I lay on the bed, I didn't cover myself or even unbuckle my sword belt. Sleep snatched me right away.

Later, I woke up alert and full of energy. I healed my hand and my wrist. I grabbed one of the bedposts, wrenched it free, and smashed everything in the room that could be shattered or bent. For the sake of thoroughness, I yanked off the other three bedposts. Then I destroyed the next three rooms on the corridor in the same fashion. Four rooms, sixteen bedposts. Those were two of the worst numbers of all. Two was a horrible number by itself. Four was two squared. Sixteen was four squared, and it was also two to the fourth power.

I hurled my last bedpost against the wall, sat on the floor, and told myself I was only thinking about these fucking numbers so I wouldn't have to think about anything else.

Of course I'd had a choice. Nobody made me do it.

Whatever deals Krak made, he could unmake. If gods could change the future, they must be able to change the past. It all depended on how much I was willing to pay. I called on Krak for an embarrassing length of time, and he didn't answer. I called on Gorlana and Fingit and every other god all the way to Lutigan, who would rather I be disemboweled than get a halfway helpful word. None of them answered.

Fatigue mashed down on me. I walked back to the terrace and lay down on the flagstones where Manon had fallen. I fell right asleep. I woke up during the night, peered around, rolled over, and went back to sleep.

Sunlight hurt my eyes when Martel woke me. He led me back to my room, which somebody had cleaned out and redecorated. Martel watched me drop onto the bed and then left. Ten minutes later, I walked onto the terrace and lay down to sleep on the place where I had killed Manon.

Somebody shook me awake in near darkness, and I felt pretty damned cold. A few inches of snow lay on the ground. Martel and Ella stood me up, and snow fell off me. They led me to a different room and put me on the bed. After they closed the door, I heard a bar drop down on the other side.

I closed my eyes for a minute, stood up, and lay back down again. I did that over and over for a while before I placed my palms against the door and shattered it to splinters. Back out on the terrace, I dropped onto the snow that covered Manon's blood, and I fell asleep.

The next time I woke up, it was daytime and still snowing. Blankets covered me, and Ella sat beside a snapping fire in front of me. She said, "Roll over so I can slide some blankets under you."

I rolled, and she slid. I said, "You were right. I didn't have to do it."

"But you did."

I nodded. "How long?"

"Three days since the battle. Go back to sleep."

Just to be contrary, I stood up, stretched, and gave Ella a hand up.

"I can't sleep forever," I said. *Not like Manon,* I didn't say.

Back inside the residence, Ella took me to a tiny room with a happy fire. She sat me beside it, covered me with blankets, propped my feet so that my toes steamed, and handed me a big bowl of soup.

I smelled the hot air rising off the soup. "Hell, I should have had you take care of me like this all the time."

"That might have been nice." She shrugged and walked out.

When I finished eating, I yelled, "Either feed me some more or set me loose!"

Ella walked back in with smart steps, took the bowl, and dragged a wet rag down my cheek. She wasn't too gentle about it, either.

"All right, stop! I surrender."

"You need a bath." She showed me the rag, which was red with Manon's blood.

I held my breath and didn't throw up.

Ella didn't say she was sorry.

A minute or so passed while I swallowed hard and sweated. "She was still there, at least a little bit."

"You can't know that." She dropped the rag in a basin of water.

"She was. That bit that didn't kill me when I walked up behind her. That was her."

Ella put her arm around my shoulders and laid her cheek on top of my head, which must have been bloody too.

I didn't care to wait for water to heat, so I bathed cold. When I went to get dressed, somebody had hauled my bloodstained clothes away. I never saw them again. Clothes had been laid out for me, sturdy and not too fancy.

I was not sleepy. I wouldn't wager that I'd ever be sleepy again. I wandered down to the barracks, and when I walked in, everybody stopped talking. It was sparsely populated, and I supposed that more than half of the guards had been killed.

I leaned against the doorframe. "Do any of you fancy drunkards want to spar?"

One man stood and said, "Love to, you lousy-ass, stinking baby-killer." Three more men and two women jumped up and started screaming some inventive abuse at me, and I learned two new insults. A dozen other guards jumped up and shouted the first ones down, and somebody among them threw a mug of beer at me. Somebody else muttered, "Ass-licking witch-lover." Everybody started yelling again, and a tin bowl flew at me. I dodged it and watched the fight.

Syd stood up and hobbled to the middle table, shouting all the way for everybody to shut up or be gutted. When she had quieted everybody to mere grumbling, she said, "Nobody will fight you. Turn around and don't come back."

That annoyed me a good deal, but I left for the stables. I took my horse out of the city for a hard ride and came back to the Residence at sunset.

That night, I ate supper with Ella and Martel. The plain meal would have horrified Mina, but there seemed no limit to the wine. I got drunk as hell. Along about my eighth cup, I said, "Did Cael come back?"

"No, should we expect him to?" Martel asked.

"If he hasn't come by now, he's probably gone forever."

"What will happen to him?" Ella asked.

"I don't know. This is a thing I've never heard much about. Maybe some god will make him a slave, or some nymph might think he's pretty and keep him in a silver cage. I imagine they'll just kill him."

Ella examined me for a few seconds, did the same to Martel, and snapped her head back around toward me. "You both are sorcerers! Perhaps one of you can ask a god about Cael."

Young Martel frowned at the table. "No god will answer me."

I smiled away from them. My bargain with Krak must have worked. "Me either." I drank another cup of wine.

I didn't pass out with my face on the table that night, because Martel had two servants drag me to bed first.

The next morning, my hangover and I wandered around and finally found Ella in Martel's dining room. "There's too damn much merriment around here. If I enjoy myself any more, I'll lose the will to go off and do stupid things."

"Are you leaving?"

"My horse is saddled and pissed off because I've kept her waiting."

"Go to Glass. Reside there for a few weeks until you recover from . . . well, Pres would love to see you."

"It's funny how many boy kings I know. No, I've already been to Glass."

"It will not be as it was. We shall build the school. Desh will need your advice, even though you doubt it. It is a thing worth doing, and worthy work brings happiness."

I couldn't help laughing at that. "I have plenty of things to do. One or two may even be worthy, if you don't examine them too hard."

"Very well. At least we'll see you when you bring us the sorcerers you find."

I shouted, "God damn it in the morning and twice at night! Don't expect to find any sorcerers in my care. I doubt I could get them to you alive. Manon didn't last a month with me." My anger surprised me.

Ella didn't speak, and the silence got uncomfortable.

I patted her shoulder. "If I change my mind, you'll see me riding up the hill someday. Don't let Pres close down the whorehouses."

"Take this gold." She held up the melted clump of gold she had carried since Parhold.

I stuck it in a pouch. "Thank you. That's kind."

Ella swallowed. "I did not expect you to accept it."

"You're welcome for that lesson. It's almost a holiday when I can teach you something."

"Bib, I don't think you're ready. Don't leave yet. Wait a few days."

"I'm sorry, darling. Nasty folks are out there waiting for me to come kill them."

Ella examined my face. Then she hugged me for a while and was sniffling when she let me loose.

"I hope you didn't get snot on my fine shirt."

"Bib, when you realize that everything you've just said is bullshit, come to us in Glass."

I kissed her forehead and walked down to the stables.

An hour later, I rode out through the Green Gate of Bellmeet and then stopped. I had been waiting until this moment to figure out where I was going. I sure as hell wasn't going to the Northern Kingdoms right away, not until Harik shared this mysterious destination with me. The Northern Kingdoms were too big to go riding around them without purpose. I decided to travel northeast toward the Empire, the very center of civilization. I possessed a good horse, a big chunk of gold, a sword forged by a god, and Harik's book in a pouch under my shirt. I could raise all kinds of hell in the busiest place in the world.

BIB'S ADVENTURES CONTINUE IN DEATH'S COLLECTOR: SORCERERS DARK AND LIGHT

A banished demigod abducting children. An underpowered sorcerer forced to fight. An impossible battle for a virtuous cause.

Bib has retreated home, wracked with grief. After dooming his own daughter, he's unwillingly dragged into a conflict with the demonic son of the God of War. And though he saves his town from the petulant deity, his tragic miscalculation allows the sadistic fiend to make off with a hoard of kids.

Enraged and determined to right his mistakes, Bib must once again negotiate with the gods for enough power to overcome his sinister foe. And if that doesn't work, then he'll just have to summon the dead...

Will Bib defeat the snarky Goliath and save the children from a horrific fate?

Death's Collector: Sorcerers Dark and Light is the third book in the hopelessly irreverent Death-Cursed Wizard fantasy series. If you like warped insults, inventive magic, and complex characters, then you'll love Bill McCurry's bloodstained quest.

Shop at: https://tinyurl.com/billmccurrybooks

ABOUT THE AUTHOR

Bill McCurry blends action, humor, and vivid characters in his dark fantasy novels. They are largely about the ridiculousness of being human, but with swords because swords are cool. Before being published, he wrote three novels that sucked like black holes, and he suggests that anyone who wants to write novels should write and finish some bad novels first. You learn a lot.

Bill was born in Fort Worth, Texas, where the West begins, the stockyards stink, and the old money families run everything. He later moved to Dallas, where Democrats can get elected, Tom Landry is still loved, and the fourth leading cause of death is starvation while sitting on LBJ Freeway.

Although Dallas is a city that smells like credit cards and despair, Bill and his wife still live there with their five cats. He maintains that the maximum number of cats should actually be three, because if you have four, then one of them can always get behind you.

CONNECT WITH THE AUTHOR

Bill-McCurry.com
Facebook.com/Bill.McCurry3
Twitter.com/BillMcCurry
Instagram.com/bfmccurry

Sign Up for Bill's Newsletter!

Keep up to date on new books and on exclusive offers. No spam!

https://bill-mccurry.com/index.php/newslettersignup/

PURCHASE OTHER BOOKS IN THE SERIES

Book 1 - *Death's Collector*
Book 2 - *Death's Baby Sister*
Book 3 - *Death's Collector: Sorcerers Dark and Light*
Book 4 - *Death's Collector: Void Walker*
Book 5 - *Death's Collector: Sword Hand*

Companion Book - *Wee Piggies of Radiant Might*

Shop at: https://tinyurl.com/billmccurrybooks

PLEASE LEAVE A REVIEW

Please leave a review on the platform of your choice!

https://linktr.ee/reviewbabysister

Made in USA - North Chelmsford, MA
1326337_9781735648798
08.09.2022 1627